D1097147

Ship It

EVIE BLUM

Evie Blum

PRINT
STATEMENT

Copyright © 2022 Evie Blum

All rights reserved

The characters and events portrayed in this book are fictitious. Any similarity to real persons, living or dead, is coincidental and not intended by the author.

No part of this book may be reproduced, or stored in a retrieval system, or transmitted in any form or by any means, electronic, mechanical, photocopying, recording, or otherwise, without express written permission of the publisher.

ISBNs: 979-8-9870758-0-7 (ebook), 979-8-9870758-1-4 (paperback)

Cover design by: Bailey McGinn
Printed in the United States of America

To N, the software ninja who captured my heart and always supports me in this sometimes hard venture called "life." We came from different places—in the world, in the way we think about a lot of things—but somehow, we work.

To my beloved mother, who read multiple drafts of my book and responded (in this order): "Wow!" and then, "Are those sex scenes about you and N?"

And to my dad, whom I love dearly. Someday, I'll send you a highly redacted version of this book. (Please, god, don't read it until then.)

CONTENTS

JANUARY 2022

QUALIFIED LEAD

There are definitely worse ways to wake up in the morning than staring into the sleeping face of a beautiful man. Somehow, I'm having a hard time thinking of any right now, especially considering I wasn't expecting to go home with anyone last night. "Shit, shit, shit," I whisper under my breath, barely moving my lips, as I lay frozen on my side in his bed, considering what to do next. I squeeze my still-blurry eyes shut, wishing I could just slip back into the warmth of my dream.

It started on a boat. Rocked gently by the waves, I rested on a roomy chaise lounge with my eyes closed. My face angled upward toward the bright sun, and like some picture in a travel magazine you see on the plane, I could feel its warmth on my brow. In the background, like a lullaby, an island instrument version of a Spice Girls song mingled with the sound of the waves. At some point, the sun had begun to feel too strong, and I had opened my eyes, just a sliver, to see what had changed.

Opening my eyes in the here and now—no waves or islands to be seen—I notice the tiniest ray of sunlight peeking through the curtains, over the bare, muscular shoulder of my sleeping companion. I hear his rhythmic inhale and exhale and take a minute to appreciate the view: warm brown hair, long dark eyelashes, an ever-so-prominent but well-proportioned nose, and broad, soft-looking lips. "Did I kiss those lips?" I start to ask myself, but I already know the answer. And for some reason, the knowing of it is connected in my mind, in my senses, with the scent of minty toothpaste and basil, of all the unexpected things in the world. Despite the unarguable attractiveness of the man next to me, my stomach is beginning to twist a bit, and I realize that if I'm going to get out of here, I should make a move soon.

This is not my usual sort of behavior. In fact, it's *very, very not* my usual sort of behavior, so much so that when I tell Camila what happened, she'll probably pass out from surprise and have to be revived with those electric paddles they use in the hospital on people having cardiac arrest. I've been impulsive in certain parts of my life, but love—sex, specifically—generally hasn't been one of them. I feel like I've had all this energy pent up inside of me. I wouldn't have necessarily classified it as sexual energy, but I guess sometimes your brain and your body surprise you.

Where did it come from? Hell if I know. If this were a therapy session, I'd probably start by talking about the unexpected death of my father a few years ago. At some point, I'd lament the isolation imposed on me—on everyone, I guess —by the pandemic. Maybe it would take a session or two to finally get around to the most recent trigger, breaking up with an emotionally-stunted boyfriend. And then we'd dig into what underlies all of it—a fear that I'll never realize my true potential, that I'll end up an old woman, looking back at a life wasted on experiences that were never truly my destiny. I doubt this guy is my destiny, but I guess I can go to the grave now knowing that at least once in my life, I had a mind-blowing one-night stand with a hunky man. Surely, as an old lady, I'll use the word "hunky." My brain obviously blew a fuse and scrambled all the signals. Yes, that must be the reason I acted like an idiot, drank too much wine, and went home with a guy I just met.

I think back to last night, while I slowly—very slowly—slide myself out of bed, channeling my inner ninja and thinking weightless thoughts, so as not to nudge my handsome sleeping partner. When Camila and I were getting ready last night, she told me in no uncertain terms that it had been long enough since my breakup with Blake six months ago, and that we had definitely spent enough time holed up at home due to the pandemic.

"You need to go out, have some drinks, and get under a guy," Camila had said.

Looks like I understood the assignment. I pull my skinny jeans up over my hips, hearing them whisper over my skin in the quiet room. I see my companion's eyelids flutter lightly. Wonder what *he's* dreaming about.

"Breakups suck, but you're young, you're hot, you're successful—" Camila had said.

"I'm not successful," I'd told her.

"Yes, you are, Sarah. You're starting a new job this week—"

"It's just an entry-level position," I'd interrupted.

"You will be running that place within a year," she said. "Now, finish your eyeliner, put on some 'fuck me' heels, and let's go have some fun."

Fun was had. Probably too much, judging by what—or whom —I'm looking at right now. I contemplate my options, quickly, and conclude the best course of action is to edge my way out of the bedroom—I'm only a few feet from the door—and do my run-of-shame the hell out of here. I take one last peek toward the bed, I can't resist, and the clock on the nightstand reads 6:04 a.m.—still really early. We could only have been asleep for a few hours. I should be exhausted from such little sleep, not to mention the energetic activities we engaged in last night, but the adrenaline of waking up next to a stranger is a force stronger than nature—maybe *of* nature—and I can feel my heart beating fast and hard. With the exception of that one sun ray—the same one that woke me from my nautical adventure, I suppose—the light in the room is dim, bluish-gray, and I momentarily admire his strong jaw, rough and unshaven, and touch my fingers to my neck, where his stubble grazed my skin as he kissed his way down my body. I allow myself just a second to try to reconcile the man who had me in his very capable hands last night with the one I see currently cuddling the blanket, clutching it childlike under his chin. Hot as hell? Yes. Still, he seems like a sweet guy. But I don't have time for guys, even—or maybe especially—sweet ones.

With a new job starting this week, I need a clear head. I've done a lot of reflection over the past six months, and I'm determined that this is my chance to start something new, something with promise, with real potential for me professionally. Nothing is going to distract me.

I tiptoe out of the bedroom and snatch my sweater from the coffee table where it ended up last night, and pull it on. I'm only a few steps from the front door—to freedom and forgetting any mistakes I might've made last night. I slip my feet into my still-damp flats and hook my fingers into the straps of my heels, patiently waiting for me near the front door. I can almost hear them snicker and whisper to me, "Job well done." I inch open the door with the cautiousness of someone defusing a bomb and just before I close it, I notice a work badge on the entry table. His name is partially covered by his keys, but I can make out "Nathan" and can see his smiling face. I whisper "Goodbye" to badge-Nathan and add a quick "I'm sorry" as I quietly shut the door.

As I make my way through the hallway and down the elevator —he lives in a high-rise—I think back. It was a good night, but now's the time for me to focus on work, on being back out in the post-pandemic world, not to get back into a relationship. With a little bit of luck, and in a place as large and diverse as the San Francisco Bay Area, I won't run into him. I step out onto the sidewalk, dodge a puddle from last night's rain, and begin to walk home. It's not far, and on the way, I stop to buy a latte.

The barista at Starbucks smirks when he notices the heels dangling from my left hand, and I shrug my shoulders and give him a sheepish look. It's not my regular coffee shop, but it is a few blocks away from Instinqt, where I'll be starting work in a couple of days. I guess if we ever go back to the office, I'll have to go to Peet's down the street instead. They call my name, and I grab my coffee. I head out the door and take a few sips. The caffeine and the fresh air do me good.

In fact, despite the unexpected experience last night—or maybe *because* of it?—I'm feeling, well, quite good. It's amazing how much things can change in a few months. After moving out from the place I shared with Blake, I found a new apartment for myself on the Alameda, not far from Camila's place. It's a few-story building, the top floor of which a contractor broke up into a number of affordable—at least for the Bay Area—one-bedroom apartments geared toward students and young professionals. I wasn't really looking to live with roommates in my late twenties, so finding a one-bedroom apartment I could afford was a real stroke of luck.

It's quite cold out this morning—it's January, after all—but the coffee and my brisk walk warm me up a bit. The walk isn't beautiful by any means—I go under an overpass as an early train rolls overhead—but it's largely peaceful and calming, being out and about early in the morning before most people have even ventured out of their beds. As I approach my block, I notice the front courtyard of the building. There's a small grassy area and fountain. The plants are all covered with water droplets, leftovers from last night's rain shower. The clean scent of the air, the coolness seeping through my sweater, the warmth of the coffee cup on my fingertips—everything, all of it—feels like renewal. And I'm ready for it.

FRESH START

"We're coming out of the pandemic," Dejohn says cheerfully on our Zoom call on Monday morning. Myself and four other new employees are starting today at Instinqt, a quickly growing startup based in San Jose. We're getting our instructions from the People team—a mighty team of one, Dejohn—on how to log in to our email and different work accounts so we can do virtual training our first two weeks and "be ready to hit the ground running" when we're back in the office at the end of January.

"You're both lucky and unlucky," Dejohn is saying. "We'll be back in office in two weeks, but we didn't want to delay all of you getting started, so you're the last people to do fully online onboarding. Two weeks from now, on Monday morning, I'll greet you all with breakfast burritos and coffee in the dining room at work. For now, you gotta make your own coffee." He chuckles to himself. But, like, really to himself, since we're all on mute. *Poor guy.*

"It actually works out really well since we'll be announcing a couple of organizational changes—promotions and the like—in a big all-hands meeting. You'll get a feel for Instinqt and get to meet your colleagues."

I'm a little nervous—it's been two years since I've worked in an actual office—but I'm mostly really excited. I'm generally an extrovert and the forced isolation of the past few years has been hard. I guess it wasn't made any easier by the fact that I broke up with my boyfriend of one-and-a-half years, Blake. When we broke up, I needed a break from men to sort of figure out who I am and what I want, when I'm not part of a couple. Even if I had been ready—which I definitely wasn't—it's not exactly easy to meet people when you're scared they could give you Covid, and frankly, I know my generation is supposed to be okay with meeting people on apps, but, well, it totally sucks.

Now that places are beginning to open up again and offices are starting to bring employees back, things are feeling a lot more optimistic than they have for a while. People are out, meeting each other, having drinks, wearing "fuck me" heels, and going home with men, too, apparently. I abruptly realize I haven't paid attention to anything Dejohn has said the last few minutes.

"—so, that's your goal for this week and next," Dejohn's upbeat voice says. "Make sure you have access to everything. Security training, specifically, is due by the end of this week. You'll be getting calendar invites to meet with your teams and your managers and if you run into any issues, I'm your People liaison, so please reach out on Slack."

I'm sitting at my desk—a simple wooden patchwork table I ordered online—and I'm facing out the window. I've learned after two years of working remote that natural light makes me look better on the endless Zoom calls, and since I'm doing my best to make a good impression at a new job, I've even put on makeup and a nice shirt, despite the fact that it's just orientation. I'm happy with my apartment. Its first noteworthy characteristic is that Blake isn't here. It's mine, all mine, and it's my safe place. Other than that, I've decorated it exactly the way I want to, with colorful paintings and mostly—probably too many —things in shades of blue. Thanks to the yearly bonus I'd gotten at Sierra, I'm able to live here without worrying too much about rent every month. It's small but comfortable.

My phone is on silent, but it's laying face-up next to my new laptop, which was delivered to my apartment via FedEx on Friday afternoon. While Dejohn continues to talk on the meeting, I see text messages start to come in at a rapid pace. Rapid is an understatement, more like machine-gun fire pace.

Camila: How's your first day going?

Me: Going ok.

Camila: So, where'd you end up Friday night?! I texted you a

MILLION times. Good to see you're ALIVE. <angry face emoji> <eye roll emoji>

Me: Sorrrryyy.

Camila: Figured it was a lost cause . . . Saw you on Find my Friends at home Saturday, so I guessed you weren't dead. Or, maybe you were, but at least you were home.

Me: Thanks for your concern lol

Camila: I'm surprised you could run on Saturday afternoon. Must've been hard to walk after Friday night, huh?

Me: Stop it! Also, quit stalking me on Runkeeper. I'm in work training. You're gonna get me fired on the first day.

Camila: What happened with Mr. Hot AF? <eggplant emoji>

Me: OMG. Stop <tears emoji> I just turned off my camera. I have to pay attention. Security training isn't comedic material and I'm lmao. Details later—promise.

Camila: You gonna see him again?

Me: No, I ran out of there.

Camila: You WHAT?

Me: I left. Later Cam, I promise.

I get back to training and muddle my way through the modules on "Creating a Safe Work Environment." The videos are corny—it's 2022, but these people are dressed like they're from the 1980s—but I guess that's better than boring, and I finish up in forty-five minutes. I spend the afternoon alternately working through the security training videos and having flashbacks from Friday night.

The thing is, when he first walked up to me at the bar, I was sure he was coming over to talk to Camila, who was already chatting with a few friends she happened to run into from her MBA program. When Covid started, everything was closed, and we all had a lot more free time, Camila determined that a full-time job at a consulting firm wasn't enough to keep her occupied and decided to do an online MBA at San Jose State. She and her friends have probably only seen each other in person five or six times in the last couple of years, but they've spent about a million hours online together doing classes and working on projects.

Decades is their usual spot since one of them knows a guy who bartends there on weekends. We went there a few times over the summer and fall when the patio was open, but it's been a few months. The music is a bit different, but fun. On Friday nights, they start with '90s music, move on to 2000s, and then make it up to newer stuff a bit later in the night.

I slowly sipped my glass of wine and watched Camila while she told a story about her trip to the farmers' market earlier in the day, where she somehow ended up encountering an angry Canada goose. She's a natural storyteller and was easily mesmerizing the people around her. I love Camila and her stories as much as the next person, but since I'd already had the honor of hearing it earlier at her apartment, I allowed my mind to wander a bit and was contemplating my new job.

It would be my first position in high tech, and to say I was nervous was an understatement. Instinqt was founded by Kevin Wong three years ago. The other founders had left relatively early on, not believing that the company would make it, but at the end of its first year, it had secured seed funding of $2 million, another respectable amount in its Series A round in its second year, and had since grown immensely. Its artificial-intelligence-powered tool for understanding people's online behavior and ability to accurately suggest purchases, related websites, and otherwise had seemingly infinite use cases, and its core product and customer base were growing by the day. Originally a B2B product, the people who had interviewed me had explained that the company was beginning to explore B2C use cases as well.

I wasn't super specific when I was looking for a new position. Growing up not far from Silicon Valley, I always knew high tech was an option but had never been particularly drawn to it. I did well in school growing up and had planned to study engineering in college. Somehow, though, I'd taken a comparative politics course in my freshman year, and had ended up switching my major to political science. At the time, I'd figured that worst case scenario, I'd go to law school. That plan, too, had changed after a post-college trip abroad. When I finally settled back down in California a couple years later, I'd ended up at Sierra Designs and Engineering. My dad's friend started Sierra twenty years ago, and he was willing to give me a chance to get my feet wet in the field. After working there for a few years with mechanical and civil engineers, I had enough street cred for Instinqt and a few other high-tech startups to give me a call. I'd interviewed with Instinqt in November and one of the engineering managers —tired of wrangling programmers and wanting to have more actual time to code—was more than happy to bring me on.

Here was my chance at an up-and-coming high-tech startup. It was exciting, but it was also extremely intimidating. I'd be working with software engineers—something new for me—and knowing that your colleagues got PhDs from Top 10 and Ivy League schools is a different story altogether.

So, I was in the middle of mulling this all over—and finishing off a second glass of wine, when . . .

I notice two guys in a booth looking in our direction. I glance away, pretending to be more absorbed in Camila's story than I actually am, and take a sip from my wine glass. I use the momentary cover to do a quick up-and-down glance of the taller of the two men, who's—shit—making his way over to us. I keep my eye on him as he walks over—looking the whole time as if he might be doing an inner pep talk—and I try not to stare. It's hard not to. He's, well, really attractive. Before I know it, he's come over and is leaning against the bar. To my surprise, he starts talking to me—not Camila.

"Um, hi," he says, and gives me a shy smile.

"Hi?" I say, smiling back, realizing I have to angle my head up a bit to meet his eyes, even sitting atop my high bar stool. I feel a little short of breath and lick my lips. I swallow and look up at him. His dark brown hair is cut short, but I can tell the top—just a bit longer —is fighting some wave. Despite it being January, his arms are a bit tan, and I momentarily wonder if he spends a lot of time outdoors.

Before I have time to contemplate anything else about him, though, he's asking me my name.

"Sarah. What about you?"

"Nathan," he says in a low, sexy voice.

"Nice to meet you, Nathan," I say, trying not to let on that I'm a little flustered. I take him in, hopefully in a not-too-obvious manner. I suppose that's one of the disadvantages of the person being hit on. You don't have to risk rejection by starting a conversation with a stranger, but you often don't have any advance warning. I hadn't had much of an opportunity to check him out before he was standing right next to me. I assume he's already done a cursory evaluation of me before coming over, and I hope I'm measuring up to his expectations. It's been quite a while since I've been in this type of situation—dressing sexy for the specific purpose of, maybe, meeting someone new, attracting their attention, and well, who knows what next?

I have on some tight jeans that accent my physical assets. I've never been typically curvaceous, but years of running have, thankfully, given me strong leg muscles and a—mostly—firm rear end. I'm wearing a cute, soft sweater I borrowed from Camila, that due to her being slightly more blessed by the bust gods than myself, has chosen this auspicious moment to slip off my shoulder. I see Nathan swiftly glance at my bare shoulder—or maybe the bra strap now making an appearance—and then quickly shift his gaze back to mine, thoughtfully giving me a moment to shrug my sweater back into place.

He's wearing jeans that fit him well and hint at muscular legs, a simple but stylish dark-gray t-shirt, and running shoes. Guys definitely win in the footwear department. I momentarily consider the tall heels I'm wearing tonight.

I can see Camila looking at me, while she continues her story, all the while giving me a mischievous smile. Nathan notices Camila's friend's SJSU sweatshirt and asks me if we're all students there. I'm craning my neck to meet his eye, and he inclines his head toward me and slouches a little.

"Well, they are," I said, gesturing to the small group, now all *cracking up at the crazy expression on Camila's face.*

"And you?"

"Oh, I'm starting a new job on Monday, actually. We're kind of out celebrating . . . and just getting out since everything's opening up again. Starting a fresh chapter, you know?"

"Definitely. Where's the new job?"

"Oh, it's at—" I begin to say, but just then Camila grabs my hand to go dance. Our song is on, and it's an unspoken vow that whenever Spice Girls comes on, whether we're at our high-school prom or on our deathbeds, we have to dance to it.

"Oh my god, I'm sorry," I say over my shoulder to Nathan, as I'm dragged away to the dance floor. He looks surprised but untroubled about the interruption.

"Cam," I yell-whisper into her ear over the loud music. "What are you thinking? I was right in the middle of a conversation."

"Don't worry about it. He's still looking at you," she assures me.

And as I glance over to where I've left Nathan, I can see she's right. He sets his drink down on the bar, crosses his muscular arms, and leans back. He's talking to his friend who's walked over. His friend is wearing a black hoodie that seems familiar for some reason, but twenty-something guys wearing black hoodies and jeans are really nothing special in Silicon Valley, so I turn my attention back to Camila, who's grinning at me wickedly.

"He is totally into you. He'll come over. Mark my words," she says.

An hour—and a few drinks—later, I'm warm from dancing. Nathan had indeed joined me, Camila, and our little group of friends on the dance floor. It's so loud, it's hard to talk, but I can tell he's into me.

"It's so hot in here," I say in his ear, fanning myself with my hand.

"Do you wanna go for a walk?" he asks me, also leaning close to talk into my ear since it's so loud.

"Um . . ." I say, looking around. I want to tell Camila that I'm going to take a short break from dancing, but she's nowhere to be found. Probably gone to the restroom. I hesitate, wondering to myself whether it's safe to go on a walk downtown at night with a guy I just met, but on second thought, I'm probably in better hands

with him than without him. He's given me a good vibe up until now. It's okay. We'll stay close by.

"You know what? Sure. Just give me a second," I tell him.

I walk a few feet away and share my location for the next 24 hours with Camila on Find my Friends, and text her "Going for a walk, don't worry, I'll get an Uber home."

"Let's go," I say, grabbing my jacket from one of the hooks under the bar on my way out.

As we leave the bar, I take a breath of the fresh, cool air. I can feel moisture in the air and wonder if we're in for some unexpected rain tonight.

"Wow, that feels so good," I say, lifting my hair off the nape of my neck with one hand. As I do so, his eyes glance down, taking me in. An almost imperceptible widening of his eyes betrays his thoughts, and a quick burst of heat shoots up my spine. I look at him coyly —"You've been caught," my eyes say—and he coughs softly, trying to cover the slip. I guess the heels Camila suggested are doing their job.

As if reading my mind, he glances at my shoes skeptically and asks me, "How are you gonna walk in those tall shoes?"

"I danced in them, so what makes you think I can't walk in them?" I joke, doing a little dance, but then wince as I realize, he's right. It's probably time for me to get out of them. I wink at him and reach into my bag to find my roll-up flats to slip on instead of the heels. I hold on to his arm—finding solid muscle under my grip—to balance myself while I switch my shoes.

"Practical," he says while helping me keep from falling over during my sidewalk footwear change. He is, unsurprisingly, sturdy. I look up at him, estimating he's a good eight inches taller than me and a lot more solid.

"So, where to?" I ask.

"Well, we could take a walk," he suggests, glancing in the direction of the park, but as we start to head that way, we can see there are two police officers talking to a homeless man on the corner and things don't exactly seem calm. He glances at me, gives me a questioning smile, and suggests that maybe we head the other direction and search for something to eat.

"I could really use pizza right now or like an amazing sandwich," I say. "I haven't eaten much today. I had so many errands to run and then as soon as I got to Camila's—my friend—she started throwing clothes and makeup at me. Is there anything good open around here?"

"I don't know . . . I mean, there's sushi, but it might be closed now. There's a taqueria around the corner. I'm sure we can find something."

We change course and begin walking in the direction of the taqueria he mentioned, finally getting a chance to talk a bit without the noise of the bar in the background.

"So, Nathan, where ya from?" I ask him.

"Well, I just moved here last year from Illinois, but I grew up in Seattle."

"Ooh, Seattle. I've been there a few times. It's really cool. I love how there's that whole island—um, Bainbridge—you can only get to via ferry."

"Well, you can actually drive there," he says, laughing.

"No, don't ruin my fantasy. I dream of one day living on an island, cut off from the world—at least a little bit—and just doing art or creating something."

"Oh," he says. "Are you an artist?"

"No," I say, laughing. "But I'm still young. Maybe I'll become one someday."

He smiles, and my breath catches in my throat for just a second at how warm it is. How warm it makes me feel inside.

"Is it raining?" I say, confused, looking up.

We've arrived at the taqueria, and the lights inside the shop are off. We're standing underneath the restaurant's awning, contemplating what to do next, and I can see a light drizzle falling, backlit by the streetlight on the corner.

"Sorry. I guess it's only open for lunch," Nathan said. "Ummm . . . I actually live really close by. But I don't know if you'd feel comfortable coming over . . ."

I'm a little torn. I've just met him, but I am feeling . . . comfortable, which is unexpected. I've felt, well, fragile since *breaking up with Blake and a bit distrustful of the opposite sex. Nathan seems normal, but I give myself a moment to consider. I can't quite read the expression on his face, but when it solidifies a bit, I see that it's uncertainty. Maybe not in what he's proposing— that he likes me is clear—but, if I'm guessing correctly, in his own level of confidence in proposing it in the first place.*

"Um, would you wanna come over? I mean, just to hang out. I can make you some food. I'm a good cook. It's definitely safer than roaming around down here late at night. I have a comfy couch. I mean—" he stops abruptly, eyes wide from embarrassment. "Sorry, I didn't mean that."

His expression is one of such utter discomfort that I laugh out loud and rub his arm, telling him to relax. I don't fail to notice how strong he is, or how, even with a look of embarrassment on his face, this guy is hot. And he is into me. Me.

"Okay, sure. Feed me, Nathan. Let's go."

❊ ❊ ❊

It's past midnight, and I'm in a stranger's apartment, waiting for him to bring me food. "Are you sure I can't help?" I call into the kitchen. Stranger things have likely happened in my life, but this is probably top ten, to be sure.

"No, it's okay. Stay there and warm up," he calls back. "I'm just heating up the pasta I made earlier. You said you're vegetarian, right? There's no meat in it."

"Yes, vegetarian," I confirm. I walk away from the large window, where I was enjoying the view from the tenth floor, and sit on his couch. I snuggle into the soft blanket thrown over it, warming up my feet that have managed to turn into popsicles on the short walk here. A woman—a previous girlfriend?—must have given it to him. This is not the sort of throw blanket a young guy buys for himself—too girly, too stylish. Must've been a birthday present or something.

As I wait, I investigate his apartment. Simple but stylish is my conclusion. Nothing too fancy, but it looks as if he's done the same IKEA-run most newly-relocated Bay Area young people do. A pop of color here and there and a few plants near the window. I take note of the small herb garden with some mint, rosemary, cilantro, and basil.

A few moments later, he comes out of the kitchen, in an apron no less, looking hot as hell—what is it about guys in aprons?—and carrying a tray. On it are two plates of delicious-smelling, scrumptious-looking pasta, an unopened bottle of wine, and two glasses.

"I'm impressed, sir," I say, smiling up at him as he unties the apron and sits down next to me.

"I saw you liked red wine, earlier," he says, holding up the bottle. "Would you like some?"

"I should probably stick with water," I say.

"Of course," he says, and gets up, returning to the kitchen for a glass of water.

While he's gone, I wonder, for half a second, where this is going. Hey, Clueless, you know where this is going.

When he comes back, he joins me on the couch, and we begin to eat. He wasn't lying. He really is a good cook. "This is delicious," I tell him.

He smiles, a little shyly, and bites his lip. "This is really out of character for me."

"What is?" I reply. "Eating pasta?"

"Oh, well, that too, I guess. I have been trying to cut carbs."

"I can tell," I say, probably a bit too bluntly, and look him up and down, definitely a little too openly.

"But I mean, like bringing a beautiful girl home from a bar—"

"You usually bring ugly girls home from bars?" I ask, giving him an innocent face.

He smirks.

"After knowing her for only a couple of hours—" he continues.

"Stop. It's okay. It's out of the ordinary for me, too," I admit. "But you know . . . I just needed to have fun tonight, and I've had fun and I think maybe . . ."

"We could have fun together?" he says, going out on a limb and flirting openly.

"Yeah," I say, more directly than I've spoken to a guy in, well, quite a while. "Yeah, that sounds good." I look directly into his eyes and garner courage from who knows where in the depths of my brain or other parts. I quickly dab the corners of my mouth with a napkin, and clutching it—as if I'm holding on to a life raft—I get even more direct.

"Can I kiss you?"

"Hell, yes," he blurts out, exhaling as if he's just been waiting for me to ask the question. He sets down the glass he's holding and moves close to me in one swift motion. His hard body is up against mine in no time, and he puts his hand behind my neck and gently angles his head and my own as he presses his full lips lightly to mine.

I'm a little bolder than I usually am. I'm not sure how to explain it. Apparently, some sort of alter-ego Sarah has taken over tonight. "Why not?" this other Sarah asks. Why not forget the pandemic and breakups from sketchy boyfriends and celebrate new beginnings, and enjoy the company of an attractive chef?

His lips are slightly parted, and I trace the opening of his mouth with my tongue—which seems to have a mind of its own. He opens them wider, and I slip my tongue into his mouth and begin to explore. He tastes faintly like mint and lemons and . . . well, whatever "I want this guy to screw me senseless" tastes like. Nathan is hot by any standard, but especially by the "I haven't slept with anyone in six-plus months" standard.

I tentatively and then more urgently let my hands drift up his pecs, to his neck, then his face, and then back down to his amazing arms and strong back. I gently bite his bottom lip, and as I release it, parting my lips for another round, he pulls back, for a moment, and takes a breath.

We look at each other, and a beat passes. "Wow," we both utter at the same time, shocking us into silence and then into mutual laughter.

"I need more," I say.

"Food?" he jokes.

"No, no food. I need more of that. That kiss. You," I say, pointing at him like an idiot.

"I think I can help you there," he says, as he lays me back on the soft pillows of the couch. "Is this okay? This is what you want?"

"Um, yes," I reply, matter-of-factly, indicating there is no place in the world I'd rather be than on this man's couch, making out with him.

"Okay, it's just . . . you know . . . I thought I'd feed you pasta and we'd talk or something and I don't know, hear about your new job or . . ."

"That can wait," I say decisively. "Kiss me again." And he does. Many times.

At some point, we move to his bedroom, and I don't know what I did in some past lifetime to be bestowed the gifts of the sex gods in this life, but it is otherworldly. Nathan must've been sent to reward me for building housing and educating orphans in a developing country last century. Maybe it's the fact that it's been half a year since I've broken up with Blake and I haven't been with anyone else for a long time. Maybe this is what being with someone new feels like, and it's just been a long time, so I've forgotten. But I seem to have lost all my inhibitions—entranced by those brown eyes of his, his calm, low voice—and whatever it is, it is fucking great.

I stare at my computer screen, realizing that the meeting has ended—we've taken a break for lunch—and I'm the only one still on the call.

Recalling it all now—dancing with him, the good conversation, the *great* sex—I ask myself why I bolted on Saturday morning. All I can come up with is that perhaps it had felt *too right*. And in my experience "too right" could turn into "too wrong" before you even realized what was happening. Waking up next to him, curled up and snoring softly, was like looking into a small window to find out what else might be inside. Something bad or something good? Can you ever really be sure? I wasn't ready for it, and it scared me. So, I ran.

BACK-TO-OFFICE

It's my first day at the office, and I open my new laptop in Instinqt's cool open workspace. The walls are bold colors, and the desks are sleek, white glass with buttons to raise and lower them, depending on your height. I'm looking out the window at the other tall buildings in the area. It's not far from where Camila and I went to the bar a few weekends ago, and I blush slightly at the fleeting memory of that night.

I'm wearing a mask. We all are. We're back in office, but there are Covid vaccination policies and mask mandates, likely for the next couple of weeks, and company policy is that in the open work space unless you're eating or drinking, you have to wear a mask. I bought a pack of black ones—despite my natural tendency to go for color in all-things wardrobe. I've gone all-out on my eye makeup, practicing my winged eyeliner methods over the weekend to add a little flair. My glasses are new—dark-red plastic—a bit of pop but still understated. I picked them up from the shop last week. I needed a new prescription anyway—the optometrist assured me that your eyes really do stop getting worse around twenty-seven. I'm almost twenty-eight, so here's hoping—otherwise, I'll be blind by the time I'm forty.

I look around and see people greeting each other, beginning to get re-acclimated. In some cases, like mine, it's our first time here in the office. I hear people laughing while they try to remember how to use the high-tech coffee maker and figure out where the mugs are stored in one of the many glossy cabinets in the kitchen area.

"Did you guys hear about the re-org?" I hear someone say in a hushed tone to a colleague.

"I heard there *is* gonna be a re-org," someone in the group replies. "But that's about it."

"Well, the weekly product meeting no longer involves Jared . . . and I went to Slack him this morning, and his account's been deactivated."

"What?" I hear a few people say at once.

I don't really know what they're talking about. I just got here, but I have heard of a Jared at Instinqt. None other than Chief Product Officer Jared Lynch, or from what it sounds like, *ex-*Chief Product Officer.

I raise my eyebrows, but figure it's none of my business, being the new girl, and continue checking my email. I see a new invite pop up for Thursday morning, "Weekly Product Review," and accept the meeting invite. I was hired as a technical program manager and sit with the product and engineering teams. My role here, as my hiring manager joked in the interview, is to "manage the chaos." *Let the chaos begin.* I gather up my laptop and coffee mug to head to my first meeting of the day.

❊ ❊ ❊

On Thursday, we gather in a conference room with a large screen at one end. The weekly product review meeting usually has twenty or so attendees: product managers, engineering managers, and C-level executives. The main idea is to update what's happening with key lines of business—status updates, any blockers or at-risk projects, or shout-outs for a job well done. This week, the meeting roster has been expanded, the person sitting next to me explains. They've turned it into a product and engineering all-hands and have included key players from sales, marketing, and finance as well. It's a big room and there are at least thirty-five people there, with another thirty to forty attending via Zoom. We can see them all—many with their cameras off, some with them turned on—just waiting to find out why we're all here. Word around the office is that Jared, the previous CPO, left—or was kicked out, some of the rumors say—and they're appointing a new interim Chief Product Officer. It's been largely assumed that someone named Matt Jones will get the position since he previously reported to Jared.

The woman next to me, Erin Park, a strategic programs manager at Instinqt, discreetly points him out to me. "That's him," she whispers. "He's a mega-douche, but he really knows his shit."

In my short time here, Erin and I have formed a pretty nice work friendship. She's about ten years older than me—close enough in age for us to relate pretty well, but just old enough for her to feel like an older sister and give me advice when I need it. She was one of the people who interviewed me back in late November, and we had a great conversation, connecting immediately. Since I began, our shared love of project planning and reporting has expanded to eating lunch together regularly, whenever we're both working from the office. We're both big fans of the taqueria just down the street. Erin isn't my boss, but she's become a mentor of sorts for me here. She's been here since the early days and has worn a variety of different hats as Instinqt has grown. She works closely with the founders and execs, but despite that, she's one of the most down-to-earth people ever.

Things settle down a bit when the CEO, wonder-boy Kevin Wong, walks in. When I got the job offer at Instinqt, I'd done a bit more research on the company, and while he's no Elon Musk, I found a number of articles on Hacker News and the like. Instinqt was hinting at going public in the next couple years, and there were plenty of people who wanted to talk to him. I don't remember seeing any pictures of him in the articles I read, but I find myself searching his face—partially covered with a mask— wondering why he seems familiar to me.

Kevin is average height for a guy and not bad-looking. Even from here, it's easy to see how charming he is and that he was born to be a CEO. He waves at a couple of people, including Erin, who acknowledges him with a slight incline of her head. Then he stands at the front of the room, near Instinqt's CTO, Maya Kapoor, and calls the meeting to order.

"So, some of you might've guessed why we're here. I know the office rumor mill has been going strong this week," he says, smiling. It's hard to tell—we're all wearing masks—but I see his eyes crinkle at the corners and can just guess that under it, his smile is 100 watts.

"Jared Lynch, our former CPO, yes former, has decided to leave Instinqt to spend more time with his family . . ."

"That's code for they asked him to leave," Erin whispers into my ear and winks.

"And we have appointed a new CPO. This is an interim appointment, but if things go well, and I'm pretty sure they will, it could become a permanent thing."

"The person we've chosen is somewhat new to the industry, but as any of you who've worked with him know, during his time here at Instinqt, he's come to know our product inside and out from his work on our engineering team. He's got a keen eye for business and that's the winning combination. It also doesn't hurt that he's a Lakers fan." People laugh.

All the time, I had my eye on Matt, and until the last second, his chest had been puffed up in anticipation and pride, obviously anticipating his name being called. But when Kevin mentioned being a Lakers fan, I saw a slight, but noticeable, confused expression in his eyes, that he quickly got in check.

"What are you doing over there in the corner?" Kevin says, looking to the back of the room. "Come on up."

My eyes now shift from Matt, who's sitting near the center of the large table in the middle of the conference room, to the man Kevin's talking to. You can tell he's smiling, behind his mask, and he stands slowly, leisurely, almost. The people closest to him are congratulating him, patting him on the back, and giving him fist bumps. "Congrats, man!" a guy wearing a black hoodie says, as he gives him a loose "bro" hug.

As he walks up to the front of the room to join Kevin, I stare like a deer in headlights at the *very* familiar body I see striding confidently up to the front of the room. I scoot as discreetly as possible behind Erin and pull a lock of hair over my eyes to shield my face a bit. *Oh, fuck.* I realize a little too late that I've said it out loud.

"What?" Erin asks, giving me a friendly but bemused look, turning her head, owl-like, behind her, to account for my impromptu hide-and-seek game.

"What's wrong?" she whispers. "Are you okay?"

I nod my head stiffly, trying to indicate that everything is okay. But everything is not okay. Nothing, in fact, is okay. At all. My limbs are all-but-frozen, and my heart is beating wildly.

I try to give her a reassuring expression, but I can feel the tension in my forehead and since that's likely all she can see—that and my wild eyes—with a mask over the bottom portion of my face, it doesn't seem to be doing the trick. She's looking completely confused by my weird behavior. I indicate with my head that she should turn back around and pay attention to the meeting. Because I cannot, *will* not, admit to her or anybody else, even to myself, that the first one-night stand of my life was in fact with the man at the front of the room—cutting an impressive figure in his fitted jeans and stylish black North Face hoodie emblazoned with Instinqt's simple logo.

"For those of you who don't know," Kevin is saying, "Nate Goldman, Instinqt's new interim Chief Product Officer."

Newly-minted C-level exec, Nathan "Nate" Goldman, the hot guy who fed me homemade pasta and took me to new heights in the bedroom. The guy I thought I'd never see again as I left his place on a cold January morning.

I hear everyone's applause, but the sound is drowned out by the thoughts racing in my head: *This is bad, but how bad is it? It's "I've-seen-him-naked" bad. No. Shit, it's "He's-seen-me-naked" bad.*

What are the freaking odds? Apparently, one-in-fuck-my-life.

NINE MONTHS EARLIER

INITIAL COMMIT

The phone buzzes, and he looks at the screen: "Kevin." Again. He's been calling daily for the last week. Nathan knows what Kevin wants. It's no secret. He just doesn't have an answer yet, and he's avoiding Kevin. Deciding that if he doesn't pick up, he'll just keep on calling, Nathan presses "Accept."

"Good morning, Sunshine," Kevin says cheerfully. Annoyingly.

"Yeah, what?" Nathan answers, a little impatiently.

"Is today the day that you make me a happy man?"

"I *will* marry you. Will you love me forever?" Nathan answers, messing with him. Kevin deserves it after the harassment he's been imposing on Nathan the last few weeks.

"Are you for real? Or are you just being an asshole?"

"I'm not gonna marry you, Kevin. You're not my type. I like them a little smaller, a little less hairy."

"I'm asking whether you're joining the startup or not, dude. I thought you just came up with a creative way to say 'yes.'"

"I don't know. You know that I have my own ideas for a startup. I'm almost done with school. I'm putting the finishing touches on the last journal article I need to get my PhD, man. I might wanna do my own thing."

"Nate, we have funding. And we're gonna go for another round early next year. We're not cash-flow positive yet, but we will be soon. It's a soft place for you to land after graduation. I know you don't wanna go the corporate tech route, not yet anyway. This way, you get something on your resume, and you keep working on your own thing in your free time." Kevin rattles off one idea after the other.

He's done his pitch to Nathan so many times, he's memorized

it. Nathan wonders if he even took a breath between sentences.

Nathan decides to indulge him, at least a little bit.

"There's free time in a startup?" he asks him.

"Mmmm . . ."

"That's what I thought."

"For you, I'll make it happen," Kevin promises.

"Why do you want *me* so bad?"

"You know, a cute girl asked me the same exact thing a few nights ago."

"Sure."

"Nate, I need some people here on my side. I've got this asshole Jared, who thinks he knows what's best for the company and doesn't seem to understand that I'm the CEO."

"Jared, your Chief Product Officer?"

"Yeah. He's not an original founder, but he acts like it, and he's good at talking to the board. I need someone to watch my back. That's where you come in, to support me."

Nathan considers what Kevin is saying. Kevin likes to get his way. It's what makes him a good CEO, a good entrepreneur, but in this case, it's not only about what Kevin wants. Nathan's been in school for the last eight—no, nine—years. He's definitely tired of it. The idea of staying in academia, becoming a professor, and starting down a path of endless peer reviews for articles or teaching some freshman-year Intro to Data Structures course sounds like torture. But he's actually been considering taking a bit of time off and traveling some. After half a decade of Illinois winters, somewhere warm sounds good. After that, he'll play some video games, work out, and cook, on loop, for about three months. Then, he'll begin working on his own startup idea.

Then again, he remembers, the world is still in the middle of a pandemic. It's not like he can jet off to travel the world so easily right now. And, well, being a student the last eight years hasn't exactly been financially lucrative. Having a job right now, especially one in his friend's company, where he knows he'll learn something, get some experience, might make some sense for now. Beyond that, he knows himself. A week of League of

Legends and cooking non-stop, and he'll be bored.

Joining Instinqt, a well-backed startup two years into its existence, might not be as good as joining *before* the venture capitals invested, but it still stands to be pretty profitable. They'll offer him good equity, even at this stage of the game. It has a lot of advantages, both financially and as a résumé builder.

He knows—from Kevin's numerous pitches to him to join— that Instinqt is in a relatively good place now. Despite being so new, and getting off the ground right before the pandemic, they pivoted to remote work like champions. Their customer list is growing, and they've just signed two well-known enterprise companies. Their chances of securing a Series B round of funding by mid-next year are very, very good.

And Nathan would probably enjoy doing something productive out in the real world instead of just hammering away at theoretical computer science research. He's ready for a challenge. He thought it would be his own startup, but joining Kevin's might not be the worst option.

"What'll be my role, huh?"

"Ooooh, coming around, I hear. You can be . . . a VP of engineering."

"VP?" Nathan says, surprised. "How do you even have that role in a seventy-five-person startup?"

"I'm the CEO. I can give you whatever title I want. It'll look good on your LinkedIn profile when you start your own thing."

Nathan is quiet for a minute, trying to run different scenarios in his head.

Kevin is quiet, waiting patiently, something he's only good at when it's the strategic choice. Nathan speaks up, surprising even himself. "Okay. I'll do it."

"Yes! Alright, let's FaceTime on Monday, and I'll go over everything you need to know. Including how we're gonna push Jared out of a moving car."

Kevin's always been pretty bold, but Nathan wonders just how savage he might be now that he's the head of a company.

"*What* did I just sign up for?"

"Don't worry about it, dude. I got your back. You got mine."

Kevin ends the call and Nathan sits there, staring at himself in the mirror. Looks like he's moving to California.

❊ ❊ ❊

Summer in San Jose is hotter than he imagined it would be, but overall, still pretty pleasant. He's starting to feel settled, after finishing up his PhD and moving out here. He didn't really have to relocate to the San Francisco Bay Area, since everyone in the company—and every other high-tech company—is still working remote anyways, but he was ready for a change, and Kevin encouraged him.

"It'll be like old times, man. Like college, except now we have more money, so we can actually drink *good* bourbon."

Nathan *has* missed hanging out with Kevin since he left Illinois for Silicon Valley to pursue his dream of founding a startup. It was risky, but things seem to be paying off. Nathan hopes it'll pay off for him, too.

"That's the great thing about a small, innovative company," Kevin's saying to the board. "We can move fast, respond to the market's needs, and not be afraid to try new things." He looks pointedly at Jared when he says this last part.

Nathan glances at Jared and catches the smug expression on his face. *He wouldn't be so smug if he knew Kevin as well as I do.* Kevin is smooth and polished, but he's also a determined motherfucker and this guy is going to go down, sooner rather than later.

Nathan has joined the meeting at Kevin's request, and if he had to guess, he'd say it's so his face becomes familiar to the board. Fortunately, or not, he doesn't really have to guess. Kevin has told him in no uncertain terms that he's getting Jared out of there ASAP, and Nathan knows who Kevin wants to replace him.

"He's holding us back. You know me. I'm not frivolous. I'm not deranged. But we have to put more resources toward the big bets, the stuff that might *not* pay off, but if it does, we're living in a golden palace, man," Kevin had explained to Nathan on a walk they took one day after lunch.

"That's not going to look really bad to the board? Kicking him out and replacing him with . . . well, your best friend?" Nathan had asked.

"Whose idea do you think it *was*, Nate?" Kevin said, giving him a pointed look.

When Nathan had shrugged, Kevin clarified. "Jerry." Jerry is the head of the board.

Damn.

"This type of thing is . . . well, it's not common, but it's definitely not unheard of for executives or even founders to suddenly figure out they want to 'explore other opportunities.'"

"Suggested to them by other founders or the board?"

"Something like that."

Nathan had been surprised, suddenly realizing just how out of his depth he was. But he knows he can trust Kevin, the same way Kevin knows he can trust him. That's why he's here. And despite the fact that Nathan didn't intend to get competitive in this role, the sound of an executive position—no matter how small the company—is beginning to sound pretty appealing to him.

Since moving out here, it's been a bit of a challenge to get to know everyone since they're not coming into the office regularly, but Kevin organizes frequent off-sites for the local employees—hikes and other day-long, mostly outdoor, activities to get the engineering and product teams together. Nathan's gotten acquainted with everyone of consequence and even though he knows that the VP title is a bit of a farce, he's making an impact already, despite his short time at Instinqt. His natural inclination is not to be impressed by fancy titles. Even the fact that he could add PhD to the end of his name now is, in large part, due to his brother David encouraging him down that path.

"If you're already a computer geek—" David had said.

"Computer nerd," Nathan had corrected him.

"Fine, nerd. Big difference."

"There is," Nathan said.

"What's the difference?"

"Well, it's a hotly debated topic—"

The look on David's face gave away his doubts.

"Maybe not so hotly debated," Nathan conceded. "But there is a difference. Computer geeks are the ones that get really excited by new technologies and tweet about it all the time."

"And nerds?" David asked, indulging him.

"Computer nerds, well, they also like new technologies, but they want to be the ones creating them. They're more . . . academic."

"So, not cooler?" David asked, laughing.

"They—we—are probably all socially stunted to some extent," said Nathan, admitting defeat. "Nerds are more introverted, I think. You gotta get to know them before realizing they analyze license plates and think about prime numbers for fun."

"You do that?"

"I do. But I also work out . . . because I like women," he had replied and grinned. David had agreed it was solid logic and the discussion had moved on.

Remembering their conversation now, he smiles to himself. They were sitting on the deck of their family home in Seattle, overlooking the Puget Sound. It was four years ago, and Nathan was trying to decide if he should just finish up his master's and call it a day or go the PhD route.

David, it turns out wisely, had advised him that if he was already doing half of the work for the challenge and fun of it, why not publish it? And if he was already publishing it, why not earn the PhD?

So, now he's Nathan Goldman, PhD and VP of Engineering, and some days, he couldn't care less. But knowing, in the back of his head, that he wants to found his own startup in the coming years, he can't help but think that the title "Chief Product Officer" might help him get funding and support when the time comes.

Nathan focuses on what's being said in the meeting now and is discreetly watching Jared, the current CPO, and Matt, the current head of product. They're both looking confident, and Nathan wonders how in the hell Kevin plans to handle the fallout of kicking Jared out. Even if he succeeds in getting Jared out of Instinqt, he'll have to deal with Matt's crushed dreams. Matt's been at Instinqt almost since the start of the company, and he probably won't take this kind of thing lying down.

Nathan listens as Kevin explains the timeline for the coming year, and he's proud of him. They've been friends for years —since the first year of their bachelor's when they ended up in the computer science department together at the University of Washington. Nathan saw Kevin wearing a Lakers t-shirt to Linear Algebra and their friendship was born. *Kevin's come a long way*, Nathan thinks, as he listens to him present. When they first met, it was clear that Kevin was, well, a little on the dorky side. But he was determined to remake his image at college through a well-planned and well-executed "fake it 'til you make it" approach. As he listens to Kevin talk, it seems like it's worked. He's made it.

He's going over the yearly budget and revenue forecast, the planned product releases, the anticipated growth in headcount and expected new hires, and when they'll start talking to potential investors for the Series B round.

"Now might not be the right time for the next round," Jared pipes up. Kevin gives him a measured look that seems to say, "*We've talked about this.*"

"Now is *exactly* the time to start talking about the round. We're growing fast, and we have to continue to do so in order to stay ahead. We've got first-to-market advantage, and don't think for a minute that our competitors aren't close on our heels. To grow, we need money," Kevin says definitively.

Nathan knows that Kevin's going out on a limb. He's showing a lot more confidence than he actually feels. He admitted as much to Nathan in a recent conversation, telling him that he wasn't sure the board was ready for this, but that he felt deep down it was the right step.

As Nathan listens to the discussion, which is decidedly in Kevin's favor, he considers that having a little courage—even when you don't feel it—might not be the worst approach in business. The board members do an unofficial vote and agree that the Series B funding talks should get started in earnest come late fall. Kevin shoots Nathan a quick look—victory—and a few minutes later, they break for the day.

* * *

"He's such a dick," Kevin's telling Nathan later, as they take a walk around the block. The sun's beginning to set, and the sky is a striking pinkish-orange hue. "I don't know why I thought this guy would be good for the product role. He's a good engineer, but he doesn't understand the business well enough. And sometimes, the main thing is to be ahead of your competitors. You gotta release new features and wow customers with the product before your competitors do it. I'm running out of ways to say 'ship it.'"

Nathan smirks. He's only been at the company a couple months, but he already knows that it's an inside joke among the engineers how much Kevin says "ship it." Sometimes it's more along the lines of "ship the fucking product release already."

But he can't fault Kevin. As the CEO, it's his ass on the line, and he's right that getting new features out, especially the ones requested by their more high-profile customers, is what brings in the dollars.

"He's stuck on the initial product vision, I think. Doesn't realize the world's changed with Covid. What worked then won't work now, not in the same way, at least," Nathan adds.

"Exactly," Kevin says. "Dude, I gotta get rid of him. I'm gonna talk to Jerry."

"Already?"

"Yeah, it's time. He's thinking about moving to Google anyway."

"He told you that?"

"No," Kevin replies. "But my buddy over there told me he was talking to some recruiter."

Nathan's impressed with Kevin's ability to have all the right intel all the time.

"So, you want a promotion?" Kevin jokes.

"Won't that be a declaration of war?"

"I'm feeling a bit Machiavellian. I also need a drink."

"Decades?" Nathan asks, gesturing with his head across the street.

"Yeah," Kevin says. "Let's sit on the patio."

❧ ❧ ❧

The bar is busy enough for early evening on a Friday, but it makes sense. It's the start of the weekend, the weather is great, and despite it being summer break, there are a lot of what looks like graduate students hanging out. There are a couple of universities in the area and Nathan knows—from living close by for a couple months—that this is one of the popular places.

A few tables over from them is a group of what seems like, if he had to guess, biology students. They have a sciency look about them, but not quite the dorkiness of the computer science majors he's used to. One of them turns around and is wearing a t-shirt with a cartoon beaker and test tube on it, confirming his guess was right.

While he's waiting for Kevin to come back with the drinks, he checks the messages on his phone and people watches. He notices a woman in her twenties—a beautiful one, with a wide smile—come in the gate to the patio and join a group in the corner. She has long, shiny, dark brown hair and as she bends down to give her friend a hug, he can't help but notice her nice backside as well. He turns his head, not wanting to get caught appreciating the view when Kevin sets down two bottles of Blue Moon on the table.

"You've been caught, Goldman," Kevin says to him.

"Doing what, exactly?"

"Being a dude," he jokes, glancing in the direction of the pretty brunette.

Nathan gives him a dirty look.

"It's been a while since Alena," Kevin says. "What happened

with her, anyway?"

"She finished school and moved to New York for work. We tried the long-distance thing for a hot minute, but it didn't really work out."

"You think about moving there to join her?"

"I didn't want to live in New York."

"What's wrong with New York?"

"Well, I guess it's more that I didn't want to live in New York *with Alena*."

Kevin raises his eyebrows.

"She was . . . fine. Nice."

"'Fine?' 'Nice?' Sounds special," Kevin says and snickers.

"Well, once she was out of sight, she also became out of mind, I guess. It just wasn't . . . *it*."

Kevin nods, waits a beat, and then changes the subject. "So, I've got a proposal for you—a *second* proposal."

"At this rate, we're gonna be married soon."

"It's the Bay Area. That's perfectly acceptable here," Kevin responds.

"You remember Danica? From UW?"

Do I remember Danica? He gives Kevin a look that clearly says *"Are you serious?"*

"You mean the Danica I dated for a few months in college and broke up with after I realized she probably had a vision board for all the ways she wanted to mold me into the perfect husband? Yes, unfortunately, I do."

"Was she that bad?"

"Let's just say that I don't need someone to manage every aspect of my life, Kev. I like how I dress. I like how I talk— or don't. And even at twenty years old, I knew what emotional manipulation looks like."

Kevin presses his lips together, and Nathan begins to worry what's about to come out of his mouth.

"Why?" Nathan asks, concerned.

"Well, she connected with me on LinkedIn yesterday, and it turns out she's working on some strategy or partnerships team at LightVerse."

"And?"

"And LightVerse's investment arm is on our short list of investors for our B round."

Kevin leans in. "I can reach out to her, but it'll probably move faster if you do it. We need to get a meeting set up. Start greasing some wheels. Feel free to grease anything else you need to get it done." He raises his eyebrows for emphasis.

"Dude, that's not gonna happen. I'm *not* interested in a Nate-Danica 2.0."

"I'm just a man trying to help you get a promotion. And get laid," he says, adding the last part under his breath.

"I heard that. I can find my own dates."

"Why don't you go talk to that girl whose ass you were admiring when I came back?"

"Maybe next time," Nathan says, glancing in the direction of the table where she's sitting now, talking to her friends.

"Sure," Kevin says, knowing his friend's personality after all these years and how likely that is to happen.

"Why don't we go back to my place and plan our *coup d'état*, then?"

"Alright, let's do it," Nathan says, taking his last swallow of beer and standing to leave. They go out the side gate of the patio, back toward work to grab their bags, and Nathan takes one last look at her. He'll definitely need to come back here one night.

DATA-DRIVEN

Summer turns to fall and things continue to move forward in the world. Covid numbers peak and then wane, and then peak again, and everyone at Instinqt is currently working from home, except for important meetings. Nathan spends most of his time working but finds time for—mostly outdoor—social activities. He hikes with a few friends he knows from school, who have also moved out here, and gets back into mountain biking, something he took a break from while in Illinois.

One thing to say for a pandemic, especially when you're single, is that you have a lot of time to fill, and he's been spending it as well as one could be. He cooks. He works out. And he's glad he's got the latter to balance out the former. He's in the best shape of his life and is enjoying the year-round good weather Northern California has to offer.

Still, it's been hard, living alone, being in isolation so much due to Covid. He's on a flight now, about midway between San Jose and Seattle, and he tries to remember the last time he saw his family. He shifts in the uncomfortable plane seat, struggling, but failing to find a comfortable position that will allow him to fall back asleep. But planes are not really built for six-foot-tall people, and he finally gives up. Exhausted as he was from his pre-dawn wake up this morning to catch his early morning flight, he was able to fall asleep for the first half of the two-hour flight. The drink cart rumbling by, though, jarred him awake a few minutes ago, and he's in some sort of limbo state—too exhausted to think clearly, but too awake to sleep. He squeezes his eyes shut against the rays of sun piercing through the window, wondering whether he can reach over and pull down the plastic shade without nudging his sleeping row-mate.

His mind is filled with all sorts of clutter: the email he sent Kevin late last night, a recent conversation with one of the engineers about what's next on Instinqt's feature roadmap, and a technical discussion he had with Maya in the office, over lunch, last week. In the middle of sorting through these bits and pieces, he suddenly remembers the last time he was home. It must've been the previous winter break, almost a year ago, when he flew out to Washington to escape the bitter cold of Illinois, only to realize that Seattle wasn't that much warmer. But spending time with his family over the holiday, just catching up and eating his mom's cooking, had been good, carefree. He realizes just how carefree now as he recalls his conversation with his mother from a couple of weeks ago.

"Nathan, darling, well . . ." his mom starts to say on their Facetime conversation. They speak a few times a week, often on his morning walk to work in downtown San Jose, but today he's at home and it's almost lunchtime. He's not sure why, but he could almost feel tension in her simple text: "Nathan, honey, call me when you can. Please."

After two minutes on the call with her, his suspicion that something must be wrong has been validated. She's been twirling a lock of hair near her ear and has a tight—unnatural—smile plastered on her face. She tugs the hair behind her ear as if suddenly becoming aware of what she was doing, and puts both hands down, out of his sight. But he can hear her begin to shuffle papers or something else. She's not usually a fidgety person, and she definitely seems agitated now.

"Mom, what's going on?" he asks, in a gentle tone. Clearly, something is bothering her.

"Why do you assume something's going on?" she replies, her voice a little higher—a little more shaky?—than usual.

"Well, you're acting weird."

"Hmmm," she replies, a look of consternation on her face. But then he raises an eyebrow, an expression he knows she finds endearing, and she smiles a bit.

"Am I that transparent?" she asks.

Nathan smiles at her and nods.

"I guess I shouldn't have done Facetime, huh?"

"Mom, can you just, you know, say whatever it is?"

She takes a deep breath, and he sees her close her eyes as if she's centering herself. Shit. What is going on?

She opens her eyes and tells him, point-blank, "Your dad has cancer, dear."

His heart drops into his stomach. That was not what he was expecting.

"Wait, what?" He thought she might tell him that an elderly relative had passed away, or someone had Covid—hopefully recovering—but not cancer. And he never would have guessed the news would be about his hearty, healthy father. He, too, now takes a deep breath and exhales, audibly."Are you sure?" he asks, hoping that there's some other explanation. That his mom has misspoken, or that he has somehow misheard. Something. Something to explain away the fear he's beginning to feel in his gut—a gnawing, clenching sort of achiness.

"Yes, well, that's a fair question, actually. If we're being very specific, he likely *has prostate cancer. He had his yearly checkup at the end of October, and he had a high PSA level–that's what they use to begin diagnosing this sort of thing. It was high enough that it* likely *is cancer."*

"Okay," Nathan says. "Okay." *His thoughts are swirling a bit, shooting off in different directions.* "It's cancer—shit," *is one of the directions.* "Prostate cancer. I've heard of that, and it's usually a good prognosis," *is the other. Before he can ask or say anything else, though, his mom continues, providing more details.*

"He had some other tests that they generally use to make a diagnosis, but he'll need to have a biopsy to confirm."

"But he seemed fine when I talked to him last weekend," he interjects. *Nathan considers himself a reasonable person, and reason, in this case, would indicate that the news his mom has just broken is likely accurate, but there's a small part of him that can't admit it. A part of him would rather deny reality and continue to hope that it's something else.*

"He . . . is fine, Nathan. I mean, he's not jumping for joy, but he feels fine. It's just good that he went in for his checkup when he did. We seem to have caught it early."

"Does David know?" Nathan's not sure why he asks. Maybe he wants to know why, if they've known about this for more than a week or two, he's only finding out now. Did David know and not tell me?

"I told him this morning, sweetheart."

"Why are you telling us and not Dad?"

"Well, because he didn't want to tell you or your brother at all. He didn't want to worry you."

"It's our right to worry. He's our dad."

"Well, as much as I don't want you to worry, either, I tend to agree with you, which is why I wanted to talk to you now. It's better for you to know." She says this last part as if she's had the opportunity —maybe many opportunities—to practice this part of her speech. He realizes that the reason she didn't tell him or David right away is because his dad likely asked her not to do so. And she's probably been trying to convince him they need to know.

"I'm sorry, Mom," he says.

"You're sorry?"

"I'm sorry you were dealing with this alone."

He can see tears well up in her eyes, but then she gives a soft, sad smile.

"My sweet Nathan. It's been too long since we've seen you. Maybe you could come home for Thanksgiving?" Her smile is hesitant now, questioning, as if she's asking for a huge favor.

But it's not a favor, he thinks now, as he sits on the plane and watches the flight attendants walk down the aisle, asking passengers if they have garbage to throw away.

Not a favor at all. Just what you do for the people you love.

He remembers her smile now when he'd told her that, of course, he would come. Her face had immediately relaxed, and her expression had turned a little happier, her smile broader. Her eyes had crinkled at the corners, and he couldn't help but think it was almost like looking at a picture of himself.

Right after the call, he and his brother David had talked and agreed that they would both come out for Thanksgiving and do whatever they needed to be there for their father and mother.

As the pilot gets on the speaker to tell them they're coming into the greater Seattle area, he allows himself to feel excited about seeing his family. It's been a long year—a long, lonely, pandemic-filled year—and despite the bad news they're facing, or maybe precisely because of it, he needs to be around the people he loves and who love him.

His Uber ride from the airport to the Goldman family residence in West Seattle allows him a bit of time to take in the outskirts of the city, and he notices how much greener it is than in San Jose. David, who flew out a few days before him, offered to pick him up, but Nathan told him to just stay at home and help his parents out. Or sleep in. That's probably what he's doing. It's only 9:00 a.m. and it's a Saturday, the weekend before Thanksgiving.

Despite the city looking gray as it always is this time of year, the beginnings of holiday decorations on the streets and in the store windows brighten things a bit. Since he last spoke to his parents, the diagnosis has been finalized. It's definitely prostate cancer—quite common for men in their sixties—and they're going to begin treatment after the holidays. To their great relief, the PET scan shows that it hasn't yet spread, but it needs to be taken care of sooner rather than later. His dad is scheduled for a biopsy at the beginning of January, so they'll know exactly what they're dealing with, to ensure the treatment is suited to the type of cancer cells.

The Uber pulls up to his parents' house, and he gets out, thanking the driver and grabbing the duffel bag he hastily packed last night before heading to bed at a late hour. Just as he begins to dig in his backpack for his key, his father opens the door.

"Hey, son," his dad greets him in a chipper tone.

"Hey, Dad," he replies, happy to see him looking, well, probably better than Nathan himself does.

"How are you?" his dad asks, taking Nathan's backpack from

one shoulder, as Nathan slides the duffel bag off his other one.

Of course his dad is asking how he is. That's just who Noah Goldman is. Even a cancer diagnosis can't keep him down or distract him from asking how his son is doing.

"I'm good, Dad," he says and draws closer to hug him. When he was fourteen, he passed his mom in height, and he's been taller than his father since he was eighteen years old, but in his father's arms, he might as well be a small child again. With everything that has happened—the long time since they've last seen each other in person and the cancer diagnosis—he feels the need for his father to comfort him, the way he would when Nathan was a child and fell off his bike or got hurt playing sports. But as Nathan squeezes him for a bit longer than he usually does, he has a faint inkling that their roles—at least in some ways—have changed. It's now his job to do what his father —and his mother—have done for his entire life: support, love, reassure, and be there when needed. Nathan pulls himself back from wherever his mind was momentarily wandering, in order to keep it—himself—together.

"How are you?" he asks his dad, leaning back a bit and holding his father out at arms' length, examining him.

"Well, your mom told you," he says bluntly. It's a statement, not a question, so Nathan simply nods to confirm what his dad already knows.

"Do you feel alright?"

"Want to go do pull-ups in the yard and see who wins?" his dad responds, smirking at him.

Nathan laughs. His dad built a pull-up bar for him and David when they were in their early teens, and since its inauguration on a cold February morning when Nathan was thirteen, there has been a long-running competition of who can do the most pull-ups each time they're all out in the yard together. His father won in the early years, but the boys—lighter, younger, and increasingly stronger—began to win as Nathan and David reached their mid-teen years.

"You know I'm gonna win, old man," Nathan jokes, letting his arms drop.

His father gives him a dirty look. "Fine, pushups."

Nathan laughs. "Fine. You might have a chance since I woke up at 5:00 this morning for the flight, and I'm tired."

"Slacker," his father declares. "I was up and had coffee made by 4:30."

With as many ways as Nathan finds himself becoming increasingly like his father, waking up early has never been—and he hopes *will* never be—one of them.

"How about we both do ten pushups, here in the hallway before Mom realizes I'm here and call it even?" Nathan suggests. He knows his dad won't give up until he's proven that he's alive and healthy.

"Got it."

They both get down and are finishing a quick ten pushups when his mom walks into the room. Nathan hears her footsteps stop somewhere behind, but doesn't pause to look, not wanting his dad to finish before him.

"You two," his mother says in an exasperated tone. "Welcome home, dear."

"Hi, Mom," Nathan says as he gets up and dusts off his hands on his pants. He kisses her on the cheek and engulfs her in a hug. He sees her roll her eyes at his father before laughing a bit.

"Go wash your hands, both of you, and you can try the lasagna I've made for later."

"Where's David?" Nathans asks.

"Oh, he was out late last night with some friends. Still sleeping."

Nathan smiles. He was right. David's still asleep. His father still likes physical challenges. And his mom still has lunch prepared by 9:30 a.m., just like she always has. It's good to be home.

✳ ✳ ✳

Having done all they can for now, Nathan spends time with his parents and David over Thanksgiving week. While they wait for whatever magic his Mom does in the kitchen on Thanksgiving Day to be completed, David and Nathan hang out, catching up, while his dad "rests" upstairs. Earlier, Noah offered to help in the kitchen, but Claire sent him upstairs to take a nap. His dad had scoffed but ultimately acquiesced. As Noah likes to say, he's been married a while and knows when his wife means business. Nathan suspects his dad is actually upstairs on his laptop since he just emailed Nathan an article from *The Atlantic*.

"So, what's happening at work, huh? Kevin still the same Kevin?" David asks. David, a few years older than Nathan and already on the East Coast for work by the time Nathan was at college, would often come home to visit during the holidays. He'd met and hung out with Kevin a number of times and was well-acquainted with his ambition, humor, and energy.

"Yeah, Kevin's the same Kevin," Nathan responds. "He's trying to kick out one of the execs and wants me to replace him. He's *also* trying to get me back together with Danica—"

"*Danica*? That hot chick from college that you dated for a while?"

"Danica, the *bossy, overbearing* chick from college that I dated for a *short* while. Yeah. She was intense."

"What was so intense about her?" his mom calls from the kitchen to where they're sitting in the dining room.

They look at each other and laugh, silently, at their mom's supersonic hearing. Lowering his tone—this isn't exactly the type of conversation he wants his mother to overhear—Nathan explains. "She wanted to have sex all the time, which, you know, *wasn't* really the problem." David snickers, and Nathan raises an eyebrow.

Claire chooses that moment to join them in the dining room, with a raised eyebrow. "You know, women and men communicate differently, Nathan."

He and David share a smile that only they know the meaning of since his mom luckily didn't overhear Nathan's last comment.

She's facing him, with her back to David. David crosses his arms, mimicking his mother's stance, and gives him a look that is spot-on the same as hers.

Nathan can't help the grin that breaks out on his face. His mother, now demonstrating her telepathic powers in addition to her excellent hearing, says, "David, you might be an adult, but I know exactly what you're doing behind my back, just like when you were a kid." Refocusing her attention on Nathan, she asks him, "Why not give this Danica another chance?"

"Mom, intense with the right person is fine, but intense with the wrong person is just uncomfortable. I don't need someone trying to change me. I already have a mother," he says, sweetly to her.

She leans down and kisses Nathan on the forehead, turns to David, gives him a stern glare, and goes back to the kitchen.

"She *was* also hot, though, if I remember correctly," David states, once his mother is out of hearing range. It seems important to him to clarify, for the record, of course.

"She was hot . . . she's *still,* well, you know . . . but when we dated, she was always trying to change me. I guess she thought I should be cooler or something. I barely put up with it when I was twenty, and I definitely don't need that in my life now."

"A relationship needs to be equal," David adds, uncharacteristically serious. "I'm not a relationship expert, but I know that much."

"Yeah, exactly," Nathan agrees. "And like, just open communication, you know? Like, you want or need something, just say it. No games."

"I get it," David says.

"Anyways, I'm more into, like, girl-next-door-with-glasses than hot-blonde-and-pushy," he says. A faint memory of the cute girl he saw at Decades over the summer floats somewhere in the back of his mind. *That's definitely the kind of woman I would be into.*

"So, why does Kevin want you to date her again?" David asks, with a confused look.

"He doesn't want me to date her, but we're trying to get into LightVerse and she works there. He thinks she can get us an intro to the right people."

"LightVerse, wow. Okay, well, be careful. You never know what an *intense* chick will do," David says, laughing.

Within an hour, they're sitting down to a late-afternoon Thanksgiving meal.

"Claire, everything's delicious. This Thanksgiving, I'm thankful for you, dear," Noah says, lovingly, to his wife.

Claire beams and reaches across the table to squeeze his hand. Nathan and David smile at each other. When they were young, they would have done what kids do when parents show affection toward one another: roll their eyes, say "gross," and leave the room. But Nathan finds as he gets older—and maybe since he and David have been out of the house for so long—that he feels a sense of comfort knowing that they have each other, that their relationship is strong.

"We'll get through it," Claire says to her husband and sons. "This time next year, you'll see, everything will be great. I have a feeling." His mom might have "a feeling," but Nathan is a bit more data-driven than she is, and he has already spent some time researching it. The five-year relative survival rate for localized prostate cancer is greater than 99 percent, better than most types of cancer. He smiles at his parents and agrees with his mom. "You're right, Mom. Everything will be fine."

They take a break before dessert and head out for a long family walk like they used to when he was young. A nutritionist for many years, his mother has his dad on a healthy eating regimen—with a few concessions given at Thanksgiving dinner —and is making him walk at least thirty minutes every day.

"Modern medicine is a miracle," she says like she's giving a TED talk. "But eating healthy helps that miracle along." She puts her arms around as many of the men in her family as she can and steers them onto their street, which has a view of the water. Nathan sees his dad put his arm around his mother's waist and she leans into him. "Thank you for the hug, dear," he hears her say, "But we're still doing another lap."

THE UNDENIABLE IMPORTANCE OF PRIME NUMBERS

It's the beginning of January, cold and gray, but mostly dry, in the Bay Area. Kevin's plan to kick out Jared has gone according to plan. The board agreed that December 31 would be his last day and he would get a nice payout and some additional stock options that would vest in the event of the company going public or getting acquired.

Kevin is planning to introduce Nathan as the new CPO on February 3, once things are in full swing for Q1, but there are whispers around the office already. Or the virtual office. Or whatever you call gossip that takes place via Slack, text, and at the end of Zoom meetings.

Covid numbers are going down and the plan is to return to the office the first week of February. Nathan's happy for the change. It's Friday afternoon, and he and Kevin are sitting in the conference room. Nobody else is on-site yet. They're strategizing over the CPO transition, the talks they're currently in with eight different potential investors, and company plans for the next three to six months.

"Dude, it's been a day," Nathan says. "We've been at it for," he looks at his watch, "ten hours. I'm hungry. I'm tired. I want a beer."

"Anything for my new CPO," Kevin says, batting his eyelashes. "You want pho? There's that new place over near the park, Pho Real."

Nathan smiles at the name. "Sure, let's go."

They get there and eat like starving men.

"How much did we eat?" Nathan asks, surveying the table after they pay for their meal. "I feel like I'm gonna explode."

"Lightweight."

"I gained fifteen pounds during the pandemic. I thought it was mostly muscle, but now I'm not so sure," he says, patting his stomach and looking doubtful.

"It's okay. Just keep working at a startup and you'll lose some weight. No time to work out but also no time to eat."

As they leave the restaurant, Nathan notices they're right across the street from Decades. Kevin looks at him, eyes narrowed. "Wanna grab a beer? I promise, no more work talk."

"Yeah, sure," Nathan says. He doesn't really feel like going back to an empty apartment tonight anyway.

It's still a bit early, but it's starting to get busy. It's the first weekend that the county has lifted the indoor mask mandate, and it looks like everyone is more than ready to venture out and see real-live human beings again.

They get a couple of beers and snag a booth near the back, people-watching, talking about work—despite Kevin's promise —and just contemplating life.

"I feel like an old man in here," Nathan says, looking around, taking in the other people around them. "They're either students or just out of college."

"*You're* right outta school."

"But I was in school for a *long* time, man."

Kevin surveys the group Nathan's looking at. "They're *grad* students, or maybe just young tech people. They're at least twenty-four, twenty-five."

"They might be, but they might also be twenty. That girl over there definitely looks nineteen. Are we dirty old men?"

"No, dude. There are some hot girls—ahem, women—here. And they've all been cooped up at home for a long time. Same as you. They're looking to connect, man." Kevin elbows him.

"Look at her," Kevin says, gesturing toward the bar, where a group is gathered around a short, energetic woman, who seems to be telling a funny story.

"Her?" Nathan says, narrowing his eyes and watching the woman. "She's cute but not really my type."

"Not the comedian," Kevin responds. "The one watching her. On the stool. She looks smart. Must be the glasses. You love that emo-I-love-books type."

Nathan shifts his gaze and sees the woman Kevin's referring to and his eyes widen. He's not sure at first, but then he sees the unique shape of her glasses and her long, glossy brown hair and realizes it's the same woman he admired on the bar patio last summer. He grins and looks at Kevin.

"See?" Kevin's nodding proudly at his correct assessment of Nathan's taste in women. "Go talk to her, dude."

Why the hell not? Nathan gets up and makes his way over to her.

He ventures over there, trying to look confident, but he finds himself suddenly over-aware of his hands, not knowing what to do with them. *Put them in my pockets? No. That's weird.* Why the hell is he so nervous? But then he's there, standing in front of her, and she has an expectant, or at least curious, look on her face.

With superb smoothness, he manages to mutter, "Um, hi."

"Hi," she replies, smiling at him. She says it like a question. His heart stops for a split second as he looks up from her smile and meets her hazel eyes.

"What's your name?" he asks.

"Sarah. What about you?"

"Nathan."

He doesn't know why, but he says "Nathan," not Nate, which is what everyone in his life except for his family calls him.

"Nice to meet you, Nathan," she says.

Sarah looks over at her friend, who's raising her eyebrows at her, and he sees her blush a bit. She's angling her head to look up at him, so he tries to slouch a little.

After talking to her a bit—she's not a student, she's starting a new job soon—"Wannabe" by the Spice Girls comes on, and her friend drags her to the dance floor. She looks back at him apologetically, but he just smiles at her, inclining his head toward the dance floor, indicating she should go and have fun.

Her being on the dance floor with her friend gives him a chance to settle his nerves. He's acting like a stupid high-school kid, butterflies in his stomach. He suspected she was attractive from afar—both the first time he saw her and this time—but being up close has confirmed his assessment. She's wearing a really sexy outfit tonight—tight jeans, a soft-looking sweater, and high heels. The dark red of the sweater sets off her long brown hair, and he's watching her—hopefully discreetly—when Kevin comes over and leans against the bar, too.

"You see?" he tells Nathan, watching Sarah and her friend dance. "These girls are ready for some fun. How old is this song anyway?" he asks, an amused look on his face.

"Must be '90s night," Nathan replies.

The song changes to another old song, and Kevin asks Nathan if it's okay for him to head out. "I ran into this woman I used to know who works downtown, and she invited me to hang out with some friends. You can come, too, but it looks like you're otherwise engaged," he says, following Nathan's eyes to where Sarah's dancing.

"Yeah, sure," Nathan replies, distractedly.

"Call me later if it doesn't work out," Kevin says, but Nathan is already walking over to join Sarah and her friends.

At first, he simply joins the group where Sarah is dancing with her friend who pulled her out onto the dance floor. The song changes to something he vaguely remembers is from the early '90s and everyone on the dance floor starts to jump around. Sarah starts to jump, too, and then she notices that he's stopped moving.

"Come on! Jump!" she says, smiling, and grabbing his hand.

When a pretty girl says "jump," you either say "how high" or just do it. He feels self-conscious but realizes that nobody else is even paying attention to him, so he just goes for it, and the whole place goes crazy for the next three minutes.

As the songs change—moving gradually from the decade he was born to the one he was in middle school—he finds himself closer to Sarah, who is smiling up at him, and touching his arm from time to time. He's loosened up a bit and being here with all these people—no, with one of these people, he's pretty sure—feels amazing.

She mentions that she's getting hot, and he asks her if she wants to get some fresh air. He's hot, too, and he wants to talk to her. Outside, they try to decide what to do, and she grabs his arm to steady herself, while she changes out of her mile-high heels. He likes her hand on his forearm. When she puts on regular shoes, she's a good half foot shorter than him, but he's liking the height difference, too, and the way her small but strong body leans into him for support.

"So, where to?" she asks.

"Well, we could take a walk," Nathan suggests, glancing in the direction of the park, but now he can see there are two police officers talking to a homeless man on the corner and things seem to be escalating. Shit. "Looks a bit busy that way. Do you wanna get something to eat instead?"

She keeps him laughing as they walk in the cool night air—she's friendly, fun—but they arrive at the Mexican place he eats at with Kevin at least once a week to find it closed. It's starting to rain and he wants to keep talking to her, getting to know her. Standing under an awning, trying to avoid the rain and keep from freezing is not going to work.

Think. Think. She's hungry. Food. I know food. I'm a great cook. That's it.

"I can make you some food," he offers. Maybe she'll say "yes." Maybe she'll hang out for a while. Maybe, well, if he's being completely honest with himself, he's open to other possibilities.

He knows he's not a serial killer, but he's still a little surprised when she agrees to come to his apartment; especially after he tells her he has a comfortable couch. He was trying to say they could watch a movie or something together, but maybe another part of his brain—or body—is thinking about the other options made possible by the presence of a hot woman in your apartment, late at night, after close-proximity dancing. When she rubs his arm and smiles reassuringly following his stupid comment, he can't help imagining her hands rubbing other parts of him, and takes a deep breath to calm himself down.

"Do you want my jacket?" he asks her. "So you won't get wet?"

"No," she answers. "I'm okay, as long as it's close."

"Just another couple minutes," he tells her, gently placing his hand on the small of her back, on the face of it to guide her in the right direction, but really because he just wants to make some contact—however small—with her body.

They arrive at his place, and Sarah sheds her jacket and now very-wet shoes near the door.

"I'll go turn on the heater and get you a towel, so you won't freeze," he says. "Your hair got wet." He lightly brushes a few locks out of her eyes and smiles at her. He rushes to adjust the thermostat in the hallway and the heater turns on. On his way back, he grabs a towel from the linen closet. "Have a seat and I'll go see what I have for you," he says, handing her the towel and heading to the kitchen. I can make you an omelet or, oh, I have some really good pasta I made. I can heat it up. Does that sound good?"

"Sounds wonderful," she says and walks over to the large windows. "I'm going to, well, I guess, dry off, and enjoy the view if that's okay with you."

"Sure. That's one of the things I liked about this place, too. You can see a lot from the tenth floor, huh?"

While he's heating up the food in his kitchen, he's trying to figure out what his goal is tonight. He had no idea this is how he'd be spending his Friday night—though he's quite pleased this is how it's going. He's thought about her a few times since he saw her at Decades in the summer, and he can't believe his luck running into her tonight.

While he prepares the tray of food, his phone buzzes in his pocket. "Dan," the screen reads. *Danica.* He sighs, hoping his luck hasn't run out already.

> Hey, wanna come over? It's late but we could watch a movie and cuddle. Oh, and talk about work, of course. <kiss emoji>

He could ignore it, but she probably already saw that it's on "Read," not to mention that she's doing a lot to help him and Kevin. He answers.

> Sorry. Just about to go to sleep. Long week.

He's just about to press send and remembers that Kevin told him she's actively working on getting them a meeting with Eden Snow, the founder and CEO of LightVerse, and so he adds "Sweet dreams" to soften it a bit before pressing "Send."

He puts his phone on "Silent," places it face down on the counter, and takes the tray to Sarah in the living room. She's sitting on the couch, cuddled up in the blanket his mom got him as a housewarming gift.

As he sets the tray down on the coffee table in front of her, she smiles up at him, and it's giving him life.

"I'm impressed, sir," she says, and he sits down next to her.

"This is really out of character for me," Nathan blurts out.

"What is?" she asks him.

Nathan stumbles through a bumbling explanation about carbs and girls at bars—Sarah gives him a curious, amused look at him the entire time. He's feeling extremely self-conscious, but also weirdly turned on by the expression on her face and he rambles along, finally finding the end of his sentence.

"We could have fun together?" he finds himself asking her, wondering when he lost the ability to speak English. He might as well follow up now with an offer to play a game of Scrabble.

But it seems she's on the same page as him. A woman on a mission, she point-blank asks if she can kiss him. Apparently, without realizing it, he was just waiting for her to ask. He takes her face in his hands, opens her mouth gently with his, and all but swoops her down like the cover of a romance novel.

He's not sure if it's the alcohol from earlier, stress from work and his need to let go, the late hour, the unwanted attention from Danica or . . . anything, really, outside of this moment. Because that's where he is right now. In the moment and grateful, like a man giving thanks at a temple, that he has this sexy, clever, slightly unpredictable woman in his arms. They're lying on the couch, Sarah mostly on her back and him on his side and half-falling off but not caring very much. They're making out with each other like teenagers—a bit hesitant, but only a bit, and gradually figuring out what works, what makes the other respond.

He can tell she's trying to hold back a bit but can't. She says silly little things here and there, making him laugh while he tries to kiss her, but he doesn't mind. She's cute, and she's funny. Maybe she's trying to mask a bit of her nervousness with jokes. He can't understand how even though it's the first time he's ever kissed her, it's so natural that he feels like he's been doing this with her forever.

"This *is* a comfortable couch," she says, her lips curling up in a smile.

"I thought I'd scared you off, mentioning my great couch earlier," he replies, laughing a bit.

"That's actually the moment I decided I *had* to come see your place tonight."

"If you think my couch is great, you should check out the bed," he says, daringly, surprising himself. He's definitely beyond the bounds of his normal abilities at banter, but for some reason, the filter he usually has in place around women is malfunctioning tonight. She's taken her glasses off, set them on the coffee table, and he's looking into her hazel eyes.

"All in good time. There are a few . . . *other things* I wanna check out first," she says, suggestively. She pushes on his chest, indicating that he should sit up a bit. He sits down, his back resting against the back pillows. She leans up, and crawls onto his lap, straddling him.

He's been admiring her for the last couple of hours, and he—his body—is more than ready for whatever comes next. He's a bit hesitant about *showing* her quite so soon, but she can most certainly *feel* him, already hard under her.

How could he not be turned on with a woman like her straddling him? She's inadvertently—or, he's beginning to suspect, not—rubbing against him. He notices as she sits atop him that the sweater she's wearing has shifted off one of her shoulders and he sees the black lace bra strap he noticed earlier at the bar make another appearance. His hands are on her hips, and he's trying not to let them roam where his mind has already taken him, so he lifts one hand to the bra strap and rubs it between his fingers.

"Do you like it?" she asks, shyly.

"Very much."

"Do you like me?" she asks, less shyly.

"Even more."

She gives him a long, sensual kiss, and then moves her lips to his jaw and then his neck. He inhales the scent of her hair, like fresh flowers, and its softness brushing his skin. He closes his eyes, allowing himself to enjoy the various sensations together.

"How are you feeling?" she asks, kissing his neck, while her hands are roaming over his chest and abs, exploring.

"I'm enjoying myself. Really relaxed."

"Don't fall asleep on me."

"I'd never," he says and opens his eyes.

"Better make sure," she says, pulling her sweater over the top of her head, revealing to him the sight of round, full breasts, held up by a mostly sheer lace bra. Her nipples are just about at eye level, and he bites his lip.

She takes one of his hands and places it on her breast. He's been doing his best to restrain himself, let her go at the pace she wants, but it's apparent now what kind of pace she's looking for tonight.

He leans forward and kisses the tops of her breasts. His hands slide down—he's been given permission, he'd say—and he grabs two handfuls of her toned ass.

"Nathan, do I turn you on?" she asks, playfully.

He looks at her, one eyebrow raised. In lieu of a reply, he wraps his arms around her, stands, and carries her to the bedroom, still straddling him, kissing her neck and chest along the way.

He hasn't been a monk since his break up with Alena, but it *has* been a while since he's gotten laid. There have been a few opportunities over the last year that he didn't take, for a variety of reasons. But he's more than ready now and can tell she is, too.

They reach the edge of his bed, and he sets her down. He wants to take off his shirt, to feel her skin on his own. He can feel her heat on his palms, as he pulls her closer, one hand on her lower back, and the other on the nape of her neck supporting her head as he kisses her. As if she's read his mind, she suddenly pulls at his shirt, struggling to get it all the way up and off of him. He breaks the kiss and rips the shirt over his head and lays her back on the bed. Finally, they're skin-to-skin—the hardness of his body melding with the softness of hers. She arches up a bit and fumbles with the clasp of her bra.

"Let me help you," he says as he undoes the clasp. He slowly pulls the bra away from her flushed body and what he sees gives him goosebumps. Lovely before—under her sweater, under her sexy bra—her now completely bare breasts, nipples rose-colored and hard from arousal, make him come undone a bit, and a slight noise of approval escapes his lips before he can stop himself. He glances away, for just a second, feeling a bit embarrassed.

"Hey," Sarah says, tilting her head a bit to catch his eye, and he looks at her. "It's fine. Look at me."

She's right. It is fine. Way more than fine. He takes a deep breath, composes himself, and gently lays her back on the bed. Her head is on his pillow, and he's lying between her legs. They both still have pants on. This situation is untenable, completely unacceptable, and they both seem to realize it at the same time, beginning to help each other get out of their clothes as fast as humanly possible. He's pulling down her stretchy jeans, and she's unbuttoning and, carefully, unzipping his fly. As soon as it's down, she's pushing down his pants and underwear at the same time, and his erection as much as springs from them. The look on her face—delighted surprise—is the most exhilarating thing he's ever seen.

She wants him. Her face—those eyes—say it all. She pulls him back in for more passionate kisses while they finish wiggling out of their pants. Their hands roam and explore the new terrain of each other's bodies. Her skin—warm before—is on fire now, and she's as soft as silk. *If she's this soft and warm on the outside, god only knows what she must feel like in other places.* He begins to explore those other places with a gentle but curious hand, and he hears her breathing speed up as he strokes her and teases out what she likes. He's happy to continue for as long as she wants, but when she reaches down and encircles him with her warm hand, slowly rubbing his cock up and down, he starts to have trouble focusing on pleasing her. It's time, he thinks, to do something they can both enjoy simultaneously. Something that doesn't require a whole lot of thought. Just feeling, doing.

"I'll put on a condom?" he asks, and he's happy to hear her immediate, breathless, response: "Yes."

He rolls over so he can open the drawer of his nightstand. It's been a little while, but he's hoping there's at least one condom still there. The odds have, so far, been in his favor tonight, and they don't fail him now. There is, thankfully, a half-full package in the drawer, and as he rolls one on, he can't help smiling at her. She's on her back, holding herself up on her elbows watching him, breasts displayed like a work of art, and completely naked now.

"Ready?"

"Yes," again, comes her answer, and she beckons him with her pointer finger, inviting him to come closer with a naughty smile on her face. *Who is this woman?* He has to restrain himself from jumping on the bed and simply entering her, then and there.

He rejoins her, lying down next to her on the bed, and she spreads her legs, seductively inviting him into her. He can barely wait to be inside of her but wants to make sure she enjoys herself, too. He rolls on top of her, holding himself above her on his forearms, and kisses her, deeply. For a split second, he wonders how it's possible to feel so comfortable, in bed, naked, with someone you've just met, but then she's pulling him—his cock—to her warm opening, and all thoughts but one escape him.

He pushes into her slowly at first, to make sure her body is ready for him. He glides in smoothly and groans. She's grabbing his butt while he kisses her lips and her neck, and his thrusts get faster. He can feel her squeezing her muscles around him and raising her hips to make sure the angle is right. It's more than right. He can barely contain himself, but he watches her face and listens to her breathing and the small sounds she makes as he moves on top of her. *Is she enjoying herself or am I just crushing her?*

"I'm enjoying myself," she assures him. *Shit.* He realizes he must have said it out loud.

She laughs and the sound of her laughter and her exhalations —just the smallest whimper—and her muscles clenching around him is too much for him.

"Sarah, I'm so close. You can't do that movement you just did, or it's gonna end way too soon."

"This one?" she asks, doing it again, teasing him.

He lets out a gasp. "Yes, that one," he says, through gritted teeth.

He's trying to think of something completely unrelated to sex to hold out long enough for her to come, too. Enumerating prime numbers might work.

"Are you close?" he asks, sounding desperate.

"Very," she says, as he continues his efforts. "It's good, really," she says. "But come. Now."

"No, I want you to enjoy yourself, too," he replies.

"I am," she says. "Really, do it. You'll help me afterward," she says, caressing his face and leaning up to give him a sensuous, full-mouthed kiss.

It's everything—but especially that kiss—that pushes him over the edge, and he releases everything he's been holding back. He's done and he's breathing hard like he's just run up five flights of stairs, as he rolls off her, still panting.

She lays on her side, body angled toward him, eyes closed and her hand on his stomach. He touches her hand and asks if he can touch her. Her eyes open, and the sweetest smile crosses her face. She nods.

He's barely recovered from his own orgasm, but he can't leave this gift of a woman wanting. He rolls her gently to her back, so he has full access to all the things he needs—that she needs —and begins to kiss her mouth and let his hands wander over her. He kisses, licks, and bites her wherever he sees that he gets the right reaction. She smiles and closes her eyes while he kisses her neck. He spends some time there, and she rewards him by running her fingers through his hair. When he moves down to her breasts and licks her nipples—gently biting them, just to see what happens—he gets a different positive reaction. She turns towards him and unabashedly pulls his hand between her legs inviting him to do more. Lower, she's slick and a little swollen from their encounter, and he parts her gently, exploring with his fingers. He feels like an explorer that has found a treasure and says so.

She giggles. "I guess there's a reason they call it pirate booty," she jokes.

It's fun and it's hot and it's sweaty and it's exhausting, and he smiles and thinks, for a second, that he has found a treasure. He continues to kiss her mouth deeply—he could do it forever—and moves his hand, first slowly and then increasingly fast, along her clit, until she, too, has come from the efforts of his hands and his mouth.

He's lying on his side, looking at her with her glasses off, finding himself wondering what her prescription is. Why? He has no idea. But she seems like the kind of woman he could get used to. She looks at him, eyes half-closed, with an exhausted grin on her face.

"Wow, Nathan, that . . . 'pasta' was really good," she says and giggles softly. He smiles at her and rests his eyes a bit while she falls asleep. When he hears her soft breathing slow to the pace of sleep, he gently gets up out of bed and pads over to the bathroom to brush his teeth. When he returns, he crawls into bed next to her and can't help himself from giving her one last, slightly open-mouthed kiss, to which she responds by saying "mmmm" in her sleep. He falls asleep with thoughts of what Sarah will look like in the morning in his head.

When he wakes, the light is dim and it's cold in the room. It only takes him a minute to remember what happened last night. Her scent is still in his nose, in his mind. *Right, her.* He smiles and starts to roll over with the intention of cuddling her, breathing in her scent more closely, and telling her "Good morning." But when he does, Sarah is gone.

STRESS TEST

A couple of weeks go by. Nathan's sitting on yet another Zoom meeting with Kevin, the third one this week, an entire *series* of Zoom meetings that Kevin, under the radar, is calling "Operation Subway." He realizes his mind must have wandered. "Nate, dude, I asked you a question."

"Sorry, dude. Ask me again. I'm ready. I must be ready. We've gone over everything ten times."

"I said, 'What's your answer for the board when they ask why *you're* the right choice to lead product, having spent most of the last decade in academia?' It's important that you get it right, that you put the right amount of focus on the business, that it's technical enough, but not too technical that you lose them."

"Kevin, I got this. Seriously. You didn't choose me for my pretty brown eyes or my—"

"Your dick?"

"What the hell's your problem, dude?" Nathan growls at him.

"That's your problem right now. You're thinking with your dick. Ever since you met that girl at the bar and then she bailed on you, you've lacked focus. We gotta get this thing right with the board. Otherwise, we're dead in the water. If I don't get Jared outta here, we don't come across as strong with the investors, and we could lose our momentum. I need you, man."

"You've got me, man."

"Okay, so give me your answer. This board meeting is a good dry-run for everything that comes after when we present to the venture capitals. You're gonna be doing stuff like this for the next six months, at least."

"Kevin, I got it, but I'm hanging up now. I gotta call my mom and check on my dad."

"Alright, dude," Kevin relents. "Send him my regards."

"I will."

He takes a quick break from work to call his mom, and she tells him that there's nothing new happening. That's actually bad news since the last update was that he has a Fever of Unknown Origin. It came on shortly after the biopsy he had in early January to determine the type of cancer cells. His dad has been insisting that he's fine, but after numerous tests and scans —Covid, strep, PET, CT, you name it—the doctors still can't figure out what's causing him to have a fever. His mom is worried.

"Mom, it's gonna be okay. We'll figure it out and we'll get him the treatment he needs." Nathan tries to sound optimistic, confident, but he's not sure he's coming across as convincing.

After he gets off the phone with his mom, he sends David a text:

Nathan: Hey, you still planning on coming out for a bit to stay with Mom and Dad?

David: That's the plan.

Nathan: Ok, thanks. I'll come up as soon as I can. There's so much shit going on at work. Kevin's counting on me to help get him through this transition period. I'll fly up right after the announcement on the 3rd.

David: No problem. I'll get there in a couple of days and hold down the fort until you can come up. Don't worry about it.

He's putting his phone down when it buzzes again. Danica.

Danica: Hey there, I'm having a hard time getting on Eden's calendar, but . . . there's an event in about a month.

He sighs. It's a long way out, but she's doing her best.

Nathan: Ok—can we get in?

Danica: Iiiii can get in.

Nathan: And . . .

Danica: I can get you in . . . and Kevin.

Nathan: Awesome. Thanks, D.

Danica: Thank you, Mr. CPO.

Nathan: It's not public yet.

Danica: <shhh emoji> I can keep a secret, if you can.

He opens his calendar app to add it and sees that she's already sent him the calendar invite, and it's the same night as the Instinqt partner event taking place in downtown San Jose.

When he texts Danica to let her know that they'll have to come late, she suggests that they all first head to the Instinqt partner event and then continue on to Willow Street in Palo Alto —where the LightVerse offices and its own event is taking place —afterward. He agrees.

Nathan: Thanks for the help, D.

Danica: Any time.

A whole night with Danica. Kevin *better* give him a raise.

He texts Kevin to let him know the plan.

Kevin: It's happening. You da real MVP.

Nathan sighs and wonders how eight short months ago, he was standing in a cap and gown holding his PhD diploma, and now he's selling himself out to an old girlfriend for Kevin to get investors.

* * *

On Thursday, the day of the announcement, he's a bit nervous. Nathan knows Matt from product thinks the job is his, and he also knows he'll be Matt's boss after this meeting. Nathan sits in the back corner with some of his current teammates and listens as Kevin talks about Jared leaving to "spend time with his family." *Something like that.* Poor bastard never had a chance against Kevin. The same probably applies to Nathan, as well.

Kevin is calling him up, introducing him, and suddenly, it's real. The culmination of their months of plotting. He smiles, trying to convey confidence but not arrogance. People are congratulating him on the new position, and it feels a little dream-like, everyone talking to him at once. As the room empties out, and he grabs his things from the back corner, he gets a glimpse of Erin leaving the room with a new employee, and wonders who she is, thinking her backside looks a little too familiar.

✳ ✳ ✳

Right after the announcement in the meeting, Nathan made a little "thank you" speech. And whether it was everyone wearing masks, my new glasses and haircut in preparation for my new job, or my taking cover behind Erin—*Wow, I'm all of a sudden so interested in the things in my handbag on the floor*—I made it out of there without him seeing me. As the meeting ended, a number of colleagues went up to congratulate him, and I made yet another ninja escape from Nathan. *Second time in a few weeks, I'm almost a professional.*

I'm sitting—more accurately, hiding out—inside a Zen booth, one of the cool little phone booths they have here to give people a private, quiet place to work in the open-office setting. It's about four-by-four feet with a high desk and stool inside and made from smooth, light-colored wood, with a tiny little skylight at the top. It even smells nice. I'm scoping a project I'm in charge of and trying to figure out if it's smart to temporarily shift some engineering resources from one team to another in order to complete it on time. Brooks' law comes to mind and I decide it won't work. Nine women can't make a baby in one month.

I see Erin's face pop into the little window in the door of the booth, and then she opens the door. She asks me if I want to join her and some colleagues for lunch.

"Sure," I say, closing my laptop quickly, indicating this is the perfect time for a break, as well as a chance to get out of the office while Nathan is still—somewhere—around here.

"Let's try that new salad place," Dreya, our UI/UX designer, suggests, as we leave the building.

"Where is it?" Erin asks.

"It's right near that bar on the corner. You know, the one the engineers go to all the time."

"Decades?" I ask, without thinking.

"Do you know it, Sarah? Have you been there?"

"Yeah . . ." I answer, my tone a bit odd. Erin shoots me a look. "Yeah, I've been there. They have good . . . music."

"Well, I don't know about that," Erin says, still looking at me intently. "But Kevin said he likes the vibe. Knowing him, that probably means he likes the women who hang out there."

I look at her, waiting for her to elaborate. She doesn't disappoint.

"Grad students," she says, giving me a knowing look.

I cringe a bit and begin to imagine Nathan—Nate—having a beer after work with Kevin and hitting on college girls. I feel a little sick to my stomach, just thinking about it. He said going home with a girl from a bar is so "out of character," when in fact, maybe I'm a complete idiot and it's totally *in* character for him.

My imagination gets the best of me, and as we walk to the salad place, I'm only half-hearing the conversation Erin and the other women are having. Dreya talks about her upcoming wedding and how planning it is completely stressing her out. Erin, not married, but happily coupled with her partner of ten years, Ryan, quips that it's easier to just get pregnant, by accident, and not get married—speaking from experience.

"Erin, how did I not know you have a kid?" I ask her, already back in the conversation and focused once again on the present.

"Yeah, well, I'm thirty-seven, and it was about time anyways, so when I found out I was pregnant, I decided to just roll with it. It was the best decision I ever made. I'm in love," she says, opening up her phone to show us pictures of her three-year-old daughter.

"Just to be clear, though, if I were ten years younger like you, I'd take advantage of it. I didn't have enough one-night stands in my twenties," she says, winking, just as we pass Decades. My eyes bug out and she laughs at me. "Are you okay?"

"Yeah, I'm fine." I speed up and walk a bit ahead of the group, trying to evaluate just how likely it is that Erin is a psychic.

We buy our salads and end up sitting in the nearby park to

eat lunch. It's a beautiful spring day. Brisk out—I've forgotten my favorite pashmina scarf back at the office—but the sun is shining. For obvious reasons, Nathan comes to mind. I remember how he suggested we walk in this very park the night we met. *Today would be a nice day for a walk with him.* I close my eyes, behind my sunglasses, and tilt my face up, just a bit, toward the sun.

"Oh, look," Dreya says. "There's Nate and Kevin."

"Who?" I snap back to reality.

"Nate, you know? The new CPO, and Kevin, our . . . CEO," she says, looking at me strangely. I glance surreptitiously in the direction she's indicating and see two men, two very familiar men, walking not nearly far enough away from us and in the direction of the park bench we're sitting on.

"Ladies, I just remembered I have to make a call. It's for my mom. I'm gonna head back. I'm sorry."

Erin looks at me like she doesn't quite believe me, but chooses to pretend she does. "Okay, see you back at the office," she says, skeptically.

I've gathered up my bag and salad container and begin walking quickly away as Nathan and Kevin get closer.

I'm just rounding the corner of a gazebo when I hear Dreya and Erin greet them. "Hey, guys, how's it going?"

Kevin says, "Hey, ladies. Team lunch and you didn't invite us?"

"Well, it's not really our team, you know. Just a little ladies' lunch. Sarah was here earlier and . . ."

❋ ❋ ❋

"Sarah?" Nathan says, and all of a sudden, the penny drops.

Sarah, he thinks to himself, suddenly realizing why the woman in the conference room earlier looked familiar. "Shit," he says in a barely audible tone. He feels a little clammy.

His uneasiness must be evident on his face, since Erin gives him an alarmed look, and asks, "You okay, Nate?"

"Yeah, fine. Sure. CPO first-day jitters, I guess," he says. "Hey, Kev, I'm gonna head back, okay? I've got some stuff I wanna take care of."

He walks quickly back to the office, looking at his phone the whole time—trying, unsuccessfully, to find her on Slack and then LinkedIn or any other social media—and narrowly missing a few people on the way on the sidewalk.

When he gets to the third floor, he grabs his laptop from his desk and heads to one of the Zen phone booths. Its name suggests one should feel calm while sitting in it, but as he sits in silence for a few minutes, it feels much more like a cell, and he, like a prisoner awaiting a sentence.

Just sitting inside thinking *shit, shit, shit* in his head over and over isn't doing much for his "zen," so he takes a deep breath. And as he's exhaling, trying to feel as "zen" as possible, he notices someone's left a soft black scarf on the stool across from him. Somehow—his mother?—he knows it's called pashmina. It seems familiar and he touches it lightly with his fingertips. He brings it closer to his nose, as discreetly as possible—just in case someone walks by he doesn't want to look like a weirdo—and detects the faint floral scent. It's familiar, and in a second, he's back on his couch, Sarah sitting astride him, taking in the scent of her hair. He can't believe his luck—not sure yet whether it's good or bad and decides to take some action. Good enough for Eckhart Tolle, good enough for him.

He opens Slack and types in Sarah's name. Here in the office, on his laptop, he's able to find her easily. *@SHoffman* pops up. Her profile pic is a cute avatar with dark-rimmed glasses. *Even in her emoji, she's cute.*

What's the appropriate thing to write in such circumstances? He looks at the screen and sees Slack's intro message:

"This is the very beginning of your direct message history with @SHoffman. Only the two of you are in this conversation, and no one else can join it."

Not exactly the very *beginning of our history.* He types the message:

NGoldman (he/him): Hey Sarah, wanted to welcome you to the company. Haven't had a chance to meet you yet, but feel free to set up some time on my calendar so we can chat about product/engineering best practices at Instinqt.

As soon as he hits "Send," he regrets it, but what's done is done. Her Slack status is green, which means she's online, which means that she might have seen it already. If he deletes the message now, it will be even weirder, suspicious. He stares at the screen for another minute, thinking. She doesn't respond. He wonders if she knows it's him, the same guy from . . . that night.

She must. She was in the conference room. He was front and center. He's unsettled.

I hope she doesn't get me fired. But then he thinks about how she must be feeling, and his conscience corrects him. *I hope she's not freaking out.*

✳ ✳ ✳

I'm freaking out and have been for the past hour. I had my backpack and laptop with me in the park during lunch and decided that I really could work the rest of the afternoon from home and that it was probably an excellent time to head out. I had walked back to my apartment and signed back on to work for a few more hours. The minute I did, I heard a familiar ping, and opened Slack.

It was Nathan—of-fucking-course it was—welcoming me to the company and asking me to set up time to talk.

He knows. But then I realized, my Slack profile photo, as well as my LinkedIn profile, is an avatar. I had squinted at the small pic, wondering whether Cartoon Sarah looks enough like me for him to know. Cartoon Sarah—with her signature glasses and long brown hair—had simply stared back me and whispered, snickering, "He knows."

✳ ✳ ✳

Nathan wants to call it a day and head home to work from there before his flight up to Seattle tomorrow, but with the announcement just having been made, his calendar for the afternoon has filled up and he's still there at 5:00 p.m., when Kevin is finishing up, too.

Nathan walks to the kitchen to fill up his water bottle, and Kevin comes up behind him.

"Busy day," Kevin says.

Nathan turns around. "You have no idea. I got twelve—no, thirteen—new meeting invites for the next week."

Kevin looks at him shrewdly, a look that, if he had to guess, means "Cut the bullshit." A second later, Nathan doesn't need to guess. "I found out some interesting info today," Kevin says.

"About what?" Nathan asks, innocently. He's not surrendering any information Kevin doesn't already know.

"So, you know how we've been trying to improve our feature release processes? Well, when you went back to the office after lunch, I stayed and talked with Erin in the park. She told me she's been working with this new TPM and that she's doing a great job so far."

"Okay."

"Her name's Sarah."

"Okay."

"So, I was curious," Kevin continues. "I mean, I was on vacation when she was hired and didn't have a chance to interview her. Anyways, when I got back to the office, I asked around."

"Kevin, what do you want?" Nathan suddenly asks directly.

"She's kind of an 'emo-I-love-books' type," Kevin says, making quote-y fingers. "Know what I mean?"

"First of all, quoting yourself is a douchebag thing to do. Secondly, yeah, I know what you mean."

"Anything happen that night?"

"Nope, nothing," Nathan says, lying to his friend—feeling guilty for it, but still doing it—for the second time in a month.

"Shame, since she works here now. And it can't," he adds, giving him a pointed look.

"Yeah, I got you," Nathan says.

Kevin stares at him for a beat, waiting to see if Nathan will say anything else. When he does, Kevin starts to walk away, but turns back to say, "Congrats on the job, man."

SCOPING SESSION

Later that night, after several minor freak-outs and a glass of wine, I'm making dinner when I realize that there's really nothing more to do here. I skip right on over four stages of grief and land, begrudgingly, in acceptance. This is the way I operate. When I screw up, I freak out until my nerves are so frazzled that there's no possible way I can continue to ruminate on the situation anymore, and then I try to—simply *must*—move on.

It happened, he's on to me, and I come to the conclusion that I'll just have to face things head-on. The next time I see him, I'll talk to him and what happens, happens. I go to bed—not calm, but accepting my destiny, whatever it shall be—like a prisoner who's lost her last appeal. And I dream.

Again, I'm on a boat, but this time my eyes are open, and Nathan is there with me.

"Sarah?" he's asking. "What are you doing here?"

"I work here," I tell him.

"Work here? What do you do?"

"I'm the chef," I tell him.

"You are?" he asks, pleased, and tells me to come with him. He wants to show me something.

Now, somehow, we're in his kitchen. He's showing me how to make pasta from scratch. He's standing behind me, so close I can feel his breath—warm, soft, and pleasant on the side of my neck. We're both facing the counter, and he has his arms around mine, showing me how to knead the pasta dough. He's massaging the dough, and my fingers, and suddenly he's even closer than I thought possible, breathing in my scent.

"I love how you smell, Sarah," he says, "Like roses." Then he traces kisses up my neck, ending just below the back of my ear. I turn

around to look at him and see he's wearing the apron.

Like a sitcom, I say romantically, "I just love a man in an apron,"
as he lifts me up to set me on the counter. I wrap my legs around him,
my arms, too, and we begin to kiss passionately in his small, cozy
kitchen. Things are getting hotter, I pull open the apron strap and
strings. I want to see more of him.

"Sarah, why did you run out?" he asks me all of a sudden. He's
looking at my face, eyebrows tensed, an expression of confusion and
sadness on his. "Why did you sneak out before I woke up? I wanted to
see you."

"I —" I begin to say, but I can't continue with the words that are
on the tip of my tongue. "I left because I was scared," I say under my
breath, but he's already gone, and now I'm back on the boat alone.

I wake up. It's early in the morning. In the dim light and
slightly chilly air of my bedroom outside my blankets, I think
about how shady I've been. Maybe he *is* a player, like Kevin, but is
it fair what *I've* done? I get out of bed—even though I know I still
have time before work starts—and decide to do something good
for myself. I put on my sneakers and a thin-but-warm fleece and
go for a run in the cool morning air.

I come back, take a shower, and get ready for work. I've
decided I'll head into the office. It's not a mandatory day, but I've
put a challenge before myself. "Do the right thing" is one way to
sum it up. I've determined that I won't go looking for him, but
I'm also not going to avoid him.

I walk to the office, and it helps to clear my head. I try to work,
try to focus, but between yawning from my early morning wake-
up and worrying that Nathan will come upon me unawares, I'm
not getting much work done.

After lunch, at the end of one of my meetings with the
product managers, I hear one of them mention that Nathan's out
today and the beginning of next week. He had to fly home to
help his dad, but he can get online if needed. Part of me relaxes,
but the other part of me—surprisingly—is also disappointed.
Hmmm. I wonder what's going on with his family, but I'm
too shy to ask them. I file it away for future reference in a

tiny imaginary filing folder labeled something like "personal virtues"—and decide to head home.

Yet again, I walk since it's nice weather out—chilly, but sunny —and I contemplate life a bit while listening to music. Work's been going well, on the purely professional front. I've been talking to everybody on the projects I manage to learn what we're doing and how we might do it better. Optimizing processes —figuring out where things are broken and how to fix them— has always been a strength of mine. It's funny that I do it so well in the professional world, but that I could sometimes use a project manager for my own life.

My breakup with Blake looms large in my thoughts. I wonder what a project manager, or anybody not blinded by his pseudo-intellectual bullshit, would've said about me deciding to start dating him and then continuing to date him for so long, once it was crystal clear that we were totally mismatched. In my head, I can hear Camila saying, "Definitely mismatched—you're awesome and he's a jerk."

While I didn't have any proof that Blake had cheated on me, I had suspected the last four months of our relationship that he also wasn't honest about a lot of things, with the primary "thing" being a woman who worked at an agency our engineering firm used regularly for special projects. They spent *a lot* of time texting and "catching up on important projects" in his words. Things being what they were in the world, it's not like they had a lot of opportunities or excuses to meet up in person, but in the spring and on into summer, he seemed particularly protective of his phone and would often stop texting and lock it when I'd come in the room.

I never shared my suspicions with anybody, not even Cam. I knew what her feelings about him had been—still are—and despite me having told her just about everything in my life since the age of fourteen, I just couldn't bear to tell her, to have her see me in that way, to see myself in that way. I'm ashamed now that I put up with the situation for so long, and also that I left with uncertainty, never really knowing what, if anything, was going on.

Just about the time I get back to my place, I get a text:

Camila: Hey, when are you coming to pick me up?

Shit. I completely forgot that we're running a 10k in Santa Cruz tomorrow, bright and early. I mentally calculate the amount of time it will take me to get ready, and while I'm doing so, I get another text from her.

Camila: Did you forget?

Me: Never!

Camila: <Laughing emoji> See you in an hour?

Me: I'll be there in 45. Ha!

I go upstairs and pack my things quickly, making sure that I have my running clothes and sneakers. I grab an extra fleece and some cute, warm clothes, in case we end up going out on Saturday night. I'm really not in the mood for it, but I know Camila. She'll probably force me to go out in order to distract me, once I tell her what's going on. I was simply too drained to even update her last night via text.

In less than an hour, she's in my car and we're on Highway 17, winding our way up and through the mountains in the direction of Santa Cruz. On the way, we talk about all kinds of things, and Camila asks me how it's going at work.

"Everyone's really nice. I mean, I don't know a lot of the technical stuff they talk about, but I think I'll get there. They seem to like my ideas," I tell her, happy that at least the, well, job-related part of my job is going smoothly.

"I know you were scared about that part," she says.

"Yeah, you're right. But it's been cool so far. They have engineers for all the technical stuff. They just needed someone to help them get going in the same direction at the same time, I guess."

"That's awesome," she replies.

"It's going great, actually . . ." I continue, beginning to think I might be overdoing it a bit. From a quick glance in her direction

—she's narrowed her eyes and is watching me carefully—I can see that she's getting suspicious, but she's holding her tongue, waiting for me to share when I'm ready.

"Professionally, things are great."

Meaning that non-professionally, things are not.

"So, why do you sound . . . weird?" she asks, picking up on the overly chipper tone of my voice, maybe also the way my left leg is fidgeting.

Caught.

"Welllll . . ."

"Sarah."

"I'm worried I'm going to screw it all up, Cam."

"What are you gonna screw up exactly? You just said you're doing great at work," she replies. "Professionally."

I can sense she's puzzling it out, and I stay quiet.

"Is something wrong with . . . someone?"

She's confused. Of course she is. Because I'm being confusing.

We've just left the winding, mountainous portion of our drive, and I pull off the highway at the next exit. I cannot have this conversation while driving on one of America's most dangerous highways. I pull into a gas station parking lot and put the car in park.

"What's going on, Sarah?" Camila asks me, leaning back against the passenger door, so she can properly cross her arms and give me a questioning look.

And so, I tell her the gist of it. How the cute guy from Decades I spent the night with, well, had the nerve to show up and be somebody important in my new company. While I tell her what happened on Thursday in the company meeting and then afterward, I'm a little out of sorts, but she maintains enough composure for the both of us and simply replies, calmly and logically, "Well, you're not dating him *now*."

It's not much, but she's offering me a lifeline to grab onto. One part of me is grateful, but the other part—the less confident, more worried part—fights back.

"But I had sex with him and then I left and now he's—well, not my boss—but he's an executive. This seems . . . messy? Like, not an ideal way to start a new job?"

"Well, I suppose you've already passed your performance review," she quips.

"This is not the time for jokes," I say in an annoyed tone.

"I think it's exactly the time for jokes," she replies. "There's not much else to do besides accept your fate."

She says it bluntly. A little too bluntly for the weary state I'm in right now, but she's right. After hours of thinking about it yesterday afternoon, I had also arrived at the same conclusion. I look at her, my lips pursed, trying to find something to argue back, some way out of all this that doesn't involve extreme embarrassment, but I've got nothing.

"Okay," I say. "I'm just gonna have to talk to Nathan and get it all out in the open—"

"Maybe not '*all* out in the open' if you know what I mean," Camila interjects, her mouth twitching.

"Yeah, you're right. Pretty sure it was *all* out in the open last time, and look where we are now." I start laughing and can't stop. "What do they say? It's better to laugh than to cry?"

"Well, you still owe me more juicy details about what shall be heretofore be known as 'that night,' but it sounds like it went pretty damn well to me. I mean, he's hot, he cooks, he's good in bed, he's got a good job . . . What *exactly* is the problem again?"

"Well, let's see. I ran out of there like a criminal and never looked back. Now he suspects that I am who I am, and I *will* die of embarrassment because the same guy I'll be sitting across from in a meeting one day soon has seen my orgasm face. He's heard my orgasm noises. Cam, this is like the literal worst, and you can't convince me otherwise."

She takes a deep breath and thinks for a second. When she's ready to talk, she looks at me, and rests her chin on her hand on the console dramatically, and says, "If you're sitting across from each other in a meeting?"

"Yes?"

"Is there, like, *any* chance you might be able to play footsie?

Like some sole-on-crotch action—"

I put my finger on her forehead and gently push her back to the passenger side of the car and then put the car into drive.

"You are banished from my car if you continue that sentence. I will leave you here at this gas station," I say, shooting her a dirty look that says "Just try me."

She's cracking up and, by this point, I am, too. It sucks, for sure, but I *am* feeling a little better. It's the weekend. I'll try to have a couple of stress-free days before I face the music back at work on Monday and embarrass myself to smithereens or get sacked. Bad choice of words, I guess. As I pull back onto the highway, I ask Camila to put on some music, and I allow myself to think about him one last time for the day, picturing him in my mind the morning I snuck out of his room—half-naked and sweetly clutching his covers. *Oh, man, this is gonna be hard. That's what she said*, the perverted little devil on my shoulder says.

❊ ❊ ❊

The weekend is great. After Camila and I finish the 10k run, it's still relatively early, and we decide to head over to one of our favorite brunch places and drink celebratory mimosas. It feels like old times, hanging out on the boardwalk and people-watching. The boardwalk is packed. It's been a mild winter, and with the sun shining bright by noon, it feels like spring is on its way. People are playing volleyball on the beach, with some brave souls even venturing into the freezing Pacific.

My mom ends up joining us and invites us to walk with her from the boardwalk over to Natural Bridges on the seaside trail.

"I know you guys ran pretty far this morning, but I need a little exercise this afternoon." Camila and I agree, despite being tired from the race earlier and beg her to walk slowly.

"You're pretending to be tired now, but I know you girls. You'll be able to find plenty of energy to go out tonight, Sarah. Buck up and spend some time with your mother."

"I don't think I'm gonna go out tonight, Mom."

"Why not? Things are finally open. You're young. You need to get out and meet someone," she says directly, giving me a look. "Right, Camila?"

Camila shoots me a look that my hawk-eyed mother notices immediately.

"What?" my mom asks Camila, and then looks at me, raising her eyebrows.

Camila knows my mom well and has become like a second daughter to her over the years. Hoffman coming after Hernandez, alphabetically, I was placed right behind her in our high school freshman geometry class. The first week of school, I had leaned forward in my desk and nervously tapped her on the shoulder to ask if she wanted to sit together at lunch. Within a few weeks, we were regularly hanging out after school and eating all the snacks my mom kept stocked in our pantry. With my dad having passed away a few years ago, she knows my mom is alone in the house, and texts and calls to check in on her almost as much as I do.

Camila looks at me—eyes wide as if to say "I can't hold up under this type of interrogation." And I jump in to save her.

"I . . . kind of have a crush on someone," I say.

"Well, good for you! Who is he?" My mom isn't one to dance around any topic.

"He's a guy I met in San Jose at a bar near work."

"Cute?"

"Yes," both Camila and I answered.

"Smart?"

"Very," I replied.

"In that case, don't go out tonight. In fact, you should just drive back to San Jose," she says, laughing.

"Thanks, Mom."

That night, even though we spent the whole day together, Camila and I do end up going out. Camila's brother, Javier, and some of his friends join us for dinner, and we all end up hanging out at some patio bar, which has portable heaters set up to keep people warm, but they aren't really doing their job.

Javier, a bit younger than Camila, is still living at home and enjoys getting to spend time with his older sister and bragging about her a little bit to his friends.

"She's getting her MBA," he tells his friends, squeezing his big sister's shoulders. Camila looks down, a little embarrassed, but I can tell it makes her feel good. It should. She works so hard—always has—and she deserves to feel proud.

I'm sitting near Camila—we're basically sitting on each other's laps trying to share warmth—and she whispers to me: "Javier's friend is checking you out." She shifts her eyes in the direction of one of his friends, who I see is, in fact, looking in our direction.

"I don't think so, Cam. He's looking over here, but it's not at me," I correct her in a sing-song voice. "What shoes do you have on tonight?"

She holds out one of her legs to show me some hot, leopard-print boots. "Well, they're no 'you-know-what' heels but looks like they'll get the job done," I tease her. I get up, feigning the need to find a restroom, thereby vacating my seat next to Camila, and throwing her to the—admittedly, very cute—wolves.

For just a minute, I wonder what Nathan is doing, and when I might run into him at the office. When I get back to the table, Camila says they're all going to go back to her house to hang out, but I decide that I think I want to call it a night.

"You sure?" Camila asks.

"Yeah, I think so."

"In that case, I'll come with you," she says.

"What about the guy?"

"Who cares?" she says. "It's been a while since we've had a sleepover at your parents' house."

We say our goodbyes and decide to walk, despite the cold night, back to my mom's place. It's late, and it takes us a good while. I tell her it's a shame I don't have my Fitbit on, so we'd know how many steps we did. She holds her wrist up. "30k, baby!"

It's been a long day and despite Camila's desire to do a

sleepover like the old days, the only thing I can manage at this point is *actual* sleep. As we lie in the queen bed that's still in my old bedroom half an hour later, I squeeze her hand.

"You're the best big sister," I tell her.

"I'm younger than you."

"Yes, but I think you're wiser."

She giggles.

"Well, you suck," she replies, sleepily. "You still haven't told me enough about your sexy chef/programmer boy. But it'll have to wait. I'm exhausted."

Good. I'm beginning to make peace with my recent decisions and their unexpected repercussions, but I'm not quite ready to share all the details. Within a minute, I hear Camila's slow, rhythmic breathing, and I can tell she has fallen asleep. After a long day—a long week—I let myself drift into sleep, too.

✽ ✽ ✽

I wake up the next morning to hear Camila talking to my mom in the kitchen.

"How are your grades, sweetheart? Doing well?"

"Yes, Lynn," I hear Camila say. "It's hard, doing the MBA at the same time as work, but my company gives me half a day a week to do some of the degree work, so I'm managing."

"That's wonderful. You've always been a smart girl. I'm really glad Sarah has a friend like you to look after her."

"Well, she's doing great, too. Kicking ass at work. And the guy she mentioned yesterday, he's this cute engineer who, well, I don't know for sure, but my money's on him just falling in love with her. He's like a thousand levels better than he-who-shall-not-be-named."

"What's his name?"

"Nathan. Goldman, I think."

"Sounds nice," my mom replies.

I hear Camila put down her coffee mug and say, "When Sarah wakes up, can you ask her if she can pick me up at my parents? I promised my mom I'd attend mass with them today before we head back. Thank you for the breakfast, Lynn. You're the best."

And then she's out the door before I can even drag myself out of bed.

WEEKLY ONE-ON-ONE

It's Monday morning, and I'm feeling relatively optimistic. I've decided that I'll come in to the office at least a few times a week since it'll allow me to meet with people and have impromptu, but important conversations more easily in person. It's only been about a week since the return to the office, but many people have already abandoned masks, as long as we're not all stuffed in a crowded conference room. We keep the windows open—I dress warmly when I come in—and things feel the tiniest bit normal, compared to what they have been for the last two years.

It's almost lunchtime now, and I'm about to close my laptop, when I hear a ping, indicating a new calendar invite. "1:1—Nate/Sarah" for Tuesday morning at 10:00 a.m. In my head, I slither down my chair into a puddle on the ground. In real life, I manage to maintain my solid state and just start breathing harder.

I've told Erin I'll go out for lunch with her—our shared love of tacos has now expanded to include the other culinary options downtown has to offer—and we're supposed to be heading out for sushi soon.

I turn my chair to the side to grab my bag and see she's standing behind me, looking at my calendar. "One-on-one with Nate, huh? What's that for?"

"Ohhhh," I answer slowly, sure she can hear the lie that's about to leave my lips. "It's probably nothing, just a new employee sync or something like that." And, then to seal the deal on my convincing deception, I close my laptop a little too hard.

We get on the elevator to go downstairs. "Skip levels are

cool. Good opportunity for professional development," Erin says. Is it just my imagination or did she emphasize the word "professional?"

She leans her small frame against the elevator wall and crosses her arms, a thoughtful expression on her face. One of her fresh purple highlights falls into her eyes, and she brushes it away. "It's just interesting. He's been here, what, nine months? I've had meetings with him. We don't have regularly scheduled one-on-ones, though."

I shrug at her. "I'll let you know afterward."

"Do you guys know each other from before Instinqt?" she asks, cocking her head to the side.

"I did . . . *not* know Nathan worked at Instinqt before I got here," I say, trying to tell the truth.

We reach the ground floor, and she stares at me, her brow furrowed, probably trying to figure out why I'm clammy-looking and speaking English like I just came from another planet.

"Did you guys date?" she asks, keeping up the interrogation.

"Keep your voice down," I yell-whisper at her, as we exit the elevator and head toward the lobby doors. "Are you a freaking mind-reader?"

"Oh my god, you dated!" Her eyes are wide, joyful even.

"Uh, well, um, no?" I say, in a questioning tone. *God, I'd never make it on a witness stand.*

"Hah," she says, her eyes bright, her face alive as if she's just discovered the juiciest piece of gossip ever. She leans in and whispers, "Did you sleep with him?"

"There wasn't a lot of sleeping going on," I mutter weakly.

We've left the building, and Erin's basically dancing around on the sidewalk by this point. If anybody is looking out the window of Instinqt three floors up, they probably think she's won the lottery and I'm the winning ticket, as she drags me away from the building.

* * *

"Tell me everything," Erin says for the fiftieth time since this afternoon.

Camila, who's just met Erin for the first time, already likes her.

"Yes, Sarah, tell *us*," she inclines her head and smiles conspiratorially at Erin. "Everything."

"She didn't tell you already?" Erin asks Camila, surprised.

"Definitely not enough details yet," Camila replies, playfully glaring at me. "Just that she went home with a super-hot guy she met at the bar a month ago and ran out of there in the morning."

Erin's eyes light up, and she's got the funniest expression on her face.

"I've been meaning to get her tipsy since then to pry the details out of her, but she's onto me and won't drink more than a glass of wine when I'm around now," she says, cracking up.

We're sitting in my apartment. Earlier in the day, Erin and I ended up grabbing a quick sandwich, with me promising to tell her what happened when we could be in a quieter, more discreet location. But I told her we had to invite Camila since she would kill me if I ended up spilling my tea to Erin before her.

Camila has become fast friends with Erin now that she's discovered her secret-revealing powers. Once she realized teaming up on me was the key to finally finding out what happened after I left her "that night" at Decades, she was all in favor of expanding the guest list to our regular gossip sessions.

Quickly recapping the part of the night when Nathan and I had left to get some fresh air and how we ended up at his place for him to serve me homemade pasta, I quickly reach the part where we, well, the part where we made out like teenagers—dry-humping and all—and ended up in the bedroom.

"I seriously can't believe you're telling me that you dry-humped Nate from work . . . like our Chief Product Officer. Nate, he's got a PhD in computer science from the University of Illinois —and he's a nice guy, but it's just so hard for me to picture him having a one-night stand. It's so—"

"Out of character?" I ask.

"Well, yes," she says. "I mean, he must be a sexual being. I've seen him talking to the LVBs at company events."

"LVBs?" Camila and I ask at the same time.

"Louis Vuitton Bag?" Camila guesses.

"Low Voltage Breaker?" I venture.

They both give me a strange look.

"What? I used to work at a civil engineering firm," I say, by way of explanation.

"No," Erin says, laughing. "LVBs, LightVerse Bitches. My admittedly mean nickname for the LightVerse go-to-market strategy team. They're beautiful and wear perfect makeup and clothes, and they always flirt with the hot engineers and executives. They know they're probably gonna be rich someday soon, and they want a piece of it. We've tested out a few GTM/partnership-type things with them, and they're insufferable. It's not really nice—I'm generally very pro-women-supporting-women—but it doesn't apply to them . . ."

"So, Nathan . . . flirts with them?" I ask.

"Well, I mean, they flirt with *him*—especially Danica from LightVerse," she says, rolling her eyes. "Nate and Kevin and all the more senior guys. I'm not sure how much Nate flirts back. You can check this week when they visit. When I was scheduling a sync with Kevin, I saw it on his calendar."

My breathing settles a little, hearing this information.

Why should I care?

I shouldn't.

He's not mine. I don't want anything with him.

Both Erin and Camila give me a knowing look, immediately sensing my exaggerated interest in who flirts with whom concerning Nathan Goldman.

"So, yeah," I continue. "He kisses really well. Like, Doja Cat 'Kiss me More' well."

Camila snickers, nods approvingly, and raises her glass of wine.

"Those heels work every time, ladies. Blake should see your hot ass right now."

Erin looks at her, surprised, but intrigued. I give Camila a "please, not now" look. Camila understands and turns to Erin.

"That might be a little too much ancient history for one night."

"So, let's hear more about *recent* history, then," Erin says, filling my wine glass.

My eyes are open, but not focused on the room or on my friends in front of me, and I let myself imagine that night . . . again. It's been a month, and I can count on one hand the number of nights I *haven't* imagined kissing Nathan—his soft lips on my mouth and neck, and his muscular shoulders under my curious fingertips.

"We seemed to just . . . click," I tell them. "I'm not the kind to kiss-and-tell—"

"Isn't that exactly what you're doing?" Camila asks, challenging me.

I shoot her a fake-nasty look. "I won't give you *all* the details, but suffice it to say that this guy, this 'computer nerd,' knows his way around a woman's body. I definitely enjoyed myself and he definitely knew it, and . . . "

I take a quick breath and surprisingly, even to me, a small tear drips down my cheek.

"What's wrong?" they say, both jumping up and coming to me. I see them exchange a look.

"It's so embarrassing. How am I supposed to face him at work? I snuck out of his house. I never would've tried to see him again. He probably thinks I'm the biggest asshole in the world."

"Does he for sure know you're the same Sarah?" Camila asks.

"Well, I guess I'm gonna find out tomorrow."

❊ ❊ ❊

It turns out Nathan—or is it Nate since I'm talking to him at work?—will be taking the meeting remotely. He's still out of town, and I'm hoping the fact we'll be on Zoom will hide my nervousness. Not likely since I have a bad habit of chewing on my lip when I'm anxious, but I'll try to keep it in check. At least I'll be able to conceal my tendency to tap my foot in intense situations.

You're in the waiting room. Your host will let you into the meeting shortly, my screen reads.

I check my hair and face in the mirror. "Okay, you can do this, Sarah. Be cool. Be cool. Be cool."

Before I can hyperventilate, he lets me in the meeting and it takes me a couple seconds to notice he's looking at me. Luckily, I'm giving myself my pep talk while I'm muted, but he cocks his head. I notice the movement on the screen and turn to face the laptop camera and his—well, there's no other way to put it— drop-dead gorgeous face.

He unmutes himself. "Hi, Sarah," he says in the calm, sexy voice I remember. How can he sound so sexy on a Zoom meeting? "Thanks for accepting my meeting invite."

"Hi Na—" I pause, not knowing whether to call him Nathan, the way he initially introduced himself to me, or Nate, how everyone else at work refers to him. "Um, hi. Yeah, of course. Nobody says 'no' to the new CPO, right?"

I *certainly didn't say "no" the last time we met.* Why can't I keep my cool around him, even on a Zoom meeting? He narrows his eyes a bit, mouth twitching, looking as if he's trying to figure me out and whether I'm thinking of what . . . *Oh my god, is he thinking the same thing I am?* He can't be. Somebody here has to act like a professional. This is such an inappropriate way to start a work meeting, and it's all my fault. He resets his face and calm demeanor.

"So, how's the new role going? You've been here now for about a month, right?"

"Yeah, it's been a month," I say, meaning the job, but also since the last time we made out and ended up naked together on his soft, fresh-smelling sheets.

I feel like I can't get enough air in my lungs and just begin rambling, "It's been really great so far. Everyone is super nice and —"

"Listen," he interrupts. "This has the potential to be really awkward. I'm not an idiot. I get that."

His previously composed tone is breaking, and quickly, as he, too, begins to talk in a hurried manner. "You gotta know that I had no idea you were going to be working at Instinqt. I mean, I tried to ask you a couple times where your new job is and I didn't know—"

"I know, really. Nathan, I mean Nate, I mean . . ."

"It's fine. Call me Nathan."

"But everyone at work calls you Nate, don't they?"

"Yeah, but I kinda like you using my real name," he admits, a flash of a smile crossing his face. I stare at those lips—trying not to think about where exactly they've been on my body—and feel myself begin to unravel a bit. My breath is shallow. I swallow, trying to compose myself before I reply.

"Okay," I say, hopefully at least outwardly calm. "Nathan. It was really not cool for me to just leave your place. I'm not like that. I'm not the type of person who—"

"Stop," he says.

"But—" I try to continue.

"No, please, stop," he insists. "Listen, that's not my usual type of thing either, so maybe we can just try to move on and not talk about it. Or . . . *think* about it." So, he *has* been thinking about it?

"Also, I can probably get fired *if* we talk about it." He grimaces. "Like, I didn't consult the HR manual, but I'm pretty sure everything we did that night is *highly* discouraged between employees, especially one at the executive level."

Without missing a beat, I ask, "Everything?" unable to stop the words from coming out of my mouth.

He looks at me, frozen. Quiet. I glance down to check if he's on mute, and then he blinks, making me realize I've simply shocked him into silence with my brazen attempt at humor, my go-to way of handling uncomfortable situations.

He suppresses yet another smile and leans his forehead into his hand, looking down into his lap. Now *I* begin to contemplate his lap, and then, realizing that's not the best track for my mind to go down, quickly bring myself back to focus.

"How about we forgive, forget, and talk about next week's product release?" I suggest, starting up the conversation again, on a hopefully more clean and work-acceptable track.

He looks up.

"Yes", he says. "I love releases."

I bite my lip and raise my eyebrows.

"I'm talking about product releases, Sarah," he says, chastising me good-naturedly.

"Me, too, Nathan. Me, too."

❊ ❊ ❊

His first meeting with Sarah—well, technically it's his second meeting with her—goes better than he expected. Awkward —yes. Uncomfortable—definitely. But much better than he would've guessed. She jokes around with him—he's sure it's to cover her discomfort—and, well, it works. It smooths over the bumpy parts, and they manage to both survive it, even end the call on a positive note.

It isn't necessary for him, as an executive, to speak to any technical program managers—TPMs—on a regular basis, but since he figured out Sarah is working at Instinqt he's been thinking about her at least a few times a day and has a hypothesis. Maybe if he just gets to know her better, has the opportunity to see her in a professional capacity, he can get all of this—whatever "this" is—out of his system and quit acting like a love-struck teenager.

Today was a good start, and he decides he'll make it a recurring meeting on his calendar. "1:1—Nate/Sarah" every Tuesday at 10:00 a.m. It's the meeting he has enjoyed the most among the wall of meetings that make up his weekly calendar: leadership team, venture capitals, and board meetings. And he definitely wants to talk to her again.

Anyways, he's usually in Seattle on Tuesdays—the tail-end of the long weekends he's been spending up there helping his parents—so their meetings will always be remote. He's hoping the somewhat-detached nature of a virtual meeting will keep him focused, professional.

About thirty seconds into their meeting today, though, he had realized how naive that thought was. Trying not to talk about the elephant in the room—their very hot one-night stand—and the subsequent disappearing woman trick Sarah performed had proved impossible. She had seemed mostly concerned with the fact that she had bolted the morning after.

Thinking back now—well, it was only a month ago—he was confused, even worried that he'd done something wrong. All the evidence had seemed to indicate that she'd woken up, full of regrets, and escaped into the dawn. He'd even told Kevin, *lied* to Kevin, when he'd texted Nathan the next day with "?????". He'd texted him back that they'd left the bar together, but then she'd gone home. At the time, he'd been hopeful that she'd contact him somehow or he'd run into her and he'd get a second chance. But after a few weeks had passed, he'd given up hope. Until that day in the park, when Erin said her name.

He's not really sure what the rules about these things are in the workplace, but he's reasonably sure that one of your colleagues knowing what sound you make when you come can't be good. That he's been recently promoted, and there's a power differential between them, doesn't help matters. Just seeing her again today sent a bolt of electricity through his body. She was professionally dressed, and she looked like a different version of herself. Still beautiful, just different—full of confidence and in her element.

He was expecting—prepared for—awkwardness during their first conversation, considering the nature of their first encounter. But the nervous tension from both of them had simply dissipated the longer they talked. They're colleagues now, and they'll just have to put the whole thing behind them, not let it affect their working relationship.

Still, he can't pretend he wasn't excited to see her again, despite the concerns he had about how the conversation might go. Her smile was as irresistible as he had remembered, and he'd noticed that she'd gotten her hair cut, which made him remember how it had fallen, so beautifully, over her bare shoulders when she had sat, straddling him, on his couch.

If only he could have had one more night with her, before all this . . .

It's the wrong thought, the wrong time, and the wrong person, but he finds himself wondering if three wrongs ever make a right.

❊ ❊ ❊

"Oh my god. Did you guys just start taking off your clothes and Zoom-fucking at that point?" Camila asks me on the phone later, after I tell her how my conversation with Nathan went.

I tell her bluntly, "I almost died mid-conversation. There is no way I can concentrate at work if this guy is around. What am I going to do? I'm gonna have to just force myself to work and that's it." I'm rambling.

"Am I expected to participate in this conversation, or you wanna just keep doing your own monologue?" she asks, snorting.

Ignoring her question, I continue. "Seriously, though, if he exudes this much sexuality on a Zoom call, I'm gonna have to leave the room if he comes."

"I think he'd prefer to come if you stayed."

I half-gag, half-laugh.

"You're just gonna have to focus your energy elsewhere," she says. And I can't find any fault. It's sound advice. And that's what I do.

PRODUCT-MARKET FIT

Nathan and I have had two meetings, both on Zoom. When he's in the office, he's usually holed up in a meeting room, talking with senior staff: engineers, production managers, or Kevin and Maya. I barely see him, but when I do, he always gives me an amiable smile, and if he's alone, comes to my desk to say hello. At the risk of sounding like Sandy from Grease, his smile is dreamy: gentle and warm. And his mouth curls up, just enough to make his eyes crinkle a bit at the corners.

I see him come out of one of Instinqt's conference rooms now, and I start to wave and smile when I see a few people coming out of the room behind him. Kevin, two of the board members I've seen around, and an attractive blonde woman I don't know are chatting, and Nathan is waiting for them to finish their conversation. He glances my way, and mouths the word "Hi," but then turns back to shake hands with the board members. The two men walk toward the elevator to leave, and it looks like Nathan is trying to say his goodbyes to Kevin and the woman, who moves closer to him and puts her hand on his arm. Seeing it makes me feel uneasy. She squeezes his bicep and angles her body toward him in a way that seems a little too familiar for this to be strictly professional. I watch them surreptitiously while trying to pretend I'm working on my computer. She's laughing at something he's saying, and I wonder what the story is.

He puts on a smile—I don't know him well enough to judge, I suppose, but it seems forced—and walks with her to the elevator. I get up, as if to go to the coffee station, and watch them from the corner of my eye. I see Erin watching me watch them, and she gives me a look that says "I got you." Super spies always need a trusty sidekick.

As soon as the elevator doors close, she gets up and walks over to me quickly. "*That* is an LVB. Danica, to be specific. She's so freaking extra."

She's extra, alright. As much as I know Nathan isn't mine and doesn't owe me any loyalty, I'm still annoyed. I bite my lip and tell her I need some air. But I don't want to risk running into them, so I tell her I'll go down the back stairs.

Erin joins me on my walk, and we go into a full-on analysis session of Nathan. With skills these sharp, we should really be working at the FBI on serial killer cases. I'm of the opinion that the "Nate" at work, while not a total fake, is definitely different from the Nathan I originally met. Work Nate exudes confidence. He's Chief of Product Nate, Business Nate, Nate that can talk to VCs with confidence and technical know-how and "wow" anyone in the room.

Nathan—the guy who meets me on our one-on-ones isn't shy, but he's calmer, less flashy, less polished. He's more vulnerable. Erin thinks that Work Nate is the real one, whereas I think the alter-ego Nathan is his natural state. She believes me, but it's hard to convince her since she's never really seen "Nathan."

At some point, she asks me, "Does it really matter? For the time being, you probably just gotta take what you can get. You guys aren't allowed to date, so just get to know both Nate *and* the Nathan you get to see sometimes."

I know she's right, but it doesn't prevent me from thinking about it—too frequently for my own good—or remembering "that night" after Decades.

❊ ❊ ❊

It's Thursday evening, and I have *nothing* going on. Camila is busy with some workshop she registered for, and I'm not quite sure what to do with myself, so I decide I might as well go grocery shopping. In addition to nothing going on, there's also *nothing* in my refrigerator.

Instead of driving somewhere to get groceries, I decide I'll just walk to Whole Foods nearby. The fresh air and a bit of exercise will do me some good since I've been working from home and sitting most of the day. It's too expensive, but it's close. I'll pick up the basics and grab something for dinner from the hot bar, and save my more serious shopping for somewhere cheaper on the weekend. I slip on some sneakers, stuff some canvas grocery bags into my backpack, and head out.

It's starting to get dark already—but it's surprisingly warm for a February evening—and I head toward the Alameda to walk on the main street toward the store. I've got my AirPods in and I'm listening to some music and half-checking emails and Twitter while I walk, when I bump into someone on the sidewalk.

"Oh my gosh, I'm so sorry!" I say to the large, sweaty person I've run into. And then I look up, and see someone—someone familiar—smiling at me. He reaches out and takes one of my AirPods out of my ears.

"Hey, there," Nathan says. "Whatcha listening to?"

I blush. Why? One, it's the first time since that night that we've been together—in person—without anybody else around. Two, I see him put my second AirPod in his ear, just in time for the song to suggest to him that I'm alone too much and wouldn't he like to share that loneliness with me? *Oh god.*

He smiles right as that part comes on. "May I?" he asks, leaning closer and looking at my phone screen, eyebrows raised. My phone screen has locked by now—thank goodness for small mercies, since right before that I had been reading some trashy article about Regé-Jean Page Camila had sent to me earlier—and he can see what's playing. "Lovelytheband?" he asks.

"Yeah," I say, smiling. "You know them?"

"No, but it's nice. I like the lyrics," he says, his mouth twisting a bit into a small smile.

While we've been talking, I've taken in what he's wearing and determined I caught him on his way out of Orange Theory. *That explains the abs. Shit, focus, Sarah.*

"Just finish a workout?" I ask. *Smooth.*

"Yeah, you ever come here?"

"No, I'm not quite that intense," I say.

"That's cool," he says, handing me back my AirPod. I take it and then take the other one out of my ear, and put them both in my backpack. "Where are you headed now?"

"I was just gonna pick up a few groceries. Wanna come?" *Who invites someone to do grocery shopping with them?*

"Sure," he says.

✳ ✳ ✳

She looks surprised—pleasantly—that he accepted her invitation to come to the grocery store. He doesn't really know *why* she invited him, but it honestly doesn't matter. He's happy for the chance to see her again, outside of work. Ideally, he would have chosen a time he wasn't quite so sweaty and disgusting, but well, you've got to take opportunities where they arise. He learned that much from their first night together. *We were both a bit sweaty then, too . . .*

He takes a deep breath and makes himself focus.

"You come here a lot?" she asks, looking up at the Orange Theory sign.

"Some," he says. "My go-to thing now is mountain biking, but it takes a lot of time to get ready and get out there, so I usually do it on weekends. During the week, at the end of a long day, sometimes I just feel like I need to sweat." *Why is he talking about gross stuff like sweat with her?*

She touches her index finger to his arm lightly, running in down his bicep to his elbow, and raises an eyebrow. "Looks like it worked," she jokes, sticking her tongue out. The touch is not meant to be suggestive or sexual in any way—she's probably disgusted by him in his current state. His heart rate had finally settled after an hour of working out, but he can feel it speed up again, just from being near her.

"You might wanna keep your distance," he says, laughing.

"You're fine," she says, reassuring him.

They walk to the store, just a few minutes away on foot, and roam around inside with Sarah picking up a few things here and there. "I was gonna just grab something to eat for dinner. I know *you're* like a professional chef, but I'm a bit . . . well, I don't know if I'm lazy or tired, but . . ."

"Yeah, sure, let's get something. We can eat together."

"Oh," she says, a bit surprised. "Awesome."

They both choose what they want to eat and stand in line to pay.

"Um, where should we eat?" he asks. He knows it's unrealistic —and probably unwise—but he kind of hopes she'll invite him back to her place. She must live nearby if she walked to the store. He's not looking for a hookup or anything. He's just curious. He wants to see what her place looks like. After all, she's seen his.

"We could eat outside here or, oh, there's a little park nearby. It's dark, but I'm pretty sure there are lights?" she suggests.

"That works."

They walk to the park, a couple blocks away, and Nathan helps her carry her groceries. They're just sitting down on a bench when a homeless man he knows from downtown walks by.

"It's so sad," Sarah says. "There are so many homeless people here. I mean, it's the same thing in Santa Cruz, but it's just hard to get used to, you know?"

"Yeah. It's the same in Seattle," he says, nodding.

They begin to take out the food from the grocery bags, so they can eat. The man is talking to himself as he walks by, and then notices them sitting on the bench. "You guys got some change?" he asks, walking toward where they're sitting on the bench.

Sarah looks at Nathan. "I don't have any cash on me. Do you?"

"No, I left my wallet at home when I went to the gym. I paid with my phone at the store."

The man is still standing there, kind of shuffling his feet, and humming to himself, when all of a sudden he says, "Hey, I know you!"

* * *

Nathan, who hasn't yet opened his food, looks sideways at Sarah, and then at the man.

"Yeah, man. How's it going?" he says.

"Okay, okay," the man says, coming closer.

"Hey, man, you like meatballs?" Nathan asks him.

"Yeah, mannnn."

Nathan smiles and stands up and walks over to him with his box of food. "Here you go. Enjoy, dude."

I look at him to ask "Are you sure?" He just winks at me and hands him the box of food he'd gotten ten minutes ago. The man takes it from him and begins to walk away. "Thanks, man. Thanks, man. Thanks, man," he's saying to himself.

"Hey, wait, you forgot a fork," Nathan calls out. I hold out the extra unused disposable fork in my hand, and he grabs it, jogs after the man, and hands it to him.

"Fork, man. Fork, man. Fork, man," I hear the man singing now as he walks away, already opening the food container to see what's inside.

It's sweet, but my heart feels heavy. Still, I smile as Nathan walks back and joins me at the bench.

"A friend of yours?" I ask.

"Something like that. I mean, we're not exactly buddies, but I give him food sometimes. Near the office."

"Hey, man," I say, scooting closer to him. "You like tofu?"

He smiles.

"Here, we can share," I say, holding out my container of food.

"Thanks, but you don't have to."

"I want to," I say. "That was thoughtful of you."

He shrugs. "Yeah, well, he has a lot less than we do, right? Always good to share."

"You see?" I say, raising my eyebrows. "You proved my point. But we only have one fork, so you might get my germs."

He raises his eyebrow as if to say, "It's a little late for that, don't you think?" and leans in to take a bite of the food I'm holding out on my fork to him.

"This is really good tofu. So much better than meatballs," he says, looking impressed.

"Really?" I ask.

His expression breaks into a smile. "No, not really," he says, laughing and raising his eyebrow at me. I feel my heart speed up just a little bit at his, well, adorable expression. "But it's fine." He scoots closer to me, takes the fork from my hand, and offers me a bite now.

I take a bite and chew. It actually isn't that good. "You're right. Their tofu recipe needs some work."

"It doesn't matter. The company's good," he says, nudging my leg with his.

He's right. We spend the next half hour talking and eating. When we finish my container of food—it doesn't take long, Nathan's a big guy and obviously eats a lot after a workout—we break out some of the groceries I bought. We eat bread and cheese and even wash some of the apples with the water bottle from my bag and eat those.

"So, tell me a little about yourself, something I don't know," he says.

"Sounds like a job interview," I joke.

"Or a blind date," he responds, and I smile shyly at him.

"What do you want to know?" I ask.

"You grew up in Santa Cruz, right?"

I nod.

"Wow, a real California girl. Do you surf?"

"Nope."

"What was it like growing up there?"

"Well, I don't surf, but I do love the beach. My mom claims as soon as I could walk, I could swim. She and my dad used to take me to the beach and we'd sit underneath the boardwalk, so it wouldn't be too sunny for me."

"Sounds peaceful."

"It was. Whenever I'm really stressed—or happy—I end up dreaming about the water. The beach and the waves, or boats. It's my mind's way of just taking me to a happy place."

"Sounds therapeutic."

"It's definitely different from up here. Things move at a faster pace in Silicon Valley."

"They do," he agrees, and I can't quite define the expression I see in his face. It's not sad, more contemplative.

"You grew up in Seattle?"

"Yeah. I stayed there for college. That's where I met Kevin. And then for grad school—god, for the last five years I guess—I was in Illinois."

"How did you survive? Isn't it a god-forsaken winter apocalypse?"

"Yeah, but I guess you just get used to it?"

"You don't sound very convincing."

"Well," he says. "Not every place can have great weather like NorCal."

"I can manage a ski trip to Tahoe once a year, but I don't really get winter sports."

"What sports *do* you like?" he asks.

"To do? I guess mostly running, yoga. To watch, basketball."

"What's your team?"

I give him a skeptical look, indicating it's a dumb question. "The Warriors, of course."

"Well, I guess we can still be friends," he jokes.

"Why? Because you like the Lakers?"

"How'd you know that?"

"Kevin mentioned it. During the all-hands. The day . . . well, when I realized we'd be working together."

A momentous day indeed.

❋ ❋ ❋

"You ever *play* basketball?" he asks.

"I mean, I'm pretty short, so I'm kind of at a natural disadvantage," she says. "But I did play pick-up games with my dad."

"You game?" he asks. He noticed earlier that someone had left a basketball near the court in the park and glances that way now.

She looks down, he thinks, to check her clothes. She's in sneakers and leggings and seems to be considering it.

"Sure. But don't cry if I beat you," she says, laughing and getting up to walk over to the court.

She picks up the ball and begins to dribble and walk toward the hoop. He joins her and they play a loose, fun pickup game for a while. She's not bad, but she—well, neither of them—will ever be NBA stars. He could easily block her shots, but why would he? It's fun. She's fun. He likes the quick, back-and-forth conversation with her. Sometimes, he finds it hard to make conversation with people, but with Sarah, it's not an effort for him. It's starting to get pretty chilly when Sarah says she should probably head home.

"Can I walk you home? Help you carry the groceries?" he asks.

"There's not a lot left," she says. "You have quite an appetite."

"I'll make it up to you one day. I promise."

"Deal," she says, winking.

They walk the few blocks back to the Alameda, and stop on the corner, under a street light, to say goodbye. He's reminded of the first night they spent together. How Sarah had been momentarily entranced by the drizzling rain lit up by a streetlight—and he, in turn, had been entranced by her—while they tried to figure out what to do next. What they did next, well, that will always be a good memory.

"This is my stop," she says. "Are you walking home, or you drove?" Nathan tells her he walked, but that's his cue. Tonight won't be the night he sees her place. Maybe he'll never see it. He'll just have to be alright with seeing her at work and if he's lucky, a random grocery store trip.

They need to say goodbye. They both know it. They both don't want to. He knows *he* doesn't want to, and he's getting the same vibe from her.

"I didn't expect to have a dinner date tonight," she says, smiling at him. *God, that smile.*

"Is that what this was?" he asks.

"I mean, a post-gym sweaty man and mediocre takeout. What more could a woman ask for?" she jokes.

He laughs and shakes his head.

"You deserve a lot better. One day," he says.

Yeah, maybe one day.

❋ ❋ ❋

Since we met up on the street last week and had our little impromptu evening picnic and pickup game in the park, I've thought about Nathan. A lot. Embarrassingly a lot. But only during non-working hours. At work, I'm busier than I ever could have imagined. Working in a tech startup is no joke. There is so much to build, so much to fix, so many ideas to explore, test, and —yes—fail on, that I have plenty to do.

Beyond the stated responsibilities they hired me for— managing a few small product development projects—Erin has been pulling me into all kinds of conversations about how to do the entire release process better at Instinqt.

"Erin, what do I even know about all this stuff?" I ask her. We're in Instinqt's small kitchen and we're making our morning coffees. Well, *office* morning coffees, I suppose, since it's already my second of what will probably be three coffees today.

"You'll figure it out."

"I took a few project management courses. I know how to run development sprints, but this is my first time working in a place that does major software releases. I don't know how to plan or deliver on such a large scope."

"We don't either. At least not well."

I give her a lost look.

"Sarah."

"Erin?"

"You're smart. You get these kinds of things. That's why we hired you. Whatever you don't get, sit in on calls. Ask smart questions. Then tell me your recommendations. It has to be better than what we're doing now."

An hour later, I sign on to my weekly one-on-one call with

Nathan.

"Good morning," I say. *You look so handsome this morning.*

"Good morning, Sarah." *I love the way you always say my name.*

"How are things in Seattle?" I ask.

"They're okay. Still just trying to figure things out. Thanks for always asking." He gives me a warm smile.

"Yeah, of course."

We've spent our first calls getting to know each other a little more, and we've only talked about work-related things a bit, but in light of what Erin told me this morning, I decide then and there that if I have the ear of the CPO, I'm going to take advantage of it, and so I quickly pivot to asking him for some professional advice.

"So, *Nate*, CPO-friend-of-mine," I say, winking. He gives me a curious look. I never call him Nate. "I was hoping we could use our time today to go over release processes here at Instinqt. You've been here longer than I have, and I'd like to hear what you think the top three problems are. Weak points. Things we're doing poorly. And any ideas for improvement. That kind of thing."

❉ ❉ ❉

Wow. Nathan didn't sign on to this call expecting Sarah to jump right into engineering best practices, but it's a side of her he's heard about from some of his colleagues and he's here for it.

"Yeah, sure," he says, perfectly willing to talk shop.

He outlines some of the obstacles that he and the team dealt with while he was working as an engineer his first six months at Instinqt as well as some actions that he thinks the company, specifically product and engineering, could take to improve.

"You can't effectively build poorly scoped features," he says. "So, heading up product now, I'm working closely with the product managers to make sure they define what they want clearly enough, so the engineers know *what* to build, what's *actually* expected of them."

"You're right. We could be doing better there," she agrees.

"I mean, from what I've heard," she continues, qualifying her statement.

"Don't be shy, okay? With your insights or your opinions. They're just as valid as anyone else's here."

She glances away for a second. Then she looks directly in the camera and replies confidently, "Yes, you're right. Thanks for reminding me of that."

Her words say one thing, but her tone says another. *Ah, not confidence. Annoyance.*

"Sorry if that sounded patronizing. I'm not trying to mansplain or anything. I just, I mean it. You're smart, and you're coming in with fresh eyes. What you see, someone else might have missed."

She nods and smiles back at him, this time, more genuinely. He waits a beat and then continues.

"Anyways, another—well, huge—part of the problem is late delivery. Working in product now—outside of the engineering bubble—I have to talk to customers, and telling them that the features we promised them in Q1 are only going to come in Q2 . . . those are hard conversations."

"Yeah, well, engineers are notoriously bad at estimations."

"You have experience with that?"

"It's not a universal truth?" she asks, smiling. "Anyways, I have a working hypothesis that the main problem here—or at least the low-hanging fruit that can help us take a big jump forward—is communication. We need to increase visibility and communication all the way through the pipeline."

"Sounds reasonable. What do you mean, exactly?" he asks.

"Well, marketing and sales are the people who know our customers, what they need and want. If product and engineering are to create things that actually matter— that move the needle, business-wise—they have to get that information in an accurate and timely manner. I think that at Instinqt we have a breakdown in that pipeline. A lot of customer feature requests and feedback on our existing features are getting lost in, I dunno, translation, and they never make it to the people who need to build or improve them."

"Right, right," Nathan says, nodding.

"But we're a startup. We want to innovate, and we're the ones that know what our technology is truly capable of. We don't need to rely *only* on our customers to determine our path forward. Some of our product roadmaps should continue to come from product and engineering," she says. "Which I know they are already," she continues. "No offense. I know you know how to do your job."

"No offense taken. You're right. We do that already, but we need to do better. If you figure out that puzzle, then, well, you can be the next CPO." He's exaggerating a bit, but talking to her—openly like this, just brainstorming better ways of doing things—he sees her in a new light. He can see why he hears her name come up in other contexts. She's smart. Knows how to get to the root of the problem.

Nathan looks at the time on his computer. They have two minutes left.

"I'm sorry to cut this short, but I need to jump to another call now. Will you let me know how I can help?"

"Yeah, sure," she says, smiling broadly.

"I look forward to future collaboration," he says and winks, and he ends the call.

LEGACY CODE

It's evening, and I'm at home, thinking about my conversation earlier with Nathan. I'm still new in high tech, and there's so much for me to learn. I'm appreciative of anybody who's willing to talk to me about the things I don't know and help me do better. I guess I just didn't realize that Nathan could be one of those people. I shouldn't be surprised, but it was like opening a door I just found and discovering a new side of him on the other side. My brain had filed him into the "unattainable romantic interest" drawer, and up until now, I had neglected to think of him in this other capacity.

I look him up online now and try to see if he has a Twitter account. No. Instagram is also a no, but I click on the first link, his LinkedIn profile. His profile page has the same photo he uses for his Slack account, and I smile at the sight of his face. I check out his professional experience—not extensive by any means, mostly teaching assistant and research positions—but look more closely at his educational experience: MSc . . . PhD . . . And *numerous* publications in academic journals. *Wow.*

I go back to the Google search page and see that a lot of those same articles are listed in the search results, alongside a seemingly endless list of conferences at which he's presented his high-performance computing research. *This guy is no joke.*

I look at the clock. It's 8:00 p.m. He's probably at the Seattle airport now, getting ready to board. He told me earlier that he was up there visiting his parents. I, well, I want to talk to him. I pick up my phone from the table and use the app to Slack him "Have a safe flight." Right away, I see "typing . . ." on the screen. He's online.

NGoldman (he/him): Thank you. Actually flying back tomorrow morning—6:00 a.m. <smiley face emoji>

SHoffman (she/her): That's so early.

NGoldman (he/him): But you like to wake up early and get out of town quick <winky face emoji>

SHoffman (she/her): Ouch . . . but not wrong, I guess.

NGoldman (he/him): So, what are you doing?

SHoffman (she/her): Just putting together some itineraries and packing lists for the off-site. Erin asked me to help out so we can send it out by the end of next week.

NGoldman (he/him): Make sure you remind people to bring swimsuits.

SHoffman (she/her): Swimsuits? It's gonna be freezing.

NGoldman (he/him): But there's an indoor pool and hot tub!

SHoffman (she/her): You think people are gonna get in hot tubs with their coworkers? What is this, WeWork?!

NGoldman (he/him): <laughing emoji> Maybe write "optional" next to swimsuits.

SHoffman (she/her): As in, you can get in the hot tub and not wear one?!

NGoldman (he/him): YOU have a dirty mind. I meant that you don't have to bring one at all, as in, not get into the hot tub.

SHoffman (she/her): Oh.

SHoffman (she/her): Ohhhhh.

I'm dying of embarrassment, laughing, with tears coming down my face in my living room. I'm trying to reconcile my professional conversation earlier in the day with him about product development best practices with what is currently happening in this train wreck of a Slack thread when my phone buzzes again.

NGoldman (he/him): Are you still there?

SHoffman (she/her): No, I died of embarrassment.

NGoldman (he/him): Don't. Some things are MUCH more embarrassing.

SHoffman (she/her): I can think of a few.

NGoldman (he/him): Can we move this to WhatsApp?

I send him my number.

❊ ❊ ❊

We're on Whatsapp now:

Me: Hi—it's me.

He sends me a "new number who dis" GIF in response.

Me: Hint—a little short, red glasses, great sense of humor.

Nathan: I'd say "a lot" short.

Me: <Tongue sticking out emoji>

Nathan: Oh, yeah, I remember you. Cute, clever brunette from Decades, right? Badass on the court?

Me: Some might say.

Nathan: Anybody would say . . . because it's true.

Me: That's sweet, but I don't always feel so clever.

Nathan: Care to elaborate?

Me: You're a curious guy tonight.

Nathan: Well, I just want to get to know you better.

Me: TBH it's sad and boring.

Nathan: I bet it's not boring.

Me: A breakup—sad one. Made sadder by the state of the world. Sprinkle in some self-doubt about my ability to make good decisions in life.

Nathan: Deep. And not boring at all. FWIW, I think you make pretty good decisions.

Me: Says the guy I had a one-night stand with.

Nathan: Now that was a GREAT decision. ;)

Me: <laughing emoji> Do you wanna talk? You're not gonna be exhausted in the morning?

My phone buzzes.

"Hi."

"Hi," I say softly.

"Why so quiet?" he asks. I can hear the exhaustion in his voice.

"Trying to make sure nobody from HR is listening in," I whisper dramatically.

"We're not allowed to talk outside of work?" he asks.

"I guess we are. You sound a bit tired," I say.

"I am, but I like talking to you." Hearing that, my heart squeezes a bit. "Why do you think I have a recurring one-on-one with you?"

"Professional development?" I joke, both of us knowing that today was the first time we've talked about anything work-related.

"Today was a great professional conversation," he says.

"Yeah, you're right, but, well, it's okay if we talk about other stuff, too."

"Like you being a Golden State Warriors fan. I can put a professional spin on that, too. Me helping you see the error of your ways. That's gonna help you professionally at some point. You said you've made some bad decisions—going with the Warriors as your favorite team—"

"When I was ten," I interrupt.

"And they were terrible—"

"Was *not* a bad decision," I say, interrupting him. "They've been amazing the last decade."

"Look how things can turn out from a rough beginning," Nathan says.

He's talking about the Warriors, but I sense he's referring to something else, too.

"Okay, I give up. You'll never be a Lakers girl," he concedes.

"It doesn't even make sense that you like the Lakers. You're from Washington."

"People are allowed to like teams from other states, especially after your own team moves to Oklahoma. What was I supposed to do?"

"I'll accept it. For now," I say, suspiciously.

"So, besides the Warriors, you've made *other* bad decisions?" he jokes.

"Thanks for not letting that one slide. I'd *really* love to share," I say sarcastically. "I enjoy talking about my hang-ups. I've heard it's a great way to impress senior people in the workplace."

"I'm not senior," he says. "It's an interim position."

"You don't think the board will approve you as the permanent CPO? Why not? You *seem* really smart."

"You say that as if I might not be," he jokes. "Well, thank you for the confidence boost, but Kevin mostly chose me because he knows he can trust me. Matt's an asshole, and Maya despises him, and never would have agreed to appoint him CPO."

"Matt? Really?"

"Yeah, super full of himself, but beyond that, there's just a lot of business stuff going on right now, and Kevin needs someone who'll 100 percent be there for him if he ever has his back against the wall."

"Hmmm," I say, hoping I've managed to distract him from wanting to know more about me.

"Sarah, I don't think you really wanna tell me. It's okay. I'm just feeling morose or contemplative, and I guess I just wanted to know I'm not the only one in the world who goes through shit."

"Oh, it's shit you want to hear about?" I ask. "Well, you've come to the right place."

"Yassss," he says, laughing. "Go onnnn."

"Well, you might've noticed I'm pretty smart," I say jokingly. It's true, though. I am actually smart. I learn new things quickly —always have. "But sometimes, I wonder if maybe I'm just book smart, you know? For the longest time, I just haven't been able to figure out what I'm supposed to do with my life."

"Seems like you're doing really well now," he says.

"I'm doing okay now, I guess. I've just made some dumb

decisions, school- and career-wise. Definitely in my love life," I say, in an uneasy tone.

"Hmmm."

I continue. "I was all set to go to college and major in chemical engineering, but once I got there, I changed my major. I had this whole plan to attend law school afterward. I even took the LSATs and started applying to law schools my last year. My parents were super happy—I mean, they were both teachers, so law sounded really prestigious to them."

"So, what happened?"

"I just got . . . derailed? I finished college early, so I took some time to travel in Europe and then Asia. Lived abroad for a while, just teaching English and volunteering. And after all that, law just didn't seem like the right path anymore."

"So, how'd you end up in high tech? I mean, besides growing up near Silicon Valley?"

"Well, after dropping out of law school before I even started, I got a job working at my dad's friend's engineering firm as a project manager. He told me that if I took some professional courses, he'd hire me as an entry-level PM. For lack of a better option, I did it, and I actually liked it. I figured out that I'm really good at just getting shit done."

"That, you are, but all that sounds good. Everybody has questions and screw-ups in their twenties, no?"

He's probably right—and I, too, used to feel that way—but the last couple years have done a number on me. It's shocking how you can go into a relationship being one person, feeling one way about yourself, and come out with a different perspective on life, on yourself.

Now I'm at the hard part. My time with Blake.

"So, my last job is where I met my ex, Blake," I continue, hesitantly. "A few years ago. We started dating a few months before Covid started and *stupidly* decided to move in together once we were all on lockdown. For the record, all the important people in my life—my mom, Cam—advised against it, but I didn't listen. It was good for a while, but then it wasn't. It probably would've ended earlier if we weren't living together, and if . . . I don't know, I was out in the world and meeting other—better—people."

"And?"

"We just weren't a good fit," I clarify. I laugh, a bit sadly.

"What's funny?"

"Well, whenever Cam hears me say 'we weren't a good fit,' she always replies, 'Right. You're a smart and kind and hilarious . . . and he's a dick.'"

"Not a fan, huh?" he asks, amused.

"No. She's known me for a long time—since high school—and she's really protective. When I was abroad, we didn't talk as much, but as soon as I came back, it was like we'd never been apart. Some friends are just like that."

"It's good to have those kinds of friends," Nathan says. "People you know have your back. That's Kev for me. It's why I joined Instinqt when he asked."

"How long have you guys known each other?" I ask.

"Since college. We met our freshman year here in Washington, and we actually both headed to UI for grad school. I stayed a bit longer than he did. He was ready to go do his own startup."

"It's amazing to think some people have such drive. Just some cool idea that they want to share with the world and—"

"Make a lot of money on?" he says, chuckling.

"I suppose that doesn't hurt, right?"

"Well, the world should just be glad he went with the Instinqt product and not his original one."

"Which was?" I ask, intrigued now.

"Well, something like Tinder, but a lot less sophisticated. And a *much* sketchier business model. Come to think of it, the only business model was that he would get dates," he admits, cracking up.

He backtracks a bit, maybe feeling he's said too much about the person who started the company we both work in. "It wasn't *actually* his idea for a startup. He was just having fun. He liked the technical challenge of creating an app."

"Well, did he at least get any dates?"

"A few? I don't remember, but he's always been able to attract women. He has a lot of confidence, not bad-looking, I guess." He pauses. "I'm the one who's always needed a push to talk to women."

I find it hard to believe that such a good-looking guy would have a hard time finding a date. But I guess so much of my experience with Nathan has been at work, where he's confident and well-spoken. Reflecting on the night he came up to me at the bar, I remember his shyness—in his tone, in his body language.

"Well, it's better to be a little shy than a jerk."

"And we come full circle," he says. "So, your ex was a jerk?"

"Do we have to talk about it?" I ask.

"I can tell *you* some bad ex stories if it'll make you feel better."

"No, that's okay. I mean, I think all the time we spent together in the house—during the shelter-in-place and *all* the time after that—plus the fact that we were working at the same company didn't help. Also, he's an engineer, and I'm not. It just brought out all my insecurities about my own, I don't know, 'wasted potential.' And instead of being a good boyfriend, or even a decent human being, and helping me through all my crap, he just took advantage of it."

There's more, of course. I recently saw on Instagram that Blake's dating—or at least the photos would seem to indicate that—the agency woman I suspected he was having an emotional affair with while we were still together. But that's not something I need—or want—to share with Nathan tonight, maybe ever.

I'm rambling and I know it, but it's almost 11:00 p.m. and it's been a long day. We've been texting and talking for a while, and for some reason, it's like my brain has disconnected and it's not comprehending that the Nathan I'm talking to is the Nate from work, the guy a few levels above me who runs the entire product department of our company, the guy who's best friends with the CEO. Still, my filter is still intact enough not to share everything that's wrong with me and all the broken pieces of me, my ex-boyfriend, my life.

All my fears and worries and tiny insecurities are flowing out of me like a broken faucet and yet Nathan's just listening and letting me get it all out.

"That sounds really hard, Sarah," he says. It's a simple statement, but it's said with empathy.

"It was," I say, sighing.

The truth is that Blake was a real asshole sometimes. The snide remarks he made sometimes, under the guise of humor, were hurtful. He took advantage of my insecurities to feel superior. He knew that I wanted to accomplish so much, but that I hadn't quite found my way yet and he held it over me in a way that someone who's supposed to love you shouldn't.

"Do you know what I liked about you the minute I saw you?" Nathan's saying now, in a quiet but sure voice.

"Um, my red heels?" I joke because I'm feeling vulnerable and sad. I don't want to feel it all so much—to bare it all in front of Nathan—so I'm seeking a way out with misplaced humor.

"Well, I can't say I didn't notice them," he admits, and I can hear the smile in his voice. "But no. It was the way you were watching and listening to your friend, Cam, telling a story to all your friends at the bar. It was clear that she likes to be the center of attention, and you were just okay with it. You just let her take the spotlight and enjoy it, while you listened calmly. And when Kevin pointed you out across the room—the first thing I noticed was your beautiful smile. It's bright and warm . . . and there's this sense of, like, steadiness. I could just imagine you having all these deep thoughts underneath, like one of those currents under the surface of the ocean."

"Damn, Nathan, that's pretty profound," I say, chuckling. I feel myself warming up, likely blushing. It's good we're not on FaceTime.

"Yeah, I guess I'm in a mood tonight." He sighs. "I'm in my old bedroom if you can believe it. My mom kept it pretty much the way I left it. I feel like I'm in high school again."

"Hmmm, let's play a game," I say.

"Okay," he says, a little unsure. "What kind of game?"

"I want to guess what you were like in high school."

"Ha, okay, well, I hope you're ready to be disappointed, because—big shocker here—I was a huge nerd."

"But that's exactly what I was gonna say!" I laugh. "Let's see. You're hot now—oh, shit, did I say that out loud?—but you're not an arrogant asshole, which means that you used to be less hot, or at least less muscular. Am I right?"

"You are." I can hear a restrained laugh in his tone, an embarrassed groan.

"So you were less hot, and a bit of a nerd—hence becoming a computer programmer—but you weren't like a super nerd. You also did some sort of sport. I'm gonna guess something like cross-country."

"Damn, you're good."

"You still run now?" I ask.

"A bit."

"Me, too, but I guess I told you that last week."

"I could tell anyway."

"How?"

"I can't say."

"Howww?" I press him.

"Fine," he relents. "You have a nice ass. Firm, but like, just soft enough."

"And when did you notice this?"

"Right about the time I was grabbing it." He laughs.

"O-M-G," I say, and he laughs at me using the initials. "This conversation is going off the rails. We can never recover from this."

"I don't know. It just doesn't seem fair," he says, in an obstinate tone. "Like, I saw you, I liked you, I wanted to get to know you—"

"You *are* getting to know me," I interrupt.

"But it's not enough," he says. "And as CPO, I don't have any say in what happens with TPMs, but I'm probably still not allowed to invite you over . . . for pasta . . . or wine . . . or . . ."

"Other things?" I offer helpfully.

I hear him sigh.

"Nathan, it's getting late. You're gonna be so tired tomorrow. Your flight's at 6:00 a.m."

"Yeah, you're probably right. Before you go, though, can you just tell me one thing?"

"Sure."

"When you came to my place that first night," he starts and then hesitates. I can almost hear the wheels turning in his head, him trying to build up the courage to say something.

"Yeah?" I ask encouragingly, not knowing whether it's something I want to answer at all, let alone honestly.

"That first kiss, the whole night, it felt different. Like, good different to *me*. Did you also feel it?"

I'm silent for what seems like an eternity but is likely only a few seconds. My heart is pounding in my ears.

"Yeah, Nathan, I did," I say softly. "Have a safe trip tomorrow." As I look at the phone screen to press the red button as quickly as I can, before I say something embarrassing, something I can't take back, I hear him say, "Good night, Sarah."

❊ ❊ ❊

It's late Wednesday afternoon, and Nathan has come into Instinqt this afternoon to work for a bit from the office. He flew in early this morning, but he needed to meet with Maya right after lunch and thought it might be good for them to talk in person. For the last couple of hours, he's closed himself up in one of the Zen booths to concentrate and prepare for an important meeting tomorrow.

When he finally looks up from his laptop, he notices the light in the office has changed, a sure sign the sun has moved in the sky to the west. He stands up to stretch and sees there are only a couple of people left—two solutions engineers— both of whom are heading toward the elevator. He packs up his things, and when he steps out of the booth, to his pleasant surprise he sees

Sarah is in the office.

"Oh! Hi," she says, in a surprised tone.

"Hey, you're here late."

"Yeah, I was working from home, but I just dropped by to grab my notebook. Forgot it the other day," she says, holding it up, before stuffing it into her backpack. "It's my project management lifeline. I didn't even know you were here."

"I've been hiding in the Zen booth most of the day," he tells her.

"Do you have a lot more work?" she asks.

"No, I think I'm good. I was just about to head home."

"Me, too."

"Would you—" they both say at the same time, and stop, smiling at each other.

"Walk?" he asks.

"Food?" she says.

"Both," he says. "Let me grab my bag."

❋ ❋ ❋

It's not late, but with the sun starting to set, it's getting colder outside. As they leave the building together and begin to walk, in the direction of Sarah's place, Nathan sees Sarah pull a fleece and scarf from her backpack.

"You're gonna do great in Park City," he jokes. "It's freezing there."

"Maybe I'll just have to find someone to snuggle with and keep me warm."

Where do I apply for that job?

"Maybe," he says.

Just then, they pass Decades, and Nathan inexplicably feels the need to open up. "You know, I actually saw you before that night at the bar."

"What? Really?" Sarah says.

"I mean, it was *at* the bar, but it was . . . it must've been last summer. Outside on the patio," he tells her.

"I wish you would've said 'hello' then. Might've saved us an interesting story."

"Nah, I like our story," he says.

She's quiet but smiles shyly at him. "I like that," she says. "*We* have a story."

When they reach the Alameda, she suggests a Mexican restaurant she knows. "We can sit outside on the patio. It's cold, but I think they have heaters."

He'd love to sit on the patio—or anywhere, honestly—with her.

They sit across from each other, and he wishes he could just grab her hand, resting on the metal patio table, and hold it. After they order and wait for their food to come, they talk about a lot of things, first and foremost, his dad.

"So, any reason you always do Monday and Tuesday meetings from home?" she asks him.

"Well, um, I've been flying up to Seattle a lot lately to help my parents," he says. "My dad's got cancer."

❋ ❋ ❋

My mouth is suddenly dry, and my throat begins to tighten.

"Me and my brother, David, are doing our best to help out, so I fly up most Fridays and then stay over until Monday or Tuesday. Then I come back and spend the rest of the week in the Bay," he says.

I find myself muttering shallow platitudes about cancer being terrible and how sorry I am to hear it. It must sound hollow— utterly lacking in meaning—to his ears. What he can't guess is that I know a thing or two about losing a parent. What I know *nothing* about is dealing with the fear of losing said parent while they age or deal with a serious illness.

I had no notice whatsoever with my dad, and even now, I don't know whether it was better that way or not. Better to know someone is dying, slowly fading away, and you have the chance to tell them just how much they mean to you? Or better to be spared what must be an achingly awful period of time while death encroaches upon your loved one, and just lose them unexpectedly? Neither is a good option.

When my dad passed away a few years ago, shortly after I'd come back from abroad, I was devastated. He was only sixty-one. He'd been out for a run and suddenly collapsed from a heart attack. The pandemic-related difficulties we'd experienced over the last couple of years paled in comparison to the loss of my warm and loving father.

I'm close with my mom, but the bond I had with my father was something really special. As a kid, he would always take me camping in the Santa Cruz Mountains, and we liked to fish together on the pier. So many of my memories of my dad are on the pier, on a boat, out swimming. It's no wonder I dream of waves, water, and boats so much.

My thoughts must have drifted because I only realize I've closed my eyes—for a second? for eternity?—when I hear his voice, in a careful, gentle tone, calling me back.

"Are you okay, Sarah?" he asks. He moves his chair to sit near me and places a hand on my shoulder.

"Um, yeah," I mumble, even though the answer is more accurately "No."

I search for more words, struggling to pull them from the recesses of my brain. "I . . . I just know what it's like to be worried about someone you love."

He nods—silent—and waits for me to continue. Rather than it being an uncomfortable silence, it invites me in, embraces me. *How does he do that?*

"Actually, that's not right," I continue, "I didn't have the chance to worry. Just be . . . destroyed, I guess."

His brow is knitted. He's listening, trying to puzzle out what I can't seem to say.

And so, I tell Nathan my story—the sad, compact version, wholly inadequate of expressing the size of the hole in your life when you lose a beloved parent without warning. Most of the time, I think I've learned how to handle my grief, but other times something triggers me, and it's like not a day has passed since the terrible call I received from my mom telling me the news.

He doesn't say much, just listens, and gives me the space and time I need to get it out. It's different from the way most people handle it. When people find out you've lost a parent relatively recently, they often feel the need to respond, to talk, but his response—intentional silence—is the right one.

I take a deep breath and pull myself together. I don't want my grief, my experience, to worry him more. His dad's situation is different. Plenty of men come back from prostate cancer and live the rest of their lives, healthy and happy.

I try to give him the same opportunity to share—if he wants to—and he does. He explains that his father was doing alright for a while, but that in mid-January, he'd begun to have a fever that the doctors hadn't been able to figure out.

"It's really weird because the PET scan is basically clean. It could be related to the biopsy he had. We don't know. We're just trying to keep checking everything we can think of. It's been pretty shitty."

"If you ever need to talk, I'm here. I mean, I don't know if you feel comfortable with that, but . . . it's true. Anytime. Really."

He smiles softly and reaches over to squeeze my hand.

"Thank you. Really. I know it's not . . . new for you, but you can talk to me, too. If you need to."

The server brings our food—chicken enchiladas for him and veggie for me. It gives us the break we need from the heavy topics we've been discussing. The food is good, but the company is even better. We finish our meal, and since I'm close to home, it makes sense for us to part ways here.

"Thanks for walking me home," I tell him.

"Well, I like . . . walking," he says, smiling and raising his eyebrows meaningfully. "Walking" seems to be code for "me."

I grin. "I like *walking,* too," I reply. "A lot."

It's a nice note to end on, and so I turn to go, but then, just as quickly, turn back.

"Nathan?"

"Yeah," he replies, a questioning look in his eyes.

"Wish your dad my best? I know he doesn't know me or

anything, but maybe it's good for him to know people are thinking about him? Rooting for him. What's his name?"

"Noah."

"I'll think about him," I say.

"Thanks," he says and squeezes my arm.

"See you at work."

A bit later, I indulge myself and imagine him, sitting near me on the restaurant patio, small lights hung haphazardly over the plants, twinkling. Almost as beautiful as his eyes. And I begin to process what we shared with each other—the longing for a father, the fear for one still here. It feels like something significant—a departure from simple flirting, something different from the night we hooked up—a real connection.

FIRST MOVER ADVANTAGE

It's been a few weeks since Nathan got his promotion and he feels like he has started to get into a flow with his new role and responsibilities, but it's tough, with all his travel to and from Seattle. He takes some comfort knowing that his main job —as stated by Kevin—is to watch Kevin's back and try to court investors. The product team is already relatively strong and he just needs to convey that to the investors when they meet and make them feel good about wanting to invest in Instinqt.

The hopeful meeting with Eden Snow is quickly approaching and with it, a night he's not really looking forward to, the quarterly partner event Instinqt hosts. They already have some connections at LightVerse—outside of Danica—but any connection that can strengthen their position with such a high-profile company and convince them to contribute to or even lead the Series B funding round will convince that many more investors to line up happily.

Normally, he'd be fine playing this game. He wouldn't say it's a natural role for him, but he's okay being #2 to Kevin's #1. Things have just gotten a little more complicated, though, with Kevin bringing Danica into play. He can't put his finger on it, but the whole thing feels reckless.

At Kevin's insistence, he's trying to keep up regular contact with her, so she'll help them out, without giving her the wrong idea. Nathan can tell she's loving the attention from him, and despite him always watching his words and trying not to ever be alone with her, she's laying on the compliments and hints pretty thick. She's as beautiful as she always was, and it seems like her good looks and assertive personality are serving her aims well—she's advanced pretty quickly at one of the major tech companies in Silicon Valley. Still, the tendency he noticed in her almost a decade ago to ignore other people's needs and desires when they conflict with her own is still pronounced. He can't wait for them to finally meet Eden Snow, so he can just go back to what he's good at: programming, talking to people about nerd stuff, and cooking.

When things get really stressful for him, he wonders whether he made the right decision, joining Instinqt when he did. He had other paths to take but chose this one. Some days, he regrets it.

Other days, though, he sees Sarah, talks to her, and thinks maybe it wasn't such a bad decision after all.

✳ ✳ ✳

It's Thursday afternoon, and since Kevin's planned a group hike for the next day for the local team—"an excellent opportunity to bond" he called it—I'm trying to get some work done today. I'm sitting at my desk drafting a project brief, something to help the team clearly scope and, then hopefully, commit to how we're going to deliver on a specific feature by the end of this half. The office isn't very busy today, but Kevin's been locked up in a large meeting room most of the morning.

Every so often, he'll come out and ask someone a question—often Nathan, who's sitting on one of the trendy little couches near the window, in the "flexible" seating setup I've heard so many of these high-tech companies like to offer their employees. So people don't feel chained to their desks—or god forbid, cubicles—and to give the workspace a cooler, more comfortable feel. Kevin's ventured out at least three or four times this morning, grabbed coffee, looked in the fridge in the kitchen area, found it wanting, and grabbed a bag of Smartpop popcorn—I've noted that white cheddar is his favorite—and gone back in the room to do Zoom calls or other work.

I've thought about offering to bring him some lunch—just

to be nice—but just as I'm about to go ask him if he'd like something, he comes out again to speak to Maya at her desk.

Nathan and I both notice he's left his lair, and as if we've both received a telepathic memo at exactly the same time, we both look at the cart with the popcorn bags. He's got a mischievous gleam in his eye, and intrigued, I walk to the kitchen to meet him. He's filling his water bottle with water and glancing over at Kevin talking to Maya.

"Not to sound too cliché, but are you thinking what I'm thinking?" he asks me.

"I was thinking about going to get the poor guy some lunch," I tell him.

"No, not *that*," he says, giving me an incredulous look. "Let's mess with him."

"I don't think I'm in a position to mess with the CEO," I reply, smirking at him.

"Fine," he says. "I'll do it. So, Option A: We hide all the popcorn. Option B: We put it all next to his laptop in the meeting room where he's taking calls."

I snicker. "Definitely Option B. Funnier. Also, guaranteed to get a response," I say, loving this playful side of him.

"Okay, but you have to make sure he doesn't notice. Go ask him a question if you see that he's done with Maya."

I nod.

He gathers up all the popcorn and turns his back, where nobody on the other side of the room can see what he has in his arms, and whispers to me conspiratorially, "Cover me."

I give him a little salute and try not to laugh.

Nathan sneaks over to the meeting room, and through the glass window, I can see him unloading at least ten bags of popcorn on the table near where Kevin's left his computer open.

He slips out, gives me a wink, and returns to where he was sitting before. I make myself a coffee, and quickly glance over at Kevin and Maya, who it seems have decided to continue their conversation somewhere more private. They head toward the meeting room.

They pull the door only partially closed and sit down. From my desk, which is closer to where they're sitting, I hear Maya ask Kevin, "You really like popcorn, huh?"

Through the window, I can see Kevin get up abruptly. He peeks his head out the door and narrows his eyes suspiciously while he surveys the room, trying to figure out who's screwing with him.

Everyone is working or talking to each other or, you know, just acting generally normal, except for two people. Those two people are red from the effort of trying not to burst into laughter, and one of them fails to do so, outing herself as the culprit.

"Nice," Kevin says, giving me a direct look, one that's supposed to look annoyed, but I can see the playful glint in his eyes. "I'll remember that, Sarah," he says as he shuts the door.

Nathan walks by my desk a minute later and tilts his head in the direction of the door to the back stairwell. I look around the office to see if anyone's noticed and then follow a minute or two later.

When I get there and close the door behind me, I find him leaning on the wall, looking way too sexy to just be hanging out in a stairwell.

"You got me in trouble," I say, swatting at him.

"No, it's fine," he replies. "Kevin's a fun guy. He doesn't care."

"You just lost me at least ten professionalism points."

"Not at all. I'm telling you. He likes you. He told me he thinks you're doing a great job. A couple of the engineers mentioned you to him."

I give him a doubtful look.

"Really," he says, bending down to look me directly in the eye. "Don't worry about it."

"Okay, if you say so," I agree, begrudgingly, and pout at him playfully.

"You're so cute when you do that face," he says, putting his thumb on my chin, just the slightest touch. "Anyways," he continues, "I'll tell him it was my idea. And, I guess it was me who actually did it, too." He's laughing. "Thanks for being my partner-in-crime, though, and taking the blame."

He turns to open the stairwell door to go back to the office, but just before he opens the door, he leans down and whispers in my ear, "I owe you one, Sarah."

✳ ✳ ✳

On Friday morning at 8:30 a.m., Kevin texts Nathan that he's on his way to pick him up. They'll carpool out to the hike location together, and it'll give them a little extra time to talk about their strategy with LightVerse and Snow.

While he makes some coffee and packs it in a thermos to go, he thinks about yesterday. It was so fun trolling Kevin in the office with Sarah. He'd managed to keep himself under control, but seeing her blush in the office when Kevin realized she was in on the popcorn prank, and then afterward, having her all alone in the stairwell recapping their shenanigans had put thoughts—*those* kinds of thoughts—into his head. When he'd leaned down to whisper in her ear, the closeness and smell of her hair almost tipped him over the edge and made him kiss her. But he hadn't.

Kevin texts him when he's downstairs, and Nathan heads out. To his surprise, he sees Kevin has someone else in the car. To his *unfortunate* surprise, he sees it's Danica. Danica's facing away from Nathan, but he locks eyes with Kevin and gives him a death stare. This is not how he wanted to spend his Friday.

Nathan gets in the back of Kevin's Tesla, thinking that at least Danica and Kevin, sitting up front together, will talk most of the way and he'll be off the hook. But Danica is mostly focused on Nathan, turning around most of the ride to talk to him about LightVerse and how she has an idea to get them introduced to Eden Snow—about 10 percent of the time—and all sorts of other things the rest of the time. She talks to him about all the great places in the Bay Area to hang out—since Nathan's new to the area—and hints at how she'd love to show him around.

When they arrive at the parking lot about twenty minutes later, he's relieved and gets out of Kevin's car quickly. Right away, his eyes are drawn to Sarah, talking to some of the engineers on the team she works with. She looks beautiful this morning: hair in a ponytail and wearing a Golden State Warriors ballcap. She has on tight leggings and well-worn running shoes, and he can barely keep his eyes off her legs and, well, other areas.

She notices he's arrived and walks over to greet him, flashing him a bright smile.

"Good morning. How's it going?" he asks. He smiles and glances at her hat. He gets the joke, sure she wore it for his benefit, just to prove a point. No matter how determined he is, he'll never convince her to be a Lakers fan.

"Great. I love this hike. Camila and I have come here a few times. Have you been out here before?"

"Yeah, it's great. The view from the top is amazing."

"The views are pretty good down here, too," she says, boldly, and touches his arm affectionately.

It's chaste, but her fingers might as well be made of fire. They both turn toward Kevin when he calls everyone together and asks if they're ready to get started.

"Try to keep up," he says in a playful tone.

"*You* try to keep up," she teases back and jogs off toward the trailhead.

✳ ✳ ✳

I'd pay a million dollars to know why Danica's joining us on the hike today, or why Nathan rode here with her and Kevin. But it's time to start the hike, so I jog over toward the front of the group, where Erin's standing. The group begins to set off on the trail, and Erin and I are hiking up the steep terrain together. We are focused on two things: one, getting up the steep mountain trail, and two, determining what the hell Danica is doing here.

We take turns scoping out the situation, which looks a lot like Nathan trying to escape Danica's clutches and her trying to keep that from happening. I notice her Lululemon-clad, fit body walking quickly up the hill in front of us. *Damn, she's in good shape.*

We're all enjoying ourselves, happy to be out in nature,

instead of in the office. We finally make it to the top about an hour later, and we're rewarded with an amazing view of the San Francisco Bay and much of Silicon Valley. The sun has burned the morning fog off the Bay, and the air is crisp, but warming up quickly. I take a seat on a large rock and pull my water bottle out of my bag. As I look out over the entire South Bay area, I think to myself that no matter how many hikes I do, the vantage point and perspective from the top of a mountain will always amaze me anew.

I turn to say the same to Erin, but she's not paying attention. She's looking in the opposite direction and nudges me in the arm. Nathan has apparently also warmed up on the climb, and he's taking off his fleece. As he pulls it off over his head, his shirt comes up a bit, and we can see his cut abs. We're both trying to look without being completely obvious when she turns back to me, and mouths "*Whoa!*" We both burst out giggling, which draws his attention. Unfortunately, he catches me staring, and smirks, pulling his shirt down, a little self-consciously. I notice Nathan's abs haven't escaped Danica's attention either.

Kevin rallies the troops after our short break and we begin to head down. Erin is hanging back a bit, so I wait for her. "Sorry, my knee's a little janky," she says in explanation to a few people who pass us. I look at her suspiciously and once they're out of earshot, say to her. "Liar, liar pants on fire. Your knee is so not janky."

"How do you know?" she says, feigning innocence. "But while we're here alone, let me just say, Girlllll. Now I understand how that one-night stand happened. Those abs though." I giggle, and we gossip, as we continue our descent.

* * *

It's easier going down the steep trail than it was coming up, but it's also easier to fall, and about halfway down, Danica trips and injures her ankle.

Nathan bends down, to where she's now sitting on the side of the path, to check on her. "Are you okay?" he asks, concerned.

He doesn't want to date her, but he doesn't want to see her hurt either. She's holding her ankle. "Oh my god, I'm such a klutz."

"Let me see," Nathan says, rolling her pants up a bit and her sock down. "Well, I'm not a doctor, but it does look swollen. Can you move it? Wanna try to stand up?"

He helps her up, and Danica looks up at him, adoration in her eyes. She tries to put weight on her ankle, but hisses out, in pain. Kevin—born leader that he is—has turned back to check what's going on and takes charge.

"You alright? Can you walk on it?"

"I don't think so," Danica answers him, but her eyes are on Nathan and she's giving him a coy look.

"Why don't you put your arms around mine and Kevin's shoulder, and we'll help you down the mountain," Nathan suggests.

Kevin has another idea. "Nate, let me take your bag, and you can carry her piggyback. It's only another twenty minutes or so."

Nathan looks at Kevin like he's lost his mind. Danica already has the wrong idea about Nathan, about all of this, and now Kevin's basically leaving him to fend for himself. Even when he's already proven himself wholly incapable of doing so when she's in the vicinity.

He looks at Danica, and she's smiling at him. She might as well be batting her eyelashes.

Nathan grits his teeth, tries not to look like he's feeling—uncomfortable, ready to murder Kevin, jog down the mountain himself, and not stop until he's home—and simply says, "Okay. Sure."

Everyone up ahead has stopped, and they're waiting for them. So, the entire office—including Sarah—is there to see him crouch down, so Danica can climb on his back. Her pants are slick, so he's holding on tight to her legs, which are wrapped around the front of him.

He sees Sarah raise her eyebrows at the scene and then give a look to Erin. He doesn't know her all that well, but he thinks it's a look of amusement, annoyance, and maybe something else, too.

They make their way slowly down the mountain. It's not physically hard to carry Danica—she's not very heavy—but his muscles are tensed, jaw clenched in annoyance, from his role in this little spectacle. The day has warmed up considerably, and his skin is damp from the exertion of the hike, the added warmth of Danica's arms around his neck, and her chest pressed up against his back.

A memory flashes in his mind, sophomore year of college, him carrying her—very much like this—back from a bar late one night, when one of her heels broke. *What is it with women and ridiculous high heels?*

It's not lost on him—maybe not on her either—that after that little escapade, he and Danica had ended up staying up for hours having the kind of drunk, energetic sex only horny, unencumbered twenty-year-olds are capable of.

He's loathe to admit it, even to himself, but there's a small part of him—a primal one, that doesn't remember how Danica acted toward him when they dated, or one that only remembers the good parts, the sex—that likes touching her. That likes the feeling of her muscular, feminine legs wrapped around his torso. And then he remembers that Sarah is seeing all of this go down. And it's these very mixed feelings—emotional and physical—that plague him during the twenty or so minutes it takes them to make their way down the mountain.

As soon as they reach the parking lot, he places Danica carefully on the ground, next to Kevin's car, shoots her a tight smile, and walks away. He needs some space, some distance. She calls his name, but he keeps going, away from the car, and sits down on a wooden railing of the fence.

He really, really does not want to ride home with Kevin and Danica. The day started out with a lot of promise, but he's given up and is just ready to head home.

He takes out his metal water bottle from his bag—still cold somehow—and holds it up to his sweaty forehead. As he opens it to drink, Sarah walks up and sits beside him.

* * *

When we arrive back at the parking area, I see Nathan sitting off to the side, on an old wooden fence railing. I walk over and sit next to him. From the side of my eye, I can see his clenched jaw and his free hand gripping the fence railing.

After a minute, I try to lighten his mood. "Wow, you're a real Superman."

But it doesn't seem to dispel his sour mood.

"You think she needs to see the doctor?" I ask.

"I wouldn't know."

"Well, anyways, I think she got the only doctor's attention she wants," I say.

He looks up at me, sharply.

"Are you teasing me?"

"I might be," I say, winking at him, and he cracks a smile.

He asks if I drove, and I tell him I did. "Need a ride?"

"I'd love a ride."

Sarah: 1, Danica: 0. At least for today.

I drive us back to the city from the hike, and our conversation flows easily. It's hard for me to believe we've only known each other a couple months, and that it all started with, well, a little less conversation, as my mom's favorite singer, Elvis might say.

* * *

They listen to one of her playlists while they drive back to the city.

"OneRepublic, huh?" he asks, looking at her phone to see who sings the song that's playing.

"Yeah, it's a little corny, but I love this song. It just makes me feel good," she replies and sings a few of the lyrics about always looking for the sunshine.

He smiles and nods. While she drives, her eyes on the road, he takes the opportunity to admire her. He's trying not to be obvious, but he can't keep his eyes off her, while she talks and asks him questions, sings, and smiles. He doesn't even notice that she never asks for directions.

She asks him what his favorite book is. "I can't choose just one," he tells her.

"So tell me two. We have some time."

He takes a deep breath. "Okay, 'Thinking, Fast and Slow' by Daniel Kahneman . . ." he hesitates. Even narrowing down his list to the top five is hard, but he makes a decision. "Frankl's 'Man's Search for Meaning.' It's hard to read, but it's important."

"I've read that, actually. My dad had it and made me read it during high school. He said it would give me perspective on life. Like the things we *think* are hard aren't really as bad as they could be."

"And that we actually have more control than we realize when it comes to how we deal with the bad stuff. If you can find some meaning in it, then you can get through it more easily," he adds.

They're both quiet for a minute, letting the moment sink in.

"What about you?" he asks. "Favorites?"

"Well, after years of reading political philosophy for school, I've spent the last five years reading mostly fiction. Favorite books is too hard, but I can do favorite authors: Kristin Hannah, Blake Crouch, Fredrik Backman," she rattles them off. "And of course, the incomparable Diana Gabaldon." She sighs wistfully when she mentions the last one.

"What does *she* write?" he asks, fascinated.

"The best romance ever," she responds.

"So, you're a romantic, huh?"

"Most definitely," she says, her eyes sparkling.

❋ ❋ ❋

When we start to get close to downtown, he says, "I can get out here if you want, so you don't have to go out of your way."

"No, it's fine. Even Superman deserves a rest. So much saving of damsels in distress is hard," I tease him.

"I saw you give me a look when Danica got on my back. I know it's funny, but you also looked annoyed."

"Not so much annoyed. I also felt a little sorry for you," I tell him.

"Why is that?"

"I could tell you were uncomfortable—not physically, but with the whole situation. I felt bad for you." I continue, digging —and not very subtly—for more information. "I'd think that carrying a beautiful woman on your back, her being in your debt for helping her out, would be a good situation for most men."

"She's not—"

"Oh, she *is* beautiful."

"Maybe," he admits, shrugging. "But I was going to say that she's not my type." He glances down at her sneakers, then at the Warriors cap she's taken off and put next to the gear stick between them. "I like women who are more down-to-earth. Beautiful," he says, catching my eye, "but down-to-earth."

I smile. "Do you like muffins?" I ask, remembering that I baked last night and brought some along. I reach to pull my bag from the backseat at a stop light. My chest brushes up against his arm, where it's resting on the armrest, and I notice Nathan trying to simultaneously check me out but avert his eyes just enough not to get caught doing it.

He gives me a bit of an embarrassed look when I open the container and offer him one. "Better than chihuahuas," he answers, taking one.

I shoot him a confused look.

"You don't know the 'chihuahua versus muffin' AI thing?"

I shake my head.

"How are you even allowed to work at Instinqt? It's a *very* important thing in artificial intelligence," he says, snickering, making me think it's not really important at all.

When we stop at the next light, he shows me his phone. I'm looking at a 4x4 matrix of pictures, some of which are chihuahuas and some of which are blueberry muffins. Apparently, this is what the brightest AI minds in the world are working on.

"This *is* important stuff," I admit, laughing.

"These are pretty good," he says, after taking a bite of a muffin. "Did you make them?"

I nod. We pull up to his building.

"I forgot you'd been to my place before," he tells me.

"Forgotten already, huh?"

He blushes. "No, not forgotten," he says, shaking his head. "*Definitely* not forgotten."

He looks at me for a second, and I wonder what he's thinking. I want to give him a goodbye kiss. I want him to invite me up to his place for an afternoon, post-hike, sweaty workout. His hair is ruffled from his hat and the wind earlier, and he's the vision of health and happiness and, something like, home.

* * *

Nathan looks at Sarah and wants, more than anything in the world, to kiss her right now. Her face is a little flushed from the hike, from the sun, and she's radiant. He's not sure, but he gets the sense that she has no idea how beautiful she is, even in her beat-up sneakers and old hat. It doesn't help that when she leaned into the backseat a few minutes ago, her breasts brushed up against him and she caught him checking her out.

He pulls himself together and leans into the backseat to take his bag. He thanks her, and as he opens the door to get out, she touches his hand. The feel of her hand on his almost makes him turn back, but he steels himself. He doesn't need to make any trouble for her, or for himself.

They wish each other a good weekend, and he goes upstairs. The whole weekend, he thinks about her but tries to keep himself busy with work and a side coding project he's been working on. He picks up his phone so many times to text her, but he doesn't. Deciding on Sunday that "friends" are allowed to share recipes, he bakes her something.

* * *

The weekend passes, uneventful and calm enough. On Monday morning, I arrive at work and, to my surprise, find a small package on my desk. I open it up. Inside are a few blueberry muffins and a little note, with a tiny, printed picture of a chihuahua. *Thanks for the ride. You saved me. Superman.* The "me" is underlined, and I smile, taking a bite of a muffin that is by far better than the ones I make.

A CLEAR-CUT VALUE PROPOSITION

It's been a busy week for everyone at work. Nathan was swamped and canceled our regular Tuesday meeting, and he knows I've been busy, too—helping with all the logistics as well as preparing my own presentation for the off-site coming up in a couple weeks. I've only caught glimpses of him here and there when I've been at the office, and so our communication has mostly consisted of Slack messages with silly, encouraging GIFs: cats hanging from branches saying "hang in there" and other random funny stuff we find on the internet.

It's Friday afternoon, and I'm working at home, looking forward to a nice, relaxing weekend and a break from the off-site planning craziness, when I get a text from Erin:

Erin: You got a cocktail dress?

Me: Why? You got a cocktail? <smiley face emoji> No dress—why?

Erin: We need more Instinqt people at the partner event tomorrow night in downtown SJ. Please come—8:00 p.m. Cocktail attire. Free drinks.

Erin: Also, N will be there. <winky face emoji>

Me: Of course, see you there.

Looks like it won't be a relaxing weekend after all, but I'm actually excited. It's been a really long time since I've been to a killer party. I spend four hours on Saturday with Camila looking for something appropriate. After trying on what feels like 150 dresses, I settle on a dark green silk number that accentuates my legs—it's short, dear god, it's short—and has lace covering the shoulders. Camila is giving me a once-over as she helps me get ready at my place. The last time I dressed this fancy was probably my bat mitzvah—okay, maybe high-school prom—and I'm a little nervous about the dress, about the event, and about, well, seeing Nathan, too. She's doing my eyeliner—something I've never gotten the hang of—and when she finishes, she evaluates her handiwork, eyeing me approvingly.

"You look hot."

"Nooo," I scoff. "But do I?" I ask hopefully, fishing for another compliment.

"Yeah. You're kinda short, but that dress with those heels is doing you some favors in the legs department. Is Nathan gonna be there?" she asks, raising her eyebrows.

"Um, yes, he is. Why do you ask?"

"Why do I ask?" she says, rolling her eyes at me. "Look, maybe there *is* some policy about not dating other employees, but the way I see it, you guys dated *before* you were an employee and definitely before he was a chief of whatever. Loophole?"

"I don't think so, but thanks for trying. I'll go, chat up some beautiful people, try to sound intelligent, and probably be home by ten."

"A.M."

"Sure, Cam. I'll let you know when I'm back in time for a movie night."

"Nahhhh. Go, charm Nathan, and bring him back here for some fun," she says, her beautiful brown eyes twinkling.

I look at her, appreciative of her vote of confidence, but wonder whether she might not be overestimating my skills with men and say so.

"Well, whatever you did the first time worked," she replies.

"True, but I might be a one-trick pony," I joke.

"You're gonna be a late pony if you don't leave now," she says, handing me my phone and bag and beginning to pack up her own.

"Thanks for the makeup," I say, leaning in toward her and air-kissing her cheek so I don't mess up my lipstick. "And you know, for everything."

"Oh, my god. Stop being so dramatic. Of course. You look beautiful, Sarah. Nathan would be an idiot not to want you," she says as we walk out of my apartment. "Talk tomorrow, okay? I want to hear what happened."

"Promise," I say, as she heads down the stairs. I open my phone to order an Uber and then head down the stairs myself, a bit more carefully than usual. I've got a tiny little purse—the kind that goes well with tiny little dresses—and some black heels on. While they're not quite as dramatic as the shoes I wore the night I met Nathan, they are certainly strappy and sexy and give me a couple extra inches.

As I arrive at the hotel, I see what looks like lots of fancy people going in. I take a deep breath, hoping to find Erin soon, and walk toward the entrance. As I'm walking up, Kevin arrives in his Tesla. As he hands his keys to the valet, he catches sight of me and does a double-take, before realizing that it's me. I guess my usual work attire of jeans and a black hoodie doesn't show quite as much as this little green dress. He blinks, composes himself, and says, "Hey, Sarah, I almost didn't recognize you. Looking really sharp tonight."

"Thanks, Kevin, so are you." He offers his arm to me. I smile at him and put my hand in the crook of his elbow and he guides me into the hotel lobby and then on into the ballroom that's been reserved for the event.

Inadvertently, it looks like we've arrived together and I'm his date. I see a couple people take note of it with their eyes and notice Nathan over near the doors out to a balcony. He's speaking with some people in stylish suits and a couple of attractive women, who look like they drink organic spinach smoothies for breakfast and kick other women's asses just for the exercise. The one closest to him turns in my direction and I see it's Danica. I guess her ankle is feeling better, judging from the heels she's wearing.

His eyes meet mine and I see him notice that I've come

through the door with Kevin. He raises an eyebrow, but holds my eyes, and gives me a slight smile, only partially concealed by the glass he's holding up to his lips to drink. Danica is trying to talk to him. Of course she is. He looks amazing in his tailored suit and pale blue button-down shirt, open just a bit at the collar. Just then, Erin comes over to say hello.

Hawkeye that she is, she follows my gaze, and then gently turns me, whispering, "Can you two be any more obvious that you want to jump each other's bones?" Kevin is still near enough, and I glance under my lashes to see if he heard. I shoot her a sharp look.

"Come with me," she says. "There are some people I want you to meet."

I'm single, but not quite ready to mingle, but as a favor to Erin, I do it anyway. The place is full of all kinds of people from different vendors we work with and potential partners—people we'd like to partner with to go after enterprise deals by combining our offerings. I can talk to anyone, but since there's a lot at Instinqt—and high tech, more generally—that I still need to learn, I feel like I'm at a trade show or some academic conference, not a party.

After an hour or so of doing everything I can to be #TeamInstinqt, I'm ready for a break from the conversation and head out a side door to a smaller balcony, away from the main room. It's chilly outside and, strangely, there's a light fog starting to settle over the city. I lean against the marble railing, next to a giant fern, and take a deep breath, thinking about the evening, and as usual, when he's in the area, about Nathan. The LVBs, as Erin likes to call them, were definitely flirting with the Instinqt and other execs tonight. Now I know what Erin meant when she said they know that they might soon be rich, so they might as well get in their good graces in time. I swear some of those women's eyes were glowing—a combination of sexual energy just waiting to be released and some enticing pheromone-like chemical that must smell like cold, hard cash. As I consider Danica, in particular, and the way she kept touching Nathan's collar with perfectly manicured nails, I begin to think that my green dress is perfectly suited to the jealous tension I'm feeling in my stomach.

"Ugh," I whisper under my breath.

"Are you talking to yourself, Sarah?" I hear a low, familiar voice say behind me.

"You scared me!" I half-yell as I turn my head and see Nathan heading toward me from the door to the balcony.

"Sorry," he says, sheepishly.

"Yes, I was," I admit, giving him a guilty smile. "Just letting off some steam."

I *feel* like there's steam coming off me—the combined frustration of seeing Nathan and Danica together, and having him, coming closer to me, looking hot as hell in his dress clothes. It's just the two of us. Alone. On a balcony. And yeah, it's making my temperature rise.

He's within arm's reach now. I'm leaning against the railing, facing him, away from the view, and he takes one of my hands gently in his and looks me up and down, from the tips of my strappy heels all the way to my eyes, with plenty of savoring stops in between. "God, Sarah, you are . . . something."

"Something, huh?" I say, giving him a coy smile.

"I'm at a work event, and I'm trying not to get fired or thrown out of the hotel for public indecency," he says, at the same time shifting his legs a little, making me notice that the public indecency comment might not be far from the truth. It's dark out here, but even in the low light, I can tell that he likes what he sees. He looks like he wants to pounce on me, and the look on his face couldn't be mistaken for anything but—

Just then, the door to the balcony opens and Kevin comes out with Danica and another woman in tow. "Hey, dude, I was looking for you. Danica and Amy are ready to go over to Willow Street." He doesn't need to say it—everyone in the Bay Area knows that Willow Street in Palo Alto is where LightVerse is located.

"They said that Eden's definitely there now—one of their

friends is his EA—and they can introduce us . . . somehow."

Eden Snow, founder and CEO of LightVerse. I can see why Kevin's putting on the pressure. At this point, Kevin notices where both Nathan and I are standing, the looks on our faces—and maybe a few other things—and cocks his head. He waits a second before saying a little lower, where Danica and Amy won't hear over the side conversation they're having, "Nate, dude, we should go. It's getting late and it would really help out, and we need the . . . you know . . . connection." He raises his eyebrows, not so subtly trying to hint they need to get out of here.

Nathan looks at Kevin and then at me, chewing on his lip, obviously uncomfortable with just leaving me here on the balcony. I take that as my cue, and I decide to make it easy for him by smiling cheerfully and as platonically as possible, touching his shoulder in farewell. "It's cool. I was just about to head home anyways. Have a good time, guys," I say, as I walk quickly past them and open the door.

"Byeeee," Danica and Amy say. And I roll my eyes, as I shut the door, knowing that Danica is going to be flirting—or more —with Nathan the rest of the night. I quickly make my way through the event room and head out into the lobby, digging my phone out of my tiny purse, so I can order an Uber.

As I exit the front doors of the hotel, and walk toward the street, into the darkness, I feel like a deflated balloon. I know —at least I'm trying to know, to admit—that Nathan and I just can't be a thing now, but it still hurts a bit, knowing he's going to spend the rest of the night with beautiful women who want him, maybe without even knowing just how special he is. What's important to him. What's going on in his life and with his family. To them, he's Nate, tech genius, IPO-bound cash machine. To me, he's something, someone, else. He's Nathan. He's a guy who's devoted to his sick father and worried mother. He's a nerd who likes to mountain bike and read serious books and try new recipes. I'm near the end of the hotel driveway, almost to the sidewalk, when I suddenly hear running footsteps behind me and turn to look, scared I'm about to be harassed or trampled by someone.

"Sarah," I hear Nathan calling. "Hey, I caught you," he pants, catching my hands in his. "Here, come here, behind this hedge." He looks excited but uncertain, and he points to a place in the beautifully cultivated gardens that surround the hotel. He pulls me to a place where the decorative lights of the driveway and entrance don't reach. It's dark, and he pins me lightly against a tall hedge, taller than the both of us. "Sarah, I have to go with Kevin. I'm sorry. I wanted to talk to you, to be with *you* tonight."

I have to admit. I'm a little disappointed. I guess I've seen one too many rom-coms, and thought he might've been coming to tell me, in some grand gesture, that he'd made his choice—me—and that he was going to sneak away with me to, well . . .

"Don't be sad, beautiful," he says, looking into my eyes, close to my face, since it's so dark. "I have to go, I'm sorry. It's related to work. I promise it's *not* going to be fun. But I wanted to give you something before you go?" he says, asking, indicating that I first need to agree.

"Well, the first thing is this." He reaches up and picks a flower from the rose trellis above my head, handing it to me as a peace offering.

"And the second thing?" I ask, hoping it's what I think it is.

"Ah, the second thing," he says, suddenly shy, biting his bottom lip.

"Is it this?" I ask, cupping his jaw in one hand and lightly stroking the fingers of my other hand on his collar bone, as I press my lips to his. He parts his lips a bit and angles his head in such a way—the exact motion he made during our first kiss that night in his apartment—that it's a perfect fit with my mouth. He slips his tongue, just the slightest bit, into my mouth, as if he's testing the waters. Slowly, he and I both gain more confidence and it becomes a full-on kiss, hungry and yearning to taste each other. He tastes like mint and lemons. *Goddamn, the same as our first night. How is that even possible?* I could inhale him, stay here in this dark garden for hours, until the end of time.

"Nate, dude!" we hear Kevin calling, and Nathan's pocket

starts buzzing.

"Nooo, I have to go, Sarah. Shit, I do *not* want to go. No." He's having a monologue with himself about his disappointment and other obligations. "Can I call you later?" he asks, touching my face softly. I know it'll be a booty call. He knows it'll be a booty call. I give him a knowing smile.

"Yes, you may," I tell him. "Be . . . *careful* tonight, okay?"

He glances back at me, as he steps out into the light of the hotel driveway and blows me a kiss. It's a bit out of character, unexpected. But I guess a lot of things about him—us—have been. I reach up to "catch it" and as I listen to him walk away, dramatic as I am at times, I pretty much swoon into the hedge.

"Dude, where were you? We gotta go," I hear Kevin ask him.

"I just had to make a call to my mom. It's late and I wanted to check that she's alright."

"Yeah, no problem. Everything okay?"

"Yeah," Nathan replies. "Everything's . . . really good."

As they walk away, I hear Kevin ask Nathan, "You notice Sarah tonight? She looks a lot different in a dress than in a hoodie and jeans, huh?"

"Dude, just shut up."

"Okayyy," Kevin replies, stifling a laugh.

I smile to myself and wonder if I'll hear from Nathan later tonight.

RELEASE MANAGEMENT

It's dark in my bedroom, but I can hear my phone buzzing on my nightstand. I paw around for it in the dark and finally find it. I'm groggy, but quickly waking up, worried that something's wrong.

I see "N" on the screen and pick up. "Nathan?" I say, sleepily.

"Hi, Sarahhh," he drawls.

"Hi, there?"

"Sarah, can I come up to your place? I think I'm nearby."

"What? Nathan, how do you even know where I live?"

"I must be just drawn to you. I used my Sarah-sense, and I found you."

What?

I'm so confused right now, but I can hear the sound of a car driving by and someone honking from the phone. I simultaneously hear the same honk in real life and realize he really *is* near my place. I get up and stumble over to my window and see him downstairs on the sidewalk, still in his beautiful suit, looking up like he's waiting for manna from heaven. There's a car driving off and a few people are yelling out the window at him in an encouraging way. *What the hell is going on?*

"Oh my god, Nathan. I don't know how you got here but go to the entrance. I'll buzz you up. Come to the fourth floor."

"Oh, Sarah, my hero, my heroine, my heroin . . ." he starts to sing.

I press "End call" and run my hands through my hair. I quickly turn on my bedside lamp and look down. I must've fallen asleep in my cocktail dress on top of my covers. There's no time to change.

I run to look in the bathroom mirror—not great, not terrible —and gargle some mouthwash really quickly. As I run to the door, a bit of last-second inspiration hits me, and I scroll like a madwoman through iTunes. *What's good make-out music?* I have a sudden inspiration and start a Glass Animals playlist and think to myself that I better open my door soon, so he doesn't start knocking on doors this late at night to find me.

I open the door and find the funniest sight greeting me. Nathan's got his suit coat off, slung over one shoulder, and one hand propped on my door jamb, like some Frank Sinatra wanna-be. I laugh.

"Hey, there, hot stuff. Whatcha doing here?"

"Sarah, I had to see you."

"Come in."

"Sarah, I had to see you."

"Yes, you mentioned that," I say in the patronizing tone one uses with toddlers. I suspect he's had a few more drinks since the last time I saw him.

"I had to see you in that beautiful dress. You kept it on. I had to see those beautiful eyes of yours and those amazing legs of yours."

While he's been talking, I've been walking backward, while he's been walking forward, and now I'm up against the wall in the hallway to my bedroom. He's leaning, above me, against the wall on his forearms, boxing me in, with his face close to mine.

"I had to talk to that . . . smart brain of yours."

I tilt my head, amused by his strange choice of words. I'm loving the compliments. The weird and—now that he's in front of me, I realize—*very* drunken way he's delivering them might even be making me enjoy them more. It's great seeing someone else, besides myself, express themselves without a filter.

"What happened to you in the"—quickly glancing at the clock to see it's been three hours since I last saw him and it's close to 2:00 a.m.— "last couple of hours?"

"We went to Willow Street, and we met Eden."

"That's good, right?"

"No," he answers. "I mean, yes. Meeting him was good, but afterward, Danica—she tried to kiss me, and I didn't like it. I told her . . . *I* want to be kissing someone else."

He says it so openly, like a little kid telling someone what flavor ice cream he likes.

"And she got pissed, and then she and her friend left, and Kevin got me a drink, or maybe a couple of drinks, and then we talked about my dad a little bit, and I got sad, and I thought of you, and how I really just wanted to talk to *you*."

He sighs but then continues.

"And then Erin was there for some reason, and I asked her where you live, and she put your address in my Uber. And now I'm here with you, Sarah, and now I can talk to you."

"So, you're here to talk?" I ask.

"Can I talk to your mouth?" he whispers, leaning in. "But like really, really close?" I laugh again. He's really funny tonight.

"Are you asking for a kiss?" I start to say, but he's already kissing me. He starts with my mouth and while it's a little sloppier than the ones from earlier tonight, the enthusiasm and intention he puts into it make up for any lack of finesse. He moves his focus to my jawline and then to my neck, and while he's stationed there, I feel his hands begin to caress my waist, the warmth of them through the thin satin.

"Fuck, this dress is the best. You're turning me on so much. You're so smooth."

He's pushed me up against the wall, and his body is on mine, and I'm pretty sure with the pressure, the electrical current surging through my body, and the warmth of his body that any minute now, he and I and the wall behind us are going to become one and be transported through a portal in the universe and come out in some alien-world where people—or aliens, I guess—just have sex all day.

His stance is wide, and our hips are pressed together. I can feel his firmness there, and I know he's turned on. With my back against the wall and his hands occupied elsewhere, he's not supporting his weight against the wall anymore. I can see his quads tensed, holding himself so he doesn't crush me, and the point of connection is exactly where it should be, and I'm wondering if an erection can actually burst through a pair of pants.

I'm running my fingers through his silky hair. I want to kiss him but his mouth is too low and focused elsewhere. He's traced kisses down my neck and he's firmly in my cleavage. And from the soft sounds coming from his throat, it seems he's thoroughly enjoying himself.

"Oh my god, Sarah, I'm gonna imagine you in this dress for the rest of my life."

"Every time I see you."

Kiss.

"At work."

Kiss.

"Before I go to sleep at night."

Kiss.

"Every time . . ." he trails off, as he continues to kiss me sensuously, on my collar bone and my chest. One of his hands cups my breast, and he begins to toy with my nipple with his thumb.

I sharply inhale—surprised, delighted, and just a little bit nervous.

"Mmm, goosebumps," he says, licking my throat.

I allow my mind to wander, just the tiniest bit. If I stay fully here, I'll have him on the floor on his back in minutes, and I'm not sure that's the best idea—all things considered. I keep saying this type of thing is not how I usually am, but I'm starting to wonder if maybe it is—at least with Nathan.

I think back to our first night. It's obvious why. The kissing, the middle of the night, the desperate-to-connect urge.

But something is different this time. It's him. It's Nathan, but at the same time, it's not. It's almost as if he's put back on his work persona—Nate Goldman, CPO—and he's acting more like the confident, "bro" guy he is when he's at e-staff meetings. There's something attractive about it, to be sure, but my thoughts drift a bit. This confident guy, doing his startup-exec thing with Kevin and Danica and her friends. I imagine her touching his collar earlier tonight with her perfect nails, and then I see them in my mind at some cool club, music blasting, them dancing together, him hugging her from behind, his arm around her waist, and her turning her head to smile seductively back at him. My blood begins to boil a little, but not in the good way it was before.

"Are you paying attention anymore?" he asks, stopping his kisses down my neck and into my cleavage, to look up at me with a furrowed brow and slightly-comical grin. "Your hands stopped moving in my hair. I liked it."

"I am," I say, smiling back, but it's not convincing. The mixed feelings swirling in my head and my body—arousal, want, jealousy, uncertainty—are not a good recipe for a hookup. *That's what this is, right?* Add in the alcohol that's obviously coursing through his veins, and my decision is made.

"Nathan, let's take a little breather, okay?"

"Okay," he says, positioning his nose near my neck and breathing me in. "I like this kind of breather."

"Oh my god," I giggle—yes, giggle. "What are you, a bloodhound?"

He grins at me sheepishly and then pulls a silly face.

"How drunk are you, or are you normally this weird?"

"Both," he says. "I just usually hide it better. Something about you makes me feel like I can just have fun. And be honest."

How's that for an alcohol-induced truth bomb?

"Let me bring you some water. I have a sneaky suspicion you might need to hydrate in order to be functional tomorrow."

I go to the kitchen and fill a glass with cool water, and when I come back to the living room, he's not there. I look around—his jacket's still thrown across the dining room chair—and then I hear footsteps in my bedroom. *He must've wandered.* I smile, the way you do when you're the designated driver and out with your friends and one of them suddenly decides to serenade a Denny's at 3:00 a.m.

I pad down the hallway and find him, looking lost, in my bedroom. "Lose your way somewhere?" I joke.

"No, I found my way to paradise. It smells like you in here."

"I *hope* that's a compliment."

"Oh, it is," he says, and sighs so dramatically, I chuckle.

"Here," I say, holding out the glass of water. "Operation hydration."

He drinks it in one go.

"Sarah," he says, confiding in me, "I know I'm a little off tonight. I don't want to pressure you, or I don't know, make any 'bad decisions,'" he says, using quote fingers. "But—" he stops.

"But what?"

"But," he takes a deep breath, "can I just lay in your bed and cuddle with you? I promise, no funny business."

He says it with the funniest expression on his face, lips pouted out, and looking up at me through his eyelashes.

I crack up. "You look exactly how I would picture someone who wants to engage in some 'funny business,'" I reply doubtfully. "But I'll allow it. Just try to behave, okay?" I chuck him lightly on the chin, for good measure.

"I'll be a very good boy," he says and puts his hands together, striking a prayer pose that is supposed to convey angelic innocence, but one that's strongly undermined by his taking a second to adjust himself a little lower.

"Mmm-hmmm," I say, skeptically. And I raise my eyebrows to indicate I know what he's all about tonight. "What are you planning to wear to cuddle in, then?"

"Sarah, I have so many layers on now, you have no idea. I will undress now, and you tell me when to stop."

"What if I don't say stop?"

"Well, then we'll just see where the night takes us," he teases and shakes his butt a little.

I think I might be changing my mind about this Nate-Nathan hybrid. The confidence is actually a really good look for him, especially when he's making jokes.

I walk over to my dresser and open my pajama/workout clothes drawer. I pull out a soft tank top and leggings for myself and begin to walk to the bathroom to change.

"Wait, before you change, can I just touch you one more time before you take that dress off?"

I walk slowly to him and put my arms around his neck. I'm feeling a little more relaxed—less worried—than before. The uncertainty, the jealous monster, has faded a bit into the background after the laughs we've shared. He places his hands lightly on my waist and leans down to peck me on the lips. "Mmmm," he says, and I can feel his lips, close to mine, curl up in a smile.

"Okay, I'm going to change and when I come back, I want you less dressed—but still dressed—in my bed, ready to cuddle."

He salutes me and begins to unbutton his shirt, and before I close the bathroom door, I see he has a sleeveless undershirt underneath.

I take a few minutes to change, brush my teeth, and wash my makeup off. *What am I doing?* What I really need is to give myself a pep talk before I head back out into the bedroom.

I don't even know where to start. Part of me is saying, "Stop, don't do this. Make him sleep on the couch." But the other part is urging me to go for it. I know it's good with him—our first night proved that. One does not simply waste a sexy, horny man lying in one's bed.

I'm still undecided when he calls my name. "Sarah, are you coming? I'm so colllllld."

He's in a rare mood tonight. I force myself to go back into the bedroom to make sure he hasn't done anything insane in his drunken state.

He's lying on his back, under the covers, with the blanket pulled up to his chin. He's grinning like a nut. There's no telling whether he's lying there with a three-piece suit on or completely naked. He looks like a little kid waiting to be read a bedtime story.

"What are you wearing?" I challenge him, eyes narrowed.

"A sock, strategically placed," he says with a straight face, and I burst out laughing.

I pull back the covers on "my" side of the bed, and lay down on my side, facing him. He's already settled his hands on my butt and gives a satisfied groan as he squeezes me. "This is so nice. Cuddling with you is the best," he says. "I knew it would be."

"But we just started," I reply.

His eyes are closed and he has a sweet smile on his face. He doesn't say much beyond a few unintelligible sounds, and he nestles himself into one of my extra pillows. Being this close to him, just being, and not making out, or bantering, or joking, just enjoying the closeness, really is nice. He's right. It *is* the best.

I see my clock on the nightstand—it's almost 3:00 a.m.—and we fall asleep to the sounds of rain outside.

✳ ✳ ✳

When I wake in the morning, it feels late, which is strange for me. I'm usually an early riser. I was simply so exhausted; it must have forced me to sleep in. I can see gray light coming in the window, where the curtain has parted, and guess it's around 10:00 a.m. I close my eyes again, yawning, and as I wake up more and my senses sharpen, I notice a few things.

One, I'm warm, very warm, specifically my backside, and I attribute that to the 185 lb. radiator I can feel and hear behind me. Nathan's still sound asleep. I guess a night like he had last night wore him out. The scent in the room is different from usual, as well. Maybe it's his deodorant or his natural scent, and it's intoxicating. I want to nuzzle him, but decide otherwise— and gently scoot out of bed to leave him to sleep longer. I decide that since he's fed me once, it's my turn, and I head to the kitchen to make coffee and some breakfast. I'm absorbed in making eggs and pancakes when I feel him come up behind me and wrap his arms around my middle.

"Good morning," he says.

"Good morning," I say, turning my head to see him and flashing him a small smile. I caress his exposed collarbone gently in lieu of a shirt collar. *Take that, Danica.*

"I slept so well last night. I've been sleeping really badly lately, but your bed is so comfortable. And, well, you were in it," he says, sweetly.

"I slept like a rock, too. I'm usually up by seven at the latest, but I guess I had a long day yesterday."

"Well, it probably didn't help that I woke you up in the middle of the night," he says, looking at me apologetically. "I hope I didn't do—or say—anything *too* stupid?"

"You don't remember?" I ask him, unbelieving.

"Um, I remember a lot," he says, with an uncertain look on his face. "I guess I'm just looking for reassurance that I didn't make a total fool of myself, or that it wasn't all one-sided."

"I'm making you pancakes."

"What does that mean, exactly?"

"It means it wasn't one-sided. You didn't make a fool of yourself, but you definitely made me laugh." I give him a quick peck on the cheek to reassure him.

"When I woke up and saw you weren't in bed, I was a little worried you ran out again," he teased.

"Well, it's a little harder to run away from your own house, right?"

"Lucky me," he says, sitting down at the counter where I've placed the breakfast I've prepared.

"Coffee?" I ask him.

"Definitely," he says, taking the mug I've set in front of him. "So, what are your plans?"

"For today," I ask, "or for life?" I sit down next to him.

"Start where you want."

"Well, today, I need to work on my presentation for the off-site next week."

"You're talking about the process overhaul for all of engineering program management, right? You need help?"

"Actually, it's in pretty good shape. All the slides are approved, but I just need to run through it a few times to make sure I don't sound like an idiot when I'm presenting."

"You never sound like an idiot. Everyone says you're super-smart."

"Everyone? I've only been at Instinqt for a month-and-a-half."

"Yeah, but some people join a company and it takes a year to even notice they're there. Other people, like you, show up and are busting balls from day one."

"What?" I blurt out. "Busting balls? Did someone actually say that?"

He tilts his head and thinks for a minute. "No, nobody used that phrase, specifically. I just meant that people can tell you know your shit and how to get other people to do theirs."

"Huh," I say, feeling myself swell with a little pride.

"Can I listen to you practice after we eat?" he asks.

I hesitate.

"Please," he says. "I don't have nearly enough meetings with you—"

"We have our weekly one-on-ones," I interject.

"You're right. Those are very important, so important, in fact, that I think we should change them from weeklies to dailies . . . maybe even in person—"

"Should I stop you there?" I interrupt, covering his hand where it's come to rest on my ass while he's been talking.

"Only if you want to," he says, giving me a naughty look.

I take a deep breath.

He looks at me, eyebrow raised, and waiting for me to answer.

"Why don't we start with me doing the presentation for you?"

He smiles and moves his hand to tuck a stray hair behind my ear.

"But there are conditions," I tell him. "You have to give me honest feedback and . . ."

He's looking at me expectantly.

"You can't steal my jokes."

"Steal your jokes?"

"Yes, they are *very* good jokes. And I won't accept someone stealing my IP." I grin.

"Agreed," he says. "But I also have some conditions."

I raise my eyebrows.

"You have to do it wearing a sweatshirt and jeans. I won't be able to focus on what you're saying otherwise," he says, letting his gaze wander over me, still in the clothes I slept in last night. He raises his hand to my bare shoulder and traces his fingertips down my side to the curve of my hip.

I snort. "Nathan, I had no idea you're such a pervert."

"You *really* have no idea, Sarah."

❋ ❋ ❋

An hour later, we've finished breakfast, showered (separately), and Nathan's sitting on my couch, with a fake-serious expression on his face, and one leg crossed over the other. "Alright, technical program manager, show me what you've got."

"Don't tease," I tell him.

"I'm not. Why would you think I'm teasing?"

"My stupid ex-boyfriend used to say shit about project managers like he didn't take them seriously. He'd say that project managers are people who just couldn't be engineers or code, so they just tell real engineers how to do their jobs."

"That's the dumbest thing I've ever heard," Nathan says. "First of all, half the time, engineers *don't* know how to do their jobs, so they really *do* need someone to help them. Secondly, I think project managers—and executive assistants—run the world, and I'm not just saying that because you're cute."

"You think I'm cute?"

"Was that not clear from our last thirty-seven conversations?"

"It was," I say. "I just wanted to hear you say it again."

He laughs. "Alright, quit stalling, Ms. Hoffman. I'm waiting to have my mind blown . . . about program management, of course. Get your mind out of the gutter."

I start my presentation, running through my intro with him, warming him up with a few company-related quips, at which he smiles, and then get into the heart of it all. I'm proposing a significant change to the way we plan our roadmap and do release management. The organizational and reporting structure would stay the same, but the types and cadence of meetings and communication deliverables is a big change in the way Instinqt is currently doing things. My solutions are meant to improve visibility and coordination.

As I finish, looking up from the presentation notes on my laptop, I see that Nathan has a thoughtful look on his face. "Sarah, did you come up with all of this?"

"Yeah, I mean, I consulted with a lot of people. I wanted to make sure I don't come off as this newcomer with crazy ideas that nobody wants or likes. Why?"

"You're so good. I can't believe you've been at the company less than two months."

"Thanks." I blush.

"Can I suggest a few revisions?"

"Yes, please."

And so, we work for another hour—he gives me more context on the product development lifecycle and potential pitfalls and improvements I can make to my proposal. It's funny, because we've spent a lot of company time talking, but I didn't realize just *how much* we could be collaborating to make things better. He's able to help me see things from the engineering side, in a more open way than some of the engineers I work with are willing to do.

It's around lunchtime by now, and I see him notice the time. "Oh, man, I gotta go. I'm so late. I gotta grab my stuff from my place. I'm flying up to Seattle this afternoon to help my parents." He's up and gathering his things, pulling on his suit pants and picking up his jacket where he left it last night.

I give him a quizzical look.

"I stayed in town this weekend since we had the partner event yesterday," he explains. "But I wanna be there at the hospital tomorrow when we get his latest results and talk to the doctor. I might just stay and work remote and fly straight to the off-site in Park City next week."

"Okay, have a safe trip. I hope that things start to look up for your dad," I wish him, touching his cheek gently and looking into his eyes.

"Sarah, it was a great night. . . and morning."

"It was," I agree.

"Bye. See you soon," I say, as I give him a kiss on the cheek and ruffle his hair like a little kid.

"Bye," he says, smiling broadly, shutting my front door, at which point, I lean against it, exhale deeply, and indulge myself in a dramatic slide down the door.

✽ ✽ ✽

I open up my phone to text Camila and Erin—I need to update them on what's happened. I'm already behind. When I woke up this morning, I had seven messages already from the two of them on our group thread:

> **Erin**: So, did my surprise package make it to your house last night?

> **Camila**: Package lol

> **Erin**: I ran into him late last night with Kevin. He couldn't stop asking me about you. I guess he knows I know?

> **Camila**: Maybe just drunk enough to risk it?

> **Erin**: Maybe. He kept saying he needed to see you, S. He made it there? Don't kill me for giving him your address.

> **Camila**: She hopes you're still in bed, sleeping off a fun night of <eggplant emoji, water drops emoji, mind blown emoji>.

11:00 a.m.:

> **Erin**: But seriously. WTF happened?

> **Camila**: <News broadcast GIF>

It's 2:00 p.m. now. Nathan's hopefully been back to his apartment, gotten his bags, and is on his way through airport security.

I text the ladies back.

> **Me**: Hey, ladies . . .

Erin: She lives!

Camila: Yeah, but she was sexed into a coma last night. She just woke up.

Me: Noooo.

Camila: WHY NOT?!

Erin: Yeah, WHY NOT?!

Me: Because I'm a lady. A one-night stand is one thing. A two-night stand? Give me a little more credit.

Camila: This calls for a meet-up with coffee, wine, dessert, or all 3.

It's 6:00 p.m. on Sunday night, and we're sitting in my living room now, with, well, all three.

"So, a hot guy comes over for a booty call at 2:00 a.m. and you just close up shop? Hide in the back and pretend you're asleep?" Camila asks.

"Noooo," I say. "I let him in. And things got . . . hot. And then I do what I do—"

"A blow job?"

"Oh my god, Cam. Stop. No, not that. Not . . . this time," I say, giving her a side-eye. Erin and I have become closer, but I'm not sure if we're quite to the point for me to discuss my go-to sex tactics yet.

"I . . . just got too far into my head. I started thinking about that chick from LightVerse, Danica, with her hands all over him earlier in the night. And he was super drunk, and I didn't want, well, either of us to regret it in the morning."

"And did you?" Cam asks.

"Did I what?"

"Well, did you regret *not* having sex with him in the morning?"

I pause to think about the question. "No, I mean, god, I still wanted him. It was clear he still wanted me. But we did other things."

"Oooh," Erin says, intrigued.

I blush. "We worked on my presentation for off-site together. Nothing sexual," I clarify.

"Sounds fascinating," Cam says, sarcastically.

"It was. I mean, he helped me so much. He's so smart but so modest. And just really supportive and encouraging . . ."

"Are you gonna tell her, or should I?" Erin asks Cam, smiling.

"What?" I say.

"You like him, like *really* like him," Cam says in a sing-songy voice.

"Is it *that* obvious?" I say dryly.

But then I get serious and ask again, this time to Erin. "*Is* it that obvious? I mean, you guys know, but what about people at work? You think they know? We'd get in a lot of trouble. Well, I think *he* would get in a lot of trouble. And people would begin to doubt my judgment, my abilities maybe . . ."

Erin answers me quickly, unequivocally. "Nobody knows."

But then her eyes shoot to one side as if she's had a thought. "Well, *maybe* Kevin knows . . . Something."

"What?" Camila and I say simultaneously. Then I look at Camila and ask her if she even knows who Kevin is.

"I'm keeping up," she says, impatiently.

"How does Kevin know?" I wonder aloud.

"Let's just say Nate was more than a little tipsy last night by the time we met them at Club Fusion, and he wasn't exactly being careful when he was talking to me about you."

She continues. "You know they've been friends forever. I don't wanna scare you or anything, but I wouldn't be surprised if Nate lets it slip at some point. The only reason he wouldn't is to protect you. Nate's a good guy. He wouldn't do anything to hurt you."

I feel a blush start to spread up my chest and can feel the warmth on my cheeks.

"Oh my god, the off-site is next week. What are you gonna do?" Erin asks.

"Good question. I have no idea. Things are starting to go well at work. My presentation next week could be the start of something really good. I can't risk that."

Camila is looking at me, with one of her looks.

"Spit it out," I say.

"If you insist, I will, thank you. I've known you, what, over a decade? I've never seen you glow the way you have the last couple months. And that includes the year-and-a-half you dated Blake. Now, you've been working at Instinqt the same amount of time you've known Nathan, but it's a little hard for me to believe that dealing with backend engineers all day long has made you this damn happy."

"Maybe just one engineer in particular," Erin offers helpfully.

"He certainly likes my back end." No one else joins in my rueful laugh.

"Sarah," Camila continues, giving me a serious look. "I wouldn't want to be in your shoes, but *my* suggestion is that you don't shut the door on this guy. Jobs change, but a good partner —someone who makes you happy and seems to value you and, well, simply adores you, the way he seems to—I think you gotta see that through."

Erin, a self-admitted easy cryer, is tearing up.

"#TeamNate," Erin says. "Any guy who takes the extra food from team meetings down to the homeless people in the park gets my vote."

"He does that?" Camila asks.

She nods. "Multiple times."

I nod, confirming, and think of the night he gave away his food in the park.

"Of course he fucking does," I say. "He's perfect."

"There are worse problems to have," Camila says, bluntly.

I avert my eyes for a second, looking at the chair he sat in this morning, where he'd thrown his suit coat the night before, and smile—a little apprehensively, but then the positive memories take over.

"I hear you," I say. And I do. And I realize that my first instinct —upon meeting him and then running away, because he seemed special, too special to stay and see it through—was right. This thing—whatever it is—with Nathan could easily derail me, and take priority over everything else.

But there are some things, some people, you can't ignore. And I say "good night" to Camila and Erin, wishing them a good week, knowing that this one, with Nathan missing from the office, is gonna be a hard one.

VIRTUALLY THERE

It was hard for him to leave Sarah earlier, after working with her on her presentation for the off-site, but he would have missed his flight to Seattle otherwise. He has sensed for a while—if he's honest with himself, since their first night together—that she's special, but every time they actually talk about something related to work, and not just flirt or make out, he's more impressed by her. He falls a little bit harder for her. For someone who has joined the company so recently, she understands what they're doing, and what they *should* be doing, really well.

David has been covering for him with his parents, while he was back in the Bay Area the last few days, but he wants to give him a break and also see his dad in person. He knows he shouldn't lose faith, but the way his dad's health has deteriorated so rapidly over the last month has made it hard not to worry that it might *not* get better.

When he gets to Seattle, he heads straight to the hospital. He'll send his luggage home with his mom and spend the night there with his dad.

"Didn't expect to see *you* here," his dad tells him when Nathan walks into the room. He's lying in the hospital bed, being checked by Dr. Thompson, the internal medicine specialist taking care of him at Seattle Cancer Care Alliance. The Goldman family has, unfortunately, become far too familiar with Dr. Thompson, but despite the bad news she generally delivers to the family, they're glad they have someone like her on their care team. She seems to truly care about his father's diagnosis and treatment. She and Nate have had a few lengthy discussions about his father's prostate cancer, diagnosis of cancer in general, and what their options are in the current situation: his father's unexplained fever.

"Hi, Nate. How are you?" she asks in a friendly tone and then turns back to his dad. "Okay, Noah, we've tried one strong antibiotic, and it doesn't seem to be making a dent in whatever infection we suspect is in your body. I'd like to put you on something different, which is also strong, but has the added advantage of potentially—hopefully—covering a few more bacteria we might be dealing with. At the same time, we're going to do additional urine cultures and blood tests to check for a few things we didn't even think about to begin with since they're very rare." His father nods at her, indicating he understands. "I'm sorry this is taking so long for us to figure out," she says, and to Nathan's ears, she sounds genuinely sorry not to be able to give them better news.

"I understand. Do your best," Noah replies. Dr. Thompson squeezes his father's hand, nods to Nathan, and leaves the room.

"So, how ya doin', son? You look like shit," he says bluntly and laughs.

"That's something coming from a guy in a hospital bed," Nathan says to his dad, who looks pale and tired but is somehow still smiling.

"Long night?"

"You could say that," Nathan admits, and pulls a chair closer to the bed and sits down.

"Now *that* sounds intriguing. Was it good at least?"

"Well, it didn't start out that way, but it got much better after midnight."

His dad snickers. "Ahhh. Who's the lucky lady?" he asks, with a noticeable twinkle in his eye.

Nathan considers whether he should tell him and decides in favor of it. "Her name is Sarah. She's . . . pretty awesome."

"So, why are you looking so mixed up?"

Nathan tells him about the situation with Danica—everything. From Kevin convincing him to contact her again, to spending time with her in hopes of her helping them meet Eden Snow, and on up to last night. It's hard to admit everything to his dad. Maybe he'll be ashamed of him for how he's acted, especially how he treated Danica.

"Well, it sounds like you acted . . . like an idiot," his dad says in his usual direct manner.

Nathan nods and looks down, averting his eyes.

"But that's what you do when you're young."

"Or when you're old, too, sometimes," his mom's voice says, behind him, in a wry tone, as she walks into the room.

"Hey, now. You have to be nice to the sick guy," his father says, taking his mother's hand as she comes close to the bed. With her free hand, she lightly touches his dad's shoulder and then brushes a lock of hair—not quite as thick as it used to be—off his forehead.

This small show of tenderness—a tiny glimpse into the life-long connection his parents share—embarrasses him just the slightest, as if he's caught them in an intimate moment, something he shouldn't be privy to. But just as quickly as he takes note of it, it's over.

"And you," his dad says, looking at him, "just apologize. Don't make any grand gestures. It sounds like she already has the hots for you. Just apologize. Be genuine. Say what you mean. And then, go after the girl you do want. This Sarah."

"Sarah?" his mom asks, obviously delighted to have returned to the room just in time for Nathan to be spilling about his love life to his dad. "Do say more."

Nathan shoots his dad a look that says "Thanks a lot." He stands up and puts his arm around his mom's shoulder and guides her out of the room.

"Let's let Dad rest. I'll tell you about her," he promises, as he glances back at his dad, to give him a reproachful look before he leaves the room.

* * *

Nathan inspects his face in the bathroom mirror as he brushes his teeth. The long days at the hospital are definitely catching up with him. He's planning on going to bed early tonight. Maybe he won't look like a zombie when he wakes up tomorrow morning. Or maybe he will.

His phone pings with an incoming text.

Sarah: FaceTime?

A smile breaks out on his face despite the toothbrush in his mouth. They didn't have their usual one-on-one this week—her being busy at work, him here in Seattle and trying to spend as much time as possible with his family. He's glad she reached out.

Nathan: Sure, but I haven't shaved in 3 days, and I'm in my pajamas.

Sarah: Ooooh, scruffy Nathan. I bet you look really cute.

Her flirty texts cheer him up a bit. He spits and rinses, then splashes his face with water, in an effort to look a little more alive, but then his phone is ringing. He looks in the mirror, and figuring it's a lost cause, he answers.

"I was right," Sarah says, without even saying "Hello." "You are cute. Scruffy, but cute."

"Not fair. You look . . . beautiful," he says. And she does.

She's wearing a form-fitting sky-blue hoodie and the zipper is partially open. He wonders what she's wearing underneath but tries to focus.

"How's work?" he asks.

"Oh, fine. Just trying to . . . you know what? Let's not talk about work. There are more important things. How's your dad?"

"Hanging in there. Not great, but mostly in good spirits. It's hard but at the same amazing to see how strong he is—mentally, emotionally—even though his body's doing so badly.

"And seeing the way my mom cares for him—she's at the hospital with him now. I hope one day I have someone who loves me as much as they love each other."

He says it without thinking and worries he's being too direct. But looking at Sarah's face—he can look at her intensely through the phone and she can't tell—and he thinks maybe it's alright he's being so unguarded. She looks right back at him and smiles softly.

"I know what you mean," she says. "We're both lucky to have —have had, I guess, in my case—parents who love and support each other so much. When my dad died—well, even now—my mom just isn't herself. It's like once you find that person—*your* person—you become a better version of yourself, more than you thought you ever could be."

"Yeah," he says. "But at the same time, you're also like half of some bigger . . . unit. Without your other half, you're just less than you were before."

They both take a deep breath at the same time, notice, and then smile at each other.

"Sarah—"

"Nathan—"

They say at the same time and laugh.

"Topic change?" she asks.

"Yeah, good idea. Let's talk about something positive. I've been sleeping really badly. I need to think about something happy before I go to bed."

"Hmmm. I can do happy." She props her head on her chin, her pointer finger across her lips, in an expression he's come to learn from spending time with her recently means she's thinking. "Favorite food?" she asks.

"Anything my mom makes," he says in a happy tone. "What about you?"

"My mom's an okay cook, but I really like salad, which sounds weird, but I just like fresh, crunchy stuff. Like taboule or a fattoush salad. It's this Middle Eastern salad that has radishes and toasted pita. It's amazing."

"Do you by any chance like Ethiopian food?"

"Kind of random, but yeah. Actually, I do."

"So my Uber driver, of all people, recommended a place to me in San Jose. We can check it out together if you want. Walia?"

"Oh, yeah, it's really good," she says and snickers.

"What's so funny?

"Well, the food is good, but it's also right next door to this dirty lingerie store, something 'Hustler.'"

"Well, if delicious Ethiopian food and a dirty lingerie store isn't the recipe for a good date, I don't know what is," he says, laughing.

"So, I can see you haven't shaved in a few days . . . Did you at least change clothes?" she jokes.

"I did indeed. These are *clean* pajamas I'll have you know."

"Show me," she says, in a daring tone. He doesn't quite understand where this is leading but is willing to be patient and see.

"Okay, they're not *that* exciting, but sure," he says and angles the phone camera where she can see the white t-shirt he's wearing with some flannel pajama pants.

"Your turn," he says.

She gets up—he can tell because she's walking, and the background of her bedroom is moving behind her as she does. She props the phone on something and then walks back from it, so he can see her whole body. She's wearing the tight hoodie that he saw before and some black leggings that accentuate her killer legs and butt. She does a little pose and says, "What do you think?"

She's flirting with him again. He's into it and reciprocates. "I don't know. I think I need to see what's under that hoodie to really be able to give a verdict." He's testing his luck, being bolder than he usually would, especially on a call, but he's had a rough week and this mini-escape from the hospital, from everything weighing him down, is just what he needs.

She raises an eyebrow. "I guess I could show you," she says teasingly, and begins to zip down the zipper, one inch at a time. "But only if *you* promise to share more later."

He's nodding, feeling like a pervert, but unable to take back his request, now that it seems like it's going to be granted. "Deal," he says, and swallows.

She moves closer to where her phone is propped and unzips the jacket all the way. Underneath, she has on a thin-strapped, white, mostly-transparent tank top. She moves even closer to the camera now, leans down, puts her hands on what must be a desk, and says, smirking, "Is this a good angle?"

It's an amazing angle, and she knows it. Her breasts are hanging freely—no bra—inside her top, and he would give up his right hand to be in the same room as her, his hands on her body. Ironically enough, said right hand has already drifted down to the hard-on he's had the past few minutes, and he doesn't know whether to hope she's going to ask to see more of him or not.

Her expression changes, and she says, "Nathan, I'm really sorry, I have to go. I have a call and it's, um, something important."

He manages to force out, "It's okay. Have a good night, Sarah."

"You, too. Sweet dreams," she says, and blows him a kiss, before ending the call.

Nathan does dream—a lot—that night, but he's not sure "sweet" is a fair characterization. His dreams pick up where reality ended on his earlier FaceTime call with Sarah. And this time, it's not a call.

He's there, in her room with her. Her lovely breasts in her see-through shirt are his to touch and squeeze as much as he wants. Dream Sarah is aroused and begins to make demands as he peels off her shirt. "Touch them," she says. "Mmmm . . . kiss them."

"Well, if you insist," he says, and she laughs. The sound of her laugh—the taste of her on his tongue it's good. It's amazing. But what turns him on the most is her wanting him so much. Her asking him to do what she likes. Her openness to him—that's what arouses him the most.

"What now?" he asks, curious to see where this will lead.

"Now it's your turn to share," she says. "Remember that you promised?"

He's lying on her bed, on his back, and Sarah is pulling his pants off and reaching for his hard cock, saying "You promised" over and over again.

He wakes up, disappointed, to say the least. He looks at his watch. It's the middle of the night. He's alone, with an erection that feels like steel. He exhales, in dismay. He tosses and turns for a bit, unable to calm down enough to sleep, when he decides to simply take care of things himself—still imagining her—since it's not like he has a whole lot of other options.

VULNERABILITY ASSESSMENT

It's been over a week since I've seen Nathan. I felt pretty bad that I had to cut our FaceTime session short, but I felt even worse about why I had to do so. Poor excuse for a daughter that I am, I had somehow forgotten my dad's birthday, and I only realized it when I saw "Mom" come up on my caller ID. We always talk on his birthday. It helps my mom, and it helps me. To make matters, and my own guilt, worse, I was in the middle of a pretty hot flirting session with Nathan. Probably best we got interrupted since it was definitely going down an inappropriate path. Definitely winning "Daughter of the Year" award this year.

With Nathan dealing with everything at home, and work being really busy for both of us, we only had a few opportunities to connect the past week and a half. It's early Wednesday morning, the morning of the off-site. I'm at home and I do one last check of my bags: laptop, wallet, toothbrush, and phone—the absolute essentials are all there. Then I check my second bag and blush, cringe, freak out: clothes, sexy underwear, condoms. *Ahhh*. This is either going to be the best trip ever or the worst, but I am prepared, at least as far as wardrobe and contraceptives go.

I order an Uber and arrive at the airport to see some of my Instinqt colleagues heading to the same gate to check in.

"Good morning," I say to some of my engineering teammates. I walk toward security and check my phone.

I see a text:

Nathan: On your way?

Me: Yes. You?

Nathan: Yep.

Me: How's your dad? I didn't hear from you.

Nathan: He's . . . stable. That's the best that can be said right now.

Me: I'm sorry. I'd hoped there would've been an improvement.

Nathan: Thanks.

A pause, and then:

Nathan: I miss you.

It takes some courage to admit it, but I summon it and write back.

Me: Me too.

Nathan: Ready for your presentation?

I send him back a Mr. T "I was born ready" GIF, even though it's a bluff. I am starting to get nervous. When we get to Park City this afternoon, we'll do all the company presentations. The plan is to get all the official, "boring" stuff out of the way on the first day, and then basically get drunk and have fun tonight. There are fun, team-building activities planned for Thursday, and then Friday people can head home, go skiing, or whatever else.

I go through security and make my way to the gate. I know I'm there when I see a few of my teammates, and Angie, our procurement specialist, standing there greeting everyone, looking at an iPad.

"Hi Sarah, let me check," she says, scrolling down her screen. "Here you are. Negative," she confirms. "Perfect. Thanks for uploading the test results on time. If only everyone was as organized as our program managers."

"What do you mean?" I ask.

"Well, I'm gonna have to jam a few sticks up people's noses this morning for the rapid test, since they didn't upload their results yet. Lucky me."

I had been roped in to help arrange hotel rooms for 110

people, create and send out packing lists, and organize the bus rides from the Salt Lake City airport to Park City, but it looks like there were more stressful jobs. Seems like Angie got the honor of ensuring everyone has negative Covid tests before the off-site.

"Good luck," I tell her and go sit near a large window that looks out onto the tarmac where a number of planes are parked. I open up my laptop to review my presentation a few more times and make any last-minute tweaks to my notes. I put in my AirPods to discourage people from talking to me. I'm generally friendly, but right now, I need some mental space.

When I finish reviewing my presentation, I determine there's nothing else to be done. It's either ready or it isn't, and I decide that I can allow myself a little frivolity and text Nathan.

Me: What's your favorite song?

It takes him a minute to text back, and I wonder if he's already on the plane. Then I see the "typing" bubble.

Nathan: Do you like Vance Joy?

Me: He's pretty good.

Nathan: Well, there's this one song. It hasn't always been my favorite, but recently it's been on rotation.

Me:???

Nathan: How about I play it for you when we hang out again?

Me: So secretive. Ok.

Nathan: What about you?

Me: Well, I already let it slip when I drove you home— OneRepublic. Don't laugh.

Nathan: I'm not. I've been listening to that song a lot the last week.

She sees that he's typing.

Nathan: It makes me think of you, so I listen to it and . . . well, think about you.

Me: Like a high-school girl with a crush.

Nathan: Exactly. Kev caught me when we FaceTimed this week and now he's questioning my masculinity.

Sarah: OMG. <laughing emoji> Thank you for that. You made my day.

Nathan: About to board. See you soon.

I'm trying to decide how to respond, but then I see Kevin coming my way, so I send a quick <kiss emoji> and turn my phone over on my lap.

"Hey, Sarah. Good morning," Kevin, wearing a Lakers hat, says as he sits down right next to me. "Ready for today?"

"Definitely. Been brushing up on my presentation."

"Haven't seen you much since the party," he says, eyes sparkling. "Have a good night?"

I look at him, numerous thoughts hidden behind my—what I hope are—neutral eyes. I'm thinking about all the different things I did that night and with whom, but when he looks at me curiously, waiting for an answer, I realize maybe he's just asking whether I enjoyed the partner event.

"It was really fun. Haven't been to an event like that before," I respond. "How about you?"

"Yeah, I had a good time. Afterward, me and Nate got introduced to Eden. Seems like he's pretty interested in what we've got going on at Instinqt."

"Wow. That's so cool. Who introduced you?" I ask, knowing perfectly well it was Danica and Amy, from what I overheard on the balcony that night.

"Oh, those contacts from LightVerse we hung out with that night. Danica used to date Nate."

Wait, what?

"She's doing a lot to get back in his good graces," he says, giving me, what I think is, a meaningful look. It's hard to tell with only his eyes and eyebrows visible above the black disposable mask he's wearing.

Or his pants. Every time I've seen them together, she could barely keep her hands off him.

Kevin doesn't say anything else. I search his face for some

indication that he's trolling me, trying to get me to spill something about what's going on between Nathan and me, but he's holding his cards close to his chest. Is his comment meant to be a warning? *"Tread lightly, Nathan might as well be your boss."* Or is he trying to give me—albeit indirectly—some other message?

He's my boss, Nathan's too, for that matter. But he's also Nathan's best friend in the world. He must know that something happened between Nathan and me. But the real question is whether he's okay with that, or not.

Not sure what to do, or say, I simply reply, "Sounds like a good connection to have. Um, I gotta run to the restroom before we head on the plane. I'll see you when we get there, okay?"

"Sure, have a nice flight."

✳ ✳ ✳

I hit the restroom with the plan of splashing some cold water on my face, but realize I'll ruin my makeup if I do, so I just stare at myself in the mirror and watch myself take a few deep breaths. *They dated? For how long? When?*

Dreya comes out of the bathroom stall. "Hey, Sarah, you okay?" she asks, looking a little concerned.

"Yeah." I plaster what I'm sure looks like a fake smile on my face. "I'm fine. Just a little tired."

She smiles. "Don't worry—you'll do great later," she says, wrongly attributing my uneasiness to my upcoming presentation and not what I just found out from Kevin. She washes her hands and leaves the restroom.

I give myself one final internal pep talk about being a modern woman. "Pull yourself together," I tell myself. "You're here to do your job, not find a boyfriend. Lizzo would be ashamed of you."

Thinking "Like a Girl" is exactly what I need to hear right now, I pull out my phone and stick my AirPods in my ears and crank it up. As I walk determinedly toward the gate for boarding, I think that love and hormones and hot guys are all nice, but sometimes you've just got to get some shit done. And that's what I plan to do.

* * *

We arrive in Salt Lake City, and I've been tasked with getting all the people coming from the Bay Area onto a shuttle to Park City. Suffice it to say, that it's easier to plan and deliver multiple product releases than get sixty-five software engineers and other supposedly highly educated people on the three mini-buses we've ordered for the purpose. By the time everyone is on —and my hair is completely soaked from the drizzle outside—all I want are some dry clothes and a warm place to defrost.

We arrive at the hotel in Park City, and everyone is given their room key. I'm sharing with Erin—as planned—and she's already there when I slide the hotel room key into the slot and open the door.

"You look like a drowned rat," she says, surprised. "Come in, put your stuff down."

"I need a shower. A hot shower," I say, but give her a quick hug after dropping all my things on what looks like my bed near the window.

We have about an hour before kickoff of the company presentations, and I need a reset. The flight was short, but I'm feeling frazzled, and I need to center myself before getting up in front of 100+ people—our Bay Area folks and the Salt Lake City-based sales and marketing teams.

Despite the Silicon Valley uniform being a hoodie and jeans, which I'm sure at least half of the attendees will be wearing, I've already decided that I'm going to dress nicely for the presentation. We'll be going out for dinner and drinks afterward, and besides, I want to make a good impression during the presentations. Never hurts to put in a little extra effort, I think, as I lay out some dark skinny jeans, a soft, fitted cream-colored cashmere sweater, and heeled boots before I head into the bathroom to shower.

After I get out, I'm feeling better. As I get dressed and put on some light makeup, Erin asks, "So, what are you so stressed out about?"

"So, basically," she sums up, after hearing about my day, "Kevin is the same as every other guy in the world, essentially clueless, and he used Danica's crush on Nate to get an in with a major potential investor."

I clarify for her, assuming that since she's so calm, she must not understand. "And Danica dated Nate, at some point in the past. She tried to kiss him the other night since she obviously still wants him. You're forgetting that part."

She looks at me, her mouth twitching.

"And she's beautiful," I tell her, annoyed that she's not more upset.

"Sarah, whose house did he end up at on Saturday night?"

"Mine."

"Who was he making out with at 2:00 a.m.?"

"Me."

"And who did he spend the night with?"

"Also me," I admit, grudgingly.

"So don't let that girl live in your head rent-free. You got him if you want him. And you got this presentation, too. So why don't you just put on your coat—it's drying over the heater—and go kick some ass?"

✳ ✳ ✳

We walk to the conference center of the hotel, where 100+ seats and a projector are set up. People are milling around, eating snacks, and waiting for things to get started.

I see Nathan out of the corner of my eye, sitting at a table near the front of the room, which seems reserved for the executive team. I can tell he's seen me and even though he's nodding at our CFO, and responding in short answers, I catch his eyes flitting over to me. He's got a slight smile on his face, which I'm guessing is meant for me, and not the quarterly numbers the CFO is probably telling him about.

Things seem to be quieting down, about to start, so I take a seat about midway back and go to silence my phone. I see I have a message.

Nathan: You're gonna do great. Drinks on me after to celebrate. <wine glass emoji>

I glance up and see Nathan looking at me, but trying not to seem like he is. I take him in and realize I still feel a bit unsettled by what Kevin told me earlier, but the expression on his face— a half smile, kind eyes trying to catch my own—reminds me of all the conversations we've had over the past couple of months, everything we've already shared. And instantly, I feel more at ease than before and smile back. Just being in the same room as him makes me feel reassured. Erin's probably right. I've got him if I want him.

But first, I've got a presentation to do, and I'm determined to kick some ass. We get started, and my time slot is about three-quarters of the way through the agenda for the afternoon. When it's finally my turn, I walk up to the front and introduce myself.

"Hi, everyone," I say. "For those of you who don't know me, I'm Sarah Hoffman, and I've been at Instinqt for about two months. I've had the great pleasure of working with a number of our product managers and engineers to come up with what I think is a solid proposal to improve how we plan, execute, and deliver our products to the market. Kevin asked me to share it all with you today, so let's get started."

I take them through my slides, explaining, answering questions, and even fielding a few opposing views. They listen as I explain how I first went about understanding Instinqt's needs, culture, and working methods and how I conceptualized a better way for product and engineering to work together on feature development and releases. They ask good questions related to the recommendations I'm making. I get lost in the challenge of it all. Like a quarterback in a noisy stadium full of fans, I know my purpose there and I get it done. After years of wondering if I'm going in the right direction, if I even know what I want and who I should be, I feel my skin prickle. This is my place. I can feel it, as I stand in front of a room full of colleagues and confidently present things I know well: process, efficiency, collaboration, and execution.

I finish to a round of healthy applause, especially raucous from my teammates, and glance over to the table at the front where the leadership team is sitting. I see Nathan grinning ear to ear. He gives me a thumbs up, and I'm on top of the world.

The program ends about twenty minutes later, and Kevin tells us that now that we've gotten all the official stuff out of the way, we're going to head over to our first social event—dinner, drinks, and karaoke.

I realize I've forgotten my heavy coat back in the room, and since it's a ten-minute walk to dinner, and it was already freezing earlier this afternoon, I tell Erin I'm going to head up to get it.

"I can come with you," she offers.

"No, that's okay. It's light out. I'll be right over. I want to drop off my laptop anyways."

I get to my room and set my things down, putting my phone in my back pocket so I don't have to take a bag. I open the door to leave and find Nathan, posed in quite the same way as he was the Saturday night he arrived at my apartment—hand on the door jamb and coat slung over one shoulder—with a rakish smile on his face.

"What? Were you just standing here waiting for me to come out so I could find you in that cool pose?" I ask.

"Never," he says, and laughs. He leans in, glances from side to side to make sure nobody is in the hallway, and pecks me on the cheek. "I actually heard you about to open the door and wanted to make you laugh."

"What're you doing here? We're supposed to head over to dinner."

"I wanted to tell you that you did a great job. Like phenomenal."

"Thanks—" I start to say when he gently pushes me into the room and shuts the door behind him.

"And to give you this," he says, dropping his coat on the floor. He cups my face between his hands and presses his lips against mine.

By this point of the day, I've been up and down so many times emotionally that I have very little reserve left, and instead of thinking of all the reasons why we shouldn't or what things about us—Nathan and Sarah—worry me or don't make sense, I choose to give in and let him kiss me. I open my mouth slightly, and his tongue—which seems as if it was just waiting for the opening—slowly joins my own, and we kiss fully, hungrily for several minutes.

"I've been wanting to do that since last Sunday," he admits. "It's been a rough couple of days, traveling, at the hospital, not to mention work, and—" he stops.

"What?" I ask gently.

"I just feel good—grounded—when I'm with you," he says, lifting his hand to smooth my hair, which I'm sure is showing some signs of our short-but-passionate make-out session.

"We should hurry to dinner," I tell him. "Only Erin will miss me, but I'm pretty sure more people will notice you're gone. Anybody who puts two and two together . . ."

"You're right," he says, a pained expression on his face. "But I have to do one thing first."

Before I can ask, he grabs my ass with both hands and squeezes.

"God, you have such a great ass," he says, groaning. He exhales, dramatically, and braces himself. "Okay, I'm good for a couple hours." I roll my eyes at him and, smiling, I open the door.

We leave the room, one at a time, just in case someone from Instinqt is around, and walk to the restaurant. We consider whether we should arrive separately, but decide that it won't raise any suspicion for us to walk in together like normal colleagues. "Normal colleagues." The kind who haven't seen each other naked. The kind who focus on product launches and quarterly sales numbers during company all-hands, rather than where all their own hands would rather be on each other's bodies. As it turns out, the whole place is set up with buffet stations and a bar, so nobody even notices our entrance.

I seek out my teammates and get some food and a glass of wine, and I'm having a really good time, chatting with a few women from the product marketing team, when Erin shows up.

"So, I know this could theoretically wait until later, but I wanted to share something I just learned," she tells me, and winks in a very obvious way like only a deranged person like Erin would.

"Okay," I reply, winking just as obviously. "Is this confidential?"

"Yeah, let's head out to the patio."

"In this weather?"

"It's enclosed. C'mon. You need to hear this," she says, giving me a meaningful look.

"So, I was chatting with Dejohn from HR, and casually asked about people at work having relationships. Turns out, Instinqt doesn't have a formal policy about it. They figure they're too small for it to matter now. What are the chances?"

"What are the chances? I don't know, something like one in," I pause to survey how many people are partying inside, "a hundred."

"First of all, that's not how probability calculations work. Second of all, if there are no *official* rules, then you can't break them."

"Why'd you emphasize the word 'official?'"

She looks like a deer caught in headlights, realizing she's slipped up.

"Well, he did mention that it's highly frowned upon. I mean there are potential conflict of interest issues, and what if people break up? Then someone could sue for sexual harassment, whether it was consensual or not."

"So, basically, nothing's changed."

"Well, no, I guess not. But there is another loophole," she says. Obviously, she's prepared.

I look at her, waiting to hear her next, likely implausible, idea.

"It's a different area code!" she says, and I can almost see a little cartoon light bulb above her head as she nods at me and waits for me to get it. But I don't.

"What are you talking about?"

"Oh, I forgot. You're like . . . Fetus-age, so you probably haven't seen 'Road Trip,' but . . ."

"Are you about to tell me it's not cheating if it's in a different area code?"

"It applies here," she says point-blank.

"No, it doesn't, but I appreciate the effort," I say, laughing. "Should I be telling your husband this is your logic? Should he worry about your next business trip?"

"Says the lady who's gonna bone Nate tonight," she replies.

"Excuse me?" I say, eyes wide.

"What Dejohn said is as good as a green light. You're an idiot if you don't go for it."

I look at her, uncertain.

"You've got the green light to bone-town, girl," she says in an official voice and pulls an imaginary train whistle.

We burst into laughter, and she takes a nonchalant sip of her drink. I'm beginning to wonder which number cocktail she's on tonight when someone opens the door to join us on the patio, and we see it's Kevin and Nathan. Noticing it's them, we begin to roll with laughter, embarrassment, giddiness, and alcohol forming a perfect storm of idiocy.

Kevin asks us what's so funny and gives Nathan a look like "That's the last time we're having an open bar."

Erin and I look at each other—seeing if the other will answer—but when I see that she's not going to say anything, I pipe up, "Just talking about . . . stuff," unable to formulate a better answer, which sends us into further snickers. We're trying to control ourselves, but we're obviously unable.

Kevin and Nathan are looking at us completely bewildered. Kevin exhales and tells us that games and karaoke are starting inside if we want to join. If nothing else, his comment distracts us from what we were howling about.

Erin heads in and Kevin follows her.

"Coming?" he asks Nathan.

"In a second," he replies, grabbing my elbow, indicating that I should stay back.

"What was that?" he asks, as I turn to him.

"I'm honestly not sure, but . . . Are you a fan of rules, generally?"

He tilts his head, trying to figure out where I'm going with this.

"I guess it depends. What kind of rules do you mean?"

"Erin has a theory that if you're on an out-of-town trip, then the rules that would normally apply back home, don't, because it's a different area code."

He's looking at me, eyes narrowed. "You're blushing. It's cute. And it makes me think I know what you're talking about," he says to me.

"And?" I say, teasingly.

"And . . . I think I could be convinced—with the right logic, of course," he says, looking me up and down suggestively, "that the usual rules don't apply out of town."

"Mmhmm," I say, raising my eyebrow at him.

"What are you thinking?" he whispers in my ear, and he's so close, I can smell his aftershave.

"I'm thinking," I whisper back to him, "why are we still here?"

WHAT HAPPENS
IN UTAH . . .

We leave the party—Nathan first, begging off Kevin's invitation to join either the games or where they're headed after, another bar—and me second, telling Erin not to wait up, that I'm going to be studying some HR policies tonight.

She gives me a naughty grin, smacks me on the butt, and whispers at me "Go get him, girl!" like the excellent rom-com sidekick role she was born to play.

I head out the side exit—feeling like a spy—and see Nathan waiting a block down, hands in his coat pockets, trying to keep warm. I catch up to him, and he immediately pulls me into a small alley between the old-timey buildings in this part of town.

"Sarah, your brain and your personality are amazing. I love them."

I give him a confused look.

"But . . ." he says, giving me a look that can't be confused for anything other than lust, "I am a mere mortal, and I need to see you naked. Soon. Like. . . in the next five minutes." As he finishes his speech, maybe to convince me of his need, he slips his cold hands inside my unzipped coat and rubs his hands over my soft sweater, first holding my waist and then allowing himself to squeeze one of my breasts.

"I have bad news," I tell him, gravely. "The hotel is a ten-minute walk, and there's no way I'm taking off my jacket, let alone my clothes, outside."

"I have a solution," he says, grinning wickedly, and swoops me up in his arms. He peeks his head out of the alleyway and looks both ways before turning right and racing off—holding me and bouncing me the whole way—toward the hotel. There's nobody out on the streets. It's 10:00 p.m., but it's a Wednesday and not high-season, and we barely see a soul on the way back. At some point, I absolutely refuse to be carried any longer, and he sets me down and we walk—quickly, excitedly, like horny people who're dying to get laid.

"I have my own room. Come on," he tells me. His room is in a different building than my own, and we sneak up the stairs, avoiding the elevator, and now I really feel like a spy.

He pulls me up the last flight to the fourth floor where his room is, and we exit the stairwell to an empty corridor. We don't really have much to worry about, since everyone is still out partying, but I still feel nervous and want to get inside. I watch, impatiently, as he looks for his key and then opens the door, and then I bolt in, before he can even get inside himself.

"Anxious?" he teases.

"Me? No. I could wait," I reply, oozing pretend nonchalance.

"Well, I can't," he says in a more serious, low tone that tells me he's already thinking about what's going to happen next.

He takes off his own coat and holds his hand out for mine. I take it off, suddenly a little shy, recalling the way his cold hands felt through my sweater in the alley a few minutes before. I hand it to him and he throws it to the side, over a chair, barely even looking in that direction. His eyes are on me. They're dark, but they're full of something else, too. There's lust there, to be sure, but if I had to guess, or maybe just to hope, I'd say it looks almost like adoration.

"Do you know what happens when you get a taste of something so amazing and then you're told you can't have it anymore?" he asks me, giving me a sly grin.

"Mmm, I don't know. Turns you into a sex addict who shows up in the middle of the night to someone's apartment for a booty call?"

We're standing in the middle of the room between the bed and the giant window that looks out onto the snowy slopes of the Iron Mountain. I can see we have a couple of options—bed, couch, hell, right now, I'd settle for bent over the coffee table—but we're not quite there yet, and I make myself focus on the delicious man I have standing right in front of me.

I still have my tall boots on, which give me a couple of inches, bringing me closer to his height. But there's still a good height difference, and now that we're close enough to touch, I have to angle my face up to look at his eyes.

He puts his hands on me, and I shriek. "You," I say, teeth almost chattering from the shock, "are going to warm up your hands before you even *think* about touching me."

"Well, I've been thinking about touching you for at least the last eight hours, so that is patently untrue. But I *will* warm up my hands before I touch you."

By the time I get my boots off, he's lit the gas fireplace in the room. I'm sitting on the couch, near the window, and rolling my ankles around to stretch them out.

"This room is a *lot* nicer than mine," I say, spreading my hands on the velvety-smooth sofa and turning to look out the window at the breathtaking view of the snowy mountain. He's holding his hands near the flame, rubbing them together. He's watching me while he does so, and it gives him the comical look of a cartoon supervillain sizing up his sworn enemy mixed with someone about to eat a delicious dessert.

"You're looking like you've got some definite plans over there," I say, amused.

"Oh, I do."

✳ ✳ ✳

He feels as if the last few months have all been leading toward this moment. Their first night together—that fleeting one-night stand—was amazing, but when he'd woken up in the morning to find her gone, well, he'd felt like shit is what.

It had knocked him for a loop. They'd had a great night—it had felt so right—and then she had vanished into thin air. But then he'd been given a second chance. *They* had. And that night

—and the rightness of it—is on his mind now as he closes the gap between them, moving toward the couch, now with warmer hands.

Nathan sits near her on the floor, right next to the couch, and begins to massage her feet, already imagining doing the same to other, more sensitive parts of her body.

"Feet hurt?" he asks her.

"Not really, but maybe I won't tell you, so you'll keep doing that. It feels great."

He stops for a second, to pick up his phone, which he's placed on the coffee table, and puts on some music. "Spice Girls, huh?" she says, raising her eyebrows. "Didn't know you were a super fan."

"I'm a super fan of you. Don't worry, it's only the first song. It gets more romantic afterward. I made it on the plane today."

"And what made you choose this one?"

"They played it at the bar the night I met you."

"Do you wanna be my lover?" she asks, raising an eyebrow, and laughing. Hearing her laugh always makes him happy, but tonight—maybe because he's been thinking about her non-stop for days—it's also turning him on. He's imagining that same voice, like soft bells tinkling, saying his name as she comes. He continues massaging her feet and moves up her calves, inside the legs of her jeans. She's laid back slightly, eyes closed, and her little moans and gasps let him know she's enjoying his touch.

He glances out the window and notices it's snowing. "Look," he tells her, bringing her back to the present. "It's starting to snow."

"It's so romantic here. You got lucky with this room," she says.

"I didn't get lucky. I upgraded it. I wanted something in a different building than the others. I needed a little space. Physical, but . . . mental, too."

He waits a beat and then continues, "And something a little nicer, you know, just in case."

"Just in case, huh? Of what exactly?"

"In case a smart, beautiful woman decided she wanted to

spend some time with me tonight."

"Looks like you *did* get lucky then."

"Correct. I'm already lucky, just having you here with me, but . . . I'm hoping to get a little luckier," he admits, laughing, and joins her on the couch, laying her back even further and starting to kiss her on the neck.

"Do you practice lines like that in the mirror?"

"I'd say I'm a natural, but that's not true. You just make me laugh, and I wanna return the favor. Seeing you giggle at my bad jokes is the best."

As he kisses her neck, the feeling of her warm body beneath his is stirring up all sorts of good feelings—both physical and emotional.

But then, out of the blue, there's a quick pang of guilt. He's worrying that he should be with his dad. He's in an undertow, his feelings the waves pulling him away from the shore. Apathy toward everything else in the world besides his father's precarious situation, and yet at the same time, desperation for connection, for comfort, for love.

He sits up, pulling her up, too. Then he pulls his own hands back from her and looks down at them, willing himself not to crack his knuckles, something he does when he's stressed or uneasy. He can feel himself closing off, but then he looks up he sees the expression on Sarah's face. She watches him intently, openly—no judgment.

"Nathan," she says, simply, in a tone that tells him, there's only vulnerability now, and it's safe. *He* is safe, with her. She reaches for his hand and holds it in her lap and just waits for him to be ready to do or say whatever it is he needs to. He takes a deep breath, gives her a small, hesitant smile, and begins to tell her about how his family told him he had to come to Utah. And more importantly, why. "Because they wanted me to be here with you."

❊ ❊ ❊

"I was gonna skip out on this whole thing," he admits. "But

David basically forced me to come. He drove me to the airport, took my bag out of the trunk, put it on the sidewalk, and drove off before I could argue." He smiles at the recent memory.

"Why? I mean, a few people still had to dial into the meetings. You could have, too. I'm sure Kevin would've understood," I tell him.

"Yeah, Kevin would've understood, but David and my mom are determined . . . well . . ."

"For you to keep living life?" I ask. I know, because it's what people told me when my dad died: "You have to try to keep on living."

"In general terms, yes."

"And in more specific terms?"

"In more specific terms, they said there's no way I'm missing a chance to 'woo' you."

"Woo me, huh?"

"Well, that's what my mom said. David might've used a little more colorful language," he says, blushing.

"Wait, so your mom and your brother know about me?" I ask, unbelieving.

"Yeah, they do. My dad, too."

"How did that come up? 'Guys, I have to tell you about this amazing TPM at work. She's gonna revolutionize release management.'"

"Nah, it was a couple weeks ago when I flew up there on Sunday night. After the partner event . . . after being at your place for the night," he clarifies. "I got there, and I was like falling asleep at the hospital, and they were asking me why I was so tired, what had I been doing the night before." He looks at me, eyebrows raised, indicating I know exactly what we were doing the night in question.

I give him a look of surprise. "You didn't tell them what we were doing the night before!"

"Of course not, not in specific terms, but I told them that I was out with a girl from work and that she was pretty cool—"

"It's true, I am," I interrupt.

"And that I'd actually known her for a couple months and . . . I think they could just tell that I like you a lot."

"I like you a lot, too,"

He smiles. "They convinced me that it's only a couple of days. That I shouldn't miss out on a chance with you. I'm here because they wanted me to be here with you."

Realizing that his family knows about me—about us—gives me a start at first. Then I look into his eyes—brown, beautiful, searching my own at this moment—and consciously take a deep breath to calm my beating heart.

"Can I kiss you?" I ask him, realizing too late it's the same thing I said to him the night we met.

When his eyes widen a bit and he smiles gently, I realize he caught it, too.

"Yes."

And wanting to give him a chance to recover from all the bad, before we move on to the good, I start with a small kiss, aiming for his cheek, but due to the height difference and just a little bit of nervousness, I end up kissing his jawline.

He turns his head and tells me in a husky tone, whose emotion I can't quite nail down, "You're really something, Sarah."

"Put your money where your mouth is?" I ask him, giving him a small wink.

His smile brightens. "My pleasure. Yours, too," he jokes and leans down to kiss my neck.

❊ ❊ ❊

I squeal and run my hand through his hair. "I love when you do that," he's saying between kissing my neck, my face, and my mouth. He can't seem to decide where to concentrate his efforts. He's lying half on top of me, holding his weight with his forearms beside me and one of his legs still on the floor, so he won't crush me. I feel like I'm sinking into the squishy couch, drowning in a sea made of pillows and sexy man.

"I wanna do this differently," I say, struggling to sit up.

"Okay, how?"

"You sit down on this man-eating couch. I'm on top."

He nods enthusiastically, eager to follow my orders. He sits on the couch and unbuttons the top few buttons of his shirt.

"It's getting hot in here."

"Yes, it is," I agree, and straddle him. He immediately wraps his hands around my hips and begins to knead my ass.

"Your ass is so sexy," he whispers, almost pained.

"Yeah, you mentioned that earlier."

I unbutton my own sweater buttons, leaving it fully open to him, inviting him to appreciate some other parts of my body.

He accepts the unspoken invitation and sits up, moving his hands up my back, under my sweater. He tips me toward him, so my back is just slightly arched and my breasts—if I may so myself—are looking pretty stunning. He seems to agree, judging by the hungry look on his face.

Sitting on him at this angle, our bodies are perfectly aligned. We're rubbing against each other, and I can feel him, feel how much he wants me. It's turning me on so much, and like I've drunk a truth serum, I blurt out, "I really, really want you. I have for—"

"A while?" he interrupts me.

"Yeah," I say, leaning down and smiling into his neck as I begin to kiss it and nibble on his ear lobe, to see what kind of reaction it elicits.

He exhales in a measured way, as if he's trying to calm himself.

"Everything okay?" I ask, playfully, from where I'm positioned in the crook of his neck, enjoying his scent, his warmth, the little nook between the back edge of his jawbone and his earlobe—and especially the slight moan he makes when I kiss him there. *I might just stay here forever.*

"Oh, more than okay," he replies, in a satisfied tone, and gently lifts my chin and face, where he can look me in the eyes. "Are *you* okay?"

My thoughts are scattered all over the place due to the

increasingly warm air and his intense gaze hitting my bare skin. But the answer to his question is easy.

"Way more than okay," I tell him and run my hands through his hair. He closes his eyes and smiles more broadly. When he opens them and blinks at me, it seems like he's come to a decision.

"Get up for a second," he says. I do.

"I wanted to pick you up in a romantic gesture and carry you to the bed, but I can barely make it out of this couch alone," he laughs, grabbing my waist for leverage, and hoists himself up.

Facing me, both of us barefoot, I'm overly aware of our height difference. He leans down and gives me a slow, sensuous kiss.

"Sarah, when you're in the room, I'm out of control. I'm calmer, but I'm also breathing faster, all at once. You're like some crazy drug that makes me insane and happy and horny . . ." he admits, laughing.

We're kissing again, deep, open-mouth, wet, and slick, and I tug on his shirt so he knows I want him to take it off. He undoes one more button and then impatiently lifts it over his head, tossing it on the ground. I rub my hands over his hard pecs, but I'm interrupted when he grabs my sleeves and pulls my sweater off.

We're skin-to-skin—with the exception of my lacy bra—still standing near the window. He begins to walk me backward toward the bed. One of his hands is on the nape of my neck, angling my head up, supporting it, as he kisses me, and the other is on my lower back to keep me steady, as I clumsily trip my way along in reverse. All of a sudden, we're falling and I grab his shoulders and pull him down with me.

"You're pretty sure of yourself," he asks. "How'd you know we reached the bed? Your eyes are closed."

"I'm sure of *you*," I say, looking into his eyes, sappily. "You wouldn't let me fall."

"You're right. I wouldn't."

The feeling of him on top of me is driving me crazy. I rake my fingernails, lightly, down his back, and he shivers. I unbuckle his belt as he fumbles with the front clasp of my bra. We both succeed at the same time and say "Yes!" which sends us into a quick burst of laughter.

I'm trying to pull down his pants, but he's distracted by what he sees in front of him. He touches one of my breasts lightly, then kisses the side of it, puts the nipple in his mouth, periodically looking up at me, to see my reaction—always checking, always gauging.

"You should work in QA. Very results-oriented and such attention to detail," I tease him. He smiles briefly, but he's in another world. His other hand is toying with my second breast, as he continues to lightly lick and nip the other.

"Nathan, I need to see more of you. Those abs are pretty fucking great, but I need more."

He's drawn out of his breast-induced stupor for long enough to comprehend what I'm asking. I pull at the front of his pants and his jeans button comes undone. He stands up, quickly, and takes a minute to get out of his pants and underwear—all at once—like a trained stripper. The intent on his face is clear, and I understand the assignment. I begin to struggle with my own lower garments, knowing they're the only thing between him and me and step two or sixty-nine of what's happening tonight. Seeing my struggle, he begins to help me. We get my jeans off, and I reach for my underwear, but he puts his hand on mine and stops me. He's staring at the red lace thong I'm wearing, and I can hear his breath catch in his throat.

"What?" I ask.

"I'm just giving myself a minute to engrave this in my memory for all eternity."

"My underwear?"

"No, you. You're so beautiful right now."

"May I?" he asks, his hands on my glasses.

"Yeah, set them over there, on the nightstand. If they break, I'm in trouble."

"You can't be that blind."

"I assure you, I am."

"I bet you can see up close just fine."

"Ernie, is that you?" I ask him, squinting at his face. I move my hand lower and grab him gently. "Your cock's so much bigger than it was last time."

He's full-on laughing now.

"You're ridiculous."

He kisses my neck and then returns his focus to the task at hand. He lays prone on my body, skin-to-skin, head-to-toe. My skin is catching on fire as he travels down my body, tracing kisses from my lips, down to my throat, and beyond. He takes his time on my breasts and then my hips are raising, of their own accord, as he kisses my hip bones and the area right above my mound.

He hooks his fingers into the red strings on the sides of my hips, pulling them down inch by torturous inch as he gets closer to his final destination, and as his tongue touches my clit, it takes all the restraint I have in my body not to explode on the spot. My mind is running even faster than my body right now, and I'm sure it won't take much for me to come. He must sense it, because, after a few playful licks and explorations of his fingers, he looks up at me and whispers, "It's okay. Let go. There's always time for more later."

As he gently parts me with his fingers, now deliciously warm, he kisses his way up my body and makes love to my breasts with his mouth, while he rhythmically touches all the right spots below. His middle finger teases my opening, and he looks at me, questioning. I feel half-conscious, like I'm in a hazy dream, rocking on a wave, but I nod at him, indicating that this is what I want.

As his fingers enter me, I feel him touch a spot that I knew existed, but that hasn't been loved or cherished for a long time. He continues to suck at my nipples and takes a break here or there to give me long, slow kisses, and I feel myself rising, like the crest of a huge wave.

"Do you wanna come?" he asks me.

"Yes."

"Tell me again."

"Yes, I wanna come. I'm *going* to come."

I feel disconnected from reality at this point, but I manage to find my own hands and put them on his cock, and it drives me wild. He's so hard, and I can imagine him in me.

"I'm coming," I say, and make all sorts of moans and cries that I can't even bother to be self-conscious about.

"Oh my god, Sarah, you're amazing," he says as I orgasm. My eyes are closed, and I see bright lights flashing. A minute or an eternity later, my breathing starts to slow. I open my eyes to see him—hand still on me, covering the area of his adoration from a few moments ago—smiling at me. His head is on the pillow next to me, and he's lying beside me. I realize we're still on top of the covers. We never turned them down.

Suddenly, I'm freezing, and I shiver noticeably. "You're cold?"

"Yeah, I don't know how. A minute ago, I was on fire."

"Can I warm you up again?" he asks.

"What'd you have in mind?"

"Get under the covers. I'll be back in a sec. I gotta drink some water, or I'm gonna pass out," he says. "The altitude here is messing with me."

While he's in the bathroom getting a glass of water, I get under the covers. The sheets are soft under my splayed fingers, under my naked body, and I let my mind wander—get dirty—thinking about Nathan's skin. Wondering how his cock can be so hard, so real, but also so soft and inviting.

He comes back into the room, and before he turns off the lamp, I enjoy the sight of his naked body. When he clicks it off, the light from the flickering fire hits his shape in such a mesmerizing way, it's the stuff of dreams. Shadows and golden skin combine, lulling me into a trance-like state, and I wonder whether his muscular body and the erection I see starting is a mirage and I'm stuck in a desert somewhere, or whether I'm actually here with him—finally—after months of imagining a night like this.

"I think," I say as he slips into the bed with me, "that you are the sexiest thing I've ever seen."

"Say more," he says, smiling at me. He's on his side, propped up on his elbow, and I'm facing him on my side.

"That bicep right there," I say, kissing his arm, "I like that very much."

"And those pecs," I continue, giving his chest some much-needed TLC, "those are very nice, too."

"What else do you like?"

I push him gently onto his back.

"Well, I already told you that your abs are every woman's wet dream," I say. "But I can tell you again," I continue as I trace my tongue over the individual ab muscles on his tensed stomach, and move to straddle him.

"These hips, I don't know if you're supposed to compliment a guy's hips, but they also turn me on, especially this little muscle jutting out right here."

"Which one?" he asks, and I know what he wants.

"This one," I say, nipping it with my teeth. I hear a sharp intake of breath from him.

"But the thing I like most of all . . ."

"Yeah?"

"The thing that turns me on so much . . ."

"Mmmhmm?"

"Surely you can guess?" I say, continuing to kiss him low, very low on his torso, getting closer to what he wants—what I want—one inch at a time.

"I think I have an idea," he says.

"It's your . . ."

"Yes?"

"It's those feet, Nathan."

"Oh my god, you're the worst. Sarah," he says, laughing but in a pained way.

I look at him and lick my lips, watching him watch me. I'm hovering over him, at his waist, his erection is brushing across my naked breasts. I put it between my breasts and rub myself up and down a little bit. I wink at him.

"Just kidding. It's your amazing cock."

"Sarah, please, just do it already," he all-but-pleads with me, unable to control himself.

And so I do and put him out of his misery. I put him in my mouth, letting my lips roll over the tip, tasting him, and I can hear him groan.

"Yes."

I begin to use my tongue in earnest, licking him from the base to the tip, while I balance myself, one hand on his hard hip and another gently holding his balls. I wrap my first hand around his shaft as I move my head up and down. I watch him, and my god, is he a sight to behold. The expression on his face is one of arousal, of course, but there's an inner peace he's radiating, with just the tiniest bit of vulnerability. I can tell he's trying to control himself, and I take my mouth off him long enough to tell him to enjoy himself, the same way he reassured me. But before I can go back down on him, he's hauling me up his body and putting his hands on my back, pressing me into him.

"Sarah, I need you."

I sit up on him, rubbing myself against him, and he reaches up, putting his hands in my hair.

"It's happening, beautiful?" he asks me with just a little bit of a smile and the sweetest expression on his face. "I'm not dreaming, right? I've dreamed of you so many times in the last two months."

He's confirming that what he's wanted for so long is now within reach and begging just the

slightest bit.

"It's time?" he says, sounding exposed, a bit raw.

"It's time," I say, leaning down to whisper in his ear.

I see him grin like a kid being given permission to eat a lollipop, and I grab my bag off the nightstand.

"Condom?" he asks.

"Yeah."

"Are you on birth control?" he asks.

"I am. You wanna go without it?"

"Are *you* okay with that?" he asks.

"Are *you* clean?" I ask.

"My body definitely is. My mind, not so much," he says, biting his lip and smiling.

I nod and reach behind me to stroke him. As I arch my back to reach him, he lets out a soft moan and grabs my breast with one hand. With the other, he takes my hand off him and lifts his hips to flip us over. Now he's on top, and it looks like the real fun is beginning.

He's kissing me deeply, and rubbing against me—not *in* me yet—and a flood of memories from our first night blend together with what's happening in the here and now. Suddenly, I can't take it anymore. I'm already so aroused that I want him in me now and I say so.

He's in full agreement and it takes him only a second to spread me wide open and lift my hips up, just enough, that it's a smooth, unobstructed entry. We'd score a perfect ten in Olympic diving with such precision. The pressure is perfect—his cock, fucking hell, is perfect—and he's moving in me slowly, giving my body, already wet and ready, a chance to get to know him again in this intimate way. I grab his ass and pull him into me. "You know," I say, between his thrusts, "your ass is luscious, too."

He laughs a little, but not to be distracted, he keeps his pace. He's kissing my mouth, thirsty for connection, arms braced on his elbows with his fingers in my hair. I feel like I'm on fire, and I'm beginning to pant and make noises under him.

"I love it when you scream."

"When have you heard me scream, huh?" I try to say, between breaths.

"The last time. I've thought about it a lot. I wanna make you do it again."

"Well, you're getting close."

"How close?"

"Really close."

Just then he lifts my leg, putting me in a position he must've learned in a Kama Sutra 101 course, and I let go.

"Yes. Yes! Oh my god, yes!"

After I've come back down to earth, I watch him—notice in a way I didn't the first time we hooked up—what his face looks like when he's on the brink of an orgasm. His eyes are closed, and there's an intense look of concentration on his face. I can feel his heart thumping under my hand, where it's gripping the hard muscle of his chest, and then I see, hear, his breath catch in his throat. It seems like he's trying to restrain himself, but nevertheless, a groan escapes him as he shudders inside of me. Oh, but it's delicious to hear because I know that I'm the reason for it. And I'm certain I have a thousand-watt smile on my face. He opens his eyes and sees me and grins back, biting the edge of his bottom lip.

"Oh my god," he says, and slowly lays down on me, momentarily crushing me, and then rolls off me, exhausted. He's still breathing hard, small beads of sweat on his forehead. "That was . . . Fuck, Sarah. I thought I was gonna die." He laughs, trying to catch his breath.

"I'm glad you didn't," I say, as I cuddle up to his side and drape my arm possessively across his chest.

I'm facing him and the window. Snow is still falling lightly outside. In the firelight, I can see the blissful look on his face, a slight smile, eyes closed. I can't remember the last time I felt this good, the last time I was this happy. In a sex-induced euphoria, I fall asleep holding Nathan, likely with a goofy smile on my face.

. . . STAYS IN UTAH

I wake, as usual, early. It's 6:15 according to Nathan's watch, but then I see by the clock on the nightstand that it's actually 7:15 local time. We're supposed to be ready and waiting in the hotel lobby for our activities today by 8:00 a.m., which means people are waking up and probably heading out in search of coffee. This isn't super-great. Despite the fact that we might not technically be getting fired yet for an inappropriate workplace relationship, today's not the day I'd planned on announcing I'm hottie for Nathan's body. I need to get back to my room, shower, and get downstairs—without first getting caught coming out of an executive's hotel room in the same clothes I wore last night.

I give Nathan a quick kiss on his bare shoulder—resist a momentary unhinged urge to bite him—and scoot out of bed to begin throwing on my clothes. They're, well, all over the room, and as I snap my bra on, Nathan opens his eyes.

"Hey, there," I say. "Not to alarm you, but we gotta get moving. I'm gonna run back to my room and try not to get caught doing my walk of shame."

"You're ashamed?" he asks, in mock-sadness, pouting out his bottom lip.

"No way. Are you?"

"Hell no. I feel like I won the Super Bowl."

He bounds out of bed and tackles me gently. *And* we're back in bed.

"Nathan, seriously, I gotta go. I'll see you soon. Promise." I wrestle myself out from under him and give him a quick peck on the nose. I open the door and peek out the door.

"Here goes nothing."

* * *

I manage to sneak my way out of his hotel building and back into my own without seeing someone I know. I'm out of breath as I bound in the door of mine and Erin's hotel room.

"I knew you were probably getting some exercise last night, but I had no idea it'd be that bad," she says dryly.

"Good morning."

"Good morning. Or perhaps *excellent* morning?"

"Definitely an excellent morning," I assure her. "I gotta get ready."

I shower quickly and get dressed in a cozy sweater and hiking boots. As we walk into the breakfast room downstairs, I tell Erin in a low tone that I should probably think of a cover story in case someone asks where I was, glancing over at Kevin getting some coffee. She tells me that she went back to the hotel and went to bed shortly after Nathan and I left the party last night, so Erin and I can always tell them we were hanging out elsewhere. Erin's always been pretty solid, but I'm beginning to think that if I never need to bury a body, I know who to call.

* * *

Our first activity for the day is the Alpine Coaster, which turns out to be the brain-child of some thrill-seeker who decided the best way to see the beautiful Utah mountains would be to streak down them at thirty miles per hour in a small cart. On the bus ride over, I'm trying not to think about the YouTube video I watched about it when I first saw the off-site agenda. It's easy since Erin is interrogating me about last night. Unfortunately, Kevin and Maya—CEO and CTO—are sitting right behind us, so I'm bluntly refusing to engage with her.

Unwilling to give up, she starts a game of the dirtiest charades I've ever seen, and when I see her doing a finger-in-a-hole hand signal with raised eyebrows, I get out my phone and text:

Me: What is wrong with you? <tears emoji> Kevin is right behind us.

Erin: So?

Me: <Peach emoji> <pointing up emoji> <lollipop emoji> <bunnies bunnies bunnies>

"This is a work of art," she says. "I'm framing it."

"What're you guys talking about?" Kevin asks, peeking over the seats.

"Nothing," I say looking directly at him. If I look at her, I'll either strangle her or melt from the pressure. "It's just a painting I did for my mom that I was showing Erin the other day."

He gives us a weird look and sits back.

I give her a "You better watch your back, we're out on a remote mountain and I could bury any evidence" look.

"You. Are. A. Mother," I say in a murderous whisper.

We're falling out of our seats laughing by the time we arrive at the coaster site, and I'm just calming down as we start to head off the bus.

Nathan walks up—he rode over on the second bus—and says "Good morning" to Kevin, who's going down the stairs in front of us. He looks up and notices me and says, "Hey, Sarah, what's up?"

"Not much, Nate. How about you?" I say with as much nonchalance as I can muster.

Erin whispers in my ear, from behind me, "Yeah, Nate, enjoy the ride?"

I turn around to glare at her, but she doesn't realize I'm stopping, and bumps into me, making me fall down the stairs.

Nathan notices, and like he's following a script from a movie, catches me before I hit the ground. The only reason I don't hit the ground is, inconveniently, because he's under me.

"Sarah," he whispers, cheeky as hell, in my ear. "If you wanted me that badly, all you had to do was ask."

"Are you okay?" Erin's asking.

"I'm fine," I say.

"I wasn't asking you! I'm asking Nate," she says. I look down, and I see that his hand is bleeding from where he cut it on the rocky gravel of the parking lot.

"You should probably get off of me now," Nathan whispers in my ear. His warm breath and the smirk I see on his face makes my face heat up. I take Kevin's outstretched hand and stand up.

I then hold out my own hand to Nathan to help him up—he's heavy—and between Kevin and me, we haul him off the ground. I take his hand in mine, palm up, to check out the cut.

"I'm so sorry," I say.

"I'm fine. I just need to go wash my hands."

"It actually looks pretty gross."

"Thanks."

I snort. "I'm just saying that I think you need a bandage. Let's go find something. Maybe they have a first aid kit inside."

We walk up together to the lodge where they sell tickets and have a small coffee shop, and I apologize multiple times for being so clumsy.

"It's okay. You didn't do it on purpose."

"I know, but I just feel like it's so obvious I'm into you. I mean, straddling you in the parking lot isn't exactly discreet," I say laughing.

"Maybe it's not the worst thing if people find out," he says, looking at me to judge my reaction.

"I think it's probably not the best idea, for now," I say, and turn to ask the receptionist if they have something to put on his hand.

After he washes his hands and we put on some antibiotic ointment and a bandage, we head back outside. Almost everyone has already gone up the ski lift—to get to the top of the mountain where the coaster begins—and I look at it, wishing I could just stay on the ground.

He sees the look on my face, and asks, surprised, if I'm afraid of heights.

"Actually," I answer, "I am."

"Have you been on a ski lift?"

"Yes, once, and it was terrifying."

"You didn't realize we're gonna go on a ski lift?"

"Does it look like I realized we're gonna go on a ski lift?" I ask, narrowing my eyes at him.

"You don't have to. But if you want to, I'll sit with you. And I promise not to rock it back and forth," he jokes.

"Not funny."

"I'll sit right next to you. I'll hang on to you so tight, you won't even be able to breathe. You won't fall. I promise."

"Okay," I say, scared stiff, but determined. "I'm ready."

"Okay, but you actually gotta get closer to get on. We're like ten feet away from the platform."

"I'm gathering up my courage."

"If you do it," he whispers in my ear, "I'll go down on you again tonight."

Apparently, I'm addicted to the pleasures he can provide because that's all it takes to get my feet moving toward the platform to wait for the ski lift.

* * *

After what seems like seventy-three minutes of torture—but what Nathan promises me was actually only seven short minutes—we arrive at the top. There are small groups of people waiting to get into the coasters. Strangely enough, now that we're up on the mountain, I'm fine. High places—as long as they're the kind assembled by Mother Nature and don't involve precariously dangling from cables—are apparently acceptable in my brain. My fear of sudden death has dropped considerably since we've gotten off the ski lift. The number of groups gradually shrinks, as people make their way screaming down the mountain in a go-cart-like contraption. Soon, only four of us are left: Erin, me, Nathan, and Kevin.

Erin and I are buckling on our required helmets and we're about to get into one of the coasters when the ride instructor looks at me and Erin and then at Kevin and Nathan. "You ladies should probably split up. These guys are kinda big, and they're not gonna fit in one together." Erin already has one foot in the coaster at this point, and the ride instructor gestures to Kevin,

"Can you ride with her instead?"

Kevin nods and tells Nathan over his shoulder, "I didn't want to spoon you anyways, dude," and jumps in behind her. They're off, and it's just me and Nathan left.

"Ready?" he asks me, holding out his hand.

"Not really, but I guess it's better than taking the ski lift down," I say and let him help me into the coaster.

We squeeze in—it's a tight fit with a six-foot-plus man behind me—and he wraps his arms around my waist, giving me a bear hug, but at the same time being careful with his bandaged hand. I give him another "sorry" look and tell him, "You're the best, keeping me from falling on my face."

"I couldn't let you mess up your beautiful face, now could I?"

I turn around and put my helmeted forehead against his. No amount of puckering my lips is enough to make mine reach his for a kiss and we laugh. Instead, he slips his hand up my short jacket and gently squeezes one of my breasts. The instructor catches us and raises his eyebrows as if to say "My lips are sealed" and pulls the lever. We careen down the mountain screaming like banshees.

❋ ❋ ❋

We've had lunch and have completed another team-building event—a scavenger hunt in the city. The engineering team won, with the combined sales and customer success team coming in second. A long day of activities following a long night of drunkenness means we're all exhausted, and when we arrive back at the hotel, everyone disperses to their rooms, desperate for late-afternoon naps. Nathan has a meeting with Kevin and the other C-levels this afternoon, but slips me his key card and tells me he'd love for me to be waiting for him when he's done in an hour.

I make my way to his room and decide that I'll take a nap, too. Last night's activities definitely kept me from sleeping enough. Once inside, I slip off my jacket and decide that before I rest, I'll take a quick shower.

I take my time getting undressed, put some music on my phone, and put my hair up in a ponytail. I light the fireplace and start the shower. The warm water feels great after a long, cold day, and I soap myself up. I'm almost done when I hear the door click. Startled—it's too early for Nathan to be back—I see him peek in the door with a grin on his face.

"Oh! I was hoping that was you," I say.

"I was hoping that was *you*," he jokes. "Any chance I can join you?"

"As a spectator or participant?"

His jaw drops. "Just when I thought you couldn't get any better, you say something like that."

He takes his shirt off in an instant and is hopping out of his jeans and boxers.

He opens the glass doors, letting in a quick burst of cooler air, and then joins me, wrapping his arms around my still soapy body.

"Is your hand gonna be okay?"

"It'll be fine," he assures me, coming close. "Press your body against me."

"What happened to your meeting?" I ask.

"I told them I had to leave early because there's a hot . . . wet . . . sex-goddess waiting for me in the shower." His speech is punctuated by kisses. I feel his lips curled up in a smile, whenever they touch my skin.

"No, you didn't."

"You're right; I didn't. But I'm not wrong, am I?" he says playfully and pinches my butt. His roving fingers trace down my spine and settle on my hips, pulling me in closer to him.

While we've been talking, the spray has rinsed off all the soap, and he starts to kiss my clean, slippery shoulders and chest, bending down in a funny way to reach them. I can tell it's uncomfortable, and I go up on my tiptoes to make it easier for him.

"Can you turn around?" he asks. "I wanna touch you from behind."

* * *

Just the thought of her hard nipples—let alone the feel of them on his wet fingertips—is almost too much for him to take. He needs to slow things down a bit, which is why he asks her to turn around. She gives him a questioning look, but he kisses her on the cheek to reassure her, and as she turns around, she bumps him with the side of her hip and smiles mischievously.

He faces her toward the shower wall, wraps one arm around her, so she won't slip, and kisses the side of her neck as she leans into him. Earlier today in the confined quarters of the coaster, he sat behind her and caressed her bare skin, under her clothes, anywhere he could, the whole way down the mountain. Since then, he's been having fantasies about what they'd do later in the day, but this particular scenario hadn't occurred to him. When he'd come into the bathroom and found her completely naked, the hot water running over her body, soaping herself up, he'd had to take a deep breath to calm himself and convince himself it was real.

The only thing between them is the warm water and it's doing its job to keep things moving smoothly. He's rubbing the front of his body against the back of her. He joined her in the shower only minutes ago, but it hasn't taken him long to get into the game they're playing.

He lets his hands roam down the front of her body, stopping to play with her nipples and then curving underneath both of her breasts, bouncing them lightly. He's enjoying himself immensely when Sarah takes it up a notch, guiding one of his hands lower, and slipping it between her legs. It's a perfect angle, an angle sent from geometry heaven. *Thank you, Euclid.* He uses one of his arms to pull her in close to him and grab her breast, all the while stroking her below with his other hand.

He's using two fingers to rub her clit and slowly moving back and forth, every few strokes, he takes a small break to massage her opening. She's moving with him, encouraging him to do more, and her hand is gripping his own on her breast. She turns her head toward him, her breath shaky, and asks if she can do something for him. He shakes his head.

"Stay there. I want you to come, while I finger you," he says.

* * *

Just hearing him say it out loud makes me groan audibly, and I stick my ass out to put me in an even better position. The length of his hardness rubs, slick, between my legs, as he enters me fully with his fingers. The pressure, the rhythm, all of it is nothing short of amazing.

He's sliding his fingers into me, fast and furious when I decide to take control. I pat his hand to indicate that I want to do something different. I turn around and begin to stroke him, pulling him—lightly, but the message is clear—toward me. There's a ledge at just the right height in the shower, and I rest myself on it and lean back, spreading my legs, an invitation to Nathan. I'm a little shocked at my own directness but feel unable to stop myself. At this point, it's a foregone conclusion what's about to happen, and I'm just leading us there. I imagine his hands on me earlier, in the coaster, as we rocketed down the mountain. Right before the instructor pulled the lever, Nathan had wrapped his hands around my waist and explored inside the waistband of my jeans, discovering the naughty underwear I was wearing.

"Do you always wear such sexy underwear on roller coasters?" he had asked and smiled.

"Just for special occasions," I'd responded.

All the way down the mountain, I could feel his strong legs wrapped around me and his arms holding me tight. In the blink of an eye, I allow myself to remember it now, but bring myself back to the present, where a wet, naked, pulsating-from-excitement man is standing in the steamy shower, eyes on me. He looks down to where my hand is stroking him, moving up and down rhythmically, and I let go to grab his hips with both hands and pull him into me in one flawless motion.

I gasp at the feeling of his hard flesh filling me, and begin to chant his name—"Nathan, yes"—to the rhythm of his thrusts like my life depends on it. Like if *I* stop, he will, and that's not an option. He's turned on—wild—and can barely keep it together. He's grabbing my shoulder with one hand, and my ass with the other, and I have a brief, admittedly deranged thought, wondering if this is how we both die—found by the hotel cleaning staff in the morning, either drowned by the shower spray or crumpled on the floor with broken necks from slipping. He's close, and I tense my muscles inside and that does him in. He comes, shuddering, and begins to gently release the pressure of his hands on me.

He takes a deep breath and wipes his hand down his face, steadying himself.

"Jesus Christ, Sarah," he gasps. "Are you human?" He can barely get the words out. Panting, more than talking.

I start laughing, giddy with endorphins, and he joins in. As we regain our breath and our heartbeats slow down, I ask him if he'd like to continue our festivities on dry land.

"Yes," he says, reaching to turn off the shower. I grab a big, fluffy towel from the small table outside the shower and wrap it around his broad shoulders. While he dries himself, I grab another towel and begin to dry my hair. While I stand there—still naked—squeezing a bit of the water out of my hair, he runs his finger down my spine, all the way to my waist, and I squeal.

"It's so wet in here, I thought we were gonna fall and die."

"The thought crossed my mind as well."

"Worth it," we say at the same time, and crack up.

"I told you last night that I won't let you fall. Look, I've even got the scar to prove it," he says, holding up his injured hand and pouting. I hold up his palm and kiss his wrist and then put his hand to my heart, pulling him closer. He takes advantage of the proximity to pick me up, wrap my legs around his waist, and carry me to the bedroom.

* * *

"Couch or bed?" he asks, still holding her and raising an

eyebrow in question.

"So soon?"

"I'm pretty sure you didn't come just now, at least not all the way."

"Closet, then."

"What?" he says, snickering.

"Floor."

"*That* can be arranged," he says, holding her tight with one hand while pulling the blanket off the bed and laying it a few feet away from the fireplace.

"No bear rug?"

"Trick question. You're a vegetarian."

"You think of everything, I'm surprised there are no chocolate-covered strawberries and champagne already chilling on the table."

There's a knock at the door.

"Who is that?" she says and begins to have a minor freak out.

"You *said* you wanted champagne," he says, teasingly.

"I was joking. It's not really champagne, is it?" she asks, unbelieving.

"I guess we won't know if we don't open the door," he says, but he does know. He's the one who ordered the food. "Stay here," he says, winking at her. "I'll go check."

He wraps the bottom half of his body in one of the towels and sees her eyes roam up and down his body appreciatively. Nathan looks through the peephole, just to make sure it's what he thinks it is, and then opens the door and pulls in a little cart with a tray on it.

"Sorry I didn't think about the strawberries," he tells her. "I did order champagne and some sandwiches. I thought we might get hungry later."

"Very practical," she says. "But sandwiches can wait. I have other plans."

"Now *you* have plans, huh? How the tables have turned," he says.

"I've had plans for two months or at least ideas. Didn't know they'd actually happen, though."

"You're a project manager. It's your job to *make* things happen."

"I certainly know how to manage releases pretty well." She snorts, gesturing at the site of recent releases with one hand while taking the champagne flute he's offering her in the other.

They laugh for a minute, just sitting on the floor in towels and drinking champagne. He sets his champagne down and leans back on his good hand, with his legs out in front of him.

"You look super-relaxed," she tells him.

"Yes. And tired," he says. "Good tired."

"Nathan, I know your family's going through a lot now, with your dad, so I just wanted you to know that I'm really happy you came here this week. Or, I guess, that your brother and mom forced you to come. To . . . I guess, at least a little bit, to see me."

He holds up his fingers close together. "Just a little bit," he says.

"How'd you end up back up here early? Why was the meeting so short?"

"Oh, Kevin was just updating us all on the investor talks. Just didn't take long."

"Something important?"

"Yeah, I guess so. I can't really talk about it yet, though . . . I'm sorry, I know that's kind of a weird thing to say to a person you just had shower sex with. But you'll find out soon, and we have more important things going on here."

"Drinking champagne?"

"Other things."

"Eating sandwiches?"

"Other things."

"Surely you don't mean . . . sex," she whispers, salaciously.

"Getting closer," he grins.

"Why don't *you* get closer?" she says, pulling him into her arms.

❊ ❊ ❊

He kisses me, tasting of champagne, and it just strengthens the buzz I'm feeling from my own. Drinking champagne, mostly naked, with a sexy man in front of a fire has to be among the top five romantic situations a woman can encounter. Feeling like I'm trying to check off half my sex bucket list in way too little time, but perfectly willing to attempt the challenge, I return his slow, intentional kisses, and he lays me down gently on the blanket. I'm facing the fire, entranced by the flickering light, the champagne bubbles still dancing on my tongue and in my head, and Nathan's fingers tracing patterns on my skin. He's not rushing anywhere or anything. It's still early in the night, many hours before we'll wake tomorrow and be forced to go back to the real world. His father's illness, the rules and expectations of work, whatever pressures the outside world with other people places on us.

We must be tired, relaxed, and just a tiny bit drunk. Somehow, despite lying on the floor, we fall asleep. When I wake, Nathan's arms are still around me. He's the big spoon to my little one. He must feel me move because his fingertips resume the tracing he left off hours ago.

"One last time?" I ask, drowsily.

"I certainly hope it's not the last time."

"You know what I mean. Make it count, Dr. Goldman," I tease, as he rolls me over on my back and crawls on top of me.

"I think I was dreaming about you," he tells me, touching himself, with a surprised little smile on his face. It's then I notice he's already *very* aroused, more than ready. I touch myself, too, while I watch him move his hand slowly up and down, readying himself just a bit more.

"Oh my god. You're gonna kill me. It's so hot watching you do that," he says, in a low voice.

"Same," I reply and bite my lip as I watch him stroke himself.

"I wanna put it inside of you and watch your beautiful face while I make you come for me, slow this time."

"Yes, please," I breathe out and smile.

He pushes himself inside of me while kissing me deeply.

Somehow, despite the minimal foreplay, we're both ready, and his movements inside of me—that start out slow and romantic —speed up. I'm there for it, bending my knees and wrapping my legs around his body. He's so deep, and I cry out.

"Is it good, Sarah?"

"Yes."

"How good?" he asks, urging me to tell him. He wants to hear me say it. So, I do.

"Fucking amazing, Nathan. Come. Now. I can't take much more."

He bites my ear playfully, and then he speeds up his pace, and my mind is blown for the fourth time in half as many days. I cry out, this time louder, unable to control myself, and I feel him shudder in me, as he, too, lets go.

DOWNTIME

We're lying together next to the fireplace, recovering from our recent exertions, when my stomach growls. Making love in such a warm environment must burn extra calories.

Nathan gives me a skeptical look. "You're kind of small to need so much food, you know," he teases.

"It takes a lot of fuel to burn this hot, baby," I joke.

Nathan asks if I want one of the sandwiches from before.

"Am I super-lame or super-awesome if I say yes? Actually, I don't care. Yes, I need a sandwich."

I go to the bathroom to clean up a bit, and come back and put on one of his t-shirts I see on top of his bag. It smells like him. He must have worn it recently. I open the cover on the tray and choose an avocado toast that looks delicious.

"Should I wait?" I ask him.

"No, go ahead. I'll be out in a bit. Gonna take a shower," he says, and he goes into the bathroom.

I hear the water turn on, and pick up my phone, which is next to Nathan's. I have a few messages from Erin, mostly suggestive emojis, a couple texts from Camila (things like "So?" "What's happening?") and another one she sent on our group text with Erin that says, "You Bs better not be keeping any details from me."

I text her back a kiss emoji. Erin responds with an inordinate number of sex-related emojis. I text them both a middle finger and a laughing emoji.

Nathan's phone buzzes on the table, and I see a string of texts pop up from "Dan."

Dan: Got your message. IMO our night went really well.

Dan: Homerun with Eden. Maybe only 3rd base for us <fire emoji>

Dan: No regrets here. Let's pick up where we left off.

Dan: And I def wanna hear more about those "other ways" you wanna help me. <wink emoji> Like the old days?

I'm trying to figure out if I smoked something and don't remember, or if someone named "Dan" is actually sending Nathan suggestive—well, there's not much left to the imagination—text messages. *Who is Da—?* Before I even finish the thought, I know. Danica. *Fucking A.*

But even in my rattled—no, shattered—state, I think "it takes two." He's as much to blame as she is. *More.*

My breath catches in my throat as something darker and heavier than simple jealousy descends upon me. For two months, I've watched Danica around Nathan, the familiarity and easiness with which she talks to him and touches him. I've wondered what exactly is going on between them, and as Nathan and I have gotten to know each other more, as we've grown closer, I've wanted to ask him but never had the guts. And then, my conversation with Kevin at the airport suddenly makes a lot more sense, and carries a lot more weight.

"Nate and Danica used to date," he'd said. "She's doing a lot to get back in his good graces." What exactly has she been doing? What has *he* been doing?

I look at the texts on his lock screen now. He told me that nothing happened between them, so what the fuck is this "third base" talk? What "regrets" would, or should, he be feeling? The night after the partner event, he'd shown up to my apartment and spilled it all. Or so I thought. He'd told me that she *wanted* to kiss him. Did he say that she *did* kiss him? But he told her *wanted* to be kissing someone else. Was that before or after something happened between them? And what "other ways" did he offer to help her out?

A bleak, poisonous feeling is swirling in my stomach and my heart is racing. Did he lie to me? Does he have something going on with her? Is he playing me?

"*He was drunk that night,*" a cynical voice says in my head. "*You don't actually know what happened before he finally made it to your place.*"

"*Very late at night,*" the voice adds, a beat later. "*Just imagine all the things they could've done together earlier.*"

I look at the champagne flute still in my hand and think about the approximately 10,000 kisses we've shared in the last thirty-six hours, and it takes all the restraint I have not to throw it at the fireplace.

My mind is racing when another text comes in. A picture. His phone is still locked, but even in the tiny thumbnail, I can tell it's a thirst trap: A selfie, angled just right to see right down her low-cut t-shirt, and she's wearing short (or *no?*) shorts. She's biting her lip and her expression is, honestly, a lot like the one I've been giving Nathan the past two days and look where that ended up.

Fuck my life. And *that* is when I throw the champagne flute in the fireplace.

Nathan comes out of the shower a minute or two later, with a towel around his waist, while I thrash around the room, moving like a madwoman through the slightly chaotic results of our recent love-making.

"Everything okay?" he asks. "I thought I heard something break. Did something fall?"

I've taken off his t-shirt, and I'm yanking on my own clothes, facing away from him, and I don't even turn around. If I do, I'll either scream or cry or both, and I feel like I'm going to shatter into a thousand tiny pieces like the champagne flute I just obliterated.

"Sarah," he says, growing concern in his voice. "What's going on? Why are you getting dressed? I thought we were gonna eat together."

I turn and shoot him an incredulous look. He tilts his head, looking confused. He almost looks comical and if I weren't about to explode, I might have the urge to laugh.

"No," I say, with no emotion. "I'm gonna go. I need to pack. I have to leave early for my flight back to San Jose tomorrow."

I'm standing there in just my bra and jeans since I can't seem to find my shirt anywhere. I'm flustered—it's clear—my skin is probably patchy red, and I'm running my hands through my hair. "Where is my . . . fucking shirt?" I say, frustrated.

"Did something happen?" Nathan's still totally confused. He almost looks cute, but that fact is completely by overshadowed by my current desire to strangle him.

He sees my phone in my hand. "Did you get bad news? A call or text or something?"

"No," I answer coldly. "But you did."

I've found my shirt by now, and I'm pulling it over my head.

"Nathan," I say, pulling on my boots, not even slowing to zip them all the way. I hastily grab my bag. "I . . ." but I can't even continue. I'm so hurt and confused and just plain livid. I take a deep breath—I need to say this, to be okay with myself, even if I can't be okay with him. "Tell your dad I wish him the best. I really hope the treatment works and he gets better."

"Sarah! Wait. What the hell is going on? Why are you acting so crazy? I thought we were gonna spend more time together before we leave tomorrow."

"Check your fucking phone, Nathan. There's someone there who'd just love to spend some time with you."

And I walk out and slam the door, wishing Nathan had never come into my life.

❊ ❊ ❊

As I rush away from Nathan's hotel room back to the one I'm at least theoretically sharing with Erin, there's a small part of me—miniscule—that hopes he'll open the door, come after me, and explain that it was somehow all a big misunderstanding. But it doesn't happen—maybe for practical reasons, it's twenty-nine degrees outside and he just got out of the shower, or maybe because he doesn't have a good excuse. He and Danica were at some point . . . something . . . and she obviously feels comfortable enough with him to send him half-naked selfies.

I want to just sit outside and be alone, but I've left my coat in Nathan's room, and there's no way in hell I'm going back there. I decide that being found frozen solid in the morning by the Park City police is at least a little bit worse than I currently feel right now, so I use my key card to open the door to the stairwell of the building where my hotel room is. It's not likely this time of night, but I don't want to risk running into anyone in the elevator. I take my time trudging up the stairs. The stairwell is dimly lit, cold, and smells of concrete and chemicals. An abrasive, unpleasant smell, well-suited to my mood right now.

I finally make it up to my floor and reach the door to my room. It's 1:00 a.m., so there's a good chance Erin will be asleep. I'm grateful because I might crumble if I have to explain to her why I came back, why my face is streaked with tears. I enter quietly and see her curled up shape, sound asleep under the blankets. With literally no energy whatsoever to brush my teeth or change into pajamas, I crawl into bed and fall asleep. But it's a restless sleep. My dreams, not shockingly, feature Nathan and start off highly sexual, but turn vicious.

He's caressing my body and just as I start to feel comfortable, a strange and sinister version of him with dark, mean eyes sneers at me and says terrible things. "Why would I ever choose you? It was just convenient. You're so easy to fool."

I wake as light comes through the curtains, too early even for me, and gasp for breath as if I've run hundreds of miles during the night, chased by wolves or worse. I'm still half asleep, but my mind is already busy. *Did they kiss? Did they do more? Did he enjoy it? Did he lie to me?*

I thought he was a good guy. *How could I have been so wrong?* I begin to doubt my own judgment. *Have I misread this whole situation? How bad of a judge of character must I be to have fallen for a guy who could be with two women in the same night?*

As a bit more light begins to enter the room, I take a look at the clock—5:57. Erin is still asleep, and I wonder what are the chances of me being able to pack everything and leave before she wakes. I'm so sad, so . . . so embarrassed. I've made a fool of myself, falling into this with Nathan. It would be one thing if I was thinking about it the same way he apparently was—a good, convenient, close-proximity lay. But the way I'm taking this news about Danica is evidence enough that I was already considering that maybe it could turn into more.

I have about an hour before I need to leave for the SLC airport, but decide that maybe I'll just go early. I could use a shower, but decide a change of clothes is sufficient. Thinking about a shower in this hotel—and with whom I shared one last night—makes me feel nauseous. I'll just brush my teeth, throw all my stuff in my bag, and head out. If Erin wakes up, I'll be on my way out, and I can just tell her that my flight changed and I'm running late for the airport.

I somehow manage to get out of there without waking her, and when I gently shut the door, I see my coat hanging on the doorknob, my favorite pashmina scarf on top of it. I put my coat on and wrap the scarf around my neck—its softness a salve, however inadequate, to my raw and tender feelings—and head down the hall to the elevator. For the first time all morning, I open up my phone so I can order an Uber. My lock screen has tons of messages on it, almost all of them from Nathan.

12:57: Sarah, what's going on?

12:59: Are you ok?

1:04: Are you back in your room?

1:09: I'm coming to look for you.

1:16: Ok, I see your scarf on the floor outside your door, so I guess you're inside.

1:22: Can you please respond, so I know you're ok?

1:25: Sarah, I know you saw the message from D. That has to be what upset you. It's not what it sounds like.

1:34: Fuck, I know it looks really bad, but I swear to god, it's totally one-sided. From HER side. Please give me a chance to explain.

1:39: I'm going back to my room.

1:54: Please text or call me in the morning. I need to talk to you.

6:15: When are you leaving for the airport today? I want to see you before you go.

It's 6:26 now. My Uber will arrive in seven minutes.

It's 6:33 when I get in the car and leave Park City—and Nathan—behind. I put my phone on silent and hide it in my bag. I need a break. I just want to get home to a normal-temperature climate and spend the weekend watching Russian Doll or some other weird, tragic TV shows to give my mind a break.

But my self-imposed phone break lasts only as long as the ride from Park City to SLC. When I get to the airport, I have to turn it on to show the airline staff my e-ticket to get my printed boarding pass.

When I open it, I see I have more messages from Nate and a few missed calls.

Nathan: I can't believe you left already.

Nathan: I need to talk to you. I need you to understand what's going on.

Nathan: I need you to understand how I feel about you.

That one makes me sit up and pay attention.

"How do you feel about me?" I type, but leave it unsent.

I turn off my phone before I go through security and leave it off until I reach San Jose.

✳ ✳ ✳

Once I'm home, I make myself a coffee and decide that maybe caffeine and sugar will give me enough fortitude to listen to the two voicemails Nathan left me while I was on the plane.

I press "play":

"Sarah, I'm not even entirely sure what to say, because I've been having a monologue with myself for the past twelve hours, and I don't know what you're thinking or feeling."

There's a pause and I can hear his sigh.

"I'm sorry you saw that, but it's really not what's going on in reality. Well, I don't know what you think *is* going on, but if it made you leave and not respond to me for twelve hours, then I can imagine what you're thinking."

"That you have something going on with Danica," I say bitterly, in my empty apartment.

"I *had* something with Danica a long time ago," I hear his voice say from my phone speaker.

"*What the hell, Nathan?*" I yell, throwing my phone on the couch, but then rush to retrieve it almost as quickly so I can hear the rest of the message.

"In college. It was only for a couple months, and I ended it. I guess she still thinks we could, I don't know, be something. I should've told—"

The voicemail is cut off there.

There's a second one.

"Sarah, god this is so hard. I don't know how you're gonna respond, and I'm just putting myself out here on a voicemail that you might never listen to, or maybe you'll share it with your friends while you stick pins in a voodoo doll version of me."

Despite my rage and sadness, a small, tired, desperate laugh manages to escape from me. But I steel myself and continue to listen, determined to feel angry. *I deserve to.*

"I'm heading to the airport soon to fly back to Seattle. My dad's not doing well. I'm not saying that so you feel sorry for me and forgive me. Just because . . . you matter to me. I want you to know what's going on with me. And I want to know what's going on with you. My world just feels smaller without you in it. Because I care about you. And I know we've only known each other a couple months, but you . . . you matter to me already. Please just call me later today? I need to hear your voice and know you're okay. And that maybe . . . maybe we can be okay."

I know he's hurting. *Well, maybe not. Maybe he's just put out because he's been caught playing at something.* I'm bitter, and I go into self-preservation mode. I turn off my phone, binge-watch "Outlander," wish I had my own Jamie, and listen to sad, sad music.

THREE WEEKS EARLIER

LGTM

Mid-week, Nathan gets a message. He's hoping either, one, that it's not his mom with bad news, or two, that it *is* Sarah with . . . pretty much anything. They've both been busy, so they've mostly been sending each other emojis or dumb memes, but she always makes him smile.

But it's option three, Danica:

Danica: Wanna see my dress for Saturday night?

Before he can respond, she's sent him a selfie, in a little black dress, "little" being the operational word.

Danica: Wdyt?

He tries to think of something he can text back that'll get her off his back but not offend her and suffices with a simple "Wow."

Danica: Can't wait to hang out Saturday.

He texts back a <martini emoji> and "See you later," hoping that's enough.

It's Saturday, and while he tries not to check his work email on weekends, he wants to review a few of the talking points he and Kevin went over, in case they come up when they—hopefully—meet Eden Snow later tonight. He opens his computer and sees he has a few new Slacks from yesterday evening.

> **@EPark (she/her)**: Hey Nate—just wanted you to know that I invited the TPM team. I know they don't usually come to these events, but thought you might be interested to know they're coming on Saturday night. Hope you can say hello and have a drink.

Nathan sits there a little confused. *TPM team?* Erin is a strategic program manager and doesn't have a team, per se.

The only person she works with in program management is . . . Sarah. *Of course. I* am *interested to know. Thank you, Erin.* He bites his lip and finds himself suddenly looking forward to tonight a lot more than he was before.

❋ ❋ ❋

He spends most of the partner event doing his job—talking to people, making connections—but no matter how hard he tries, he seems to be unable to get any closer to Sarah or any further away from Danica. Almost two hours pass before he has a chance to break away—begging a restroom break—to follow Sarah out to the side balcony he saw her heading toward a few minutes ago. Their time alone doesn't last long, but he does manage to give her a compliment, far less eloquent than everything he was thinking he would say to her. *Smooth.*

Just when he begins to calculate the odds of anybody inside noticing if he just starts making out with her here on the balcony, right now, Kevin—and his new LightVerse entourage, Danica and Amy—join them and his fate is sealed. No Sarah, at least not now. They're heading out for Palo Alto now, where Danica has confirmed Eden Snow is having dinner tonight.

He can't just let Sarah go, without telling her—without showing her—what he wants. What—who—he wants tonight is her.

Luckily, she's on the same page as him, which makes it that much harder to leave her in the hotel garden. But before things can proceed, Kevin's calling his phone and then his name, from somewhere on the other side of the hedge.

How am I leaving her here by herself when it's the last thing on earth I want to do?

But he does. He leaves. Kevin must know Nathan is lying when he tells him he was calling his parents. Nathan *knows* Kevin knows because Kevin is a snarky asshole at his core, who can't help but make a thinly-veiled comment about how great Sarah looked tonight.

He tells Kevin to shut up and tries to accept that he just has to make it through the next couple of hours for Kevin's sake, for the company's sake. He wonders what price he'll end up paying, as he looks toward the entrance to the hotel where Danica and Amy are waiting for them.

"Let's go," Kevin says cheerfully. "The night is young." Nathan wants to wipe the smirk off Kevin's face, but just swallows and follows him up to the driveway to wait for the valet to bring Kevin's Tesla.

❉ ❉ ❉

On the ride from downtown San Jose to Palo Alto, Nathan sits in the back seat of Kevin's car with Danica. She's talking to him about all sorts of things, and he's trying to be respectful in his responses, but not so much that she'll keep talking. She talks. A lot.

At one point on the ride, Danica, Kevin, and Amy, who's sitting in the front passenger seat, discuss how it is working at LightVerse. Nathan takes the opportunity to close his eyes, hopefully hinting to Danica—should she decide to start up again —that he's resting. With his eyes closed, he thinks about Sarah and how beautiful she looked when she walked in the door of the hotel ballroom earlier. He thinks about their brief—but hot— make-out session in the gardens, before Kevin interrupted them. He allows himself to imagine how things might have progressed had he and Sarah been left undisturbed.

They're stopped at a traffic light when Kevin mentions they need to find parking. He opens his eyes and looks out the window. Expensive cars as far as the eye can see. *Palo Alto.* And a homeless man, sleeping on the sidewalk on a side street, next to the picture window of a high-end home goods store. *Also Palo Alto.*

He glances away and notices Danica looking at him, thoughtfully, and smiling.

"You're cute when you sleep," she says. "I'd forgotten that."

He realizes she's referring to when they dated in college. He gives her a stiff smile.

"Then again," she says, leaning over to whisper in his ear suggestively, "we didn't do a whole lot of sleeping back then." Alarms bells go off in his head.

When they find a place to park a few minutes later, Nathan is more than happy to get out of the car and put some space between himself and Danica. They walk over to the area where the LightVerse event is taking place, and Kevin and Nathan start to head toward the club entrance, but Danica stops them and tells them that Eden is actually having dinner with some people at the restaurant on the roof. Kevin exchanges a look with Nathan, like, *"See, it's all worth it. We're gonna get what we need tonight."* Nathan nods and they follow her into the elevator.

When they reach the top floor, a *very* nice place that so seamlessly blends the outdoors with the indoors, he can't quite pin down where they are, they see a group of people, including Eden Snow, in the corner of the rooftop terrace. Danica confidently walks over to a woman sitting with the group and gives her a hug and kiss. The woman gives her a knowing smile and begins to introduce Danica and Amy—both LightVerse employees.

"Stars on our GTM strategy team," she says to the group. "Who are your friends?" she asks Danica, knowing the answer already.

"I'm Kevin Wong and this is Nathan Goldman," Kevin says in a natural manner, but one that Nathan is sure he rehearsed in front of the mirror at least a hundred times. "We're with Instinqt. I'm the CEO and Nate's our Chief Product Officer."

A man sitting next to Eden leans in and whispers something to Eden, who then speaks up. "I think your name came up this week, during our e-staff meeting. In the AI space, going for a Series B, soon, right?"

Nathan knows that Kevin could not have asked for more. This is the opening, the chance, he has probably had wet dreams about. Kevin smoothly walks over to Eden and begins to talk with him more, and Eden invites him to sit.

"We're just having dessert, but you guys are welcome to join us for a bit, if you'd like."

Kevin glances at Nathan and raises his eyebrows just the slightest bit, an expression Nathan knows means, "Fuck, yeah," and Nathan smiles and says they'd love to. He has to admit it—Danica has pulled it off. She's gotten them the connection they need. They're literally sitting at dinner *with Eden Snow* talking about their startup. He looks over at her, so he can whisper "thank you" and notices she's already looking at him with a pleased expression on her face.

❅ ❅ ❅

Despite all his best intentions, Nathan finds himself sitting on a sofa with Danica draped around him in the corner of a club on Willow Street come midnight. They ended up spending half an hour at Eden Snow's dinner, talking business, technology, and more with Eden and his dinner companions. And Kevin and Nathan left—utterly dumbstruck by their good luck—with the name and email of Eden's executive assistant and an invitation to set up a meeting to talk more.

Kevin is in a great mood, envisioning the next big step for Instinqt, and he's bought them all another round. Nathan, frankly, is ready to leave now but hasn't yet been able to escape either Kevin's clutches or Danica's.

"One more drink, and then you can go home to bed, Dr. Goldman," Kevin, says in a sing-songy voice while putting his arm around Nathan.

"*Dr.* Goldman?" Danica says. "Nate, I didn't realize you'd finished your PhD. Impressive."

"Yeah, it's okay," he says, with a tight smile.

"You know," she says, talking closely to his ear, due to the loud music. "I've never slept with a doctor."

Kevin seems to have overheard, and when Nathan slowly turns his head away from Danica to ask Kevin to save him, Kevin's looking at him with a maniacal smile and amusement in his eyes.

"Me, either, Nate," he says, drunk, and cracks up.

Nathan decides it's time to go and swivels around to see if

he can scoot by Danica, who's barricaded him in the couch area they're sitting in. Just as he turns his head, she leans in, takes his hand, and places it high on her inner thigh—very high.

"I think we should give things another chance, Nate, don't you?" she says. "Back then, we were just kids. Now, well, we know a lot more, don't we?" Not waiting for him to answer, she leans in and kisses him with full, eager lips.

It takes him a moment to register what's happening. He'd like to say that he stopped her immediately, but he doesn't. Danica and her mouth know what she wants. She knows what she's doing—well. Like, back when they were in college, but she's even more sure of herself now than then, the benefit of eight years of experience under her belt. What's under his belt is what he's thinking with.

But some piece of his mind is still in the present, still working, despite all the blood going elsewhere. It's late. It's loud. He's had more than a few drinks, and it's been a long night. His body —primed now for earthly pleasures—is at odds with his mind. His thoughts are muddled, and his muscles, taut, are tense for the wrong reasons. It's as if he's been swimming through rough waters, trying to reach a shore, and he's exhausted—physically, emotionally. He's happy for Kevin, but he doesn't want to be here in this club right now. He doesn't want to keep playing this game with Danica for Kevin to achieve his own dream. He doesn't want to be kissing Danica.

And that is the thought that drags him from the warmth of her mouth. He opens his eyes, and he knows. He doesn't want to be kissing her. He doesn't want to be kissing *her*, because he wants to be kissing someone else.

"*What* did you say?" She's looking at him, eyebrows raised in shock.

He realizes with a start that he's said it out loud. *I want to be kissing someone else.*

"I'm sorry, Danica."

"You're *sorry*?"

Nathan just stares at her dumbly, silently. He's at a loss

for words. He imagines he's already, inadvertently, said the important ones. He turns to see Kevin and Amy, who were talking and joking up until a few seconds ago, staring at him.

"What's going on, Nate? You okay?" Kevin asks.

"No, he's not okay. He likes to play games," Danica says sharply, shooting daggers at him with her eyes.

Nathan, still shocked, thinks to himself that she's right—partially. He *has* been playing games, but not ones he enjoyed.

"Should we go?" Amy asks Danica, looking uncomfortable with the whole situation unfolding before them.

"Yes," Danica says, getting up and grabbing her bag. Never one to let a good opportunity for drama go to waste, though, she leans down to stare at Nathan eye-to-eye, giving him a front-row seat to her cleavage, and whispers, "You should really learn to relax and appreciate a good offer, Nate."

"Danica, I'm so—" Nathan says, starting to apologize.

"I'm outta here. I don't have time for this shit."

❊ ❊ ❊

Kevin and Nathan are just staring at each other, wondering what just happened when suddenly Kevin just starts laughing his ass off. Nathan is still shell-shocked, but seeing Kevin absolutely lose it starts to make him laugh, too. And they're both red-faced and cracking up for a few good minutes before they're able to talk normally.

"I'm sorry, dude," Kevin says to him.

"What are *you* sorry for?"

"For making you contact your crazy ex-girlfriend and making you hang out with her and . . . whatever. She's hot, and she did us a real solid, but god damn, I forgot how erratic she can be."

Nathan sighs and takes a sip of his cocktail. "She's not crazy. She just . . . she knows what she wants, I guess." He wonders if he shouldn't be more like her, at least in that respect. "Well, I guess you got what you needed with Eden, huh?"

"If she doesn't sabotage us," Kevin says, glancing nervously over to the door Danica and Amy left from a few minutes ago.

"She won't. It wouldn't look good for her either."

"Yeah, I guess you're right," Kevin says, nodding.

"Weird night, huh?"

"Weird. And I know you just got blasted by Danica, but . . . it was still a good night. Can you believe it? We just had dinner with Eden-Fucking-Snow. And did you see Jason Calacanis at the next table?"

"Yeah," Nathan replies, trying to muster the enthusiasm he knows Kevin expects from him after such a night.

But he can't help but put his head in his hands and run his fingers through his hair. He's exhausted—physically and emotionally.

"You gonna be okay?" Kevin asks.

"I will. I'm just tired, man. And I was hoping tonight might end a little differently, I guess. And . . . there's just all this shit going down with my dad. I must be a sad drunk, huh?"

"Well, if you wanna talk about it, we can leave, go somewhere quieter."

"Nah, it's okay. I need a break from thinking about it," Nathan tells him. "And all of this," he says, moving his hands in a vague manner meant to include the club, Danica, maybe all of Silicon Valley. Just then their colleague Erin—of all people—walks over to their table with a guy who has his arm around her waist.

"Hey, guys. Keeping the party going?" she asks.

"How are you still out? Don't you have kids?" Kevin asks.

"We have a kid," she says. "And this," she gestures at the man with her, "is my partner, Ryan. Life doesn't end when you have kids, Kev. We got a babysitter for the night, and we're pretending to be young again. Amy from LightVerse told me earlier this week that they were having a party tonight and put us on the guest list."

"Small world," Nathan says.

"Mind if we join you?" Erin asks, and sits down, inviting Ryan to do the same, before they have a chance to respond. "What are you guys doing all alone anyways?"

Kevin and Nathan exchange rueful glances. They're all silent for a beat, when Nathan, deciding that he is the master of his own fate, has a sudden inspiration. While Kevin talks to Ryan, he asks Erin if she knows where Sarah lives.

"I do," she tells him, eyes twinkling.

"Here, type it in my phone. I'm going over there."

"You are? You know it's almost 1:00 a.m., right?"

"You're right. I probably shouldn't."

"No, no, no," she says quickly, with a sly grin. "You definitely *should*. I'm just saying that if you go now—*when* you go now—you better bring your A-game."

Nathan grins like a little kid, and promises her, "I'll do my best," as he hands Erin his phone and waits for her to type in Sarah's address.

✻ ✻ ✻

"Nate?" the Uber driver asks when Nathan opens the backdoor of the car.

"Yafet?" Nathan asks, looking at his phone and then the driver.

"Yep. You're going to the Alameda, right?"

"Yep."

"Okay, I got two more to pick up going to downtown San Jose."

"What? No, I'm in a rush," Nathan says.

"You must've accidentally chosen Uber Pool, man. I already accepted their ride. I can leave *you* here, but I gotta pick them up around the corner."

"Ahhh, no. Can you at least drop me off first?"

"If it's okay with them, it's okay with me."

They pick up two people—a man and a woman—around the corner, and Yafet and Nathan ask if they're okay going to the Alameda before heading downtown.

"That's cool, man," the man answers. "It's on the way."

"He's trying to meet a lady," Yafet shares.

Nathan shoots him a look. What did he expect? *I guess Uber driver confidentiality isn't really a thing.*

"It's a little late for a hot date," he says, "But—"

"Dan, it's not a date if it's after midnight. It's a booty call," the woman says and cracks up.

Dan and Yafet all look at him knowingly and try not to laugh.

"It's not a booty call," Nathan says, trying to defend himself. "I really like her."

The woman, who introduces herself as Noelle, says, "Those two aren't mutually exclusive."

Yafet, who's obviously already invested in his story, asks, "She know you're coming, man?"

"Uh, no, not really, but I'm pretty sure she'll be happy to see me."

Yafet laughs. "You don't sound so sure. And you better hope she *is* happy to see you. It's one in the morning. In Addis Ababa, you come to a woman at one in the morning, it don't end well."

Nathan laughs. "Well, I'm pretty sure she'll let me in, and once I'm there, I can make her happy."

"TMI, man. TMI."

The group continues to talk the whole ride there. Dan and Noelle ask him questions, and he answers freely. "Her name's Sarah. She's amazing. We work together, but it's not like that. I *think* she'll let me in." Nathan knows he's had too much to drink tonight. Before he left Palo Alto, he took one—or two?—shots of "liquid courage" at the insistence of Kevin, Erin, and Ryan. It all felt like a movie scene, where the guy decides to go after the girl and he's got the whole bar cheering him on. In this case, it was three people—and he had just met Ryan, who seemed like a nice enough guy. But it was enough to make him go. And once he's there, he'll figure it out.

In any case, he's telling the people in this Uber more about his feelings for Sarah than he's even shared with Kevin, but it feels great to get it out. They're good-naturedly listening to him and giving him some advice on what to say and what definitely *not* to say. When they pull up to Sarah's building, he gets out of the front passenger seat, and they all roll down the windows and wish him luck. He bows like an idiot—god, he's drunk—to say "goodbye," but then sticks his head back into the rolled-down window and asks Yafet, "What's the name of that restaurant you told me about?"

"Walia, man. You take her there on your next date," Yafet says and peels out.

Nathan's here, wherever here is. He realizes that he forgot to ask Erin earlier which apartment Sarah lives in, but he's come this far, and such a small—though, admittedly, important—detail won't deter him. He's feeling pretty damn good, so takes the bull by the horns and simply calls her.

❊ ❊ ❊

When Sarah answers his call from downstairs, he says all kinds of crazy things—he's sure of it. But his purpose now is singular—see Sarah—and he's almost there. He can't waste time or energy on beautiful words or even words that make sense together.

She invites him up, and he miraculously makes it to the right floor on the first try. He's waiting at her door when she opens it, doing his best Frank Sinatra impression, coat slung over his shoulder.

He might look cool—let's be honest, probably not—but he loses it the moment he sees her, still in that killer green dress.

"Sarah, I had to see you," he says once and then again.

He comes into her apartment and has her pinned to the wall in the hallway in no time. But they aren't kissing yet. Just talking. Sarah wants to know what he's been doing since he saw her last, and a wave of embarrassment washes over him as he thinks about what happened at the club. But in the state he's in, there's no lying, and he tells her—point-blank—about Danica wanting to kiss him and how it wasn't what he wanted and how, when he shared that news with Danica, it didn't go so well.

Now—here—things are going well, very well even. His hands, his lips, are all over her, and when he feels goosebumps pop up on her skin, he tastes her, licking her throat like an ice cream cone, thinking she's the best flavor he's ever tasted.

Sarah seems really into it—into him—until she's not, and

even drunk as he is, he can tell she needs a break. While she goes to the kitchen to bring him a glass of water, he steals down the hallway to her bedroom, and when he gets there, the heady scent of her hits his nose and he feels like he could pass out and stay here for the rest of his life.

When she joins him, he's not sure how, but he finds himself asking if they can cuddle in her bed.

"I promise, no funny business," he assures her.

She gives him a skeptical look and laughs. Apparently, he hasn't been all that convincing of his utterly pure motives in his sales pitch. He can feel he still has a hard-on—maybe she knows, too—so he supposes she's probably right to doubt his intentions. He's doubting them himself.

While she's in the bathroom changing, Nathan undresses to his undershirt and boxer briefs and crawls into her warm bed— he pulls the comforter up to his chin and feels like he could die happy there.

As Sarah joins him under the covers, and he hears rain begin to fall outside, he swears this is what heaven must feel like: cuddling with a kind, smart, sweet-smelling woman in the warmth of her soft bed. *I wonder what she loves.* He begins to drift off to sleep, his arms around her. *I wonder if she could ever love me.*

BUG FIX

It's been a week since the partner event and everything went down. With Eden Snow—good. With Sarah—very good. With Danica—decidedly not good. He's in Seattle and has been all week. It's Saturday night. His mom is at the hospital with his dad, and David's out with some friends from high school, who still live in the area.

He's staring at his computer at a blank email. He doesn't know why it's taken him six days to just write a simple apology to Danica, but he's guessing it's because he acted like a jerk, and sometimes admitting that to yourself takes some time.

He's texted here and there with Sarah all week. And their FaceTime conversation, well, that was a very welcome distraction. When he's not actively communicating with Sarah, he's thinking about her, and thinking now, about the night Danica kissed him, is putting him in a sour mood. Hell, he could've easily hit second base and headed to third if he hadn't come to his senses in time. Thank god, he stopped. He could blame the fact that he'd had a lot to drink, or the stress he was under from Kevin, or maybe even some primordial urge that a heterosexual man feels to procreate when an attractive woman offers him her body, but he's also just got to man up and take responsibility for treating her unfairly and fucking up.

He takes a deep breath and sets himself to the task.

Subject: Apology

No sense in beating around the bush.
Hey Danica,
I'm sorry it's taken me all week to write you, but I wanted to let you know that I'm sorry for . . .

"Shit, what am I sorry for?" he asks himself. "Kissing her back when she kissed me?" *Well, that's a start.* But it goes back further than that—the months of leading her on. He didn't do it on purpose, but now—too late—he realizes he should've told Kevin to reach out to Danica himself. What had she said on Saturday night? That he was playing games. *Ironic.* That's the main reason he'd broken up with her in college, for the mind games she had played with him back then. He *has* been playing games with Danica, and it's not cool. He takes a deep breath, hoping it will clear his head a bit. He can't go back in time, but at least he can try to do the right thing now.

He continues typing.

I'm sorry for giving you the wrong impression.

He could tell her that there's no way for him to pursue something with her since he's interested in someone else, Sarah, but it's definitely not a good idea to put Sarah on Danica's radar. He's not sure what she might do, but Sarah doesn't need to get pulled into this.

"Right now's not a good time for us to get together . . ." No, that's wrong, and he deletes what he's written. That'll give her the impression that there's a chance later on, and if there's anything he's sure of, it's that their short fling in college is not something he wants to repeat. She was unreasonable back then, tried to make him do things and act in a way he didn't want to, but it doesn't excuse his behavior now, seven years later. No wonder she was hurt, angry.

I'm sorry for giving you the wrong impression. You're great, but I think we're . . .

He's had writer's block in the past, while writing journal articles for his PhD, but this is a whole new level of difficulty. High-performance computing has nothing on groveling to an ex-girlfriend determined to get back together with you but whom you can't annoy or offend since you need her help getting your startup funded. Fuck.

. . . just meant to help each other in other ways.

Friendship, he means, though—honestly—he'd rather not. He re-reads what he's written. It certainly won't win any Pulitzers, but he hopes she gets his intention, the fact that he *is* sorry for being such a douchebag. He hits "send" and goes downstairs, feeling a little bit better, and makes himself some dinner.

HIGH RETURN ON INVESTMENT

He's not quite sure how he ended up in his parents' car with David driving him to the Seattle airport, but here he is.

"Bro, you're going," David's telling him. "I've got things under control here. Nothing's gonna happen in two days. Dad's stable."

Nathan begins to protest, but before he can utter a word, David tells him, "Mom agrees with me."

"It's just a stupid off-site. I don't have to go."

"I'm sorry. Was I not clear? Nobody cares about the off-site, but we do care about you getting some tail from Sarah. Well, Mom didn't say it in those words—"

"Mom definitely didn't say it in those words."

"Hey now, I'm all for whatever happily-ever-after comes after, well, you know. But, dude, I've never seen you look simultaneously so miserable from missing a girl and so dopey from being obsessed with her. You gotta go."

"Maybe I look miserable because our father's in the hospital?" Nathan says, challenging his logic.

"You can try to play the 'dad card' but he agrees with us. You're going. I'm just as worried as you are, but you heard what Dr. Thompson said yesterday. They're narrowing down what it could be, and after the . . . well, I don't remember what the scan is that he's having today, but whatever it is, it's likely to show what she suspects it is and they'll be able to give him the right treatment. He might even be out by the time you come back this weekend. So, go, do your startup thing, try not to act too much like a dork, and maybe Sarah will be as into you, as you obviously are into her."

And that's how he finds himself on a plane to Salt Lake City and then a taxi to Park City to the company off-site.

Once he arrives at the hotel, he checks in and asks for a room upgrade. "I'll pay for the whole thing myself," he tells the hotel receptionist. "Any special requests?" she asks.

"No, well, maybe in a different building than the rest of the Instinqt rooms. Just want a little quiet the next couple of days," he explains. *Or some necessary privacy.*

A little later, he heads to the large conference room they're all supposed to meet in for the afternoon and walks to the front of the room to greet Kevin.

"Hey, bro. How are you? How's your dad?" Kevin asks immediately.

"He's okay, I guess. My family told me to come. Get my mind off things there for a little bit."

"Understood. Well, take whatever breaks you need for any calls or whatever. But . . . thanks for coming, man. It means a lot to me, the support—all the, uh, 'trouble' you go through for me," he says, raising his eyebrows and they both know he's talking about recent events with Danica.

"It's okay, man. I think I smoothed things over with her. I sent her an email and told her I hope there are no hard feelings, that uh, you know, sometimes things get outta hand, and . . . it should be okay now."

"Yeah, I think we're alright. In any case, conversations with you-know-who," he says, meaning Eden, "are going very well. I'll tell you more later tonight. Catch me after the social event, okay?"

Nathan nods and they both head toward the table at the front of the room, where the executives will be sitting off to the side this afternoon since many of them need to present. He sits down next to the CFO, who talks to him about the numbers they need to be hitting in the first half in order to have a strong case with the investors they're approaching. He's half-listening to him, but the other half of his attention is focused on looking for Sarah in the group of over a hundred Instinqt employees. He sees her walk in and sit down about six rows back. He's looking forward to hearing her present today. He knows from their run-through in her apartment that she's well-prepared.

He excuses himself from the conversation, pulls out his phone, and types her a quick text message. He wants to tell her a lot more, but settles for a quick "You're gonna do great." He looks up from his phone to where she's sitting and smiles at her encouragingly.

Sarah presents near the end of the afternoon schedule. He's been hearing for weeks—from engineering, from product, from pretty much anybody who works with her on a regular basis and even those who don't—what a great addition she has been to the Instinqt team. And he couldn't be more proud of her, listening to her run through her slides like she's been doing this for a decade. Her ideas for streamlining processes at the company are a combination of big bets and simple, easy-to-follow prescriptive methods, and he can see Kevin and many of the team leads, nodding their heads in agreement, impressed by her recommendations.

The presentations are over now, and people are hanging around, waiting for someone to tell them what to do. Nathan sees Sarah say something to Erin and then slip out. He tells Kevin he'll meet him at the restaurant in a bit, and heads out—as inconspicuously as possible—to follow Sarah.

He doesn't know what room she's staying in but sees her head into one of the hotel buildings. He watches the elevator go up, knows she's on the fourth floor, and takes the stairs up after her. By sheer luck, he sees her door close, just as he's opening the door from the stairwell onto the fourth floor. Otherwise, he was gonna just start knocking on doors. He hopes he's not breathing hard as he knocks and hears her footsteps walk toward the door.

She opens the door, surprised, but happy, and asks what he's doing here. He's here because he wants to tell her how well she did on her presentation, but if he's honest with himself, he's here because he feels a visceral need to put his hands on her, his lips on hers. He gently pushes her into the room and closes the door. He's been thinking about her—fantasizing is the better word—for the last ten days and now that he's got his hands on her, he doesn't know if he'll ever be able to take them off.

He kisses her deeply, hoping that it gives her some inkling into what he's been thinking, how he's been feeling. It's a kiss that he hopes tells her what he feels for her on the physical level, but it's something beyond that, for him. He's desperate—not just for a connection with her—but from everything going on right now. Somehow, this person who came into his life two months ago is some sort of centering force for things that seem to be spinning out of control. When he's happy, he wants to tell her. When he's aroused, he wants to be with her. When he's sad—worried that things won't get better—he wants to lean on her.

When she tells him they should go to the company dinner, he's disappointed. He was hoping they could just hole up in her room and, well, stay there forever is what. But he agrees that they have to at least show up—otherwise the ruse would be up —and he leaves her room, ahead of her, and waits for her to join him so they can walk to the restaurant together.

He spends the first hour mingling with everyone, talking to employees from the Salt Lake City office. He also catches up with people from the San Jose office he hasn't seen while he's been in Seattle the past ten days.

At one point, Kevin pulls him aside and guides him outside to the street, where nobody can hear their conversation. He updates him on the latest with Snow.

"He's saying that for them, it's a no-brainer to invest in us, but," Kevin pauses, meaningfully, "there might be something more."

Nathan doesn't catch his meaning, and Kevin elaborates. "You can't tell *anyone* this, but they're thinking that they might want to buy us."

Nathan can't believe it. He's only been at Instinqt for nine months, Instinqt has only existed for three years. Maybe Kevin Wong *is* the "wonder boy" all the tech magazines have been calling him.

"Dude. That's unbelievable. Congrats."

"Well, it's far from a done deal. I've got a meeting with him on Monday morning to continue the conversation. Anyways, it's pretty fucking cool, huh?"

"Cheers," he says, raising his glass and clinking it with Kevin's.

They head back inside and Kevin and Nathan continue to talk, in low voices, while they walk toward the balcony near the back of the restaurant. Nathan saw Sarah head out there with Erin a few minutes ago, and he's had enough of hanging out with people he doesn't care too much about.

With the news Kevin just broke to him, he's feeling like anything is possible and would like a one-on-one consultation—location and details TBD—with Sarah to see if she might agree.

They open the door that leads out onto the patio and hear Sarah and Erin laughing like hyenas at the other end of the enclosed space. Kevin hesitates in the doorway and says in a low voice to Nathan, "Remember when I told you that it's a shame that you never hooked up with Sarah before she started working for Instinqt?"

Nathan remembers well, and wonders where this is going.

"Well, if we *do* end up getting acquired by LightVerse, it's a much bigger company, and you'd likely be working in different departments, you know?"

"Okayyyy..."

"I'm just saying, maybe things could work out for you guys then..."

"Yeah, maybe," Nathan says, "We'll see, I guess." Kevin means well, but what he doesn't know is that Nathan's already way past the point of no return with Sarah. Instinqt, LightVerse, Metaverse. He doesn't care. If he's learned anything in the last couple of months, seeing his dad go through everything, hearing his dad's doubts about whether he'll make it out of all of this alive and how the thing that'll hurt him the worst is knowing he'd be leaving his beloved wife behind, seeing his mom's pain at what his dad is going through physically, mentally, and emotionally—well, life is too fucking short, is what Nathan has decided.

And as Kevin walks over to Sarah and Erin to ask them what's so funny, and he hears Sarah's infectious laugh again, he knows what he has to do.

❊ ❊ ❊

He wakes in the wee hours of the morning, wondering how he survived the night, how he survived her perfect body, her razor-sharp wit, her empathy that made him feel entirely understood but never pitied. Last night . . . well, it's what he's been dreaming of almost nightly for the last two months. And the reality was a hundred times better than he imagined it could be. Kissing her, licking her, tasting her—on her lips, her breasts, her most private and vulnerable places. His hard cock in her soft, but determined hands, her wet, warm mouth, and finally inside of her—welcoming and tight—opening, as she screamed his name. It's more than Nathan could've hoped for.

In the pale moonlight coming in from the window—the curtains are still open—he sees goosebumps on the cream-colored skin of Sarah's back and shoulder, and gently pulls the blanket up around her. She stirs a bit in her sleep, and giggles softly—she must be dreaming. His heart clenches a bit, and he snuggles up behind her and falls asleep.

The next day, a lot of things happen, but the most important thing is that Sarah is still with Nathan in bed in the morning when he wakes up. And that—while seemingly trivial—feels like a monumental win to him, all things considered.

As he sits in a hotel conference room now, with Instinqt's senior leadership team, listening to Kevin recap what's happening with the investor talks, he rubs his injured hand and thinks to himself that it's a good thing Sarah's more coordinated during sex than climbing down stairs, or he might've gotten a bandage elsewhere.

Without explicitly stating that Eden Snow is the investor potentially interested in acquiring the company, Kevin tests the waters with the Instinqt C-level executives and asks—if something unexpected happened, an offer to acquire us?—who would be in favor.

"A lot depends on the terms," Maya says, logically.

"Okay, just for the sake of discussion, if it's over $300 million, are we in?" Kevin elaborates.

Maya's eyes go wide and she nods, as do the others. Kevin gives Nathan a look, and he sees him give a slight smile. He can almost see the dollar signs in Kevin's eyes and gets up to leave.

404

Nathan turns on the hot water in the shower and leans his forearm on the wall, resting his head on it, and letting the water run over his back. He's exhausted. He's only twenty-seven, but he's pretty sure that even a younger version of himself would be tired—at least a bit—after all the sex he's had with Sarah the last couple of days. He allows himself to momentarily contemplate all the positions they've done it in the last two days, and all the surfaces they've done it *on*—most recently, on the floor, in front of the fireplace. He smiles to himself. *I'm gonna need more calories to keep this up.*

He's looking forward to eating something quickly, cuddling with Sarah, and collapsing into sleep as soon as he gets out of the shower. Remembering what he was doing in here a few hours earlier with Sarah, well, *that* is something he'll never forget.

He's certain—like, knows it in his bones certain—that it's never felt this right with someone. What he feels when he's with Sarah—talking to her, touching her, listening to her jokes, and watching her while she works—it's on another level. It has been a hell of a night, a few days of bliss, sexual and otherwise.

He's just about to turn off the shower when he hears the sound of glass breaking. He steps out, grabs a towel to dry off quickly, and then wraps it around himself. He's got a smile on his face—he has for the last two days, spending so much time with her—as he opens the door and asks her if everything's okay.

Sarah's facing the window, and she's pulling on her clothes.

"What's going on?" he asks, his growing concern likely evident in his voice.

She turns to him, stone-faced, and tells him she's leaving, that she has an early flight. She's still not dressed—she can't seem to find her shirt—and she looks super pissed off. Nathan's completely at a loss. Not even ten minutes ago, when he went into the shower, she was fine. Now she looks ready to break something—and then he surmises she did, judging by the broken glass he sees on the stone of the fireplace.

He's trying to figure out what's going on, but she's tight-lipped, not giving him a lot to go on. He asks if she got bad news —maybe something terrible has happened, but even some sort of family emergency wouldn't explain the anger he sees on her face.

She's found her shirt now, and he notices his phone lighting up on the nightstand. He sees Sarah holding her own phone and asks her if she got bad news. Maybe someone texted her, called her, while he was in the shower.

But that's not it. She says something he doesn't understand about wishing his dad her best and then all-but-yells at him, "Check your fucking phone."

He's walking to the door, to follow her, but as she slams the hotel room door, he doesn't know whether to go after her—he's in his towel—or check his "fucking phone" the way she told him to.

He's standing still, dumb-founded, in the middle of the room, and as he turns to go get his phone, he wonders if maybe Kevin sent him something. Did he say something about the exit? But why would that make Sarah so angry? But then, all of a sudden, he knows. He doesn't know *how* he knows, but he does.

He opens his phone and sees Danica's texts—her half-naked selfie. He sits down on the bed, and puts his head in his hands. "Fuck," he says out loud. "Fuck, fuck, fuck."

He wants to break something, but it takes him only a minute to go into action. He pulls on his pants and a sweater and grabs a jacket, just in case. It's probably freezing out, and Sarah just ran out of here without her coat.

He's texting her:

Nathan: Sarah, what's going on?

Nathan: Are you ok?

Nathan: Are you back in your room?

She's not answering, but he can't just let her go. Where is she anyways? He decides to head to her hotel room and grabs her coat on the way out. She must be in her room. It's the only reasonable place to be at this hour of the night since it's freezing outside. When he reaches her floor, he sees her scarf laying outside the door. It must have fallen. He's tempted to knock on the door to make sure she's inside, safe and warm. To see if she'll listen to him, let him explain. But Erin's probably there. They're sharing a room and it's past one in the morning.

Nathan: Can you please respond, so I know you're ok?

No response, not even "left on read." He knows it looks bad. More than bad. He doesn't know what Sarah's imagining, but it can't be anything good. How could Danica twist what he'd said and mess things up like this?

But as frustrated as he is with her, he's even angrier with himself. He never should've allowed Kevin to convince him to get back in touch with her. He knows how Danica can be, but he has no one to blame but himself. At any point along the way, he could've cleared things up, stopped the interactions with her, but he didn't. He went right along with it, like an idiot. And now, the one person he would never want to hurt is sitting on the other side of the door from him, not speaking to him, not even willing to read a text message from him.

How can I have screwed this up so badly? He walks back to his room, completely and utterly dejected.

He lays down on the bed, resting his head on the pillow Sarah used last night, and it still smells like her. Her shampoo, her deodorant—just her. He curls up and dreams terrible dreams.

He's chasing Sarah in the snow. She's wearing a thin, white dress, and she's shivering. He wants to reach her, touch her, and wrap her up in his arms to warm her, but every time he thinks he's close to catching her, the winter storm blows her further away.

Nathan wakes—cold and uncovered—at 6:10 a.m. He

immediately looks at his phone to see if she's responded and is disappointed to see that she hasn't. He sends her another message, one last-ditch attempt at connection, to ask her when she's leaving for the airport and if he can see her. But there's nothing, and he falls back into a restless half-sleep. He wakes less than an hour later and goes to Sarah and Erin's room.

Erin opens the door, sees his face, and asks, "What the hell happened?" He exhales loudly. "Sarah's already gone," she tells him.

Nathan nods, grimly, and then leaves. He texts her a few more times and even tries calling, but it's radio silence from Sarah. He decides that the only thing to do is to pack his bags, grab a coffee, and then head back to Seattle to his family.

She's gone. There's nothing for him here.

CLEANING UP
THE BACKLOG

It's evening, and Nathan's already in flannel pajama pants and a t-shirt, after a long day at the hospital with his dad. He's sitting at his desk, in his old bedroom, upstairs. He grew up in this house, and in high school, his parents let him take over the top floor as his bedroom. On one side, he has an amazing view of the water. The other side, where his desk is placed, faces the tree-lined street.

He's been back for a few days, but besides his regular treks to the hospital, he's barely left the house. He's texted Sarah a few times to tell her he's sorry. He could see on his phone that she'd seen them at least but isn't holding out much hope for a response any time soon.

He's half-heartedly checking his work email and considering whether he should go downstairs to make some food for dinner. He was with his parents for a long time today until his mom finally made him go home. David left at the same time and is probably out with friends, his preferred method of disconnecting and taking a break from the long, worry-filled days at the hospital.

Nathan puts off going downstairs for another few minutes and is about to text Kevin when he hears a car door close outside. He glances out the window to see who it is, maybe an Amazon Prime delivery, and is completely shocked to see Sarah standing on the sidewalk, as an Uber drives away. She's checking something on her phone and then looking up at the house.

It's already getting dark outside, and he looks at her

squinting, probably trying to make out the address. He's down the stairs and opening the glass-paned front door before she even makes it all the way up the front walk.

"Hi, Nathan," she says calmly and cocks her head to look at him, taking in his disheveled appearance and unshaven face. She doesn't smile, but she also doesn't look angry. "You look tired," she says, bluntly.

He's looking at her, bundled up in a fitted, dark-red jacket with a bag slung over her shoulder. She looks beautiful. That is the first coherent thought he has. The last time he saw her, her face was streaked with tears. She might as well have had steam coming out of her ears. She's on the small side, but damn if he wasn't just a little bit afraid, underneath the confusion he felt that night in Park City.

He walks out to her barefoot, goosebumps rising on his skin from the cold evening air, or maybe just from being close to her. It's been four days since he touched her—though, it feels like an eternity—or even heard her voice. The last actual conversation they had was just after she'd seen the text—the stupid text— from Danica. Since then, it's been only one-way text messages and voicemails. Has she even heard them?

She's close to him and looks up at him, putting her hand on his bare arm. Her warmth feels good. It's comforting. And he's brought back to the present.

"I know, I'm . . . I am tired." He looks at her, still shocked to see her standing in front of him. "What are you doing here?"

"Well, I'm not here to see the Space Needle." She smiles, a little warily.

"Of course. Come in. It's cold out here."

"You're the one wandering around outside half-dressed," she says, more warmly.

They go inside and head toward the kitchen. Nathan makes some hot tea for both of them and sits down at the dining table, him on one side of the table and Sarah across from him on the other.

They take a sip of the too-hot tea at the same time, and then both smile a bit at the timing. He looks at her hands, wrapped around the mug, warming them up, wishing he felt comfortable enough to put his own hands around hers.

"How's he doing?" she asks. *Of course she does. Because that's the kind of person she is.* Thoughtful, empathetic, sensitive— sometimes *very* sensitive.

"Well, he looks terrible," Nathan says. "But one of his doctors brought in a rheumatologist yesterday, and they think that it might be some sort of auto-immune reaction that's causing him to be so bad off right now. They never found an infection, but said it could've been the month of antibiotics he's been on that cleared it up. He still has a fever, so the rheumatologist thinks it might not be *just* an infection. They did some blood tests yesterday afternoon. We're just waiting on the results to see if they confirm the auto-immune hypothesis."

"Well, I hope it's good news. Just knowing what it is will be a step in the right direction, right?" she asks in a hopeful tone.

He looks at her. She has a hesitant smile on her face, but he can see pain in her eyes. He thinks at least part of it must be because she's remembering her own dad, taken too soon from her life. Certainly, Nathan has played a part more recently.

"Yeah," he says, looking at her and smiling a bit. Her optimism is contagious, and it helps him think a little more positively, seeing the situation through her eyes.

They sit in silence for an awkward minute or two, drinking tea, and probably both wondering who's going to go out on a limb first. Suddenly, as she often does in conversations, Sarah just asks what she wants to know. No equivocation whatsoever.

"Did you ever give Danica the impression that you'd get back together? Or . . ." She stops, twitching her leg back and forth, in an agitated manner. Her jaw is tensed and she seems to struggle to continue, finally spitting out, "Just hook up?"

"No," he answers immediately, but then he's silent and thinks back to a conversation he heard Kevin having with Danica when he'd rejoined them after talking to some other product people at the partner event.

They'd been leaning toward each other, conspiratorially, and he'd heard Kevin saying, "Nate's single now. And it's been a very long time since he's been out on a date. I'm just sayin'. . ." When Nathan had joined their little group, Kevin had coughed and changed the subject.

Later that night, when they'd been waiting at the club bar for drinks, away from Danica and Amy, Nathan had asked, "What the hell were you saying to Danica about me earlier?"

"It's fine. She's not looking for anything serious, at least not now. I know you've got a thing for Sarah, but it's not smart, man. Dating someone you work with. Just trying to help out," he had said, looking Nathan directly in the eye.

Nathan had given Kevin a hard look, and told him, "I don't need your help, and I can make my own decisions. I'm here for another half hour and then I'm going home." But then what happened with Danica, had happened, and he hadn't ended up at home, but at Sarah's acting like a drunk idiot, though evidently a likable one.

"Why are you so quiet?" Sarah's challenging him, in the here and now. "Something to share?" Her tone is different than he's ever heard. She's angry—well, that emotion he's definitely seen, and recently—but she also seems to be feeling vulnerable and doesn't seem to like it.

"No, I didn't tell her that I want to get back together or that I want to sleep with her. But . . . Kevin might've said some stuff that I didn't correct, at least not quickly enough."

"Did you kiss her?" she asks directly and then waits silently for him to respond.

"No, I mean, she kissed me—"

"That's the same thing, Nathan."

"No. No, it's not," he insists. "*She* kissed me, but I didn't want to kiss her. I told you that."

"When you came to my house, you told me she *tried* to kiss you. That would mean that no kissing actually happened. But kissing did happen, didn't it?" she demands, and he can see a flash of anger in her eyes.

"Yes, but I-I stopped it—and I came to you."

"Why didn't you just tell me the truth? That *you'd* kissed . . .

that *she'd* kissed . . . that you'd kissed each other—" She stops abruptly, unable to figure out what exactly she wants to say, and flustered, she throws her hands down.

She exhales sharply. "I'm going for a walk."

"*What*? You just got here."

But she's already up and walking toward the front door, pulling on her red coat. He's still in a t-shirt but has the presence of mind, this time, to grab a jacket slung over the banister on the way out and pull on some shoes near the front door. She's already walking down the sidewalk away from the house when he makes it out the front door and he has to jog to catch up with her.

"It's cold, Sarah," he says, coming up beside her, and leaning down to look directly into her eyes.

"I need the fresh air." Something comes across her face and she rolls her eyes. "Last time I said that to you, we ended up at your place and slept together. I should probably watch my words, huh?" she huffs out.

"No, no, no. Don't say that," he says sadly, placing his hands on her arms, tentatively, testing the waters.

She looks at him. He sees something in her eyes besides the anger and the hurt, something that tells him he has to be as direct as she usually is.

"Why did you come here, Sarah?"

She looks at him, silent.

He repeats the question. "Why did you come here? Why did you come here now? After not speaking to me for days, not even responding to a text message?"

"*Why* did I come here?" she almost yells. She's holding back tears and pressing her lips together. "I came here because I care about you, Nathan. Even after you hurt me. You acted like a jerk. I opened myself up to you and thought that you were different. Special. Special to *me*. But you lied—"

"I didn't lie. I didn't say—"

"So you weren't clear, then. In a way that makes *you* look better, like it's Danica who's to blame, and like nothing happened, like there's no . . . history. But there is, isn't there? There's history. Maybe there's still attraction. And something did happen," she says, and he sees tears in her eyes. She looks down, trying to hide them. "I shouldn't have come."

"No, just no," he says, getting frustrated. "Why'd you come here now, if you thought there's no hope? If you think I'm a lying asshole—" he starts to say.

She breathes in and then out, slowly. He watches her and stays silent, giving her a moment.

"Because I don't. I don't think you're a lying asshole. I think . . . I think you were an idiot," she says, releasing the last word in a burst of air, like a balloon popping.

"Well, join the club. My dad also told me I'd acted like an idiot," he says. He ventures a slight, apologetic smile, and bends down directly in front of her, so his eyes are level with hers. He lifts her chin so he can look directly into them.

"Come back to the house. Let's talk. Please?"

She nods, grudgingly, and wraps her arms around herself to warm herself. They walk back in silence, and go inside, he hopes, to try again. They sit—again—at the kitchen table, where their mugs of tea sit abandoned, already cold. Sarah sits, once again, across from him and looks down at her hands. Nathan looks at her and waits until he thinks she might be willing to listen to him.

"Sarah, I'm sorry. I communicated . . . really badly to you. Also to, well, Danica. But you should know that I've apologized to her. That's why she sent me that text—"

"I'd be curious to see the type of apology that gets you a half-naked selfie," Sarah says, still obviously pissed off at him.

"Well, I certainly didn't pour my heart out to her. I'll show you if you want," he offers. "I don't have anything to hide."

"No," she replies abruptly. "I have to be able to trust you. If we don't have that—"

"Fine, I'll tell you, then. I told her I was sorry if I gave her the wrong impression and that she's great—"

"So, she's great?" Sarah bristles, her eyes wide in surprise.

"She's *not* great. I mean, she helped us. I'm thankful for *that*. But her personality is, at best, *just* okay."

She snorts and shakes her head. Her face is slightly flushed —from tears, from anger—and he can feel the tension in his muscles from the effort of not reaching out to touch her, to try to calm her.

"So, you apologized?" she asks, and he thinks maybe she's slowly coming to terms with his good intentions but terrible implementation.

"Yeah."

She rests her elbows on the table and then looks down, propping her head in her hands.

"And then she got half-naked for you?" Sarah says. Now she's closing her eyes and massaging her forehead, just above her eyebrows, with her fingers. The type of movement one does when dealing with an idiot, he supposes.

"Uh, yeah?" he says, not overly sure if this line of questioning is helping or hurting his case.

She looks up at him. "You have quite a way with women, Nathan," she finally says, amusement creeping into her voice, despite her obvious attempt to quell it. He can tell she's becoming a little less angry with him. But she's trying to conceal her smile. She's going to make him work for it, and sitting there with her lips pursed, she's the most adorable creature he's ever seen.

"I'm sorry, Sarah. I was an idiot. I just got dragged into this whole thing by Kevin. I'm not blaming him. I'm a grown man. But it's the first time I've been in a situation like this— a startup, dealing with investors, adulting around like a stupid motherfucker when I have no clue what I'm doing. And then you come into the picture, and suddenly none of the other stuff even feels important anymore. I see you in the office, making coffee, and even the sight of your hair in a ponytail makes my heart beat faster. But at the same time, I've got this other woman texting me, and I'm trying to not ruin Kevin's chances with Eden Snow. And there's also—"

"Your dad," Sarah says, looking at him. She seems to be wrestling with an urge and finally gives in to it. She gets up and moves to his side of the table to sit down next to him. He nods. She turns to him and grabs his hands, holding them in her lap. "I understand."

"You do?"

"Is there anything else I should know?"

Here goes nothing.

"She kind of put my hand up her skirt that night."

"What the *fuck*, Nathan?"

Shit, back to square one.

"It was just her thigh. I swear to god, nothing else. Please, Sarah, don't be mad. I'd almost forgotten about it, but you want the whole truth and nothing but the truth, and so help me god, I'm giving it to you."

She puts her hands on the table—as if bracing herself—for anything else he might admit.

"Is there *anything* else, Nathan?"

He continues quickly, honestly. It's not going to be easy, but it's the right thing to do—the *only* thing to do. Complete and utter honesty.

"She put my hand up her skirt, but I didn't leave it there. She kissed me, and being a fucking drunk idiot, I kissed her back for a minute—less than a minute—and when my mind cleared, from the surprise of it all, it's like all my thoughts and body came together and I realized she's not . . ."

"What? 'She's not' what, Nathan?" Her voice is sharp but shaky.

"She's not *you*, Sarah," he spits out, finally saying the most important thing of all. "Don't you understand? *You*—you—are the only one that matters."

Sarah looks at him and then focuses her gaze on her hands, still clutching the edge of the table. She inhales and exhales. She might even be counting backward from ten or something, he's guessing, from the amount of time it's taking her to respond.

He puts his hand on her shoulder, and when she doesn't move

away, he turns her chair toward him, as he slides off his own chair, onto his knees directly in front of her. He scoots closer to her, positioning himself between her knees, wraps his arms around her torso, and looks up at her.

"Will you give me another chance?" he asks her in a careful, quiet tone.

She's silent, for more than just a moment. He waits. She finally replies, "You gave me one, didn't you? After I left your place that first night. I left you for what I thought was forever."

"I . . . I guess I did," he replies. "I honestly never thought about it that way."

"Well, I did. *I* do." She takes another deep breath and seems to come to some sort of decision.

"Yes, I'll give you another chance. But I swear to god, Nathan, if something like this ever happens again—"

"It won't. I won't hurt you, Sarah," he assures her.

He stands and pulls her up into a bear hug. She wraps her arms around his waist, and he can feel she's still tense. He rubs her back and she begins to soften and then lays her head on his chest.

"I won't hurt you," he repeats softly, into her hair. "I promise."

❉ ❉ ❉

It's after dinner—Nathan cooked—and they're lounging in his bedroom upstairs. He's sitting in his desk chair, leaning back. Sarah's on his bed, on top of the covers, already in her pajamas— a tank top, with a hoodie on top, and some leggings.

"I still can't believe you came. Just when I thought you couldn't get any better . . ."

"Be careful how you finish that sentence. I remember the last time you said that . . ."

He grins, the corners of his eyes crinkling, remembering, too, that it was right before what in his head will forever be known as "the shower scene." He crosses his arms and asks if he can join her on the bed.

"It's *your* bed," she says, scooting over to make room.

"Yeah, but I guess I just don't know exactly where we stand." He walks over to her and flops down on the bed, making her bounce up a little.

"Yeah, I'm feeling a little fragile, too."

"What helps 'fragile?'" Nathan asks.

"A wise man once said that one of the best feelings in the world is cuddling," she replies, giving him an adorable look.

"I'm pretty sure that 'wise man' actually wanted to get laid, but fell asleep before the festivities could commence."

She laughs.

"Are you saying I wanna get laid?" she asks.

"Nah. Honestly, it's probably not the worst idea for us to just cuddle tonight. Maybe it's being in my high-school bedroom, but I'm feeling like the simple stuff is enough for some nights."

"I couldn't agree more," Sarah says, yawning, obviously tired from the travel and events of the day. "Let's get under the covers."

"Okay, but first I wanna play a song for you." He gets up to grab his phone.

"OneRepublic?"

"Not quite."

"What is it?" Sarah asks him.

"Remember you asked me what my favorite song is? Well, I heard this one about a month ago, and . . . when I hear it, I . . ."

"You what?" she asks.

"Well, just listen. I think it speaks for itself."

He opens his phone and finds the song he wants. As the song begins to play, Sarah says that it sounds familiar, and he tells her it's the acoustic version of a song called "Missing Piece."

"So, this was the Vance Joy song you mentioned?"

He nods.

"You know I love water," she says, noting all the lyrics about waves and tides.

"I do," he says. "I kind of feel like a wave brought you to me. Like you washed over me, and I just couldn't not pay attention."

"A tsunami, maybe," she jokes.

"Maybe some days, but mostly not. Mostly a calm wave that I know will bring me back to shore if I ever get too far out in deep waters."

She has a thoughtful expression on her face.

"That's about as poetic as I probably get," he says. "I wish I could write you a song, but alas, no musical talent here."

She touches his face and smiles. He can tell she's listening, concentrating on the lyrics of the song.

"I *could* write you a computer program, but I'm not sure how many chicks go on dates with guys after being impressed by their coding skills."

"It must've happened at least once, no?" Sarah jokes.

He holds her in his arms as the song fades away and goes on to another on a calm playlist. They both know that there is a lot that still needs to be addressed, talked about. Bit by bit, they begin to touch on the last few days, the last few months—edging close to the sensitive places in their minds and hearts, and gently stepping back, when it feels a little too real, a little too painful.

After one such uneasy venture into rough waters, in which Nathan tells her about his history with Danica and how the last few months have gone down, it seems to him that Sarah is accepting, but still unsettled.

"There's something else, isn't there?" he asks. "I thought we were having the best night of our lives. At least, I was. Why didn't you let me explain?"

Sarah tells him—hesitantly at first and then opening up more, understanding that she's safe with him, that he's not her ex and that he won't use anything against her—the longer story about Blake and how she suspected he had cheated on her, if not physically, then emotionally.

"I guess I knew it was a sensitive spot for me, but I've never told anyone about it, so it's like, it was only this half-real emotion for me. I didn't realize just how . . . painful it all actually was for me until I was faced with something like it again."

"But it's not like that," Nathan tells her, desperate for her to understand, to believe him fully. "Danica's not my girlfriend.

She's not . . . well, anything beyond an old acquaintance. Kevin asked me to connect with her, so we could try to meet Eden Snow. Now I know I should've avoided the situation altogether, or at the very least, been more clear, but well, I'm not always the best communicator."

She nods, smirks, and raises her eyebrows as if to say "That's an understatement."

"I'm not you," he continues, desperate for her to understand that he never meant any harm, to Danica, to her, to anybody. "I don't know the right thing to say in every situation, how to just make people understand—or do—what I want, the way you seem to."

"You communicate just fine . . . well, normally," she clarifies, giving him the side-eye. "I should've talked to you. I should've asked and let you explain," she admits. She squeezes his hand. He squeezes hers back and brings it up to his mouth to kiss it.

She continues. "I have a confession to make. I totally stalked you on the internet."

"Of course," he sniffs out. "But as confessions go, that's not much of one."

"You're like a big freaking deal in computer science . . . stuff. You didn't want to stay in academia?"

"Nah, I could've, but Kev was hell-bent on me joining him, and I think every programmer secretly—well, openly—dreams of being part of a successful startup at some point, so I thought Instinqt might be my chance."

"So you ended up here."

"So I ended up here."

"You think you made the right decision?"

"I think there's nowhere I'd rather be than right here, right now, so yeah, I think I made the right decision," he says, kissing her on the forehead. "What about you?"

"What about me?"

"Did you make the right decision? I know you're always worried about that," he says, smiling warmly.

"With you, I'd say it's been a mixed bag. I definitely made

some bad decisions."

Her face is scrunched up a bit. She's feeling uncomfortable.

"What?"

"Well, sneaking out of your place that first night, or morning after."

"You're right. Terrible decision. Worst decision ever," he teases, pinching her lightly on her side, near her waist.

"Look at the mess I made."

"I don't know," Nathan says. "What if you'd stayed, and I'd made you breakfast that morning, and we'd actually talked instead of just..."

"Screwing like bunnies?"

"Sure, instead of that. We'd have figured out that we were both working at Instinqt and things might've been okay, but maybe they wouldn't have."

"So, you're saying it's good I ran away before you woke up?"

"Well, it made me feel pretty shitty, actually," he admits. He doesn't want to make her feel bad, but his face is likely showing exactly how bad he felt at the time. "Like I was some sort of mistake."

Her expression falls. Sadness? Shame? He touches her face, softly. And she meets his eyes.

"You could never be a mistake, Nathan. I was stupid at the time. I'm not sure if I should say I should've done things differently, because—I don't know—maybe things are okay, or will be okay now. But you're too... you... to ever be a mistake or a bad decision."

He nods.

"Please forgive me," she says.

"You're already forgiven, Sarah. From the moment I saw you on our first Zoom call, and your smile, it was all gone. All the bad feelings. I just want us to try to make things okay now. From now on."

She kisses him lightly on the lips and pulls him to lie down. She tries to wrap her leg around his large, muscular body, which amuses him but makes him feel warm and loved. They fall asleep quickly. It rains that night, and the wind slams against the windows. It sounds as if the sea has come inland to them, but they feel anchored by each other and sleep peacefully.

❋ ❋ ❋

They wake in the morning, early, and Nathan goes downstairs to make some coffee and a quick breakfast. It looks like David didn't come home last night—that or he's already gotten up and left—so he calls to check on him, putting the phone on "speaker" so he can use both hands to cook the eggs and toast.

"You okay?"

"Yeah, fine. I'm at the hospital with mom," David responds.

"You'll never believe who's here."

"Sarah."

"How do *you* know?" Nathan asks him.

"How do you think she got our address? She called the house Sunday night—I guess Mom and Dad's landline is still listed on the internet—and said she wanted to fly up. So I gave her the address."

"I'm gonna kill you. Why didn't you tell me?"

"I wanted to make sure you couldn't screw it up before she got here."

"Fair point," Nathan concedes.

"Come to the hospital now. I was just about to text you that we got the latest blood results back. It's positive for the auto-immune reaction the doctor thought it might be."

"Wait . . . that's *good* news."

"It is. We know what it is now. They're gonna start him on steroids right after lunch."

Nathan's talking on speaker while he gets dressed and looks up to see Sarah standing in the kitchen doorway. She's heard, too, and she's smiling and giving him the thumbs-up sign.

"We'll see you soon, okay?"

❋ ❋ ❋

Nathan drives them to the hospital, and on the way, he points out different places—his high school, his mom's favorite restaurant, and the gym where he and his dad used to play basketball.

"I always thought Seattle was just gray and lonely," she says, sounding impressed by the sights.

"Well, it *is* gray a lot, but it's getting less lonely by the minute," he says, grabbing her hand and squeezing it.

Due to Covid precautions, they're not allowed to have more than two people at a time in the hospital room, so David and his mom come meet them outside in a large garden near the entrance.

After a quick introduction, Claire—tall, gray-haired, and beautiful—grasps Sarah's hands, and pulls her in for a hug. "You . . . are beautiful, my dear," she whispers. "And I hear you're very smart, too. No wonder Nathan's enamored with you."

Nathan shares an exasperated look with his brother, and then takes Sarah's hand and leads her to a picnic table, where they can all sit down.

David updates Nathan with the new diagnosis and the proposed care plan—steroids, continued monitoring, and with the improvement they hope for, Noah could be home in a few days to recuperate before starting the treatment he needs for the prostate cancer.

"Oh, I have to get back home soon. It's a shame I won't be able to meet him," Sarah says.

"You just got here," Nathan says, rubbing her leg affectionately. She smiles but looks a bit uncertain.

"Yeah, well, it wasn't exactly a planned trip. I've just got a few things I need to take care of this week."

He can't tell whether she actually needs to get back, or whether everything that's happened recently is all simply a little too much for her, but squeezes her hand and gives her a small, reassuring smile.

"Well, you're welcome to stay as long as you can, Sarah. We have plenty of room. As for meeting Noah, I could ask the nurse if it's okay for you to come up. It's probably fine as long as it's during visiting hours and we don't all go up together," Claire says with a reassuring smile.

"That would be nice. I actually brought him a small gift," Sarah says, pulling a tiny package out of her bag.

✻ ✻ ✻

Half an hour later, Nathan is introducing Sarah to his father. "It's really nice to meet you, Noah."

"It's nice to meet *you*. I've heard a lot about you."

"Have you?" Sarah says, intrigued. "Well, I've been warned by the nurse that I'm not really supposed to be in here, seeing as I'm not family, but I wanted to give you something."

She hands him a small organza bag with drawstrings. Noticing that his arms and hands are in a maze of tubes and tape, she offers to help him open it.

"It's called a *hamsa*. It's a charm for protection or healing," she explains, a bit shyly. "I got it from a friend when I was sick a while ago. And I thought, well, I just thought it would be nice for you to have it."

Noah smiles warmly at her and then gives Nathan a meaningful look. "You were right. She *is* special," his look seems to say. "Thank you, Sarah. This is very thoughtful."

"I wish you a full recovery, Noah. I'll be thinking about you," Sarah says. She squeezes his hand and then walks to Nathan, where he's standing by the door.

"I'll come back this afternoon, Dad," Nathan says.

"No, spend some time with Sarah, son."

His dad's right. He's still not sure whether he's been forgiven, how exactly Sarah's feeling, or what will happen, but she's here. That's one step in the right direction, and he plans to do what he can to begin to repair things.

M&A

It's been almost a week since I flew back to San Jose from Seattle, after staying just one night at Nathan's house. Nathan was very surprised to see me arrive at his house. I was almost as surprised myself.

After I'd flown back on Friday from the off-site in Park City, I'd puttered around the house for a while, trying to keep myself distracted. Eventually, I poured myself a glass of wine and taken a long, hot bath. All I needed was to start blasting "All by Myself," and I'd have had myself a real "Bridget Jones's Diary" moment.

On Friday and Saturday, I'd eaten my fair share of Thai takeout and watched a good amount of TV, but by Sunday morning, my exhaustion from the intensity—both physical and emotional—of the trip had worn off. I decided to go for a run. Maybe it would clear my mind. At the very least, it would burn off some of the 10,000 calories I'd consumed over the previous couple of days.

I took my phone from the charger, guiltily glancing at the scores of texts that had come in from Nathan, Erin, and Camila. I'd let Erin and Camila know that I was fine—pissed off, sad, confused, lacking faith in the whole male species, but fine, and that I just needed some time to disconnect. They were curious for details, but both gave me the space I needed to work through everything.

I hadn't responded to Nathan. I was distraught, and every time I closed my eyes, I was bombarded by memories. Nathan and me kissing, playing basketball together, him catching me as I fell down the bus stairs, his smile and him laughing at a joke I'd told him. These memories brought tears to my eyes. But others made my stomach turn. Danica's arm draped around him in the hotel ballroom at the partner event, her legs wrapped around him when he carried her the day of the hike, and, of course, the text messages and selfie I had seen come in while he was in the shower.

I went for a long run and then, when I got tired, I just kept on walking. I ended up near Instinqt, and therefore, near Decades and Nathan's place. Then I began to remember the good things about Nathan. How he didn't think twice about giving away his dinner to the man we'd seen in the park. How he brought me muffins. How he'd told me that he wouldn't let me fall, and how he hadn't.

I'd stopped in the park and sat on a bench. I read all his texts again and listened to the two voicemails he'd left. The varied thoughts that had been pounding in my head since I had last seen Nathan—like the discordant notes of a terrible orchestra —had finally quieted, and in this new silence, I listened to his voice, audibly desperate:

" . . . you matter to me. . . . My world just feels smaller without you in it. Because I care about you. . . . you matter to me already . . . I need to hear your voice and know you're okay . . . maybe that we can be okay."

"I need you to understand what's going on," his text message had said. "I need you to understand how I feel about you."

Even now, a week later, I'm not entirely sure how I arrived at the decision to fly up to Seattle when I did, and especially why I didn't let him know I'd be coming. It was a combination of thoughts and experiences that led me there.

Deep down, after hearing what he said, how he'd tried to make amends, I knew he couldn't be what the deepest, worst, most vulnerable parts of me had imagined. He may have hurt me, but he didn't do it on purpose. He had acted recklessly, for sure, but that he cared was obvious.

I thought about what he'd told me about his family, how they'd encouraged him to come to me. I thought about how he'd joined Kevin's startup to help him achieve his dream, and how he'd helped and encouraged me professionally over the last two months.

And then a text from a number I didn't know sounded on my phone. "Maybe: Kevin Wong" it said when I opened it.

> **Maybe Kevin Wong**: Hey Sarah, sorry for bothering you on the weekend. Just wanted to know if you've heard from Nate re: his dad, re: life?

And then another, two minutes later:

> **Maybe Kevin Wong**: I know you guys talk a lot. Have you checked in on him?

Kevin's text is likely what tipped the scales in Nathan's favor. It strengthened my sense that everything that had happened was just one part of what Nathan was going through.

And that's why I went—because I cared about him, too, and whether or not we would end up together, he was hurting and I wanted to be there for him.

❇ ❇ ❇

His dad was discharged from the hospital yesterday, and the plan is to monitor Noah's recovery at home. For the next few weeks, a nurse will come to check on him every couple days, and if all is going well, he'll be able to undergo prostate surgery in about six weeks.

Nathan texted me this morning that he's flying back tonight, and I've been pacing around my apartment the whole day— with the exception of a run I went on earlier to try to get some nervous energy out. I should be focused on work—we've got a major feature release coming out in two weeks—but I can't concentrate.

My mind wanders to the night we slept, *actually* slept, together in his bed in his parent's house in Seattle. I wondered at the time if he would think I was lame or withdrawn for not wanting to have sex with him, but when I'd told him I felt fragile, it was the truth. The whole mess with Danica brought back so many of the insecurities I had felt when I was dating Blake. When we were together, I had always felt like I was in some competition, one that I was perpetually losing.

Until everything exploded that night in Park City, Nathan had never made me feel that way. I'd always felt like I was something, someone, special to him. But all those positive, romantic, flirty feelings were shaken, and in their place, the seeds of doubt, jealousy, and potential betrayal sown. The realization that there *had* been something between Nathan and Danica, at some point, had me asking myself, "What if there's *still* something there?"

When her texts had come in, in a split second I'd pictured every scene I'd ever witnessed of Danica talking to Nathan or touching him, laughing with him. Anything that might *not* have happened but that I could imagine was also fodder for my insecurities: scenes of them pressed together on some club dance floor, in some imagined steamy make-out session mere hours before he showed up at my place that night, all on a disastrous loop in my mind. All of it flooded my brain and my heart and made me doubt him—doubt us. We started physical, I'd thought. What if that's all it was to him? A good, satisfying fuck.

We talked for hours the night I flew up to Seattle, and I came back, feeling as if we'd resolved things—no bitterness, understanding what had and hadn't actually happened, but still so unsure about how exactly we'd move forward from there.

Back home, it almost doesn't feel like Park City or Seattle were real life. What if the physical connection we had in Park City was just that—physical? What if the emotional honesty that I think we managed to forge in Seattle doesn't hold up back in the real world? Here, where we live, where we work. Old fears have a way of keeping a grip on your heart. Even now, after I think we've resolved things, I find myself wondering, "What if I'm not good enough?" And even worse, "What if what I *think* we have isn't even real?"

I'm at a loss for what to expect now, what to do. I text Camila.

Me: He's coming home tonight.

Camila: Duh, I have it marked on my calendar.

Me: You do?!

Camila: Well, not a real calendar. An imaginary one in my head. There's also an imaginary dick pic drawn on the date, too. Cuz someone's getting laid tonight.

Me: Can you be serious?

Camila: You're nervous. You always laugh at my dirty jokes.

Me: C, what do I do?

Camila: Wise philosopher says: Follow your heart.

Camila: Horny philosopher says: Follow your sex drive and do what feels good.

Camila: I think, in this case, both philosophers lead to the same conclusion.

Now Erin is texting me, too:

Erin: Did you see this? https://techcrunch.com/2022/03/28/rumors-of-instinqt-acquisition-by-lightverse/

I click and read the article, citing a confidential source that LightVerse is considering acquiring Instinqt. That can't be right. Nathan told me that Kevin was talking to them about leading the next funding round, but an acquisition?

Me: Is it true?

Erin: Oh, shit. Look at this one https://www.cnet.com/news/social-media/lightverse-acquires-startup-instinqt-for-upwards-of-300-million/

Erin: We're officially gonna be rich! We have an exit, baby!!!

I text Nathan.

Me: Have we been bought?

The text stays on "Delivered" for more than twenty minutes. He must be on the flight already. I can hear my Slack notifications going off like crazy from my work laptop. Looks like we've been bought.

＊ ＊ ＊

It's 9:00 p.m. and my phone rings.

It's Nathan. "Hey, I'm outside. Can I come up?"

"I didn't know you were coming over tonight," I say, trying not to let my voice betray how delighted, also how nervous, I am.

"Well, you're not the only one who can surprise people."

"I'll buzz you in."

I open my front door and wait for him. He gets off the elevator, rolling his suitcase behind him.

"You didn't even go home first?" I ask him, letting him in.

"I couldn't wait. I had some news for you, but from my texts, it looks like you already heard." He takes off his fleece and places it over the chair.

"So, it's true?" I ask, coming up to give him a hug hello. I let my arms drop, but decide that it's been too long since I've touched him, and let my hands rest on his biceps, lightly rubbing them up and down with my hands. This—the being with him, close to him—is where I feel comfortable. Touching him, looking into his eyes, the worries—of what we've had, what we are, what we might be—begin to dissolve.

"Yeah. Not to quote our friend who-shall-not-be-named, but that Saturday night apparently did go pretty well."

I pinch him on both arms.

"Ow!" he says. "Too soon?"

"Way too soon," I say, swatting him lightly on the chest. He clasps my hands and pulls me to the couch.

"Kevin and the board have been talking to Eden for a few weeks, and they still need to do due diligence, but they signed a term sheet, and somebody must've leaked it. Looks like they're buying Instinqt."

"For over $300 million?" I say, eyes wide.

"I don't know exactly," he says. "That part has to be just speculation at this point. Either way, it'll be a lot."

"Are you a millionaire now?"

"Not by a long shot. I joined way too late for that kind of equity. Maybe I'll be able to buy a new car now or something."

"Wow, Kevin must be on the moon."

"Well, he's freaking out since it's still a few signatures from being final, but definitely happy," he says, calmly. Not at all the tone I'd expect from someone who probably just got a ton of money in stocks.

"Oh, and I'm out of a job," he continues, giving me a sheepish look.

"Wait, what?"

"Well, as part of the acquisition, they figure out who they need from the old company and who they don't. They want Kevin—which is unusual because a lot of times they kick out the old CEO—and Maya, since she knows all the technical stuff and has a lot of connections, but they don't really need a senior product person, especially not one who's only been in the position a few months."

"Oh, no. I'm sorry."

"Don't be. It's okay. They said I could stay on as a staff engineer, but I told them it's time for me to move on."

"Why?"

"Well, for a couple reasons. I've got my own idea for a startup —something in the medical field and big data analysis. And I think now might be a good time to go for it."

"Wow."

"You wanna hear the second reason? I think you'll find it very interesting," he says, looking at me with an eyebrow raised. He's trying to intrigue me, and I'm tempted to say "No" just to tease him, but my interest is piqued. I take the bait, but not without messing with him a little bit first.

"Okay, tell me," I say, sliding onto his lap and putting my arms around his neck.

He laughs. "Nah, I'll tell you in the morning after we've screwed each other senseless." He suddenly flips me over, pins me to the couch, and begins to kiss me energetically. "Oh, I guess I've kind of given it away," he says, making a silly face at me.

"Is that the plan?" I say, giggling, as he continues to kiss my mouth and unbutton my shirt.

"It is," he says, between kisses, "Because . . . as of 4:00 p.m. this afternoon . . . I'm no longer an Instinqt executive."

He's now pulling off his own shirt over his head, as quickly as he can, and the look in his eyes leaves no doubt about his intentions. "And now there's no reason in the world for us not to do *this* as much as we want. And I think that's a *very* good second reason not to continue working at Instinqt with you."

We're making out like it's our high-school prom and my couch is the backseat of a car when he says, "Your body is so amazing. I just want you all the time." My body is responding to his, happy to hear it, but some small bit of my mind seems to feel differently, and I tense, just the slightest bit, in his arms.

He notices and sits up, gently pulling me up with him. He takes a deep breath and looks me directly in the eyes. "You know it's not just physical, right? You *need* to know that. When you left Park City, I thought I'd screwed things up forever."

I'm trying to look at him, but my thoughts are swirling, and it's hard for me to make my eyes meet his. He lifts my chin, gently, and locks eyes with me.

"Are you listening to me, beautiful?"

"Yes, I'm listening."

"It's you," he says. "Only you. Never anybody else. You're so much better than anybody else, don't you know that? Anybody that might want to be with me, anybody else I've ever known."

I look at him, wanting to believe him, but not quite there yet.

"If you let me, I'll do anything, spend however long it takes, making sure you know that."

I look into his eyes—completely willingly now—and I touch his face. This man, whom I've known for a little over two months, has somehow become such a big part of my life in such a short time. I kiss him, slowly and deeply. My thoughts about him are all over the place: sex, and warmth, and vulnerability, and happiness, and fuck, *love*.

"Nathan," I say, almost a whisper. "You know the voicemail you left me?"

He nods, a little sadly, maybe thinking back on when he left it and why.

"My world is also smaller without you in it. It's simple. I want you in it."

I kiss him deeply, again, and he picks me up and takes me to the bedroom to do more than just cuddle.

❊ ❊ ❊

We wake early in the morning. The light outside is still gray. I don't have meetings until later this afternoon, and I've marked myself "out of office" until noon. Nathan, well, I guess he's out of a job, or his own boss now. A startup founder, apparently.

We're lying in bed, completely naked. I kiss him.

"How do you already taste like toothpaste? Did you get up and brush your teeth before I woke up?" I ask him.

He looks at me. "Sure, why not?"

"How can you suffer kissing me with my morning breath?" I ask, rolling over to grab my ever-present cup of water from my nightstand and taking a sip.

"You taste delicious, Sarah. All the time, everywhere. Come here," he says, and rolls me back to him, making me almost spill the cup of water I'm holding.

"Hold on, partner," I say, stretching to put the cup back on the nightstand.

Nathan's lying on his back, and I'm on my side now, my leg across his lower body, and his arm around me. He alternately strokes my hair and my breasts.

"I just don't get tired of them," he's saying.

"That's good news," I say and giggle.

"I love when you laugh like that. It warms my cold little programmer heart and makes me want to be not-quite-so-anti-social."

"You're not anti-social. That's just a line you say so you can have more time to code or, I don't know, prey on unsuspecting project managers."

"Prey?"

"Well," I say, examining a bite mark on one of my breasts. "It certainly looks like there was a predator in here last night."

He scoots down and out from under me and rolls me onto

my back. He lifts my breast gently and kisses me where he left a mark. Then he moves his lips, already curving into a smile, from the bite mark slowly over to my nipple, and begins to lick it, looking up at me. "Mmmm," I say. "I might forgive you if you keep doing that."

"In that case, I'll continue, but I'll be gentle this time," he says and moves to the other breast. While his mouth concentrates on the delights the upper part of my body has to offer him, one of his hands glides down between my legs, and he begins to stroke me gently.

"If this is unemployment, I may never go back to work," he jokes.

I'm beginning to breathe a little unevenly, and ask him, "Shouldn't you be concentrating?"

"I'm very good at multitasking. Wanna see?" he says. He dives under the covers and begins kissing me on my hips, and then my lower abdomen, tickling me.

"I don't trust you down there. I wanna watch you," I tease, kicking the covers off, so I can see him go down on me. Seeing his muscular arms and shoulders, push my legs wide open—part me —for the pleasure I'm about to experience is such a turn-on. "Are you hard?" I ask.

"I'm in the same room as you," he says, as if the answer is obvious.

"Are you telling me you got an erection every time you saw me making coffee at work?" I ask, laughing.

"No, but you weren't naked at work."

"True," I say.

"And I wasn't sitting between your legs with the view I have now. So, short answer, yes, I'm hard."

"Then put it inside of me."

"Already?"

"Yeah, already."

"Okay," he agrees. "But let's try something different."

"Are you planning on putting it in my ear this time?"

"Can't you ever be serious?" he says, and groans good-naturedly.

"Rarely. Don't you love it?"

His face stills and he looks at me seriously. "I love . . . you." I look at him, wide-eyed. It's too early, much too soon. "I'm beginning to," he clarifies. I see the nervous look in his eye, like he's thinking he shouldn't have said it, and that the "beginning to" remark is his concession, his attempt to calm me, help me not freak out.

I take a beat to think, but instantly realize that this isn't one of those things logical, ordered thinking can help you sort out. "I think I might love you, too, Nathan." He smiles at me. Then I whisper, "But not enough to let you put it in my ear."

He laughs, nibbles my ear, and flips me with ease to my side. "Well, we'll just do this instead." He positions himself behind me, spooning me, and after a minute or two of adjustments— mostly that he's making—because I'm too distracted by the one hand that's stroking my clit and the other that's rubbing my nipple lightly, he enters me. And we rock and rock, like a boat in the sea, until we've both come and all the waves have hit the shore. And then we rest.

❊ ❊ ❊

Around 10:00 a.m., we finally make it out of bed. I get out of the shower to see Nathan looking at his phone, and he tells me that Kevin has scheduled an all-hands to announce the exit at 11:30.

I look at the clock. "That's less than an hour. We gotta go."

"Think we have time for one more round?" he asks, giving me a questioning look, and getting up to smack my towel-covered butt.

"Nathan, get dressed, you sex maniac. We'll have time later for all of your other ideas."

"Are we gonna go in together?" he asks.

"What do you think?" I say, unsure.

"I say . . . let's do it."

"You don't care? Don't you think—" I start to ask, but he

interrupts me mid-sentence.

"You're my bae."

"Do you even know what that means?" I ask, cracking up, wondering when he suddenly decided to start using slang.

"I know stuff," he tells me.

"You know a lot of stuff," I say suggestively, snuggling up to him and thinking back to our earlier activities.

"Well, what I definitely know is that I don't care what Kevin or Instinqt think about us. I'm outta there. Kevin's getting his dream, and I'm getting mine," he says as he pecks me on the cheek and heads to the shower.

GOING LIVE

We show up at the office, shortly before the all-hands. Most everyone who's going to attend in person is in the office already —it *is* a regular Wednesday after all, and it's safe to assume most people were not at home sexing each other up for the last twelve hours like Nathan and I were. Still, I'm not quite brave enough to show up holding hands, but we come off the elevator together, and as luck would have it, Erin's looking up her computer.

The look on her face tells me that it is not in fact luck, but intentional. She's probably been watching it like a hawk for the last three hours. When I got up this morning, I saw a group text with me, Erin, and Camila, and Camila had definitely updated Erin on what was maybe—likely? definitely?—going to happen last night, once Nathan was back from Seattle.

I give Nathan a quick farewell, as he heads toward Kevin's desk, and I walk to my own desk to set my things down. Erin walks by me, and before I can sit down, she swoops in and basically drags me to one of the smaller meeting rooms. "What happened?" she demands.

"Do you not have Netflix or something?" I ask her. "Am I—are we—your only entertainment?"

"You know I ship you guys, so quit avoiding the question," she says and smacks me on the arm. "*Something* happened?"

"Something happened . . . a few times."

"Mmm-hmmm. And?"

"And, it's not official yet, but Nathan is no longer going to work for Instinqt and . . ."

"What?" she says, her eyes widening.

"I'm pretty sure . . ."

"Spit it out, Hoffman!"

"That I love him?" I say in an uncertain tone. "And I think he loves me. He said so."

Erin's already wiping her eyes.

"So much better than Netflix. I'll see you in the all-hands," she says and quickly kisses me on the cheek as she leaves and heads toward the restroom, likely to fix her now-ruined eye makeup.

* * *

A few minutes later, people begin to leave their desks and walk to the large conference room. There's a buzz of nervous energy in the air. Probably a few people here are drafting their resignation letters in their heads, having recently become millionaires.

Right before I head in, I go to make a quick coffee in the kitchen and overhear Kevin and Nathan talking around the corner.

"Dude, you're sure? I know it's not an executive position, but there's still a lot to be done. I need you there."

"Thanks for the chance, man," Nathan's telling him, in a hushed tone. "But it's time for me to do my own thing. I've got an idea for my own startup, man. You'll be on the board when it actually becomes something."

"You sure?"

"Yeah, I'm sure."

"You look really happy, man. You're starting to hurt my feelings. Were you just waiting for your chance to escape?"

"Nah, I just spent the last twelve hours with Sarah. I could get used to *that* life."

"I knew something was going on between you two," I hear Kevin say. They're walking to the conference room now, and I see Kevin turn his head and notice me standing there. We catch each other's eyes, and I blush. He smiles, raises his eyebrows as if to say "Way to go," and gives me a nod, approving. I think back to our conversation at the airport, the morning of the off-site. *He was rooting for us this whole time.* I smile back at him.

I walk into the room, one of the last people to arrive. It's the same room where less than two months ago, I saw Nathan for the second time in my life, and wished nothing more than to escape his notice and never see him again. Nathan's sitting near the front and looks up at me—smiling broadly. Kevin and Erin notice, and they both laugh, shaking their heads.

"Good morning," Kevin says. "For those of you who are living in caves and might not have heard"—everyone laughs —"LightVerse is buying us. We're now a part of a special group of startups: the ones who succeed. The ones who exit or IPO. And it's due to all of you. So, the first thing I have to say is thank you. Thank you for working your asses off and getting shit done!"

He goes on to tell the short version of how they originally talked to Eden Snow, in hopes that LightVerse would agree to lead the Series B round, but that Eden expressed an interest in acquiring Instinqt due to its products and the reputation of its team. "And the rest is history. So, there are gonna be a lot of changes coming, but folks, we did it. Congrats."

❉ ❉ ❉

Nathan leaves the office early—he hasn't actually been back to his place since arriving, and it's been a while.

"My poor little basil plant is probably dead," he says, giving me a humorous remorseful look.

"I'll see you later tonight?" I ask, standing close to him, near the elevator.

"Yeah, come over when you're done with work. I'll make you dinner."

I look at him, not sure how to say goodbye, now that, I guess, we're actually officially together.

"Can I kiss you goodbye?" he asks.

"As long as it's PG-13."

He groans. "I'll do my best." He leans down to kiss me, sweetly, more than a peck, but perfectly respectable for a boyfriend kissing his girlfriend in a place where he no longer works.

"Bye, Nathan."

"Bye, Sarah."

❈ ❈ ❈

Nathan and I spend a lot of time together over the next week. The next Friday, he sends me a text at 3:00 p.m.:

Nathan: Done with work? Wanna make it an early Friday?

I would like nothing more than to make it an early Friday, and I text him back.

Me: Sure.

Nathan: I have a surprise.

Me: Afternoon delight?

Nathan: You really have a one-track mind.

Me: That's funny, coming from you.

Nathan: I love coming from you.

I laugh as I sling my backpack over my shoulder and take the elevator downstairs. When I get there, he's waiting for me in his car, out in front of the building.

"I wanna take you somewhere," he says. "Can we run by your place so you can change clothes really quick? You need warm clothes and comfortable shoes."

"Yeah, let's go."

I run up and change into jeans, a fleece, and some running shoes, and race back down.

"I wanna take you on my favorite hike out here. We won't do the whole thing—but I think you're gonna like it," he's smiling at me, like a little kid with a surprise.

We drive for about twenty-five minutes, up into the Santa Cruz Mountains, a bit southwest of San Jose. We're up on the Skyline portion of the Coastal Range, an area full of giant, resplendent redwoods, and we park near the entrance to Castle Rock. We get out of the car, taking our things from the trunk, and he puts on a pretty big backpack.

"What do you have in there?" I ask, eyes wide.

"I brought food. Homemade," he adds.

I smile. We start the hike—and almost immediately, the

temperature drops under the closely situated redwoods, and I'm glad I've dressed warmly.

"So, what's the startup idea? You said something in the medical field, but what're you thinking?'

"Well, going through all this stuff with my dad, I just keep thinking that with all the different medical tests and genetic information we have at our disposal today, shouldn't doctors have some way of viewing all that information in one place, so they can understand it and use it for better diagnoses? What if there was some really powerful data analytics machine that could understand what's important and what's just noise? And then the important stuff shows up in a dashboard that medical staff use to catch early instances of diseases, cancer or otherwise, so people could get *really* early treatment? Like, maybe they could catch super early *pre*-stages of cancer and other things, so monitoring and treatment happen earlier and they're more effective."

I've stopped and I'm looking at him, taking in what he's said.

"Nathan, that's really awesome. How . . . well, you're not a doctor or biologist. Who's gonna help you?"

"Well, I've gotten closer with one of my dad's doctors, and she's gonna help and also connect me with a lot of people who know a lot more about this stuff than I do. And I'll bring the mathematical and tech tool part to the table."

He looks at me. "And you."

"Huh?"

"I want you to help me. If you're willing?"

"Me? But I don't know anything about any of this—I'm not medical. I'm not a programmer. What could I possibly do?"

"All the stuff I don't know how to do. The stuff that you're naturally great at. Sarah, you have this unbelievable ability to look at problems and begin pinpointing where you can get started solving them. And beyond that, you're confident . . . and well-spoken. You connect quickly with people, because they can tell you're genuine."

He continues. "I'll definitely have a place for you, *if* you want it, in the startup, once it actually *is* one. You'll be presenting to VCs and the board, and I'll just be enjoying the view from behind."

"Did you just say 'enjoying the view?'"

"I meant, to say, I'm perfectly fine being the one behind you."

"That's not too much better," I say, smirking.

He suddenly stops me and pulls me close to him. "You know what I mean." He kisses me roughly and grabs my butt. "So quit giving me a hard time."

Speaking of hard times, I'm close enough I can feel his "hard time."

"Really, just from *touching* my butt?" I say, raising my eyebrows.

"Honestly, sometimes it happens from just *looking* at your butt," he says, swatting it one last time, before pulling me up a rock to continue the hike.

As the hike begins to get steeper, I joke with him, "You're gonna make me work for dinner, huh?"

"You've already been working *really* hard the last couple of weeks," he says with a twinkle in his eye, walking right behind me and helpfully assisting by pushing on my butt since we're on a narrow portion of the trail that winds around the mountain.

"See that tree line up there? That's where we're going."

Seeing that it's not that far, and thinking that with him carrying a heavy bag, I've got half a shot at beating him, I yell, "Race you to the top," and take off running. It's quite steep, and I'm no slouch, but he overtakes me the last ten feet and turns around, panting and smiling, little beads of sweat breaking out on his forehead.

"Usually, when you're breathing that hard, it means we're just about done," I tease him, struggling to breathe. The last few steps, I slow down, fall into his waiting arms, and take advantage of the closeness to pinch *his* butt. He takes my hand and pulls me up the final stretch to the top.

"So, there's a whole trail out here where you can see some waterfalls—little ones—but I knew we didn't have a ton of time

before sunset, and I wanted us to have some time to enjoy this."
He's looking westward, out across the horizon. If we kept going
west, we'd hit Big Basin and eventually the Pacific Ocean.

The sky is a beautiful combination of pink, purple, and orange
from the sun beginning to make its way down. We sit down next
to each other on the large rock that juts out and just enjoy the
silence. Daylight savings time started a few weeks ago, so we've
got some time to enjoy ourselves before we head back.

"My dad's doing better," he says, grabbing my hand and
intertwining his fingers with mine.

"That's wonderful. What a relief, huh?"

"I was gonna fly up this weekend, but my mom told me to
stay. I think she wants to make sure I spend enough time with
you. Make sure you're convinced of all my stellar qualities, before
leaving you for a weekend without me."

"Well, you do have *many* stellar qualities," I admit. "You're a
good cook, you're a very good computer scientist—at least that's
what I read on the internet. You always smell nice, you're a
mensch—"

"A *mensch*, huh?"

"It is one of the most important things, you know."

He smiles.

"Oh, you're pretty good in bed."

"Only *pretty* good, huh?"

"I could be convinced otherwise. We might need to spend
some time on that one tonight," I say, placing my hand on the
inside of his muscular thigh, and circle my fingertips on his
upper leg. It must tickle him since he places his hand over mine
to still it. But he doesn't remove it.

"You said 'good cook' first, so let me feed you. Gotta keep up
my good reputation," he says. He unpacks the food he's prepared
and brought along. I'm not sure what it is yet, but it smells
delicious.

"I rarely say 'no' to offers of food."

"And I noticed you also said 'good in bed' last. You don't
usually say 'no' to those offers, either." He nudges my shoulder

playfully.

But I'm in my own head, a bit, and nod a little while I think aloud. "Well, that's where we started, I guess, in bed. I *was* joking. You're amazing in bed—"

"*We're* amazing in bed," he corrects me. "It does take two."

"Fine, *we're* amazing in bed, but well, that's what happened first. The more time I spend with you, the more I realize that . . . it's all the other things you are and how we fit together that makes that part so great."

He turns, takes my face in his hands, and kisses me gently, slowly. "You're right. We do fit together, Sarah."

We eat our dinner and watch the sun begin to set. "We should probably head back," he says. "It feels a little damp in the air, and I think there might be rain forecasted for tonight."

"I don't mind the rain," I reply.

"Oh, I'm sure we'll find something to do," he says, suggestively.

"That's probably true," I reply. "But it's not what I meant."

He gives me a questioning look. "Sometimes, unexpected rain changes things for the better," I say, thinking of the night we met and how it forced us indoors and down a path we might not have chosen otherwise.

He catches my drift and gives me a kiss on the cheek. "In that case, I'm always in favor of rain."

He packs up the food and then holds out a hand to help me up.

"So, what do you think? Will you help me with the startup? Make sure I don't do anything ridiculously stupid and end up destitute and disgraced?"

"You know how you're always saying that you won't let me fall?"

"Yes?"

"I won't let you fall, either, Nathan," I say, meeting his eyes. I touch his face and smile and see him do the same, a bit bashfully.

We start the hike back and walk hand in hand, as the fiery sunset slowly fades at our backs and dusk falls on the forest. We're getting close to the trailhead, when Nathan suddenly stops and pulls me into a hug.

"What are *you* smiling about?" he asks.

"Oh, well, I was just thinking that you and me. We're a little like a software release at work."

"How so?"

"Well, *we* went a little out of order," I answer, smiling mischievously at him. "But more or less, you build it, you test it, you fix the bugs, and then, when it's ready, you just—"

"You ship it," he says and kisses me.

Exactly.

ACKNOWLEDGMENTS

As noted in my dedication, I have a very special "N" in my life. Much like Nathan from the book, he is a software engineer. But he is so much more than that. I could write a whole book—maybe I will one day—about him and just how badass he is. More than anything, he has helped me go after my dreams: ones I knew I had and others that I didn't. He has opened up my world in so many ways, and I know he would say the same about me. He might have introduced me to Silicon Valley, but I introduced him to the Redneck Riviera, and we're both better people because of it. When I first met him, I made him laugh, and all these years later, I feel so, so lucky that we're still laughing. Creating a life with him has been pretty epic up until now, and I can only hope it continues on this path. Thank you, love of my life, for always supporting me and being the hottest guy ever. Oh, and for the 47,000 dishes you've washed during the pandemic.

I have to thank my mom for reading everything I write and always telling me how much she loves it and me. Mom, you crack me up. You are the best mother a girl could ask for. I'm sorry if I embarrassed you by making you read the sex scenes I wrote, but I know I've made you proud by sharing my writing with the world.

Thank you to my wonderful dad for being a *mensch* and always encouraging me to be who I am and choose the life I want, even if it's not what others are doing. Dad, the way you have lived your life—always trying to treat people the right way—has shaped the person I've become and continues to guide the decisions I make every single day.

Thank you to my stepdad for encouraging a love of reading and writing throughout my life. The modest library you created in our home—chock-full of Stephen King novels that a kid definitely should not have been reading—and always seeing you and Mom reading laid the foundation for me for a lifetime of loving books. And to my "wicked" stepmom, Janet, who will unfortunately never read this book, but will always, always be in my heart and thoughts.

To my completely and utterly wonderful parents-in-law, whose lifelong love story surely deserves its own novel (I'll try writing it one day). Thank you for welcoming me into your lives with indescribable openness and love from the moment you met me.

E, though I didn't realize it when I started writing, the challenges that you—that we as a family—faced this year with your health pushed me to integrate into this book an exploration (though limited) of how a family copes when a beloved parent faces illness. Thank you for always being the ultimate human being: intelligent, thoughtful, patient, and giving. May you be healthy and happy for many years to come.

M, I cannot imagine a better mother-in-law. Your determination to succeed in all areas of life is truly inspirational. You have supported me in everything I have ever needed since you came into my life, from helping me through new immigrant challenges to stuffing sandwiches in my mouth while I struggled to nurse newborn babies. Thank you to you and E for creating and raising such a wonderful son.

To my three amazing daughters, words cannot describe how proud I am of the people you are and continue to become before my very eyes every day. Thank you for being so proud of me for writing this book (even though I won't let you read it yet), and for always encouraging me to keep moving forward, even when things get tough. Being your mother has taught me so much about love, and I am so lucky to be your mom.

On the writing front, thank you to my editor Maxine Higginbotham for supporting me throughout my writing journey and always encouraging me and pushing me to dig in more. Thank you for taking my "book baby" and helping me raise it. I apologize for all the wrong em dashes. I'd like to say I'll improve, but I probably won't.

Thank you to Bailey McGinn for the fun, lovely cover art that helps bring to life the characters I created. Seeing Nathan and Sarah for the first time outside of my imagination blew my mind. You unknowingly illustrated me and my husband without knowing what we look like, and it makes me laugh regularly.

Thank you to Jen Boles for your careful attention to detail. 90,000+ words is a beast, and I appreciate your help in taming it.

Thank you to my friends and beta readers: Suzy, you've been a kickass bestie since middle school, and I'm so lucky you're still in my life; thanks to Avital for reading this in less than a day and being such a great cheerleader for what I hope will become the "high-tech romance" genre; and many thanks to my other early readers: Kacie, Sharon, Meghan, Paulina, Ashlee, and all my December 2010 ladies.

To Noelle, you devoted your very limited time but gave me invaluable feedback and helped me elevate this newbie writing project to something (I hope) respectable. You told me you couldn't wait to see this sucker published with a beautiful book cover. Hope you like it!

✳ ✳ ✳

I can't possibly list all the amazing innovators, teachers, and friends I've met along my startup journey, but I'll try to name a few. Thank you . . .

To Nimo for giving me a foot in the door to the startup world and letting me manage all kinds of shit I had no business managing, but which allowed me to learn a ton.

To Shahar for taking me on even though you (wrongly) thought I was arrogant in my first interview. You telling me that I could "swim in any water" has stuck with me and given me the confidence to do hard things I might not have tried otherwise.

To Aleks for teaching me everything about wrangling engineers and product managers when I barely knew the difference between frontend and backend. Your friendship and support are incomparable, and I hope we'll continue to share a million more cat memes in the years to come.

To Dana for helping me find my career path in tech and always being an amazing advocate for me. And to all the other startup goddesses (I don't know if this is a thing, but I'm going to make it one) who have taught me so much along the way.

To all the amazing teams who have entrusted me with their processes and allowed me to learn and build cool shit with you. Thanks for throwing a few pity laughs my way during daily stand ups and agreeing to try all my crazy virtual happy hour games.

❋ ❋ ❋

And to you, all my readers: thank you for taking a chance on me and my book.

AUTHOR'S NOTE

A portion of the proceeds from Ship It will be donated to charities supporting food insecurity and hunger issues. Since childhood, I have been especially attuned to the issues of hunger and homelessness. I attribute it to exposure at an early age to those in need—my local Jewish community volunteered each Christmas day to prepare and serve meals in a local center for homeless men—combined with stories from my own parents' childhoods when money was sometimes scarce. As an adult, traveling throughout the world and living abroad, I witnessed need, hunger, and homelessness in almost every place. Even in Silicon Valley, arguably one of the wealthiest places in the world, it pains me to see homelessness and wealth disparity every single day. There is no way to solve this issue for good, but the Jewish teaching of *tikkun olam* (translated as "repairing the world") has guided me for many years, and it is my goal to at least do my part to help. Thank you for buying this book and helping me make a small difference in this issue people face all over the world.

ABOUT THE AUTHOR

Evie Blum

 Evie grew up on the beautiful Florida Gulf Coast and has been an avid reader her entire life. After finishing her bachelor's degree, she decided to explore the world and ended up moving to Israel, where she lived for almost a decade. While there, she earned a master's degree in political science, worked in academia, founded her own translation and editing business, and married a pretty awesome guy.

Their path led them to the San Francisco Bay Area, and Evie found her way into the world of high tech. She helped found and grow a hardware startup, was part of a successful software startup exit, and participated in an IPO.

The pandemic gave her plenty of time–and reason–to want to escape reality, and she read approximately a million romance novels, including the entire Outlander series . . . twice. Deciding she wanted to try her hand at writing contemporary romance, she began her first fiction work this year. Figuring that the world can be a pretty rough place sometimes, she set out to add some positive energy to it by writing a fun, (somewhat) realistic love story set in a Silicon Valley high-tech startup. Ship It is her first fiction work, and she's already hard at work on the sequel.

You can find her online at evieblum.com or on TikTok at @EvieBlumAuthor.

Made in the USA
Monee, IL
12 May 2023

33218671R00173